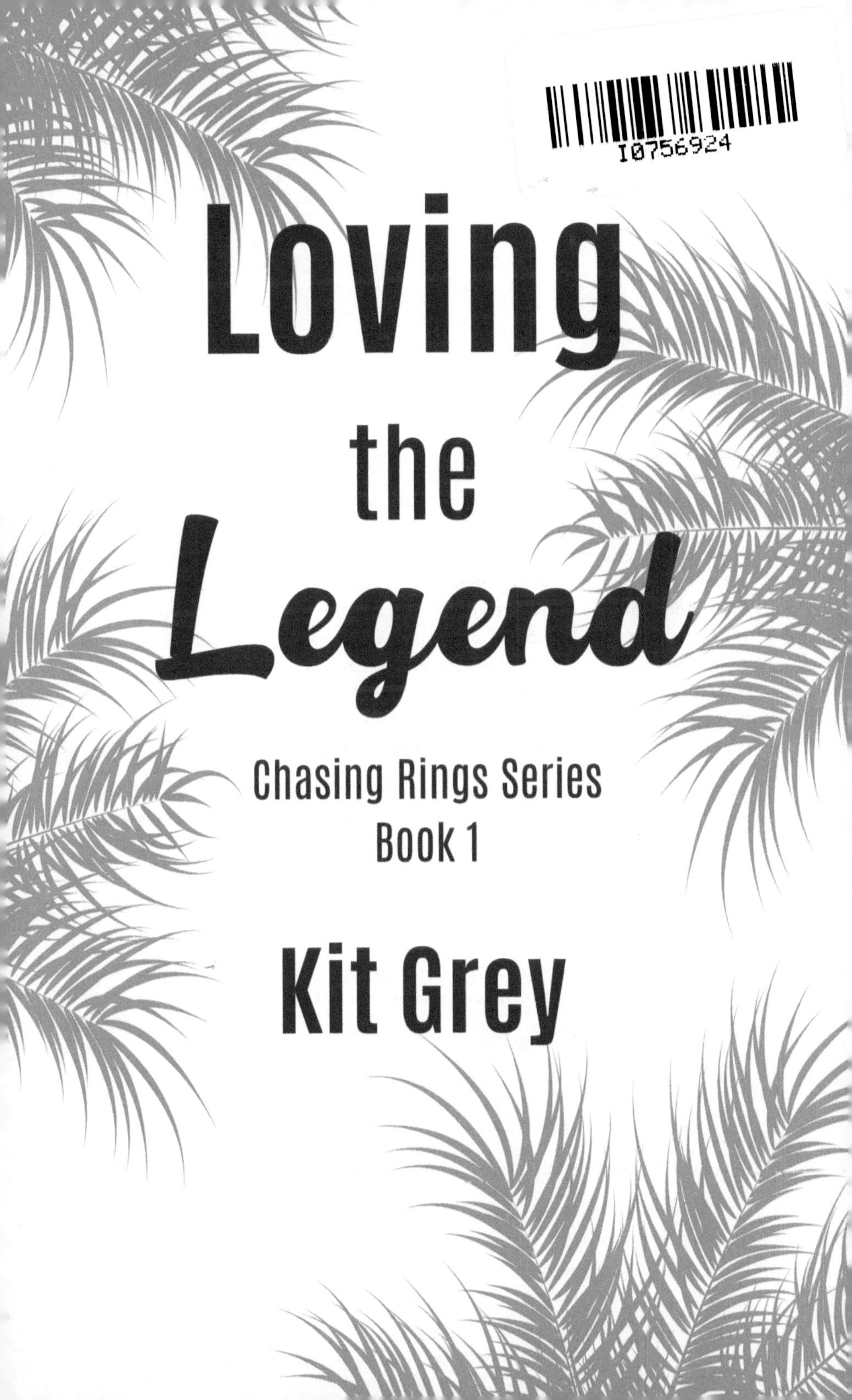

Loving the Legend

Chasing Rings Series
Book 1

Kit Grey

Disclaimer

The views in this book in no way reflect the views and principles of the National Basketball Association (NBA) and National Collegiate Athletic Association (NCAA), as it is a work of fiction. The author endeavored to portray aspects of the NBA schedule, rules, and regulations as accurately as possible. However, creative freedoms and liberties were taken for the plot purposes of this book. The teams, players, coaching staff, and agents, within this work and series, are completely made up and fabricated so as not to misrepresent the policies and values, curriculum, or facilities of real institutions.

Content Warning

Loving the Legend contains depictions of grief related to the tragic deaths of parents and a childhood friend. The deaths are described in two separate flashback sequences. The book also contains references to depression, drug overdose, suicidal ideation, self-medicating on prescription sleeping pills, mild dubious consent, parental abuse (flashback of side character), cardiac arrest and surgery of a loved one, single use of F-slur written as "fa—", MC glimpse of a MF sex scene, and homophobia. There are multiple explicit sex scenes. Reader discretion is advised.

For N, your luminous spirit is a lighthouse for my mercurial and restless soul.

Also, N, it's seven a.m., and I dared a glance at you and lost consecutive trains of thought.

After a decade of this madness, I must insist that you take your beauty down a notch.

I'd rein in my crush, but...Ah, you just smiled...

Where was I going with this?

How often have you sailed in my dreams.
And now you come in my awakening, which is my deeper dream.
Kahlil Gibran

Prologue

S ome beliefs erect new worlds, while others ravage and embitter. I used to believe that the day was mine to claim. I never thought much about beliefs until I lost that one. It was the last golden morning in the dead of winter. I woke up to the aroma of Mom's chocolate, almond, and banana pancakes. Reaching for my phone, I paused when my fingers scraped a stack of papers that weren't there when I fell asleep. I stared in disbelief at a marked-up version of my essay on Garrett Morgan. After finishing it at midnight, I sent it to Mom to proofread. I thought we'd look at it together over breakfast, but she beat me to it.

When does she sleep?

Dad's melodic baritone voice crooned along to a Stevie Wonder record. His voice sounded more like his old Otis Redding records than Stevie, with its gravelly, soulful inflection. His burly footsteps approached my room. I tossed the papers on the nightstand and scooted under the covers, pretending to be asleep. My door creaked open. Dad did the thing where he watched me for a minute or two before he woke me up.

I grinned and belted out the first line of the chorus in tune with the record. Instead of startling, Dad chuckled and caught the next line singing along. We continued singing, alternating lyrics until we belted the last verse together. He approached my bed and sat down facing me. I extended my arm, our knuckles meeting halfway for a kiss.

"My son, what kind of day will it be?"

He'd asked me this every day since I could remember. Even when he traveled for business, he called before school to ask. I peered out the window, thinking it over. The snow had been enchanting when it had fallen four days before. Now icicles descended from the windowpane like stalactites. I shivered, knowing I'd be out there within the next hour, ensnared by the elements. With an exhale, I nestled deeper under my blankets as the warmth of central heating washed over me.

Closing my eyes, I imagined the day ahead. With Mom's edits on my paper, there was a good chance I'd get an A. I'd play the best ball of my life later that day. I might even surprise Mom and Dad by attempting the windmill alley-oop shot we'd been practicing. I'd shake the feeling I was missing a secret ingredient to nail the shot.

A surge of electricity spread up my spine and swished around my stomach.

The thrill of impending victory.

"It's gonna be lit," I answered.

"What's that?" Dad tilted his ear toward me. "I didn't quite catch it."

This was a thing he did. He wanted me to proclaim it like a battle cry. He asked again, "WHAT KIND OF DAY WILL IT BE, MY SON?"

His voice reverberated through me like wildfire, igniting a resounding cry. I jolted upright and yelled, "IT'S GONNA BE EXTRAORDINARY!"

We both growled and flexed, hyping each other up. Dad's muscles were far more impressive than my own. My growth spurt hadn't kicked in until my senior year of high school. Out of nowhere, he made the strangest high-pitched sound like an elk. It killed me every time. We both ended up on our backs. I laughed so hard I snorted, which made Dad wheeze with laughter.

Then Mom thundered down like a storm. "Morris! You had one task this morning—get Ty up and in the shower by 7:15." Her gaze pierced me next. "You're a year shy of college. It's high time you learn to get yourself up on time."

Mom was our captain. I don't think Dad and I would've fared well if left to our own devices. We'd easily get lost watching video compilations of funny animal sounds until we ran late. I was, of course, speaking from experience. The minute Mom's feet hit the floor, she attacked the day with such feverish haste that she made a peregrine falcon look like a sloth. She conquered more before six o'clock in the morning than the average mortal. Dad was tenacious but wired more loosely. Whereas Mom's day began with an urgency to check tasks off a never-ending list, Dad preferred to ease into things. Mornings for Dad involved laughter and singing—always singing. Time may have governed Mom's day, but it would have found a mutinous subject in Dad.

Before I could retort that I *did* wake myself up on time, Dad piped up. "My dearest love, the aroma of your cooking was so delightful that I lost focus on my task. It bears me grave torment to know that I've disappointed you. Bleak is the hour that I've displeased my queen."

He bowed his head before Mom in an act of penance. This charade never worked. She sniffed drivel more reliably than a bloodhound tracked a scent. I snickered, and then Dad tilted his gaze toward me, and it was game over. We burst out laughing.

Mom huffed out a breath as her eyes rolled skyward. "Tyler, you have one minute to get in the shower or no pancakes."

My stomach grumbled in protest. "Hey, wait—"

"57 seconds," she replied, signaling for me to zip it.

I charged out of bed and sprinted for the shower before she crossed the threshold of the door. There was a ninety-nine percent chance it was a bluff, but those odds were steep for her pancakes. A blue whale lived inside me, crashing its monstrous body around on a mad hunt for fluffy goodness.

I slipped on a book, but Dad extended an arm, breaking my fall.

Mom winced.

"I know, I know." I waved it off. "I'll organize them when I get home."

"It's become an obstacle course to reach your bed. I almost broke my neck dropping off your essay earlier."

I slung my arm around her neck. "How do you do it? You have a clone, right?"

Her head fell back as she cackled.

"A secret identical twin sister? A time machine?"

"I wish," she replied, threading her arm around my waist.

"Thanks for editing my essay. You da bomb, even if you didn't say good morning to your only kid—tsk, tsk." I palmed my wounded chest, and she snickered.

"And now you're laughing at my pain." I sighed. "It's this kind of egregious behavior that makes a guy feel unloved."

"Egregious," she repeated with a nod of approval before angling her face up to kiss my cheek. "Two points."

"Yes!" I fisted the air.

Mom dealt out points every time I used an SAT word. I racked up the points like a championship ring was on the line.

"What else you got?" she asked.

It wasn't enough to throw one in a sentence. I scanned my brain. I needed to make it relevant to the conversation.

I snapped my fingers. "On the matter of my bruised heart, I

must seek recompense in the form of extra chocolate in my pancakes."

"Boom!" She patted my chest. "Three points."

"Ha!" I spun around. "Dad, five points!" I lobbed an imaginary ball his way.

He caught it, hit a behind-the-back dribble, and released.

"Swish," Dad shouted while Mom coughed, "Air ball."

I burst out laughing. "Cold, Ma!"

Dad shook his head. "It's the Bahamas out there"—he pointed to the frosted window—"compared to in here."

Mom blew him a kiss, a playful smirk on her lips. "I was joking, honey. It was all net."

Her gaze snapped back to me. Mom's facial expressions were a language. This one said "Did I or did I not tell you to get in the shower?" I bounced off the wall and stood up straight.

"Yes, ma'am, yes!" I saluted her and raced toward the bathroom, hitting a between-the-legs crossover with my imaginary ball.

"Ty," Mom called.

I spun around.

"Good morning!"

I rubbed my fake bruised heart and kissed the inside of my palm. I made a loud smacking noise before I launched the kiss at her. She rolled up to her tiptoes and pretended to catch it just as Dad eased behind her and wrapped her up in a hug.

THE SCHOOL DAY FLEW BY, AND IT WAS GAME TIME BEFORE I KNEW it. I felt unstoppable as I hit the easiest thirteen points of my life. As I raced up the court, the opposing team's center moved in to defend me. I feinted left but spun right, creating enough space to rip past him and charge toward the rim at breakneck speed. The crowd's noise reduced to a murmur, heightening the thumping in my heart.

I signaled to my teammate to lob me the ball.

Don't choke.

You got this.

I launched myself through the air, and the second my hands gripped the leather, I knew the next fifteen seconds were mine. Never mind that I attempted the play a hundred times and landed only a handful.

Time to light up.

The opposing team's point guard jumped up to block me, but my teammate intercepted him mid-air. *Clutch.*

I kicked my heels toward my butt and arched my back to get more height. A deep belly roar thundered out of me as I wind-milled my arms 180 degrees and hammered the ball through the net.

"Hell yeah!" I yelled as I swung from the rim.

My feet barely dusted the floor before I launched myself back in the air, chest bumping my teammate. I signaled to the crowd to get louder—and damn, they delivered. Their cheers reached a crescendo, bouncing off the walls and up my spine through my fingertips.

I searched the bleachers for my parents. They had to be out of their seats, going bonkers. They cheered the loudest. I froze when my gaze landed on the empty seats in their usual spot.

"Yo, that was fire!" My teammate yelled as he smacked my chest. A shadow crossed his face when his gaze flicked past me. I trailed his stare to a pair of cops speaking with Coach.

Coach pressed his hand over his mouth as he scanned the court. My stomach dropped when his gaze landed on me and he waved me over. I searched the bleachers again for my parents but knew they weren't there. Somewhere deep inside, I knew something terrible had happened. Coach's mouth moved, but all I registered was—*accident, parents, and hospital.* Then, the school counselor, Ms. Jenkins, appeared holding my book bag.

The bubble of cold condensation from my breath blanketed the smeared, dried blood on the glass partition of the police car as we were transported to the hospital. Ms. Jenkins patted my shoulder and reassured me everything would be okay. I never felt less okay in my life. She asked if I had any family in the area since both of the emergency contacts on file for me were my parents. I mumbled something about Uncle Adam in New Jersey. She asked me for his number, and I unlocked my phone and tried to type in his name but failed three times. My hands couldn't stop shaking. She reached for my phone, located his number, and hit the call button. I overheard Adam gasp and then utter, "Oh my god," as Ms. Jenkins shared the news and hospital details. She handed me the phone. Hearing Uncle Adam's voice break caused the sob I had been holding in to rip loose.

"It'll be okay. I'll be right there with you. I'm already in the car. I love you," he said. My whole body trembled as I tried to clamp down the storm that threatened to break loose.

Ms. Jenkins and I were in the waiting room for an eternity when the doctor, a bleary-eyed woman with salt and pepper hair, came in and introduced herself. Ms. Jenkins asked if she had any news.

I heard the words—*injuries too severe, deceased, seven minutes apart.*

I flew out of my seat. "That's bullshit. Take me to my parents!"

The doctor repeated the same information. She delivered it with a bloodlessness I'd never forget. Ms. Jenkins shared the news with Adam when he phoned from the road. His eyes were bloodshot when he arrived. I clung to him, sobbing, "Please, God!" until the room spun. I wanted out of this sick nightmare. I wanted to swim toward the horizon until the current pulled me under. Land held only darkness and a cruel God.

Mom once said that she stopped fearing death a long time ago. She said it would be as easy as falling asleep.

A false belief.

I imagined her mangled body hanging out of the windshield.

Adam went alone to the morgue to identify their bodies. As I watched him disappear past the waiting room doors, I caught the reflection of my basketball jersey in the glass pane. And it hit me—they were killed trying to get to my game.

They'd still be here if they had a different kid with different dreams. It should have been me in there. They didn't deserve this. I ripped off my jersey and flung it to the floor. The block "Washington" on the back made me lurch to the waste bin as sick bubbled up. I crouched, burying my head between my hands, and gasped for air as my stomach spasmed. A firm hand pressed against my back. I couldn't bring myself to meet Adam's face. His silence snuffed out the last ember of hope that my parents weren't lying lifeless on the other side of the doors. The hospital's social worker pulled him away to discuss becoming my legal guardian.

I glanced at the jersey. Tonight's game took them from me. A stupid fucking game. I clenched my fists. I'll never touch a ball again.

Then I heard Mom's voice as clear as the ambulance siren outside. "Washingtons don't quit," she always says...said...

I dipped my head between my arms and sobbed. I couldn't face a world where they're relegated to the past tense.

She *says*, "Even when you're sinking through life's muck, you reach out for help and keep going."

But that was a belief, and I no longer trusted them. Dad lied to me. The day was never ours to claim. We didn't stand a chance.

Beliefs are lies. They're the tattered veils we cloak ourselves in to ignore the truth. From the day we're born, we're one step closer to being murdered by a drunk driver. We're one step closer to bleeding out on a metal slab surrounded by strangers. I clenched my eyes shut. They deserved so much more than what they got. They deserved to grow old and see their kid go to college. I promised myself years ago that they'd never have to work for money when I went pro. God, they worked so hard all of their lives. They wanted so much for me.

I wiped my eyes and stared at my name written across the soiled jersey on the floor.

Washington.

They mattered.

Their sacrifices mattered.

Their hopes and dreams for me mattered.

I couldn't fathom facing a life without them, but if I somehow managed to pull through, I promised that I'd become who I said I would until death took me.

No matter the cost.

If I can't do that, I don't deserve to be here.

Chapter One

Five Years Later

Tears blur my vision as I shake off the throbbing in my nose. There was a slim chance I'd escape this game without at least one injury. The Arsenals never met a bone that they didn't want to bruise. I intercepted a pass in the first half, causing a loose ball. I dove for it. Chest sliding across the floor—fingertips a hair away from gaining possession—when a heavy force sent my face ricocheting off of the floor.

"What the fuck!"

My eyes stung as the taste of metal filled my mouth. I craned my neck and groaned when my face met with a dripping wet jersey. I shoved the opposing shooting guard, Chief Dickhead, off of me and slithered forward to take possession of the ball. I flipped to my back and scanned the floor for an open teammate when another blunt force, this one against my chest, had me buckling forward and choking for air.

The referee—who finally woke the fuck up—called a flagrant foul against Chief Dickhead for excessive contact, sending me to the line for two free throws. I tried to scrape myself off the floor, but a sharp pain locked me in place. Being bludgeoned by a steel bat had to be less excruciating. I hooked an arm around the necks of my two teammates, and on the count of three, I groaned as they set me upright. I zeroed in on the team doctor barreling toward me. She stuffed my bloody nose with cotton and rubbed pain relief cream on my torso.

"This doesn't look good. You should sit—"

"Chill, Doc. I'm good," I cut in.

If we have any chance of winning this game, then I have to be good. Not just good—incredible. And we need to win this game. *I* need us to win this game. This year, I'll announce my plan to enter the NBA draft, and I've spotted pro scouts in the stands. I've balled like my life depended on it for the last four years. Tonight is no exception. I've posted a career-high of thirty-eight points.

We're up one point, and it's our possession, with less than twenty seconds left on the final game clock. No time to mess around, I yell to my teammates to get locked in. Laced with adrenaline, I race up the court. Cam feints passing the ball to me but passes it to our shooting guard instead. Only it's intercepted by their power forward. *Fuck!* He flies down the court and tips it into the rim, taking the lead.

My heart is pounding like a war drum. Cam catches the next possession and wings the ball to me. I glimpse the game clock. This game boils down to the next eleven seconds. Their power forward may have five inches on my six-foot-four-inch height, but he is no match for my speed one-on-one.

He gestures to my nose. "Ain't so pretty anymore."

I evade his reach by crossing the ball between my legs. "You're welcome to hop off my dick anytime."

Jaw clenched, he pushes forward as I step back and release a long three-pointer.

A collective gasp rises from the crowd.

I flinch when the game clock buzzes, signaling the end of the game.

I ignore the voice in my head telling me I should've run it in, and glue my gaze to the ball as it hurdles through the air.

Why the hell did I shoot a long three?

Regret coils around my throat.

My gaze drops to the floor—if I keep looking, I might pass out. Honestly, passing out doesn't sound half bad right now.

A rushing sound echoes through the arena.

My head pops up, and I palm my temples in disbelief as the ball emerges through the bottom of the net.

We did it.

No fucking way.

We did it!

My legs are about to give out when I'm tackled by my teammates and hoisted into the air.

My ears ring from the roar of the crowd.

Ain't nothing like home court.

I wince when someone slaps my chest.

"Easy, easy," Cam yells, but the guys are hyped.

I search the stands for my parents. Seconds of parsing through a sea of faces, and it hits me like a freight train—they're not here. My eyes sting as I scan the bleachers. The fact it's been five years since their deaths is meaningless. I've learned that grieving isn't a linear process, and time has fuck all to do with healing wounds. I rest a peace sign against my heart, a gesture I make after every successful game—a reminder that every point and every win is for them.

Cam's mom is in the crowd screaming her lungs off, standing beside his girlfriend. Dillan's four siblings and parents are up there, with a few of my teammates' families. Uncle Adam wanted to attend, but it's difficult for him to make many of my games as a firefighter. I know I'll have a message from him when I get back to the locker room. I'm about to tap my teammates to drop me back to the ground when I see in my peripheral vision something, or rather someone, who can't be here. My gaze doubles back to the corner of the gym, where I lock on a tall figure standing by the door. I wipe sweat from my eyes. My head tilts to the side, unsure of what it's seeing.

Lo-and-behold, there in all of his glory is one of the most talented basketball players on the planet, Sid "The Wonder Kid" King, and he's staring right at me.

Holy fuck!

Goosebumps cover my skin. When our gazes lock, he raises his eyebrows and smiles. I've seen that half-smile, half-smirk plastered on magazine covers, social media, and ESPN interviews. Though this might be the only case in history where an airbrushed magazine cover pales in comparison to the real person. I can't look away.

His black beanie is worn low, framing his arched eyebrows. He's wearing a tailored, single-breasted overcoat with the collar up, an all-black tracksuit, and black Jordan 11s. It's the most understated look I've ever seen on him. He's clearly dressed to avoid cameras.

Sid tips his head in my direction, then pushes back on the door, turns, and walks out of the gym. It's like I just glimpsed a TV screen, not my real life. Just this morning, Cam sent me a text that read "Bad MoFo" and included a link to a commercial that made my jaw drop. It features Sid, who plays the position of a power forward for the Miami Marvels, playing one-on-one basketball against himself to Labrinth's "Mount Everest." The green screen technology that allows people to play their looka-likes on the screen is trippy. One version of Sid is shirtless, clad in gold basketball shorts. He plays offense with graceful aban-don, effortlessly knocking down an under-the-leg dunk from the free-throw line in slow motion, showcasing his athleticism and power. He bounces off the rim and hits a swagged-out, cele-bratory dance.

The other Sid, dressed in a blank tank and matching basketball shorts, steals possession of the ball and shows off his insane ball handling. He executes a lethal dribble combination by pushing forward, crossing the ball to his right hand, and stepping back, crossing the ball between his legs. He evades Shirtless Sid's steal attempt by swapping the ball behind his back before firing off a half-court three-pointer that's nothing but net. Instead of dancing, he drills Shirtless Sid with a cold-blooded death glare. A baritone voice cuts in saying something like "Want to know the secret to becoming the greatest athlete in the world? Compete with yourself." The commercial ends with both Sids walking out of the gym together.

"Anyone ever told you we look—"

"All the time! Except I'm more handsome," interrupts Shirtless Sid with a wink.

My balance tips as my teammates return me to the ground. Cam tells them to hold up as his mom lines up to take a picture of us. Leveled back in the air, I glance around to see if anyone else caught sight of Sid, but everyone is absorbed in the celebration.

Did one of the most famous basketball players in the league really just roll up to watch our game? My heart is racing like it wants to escape my chest to chase after him. I have to know if I imagined him.

I pat my teammates' shoulders. "Yo, let me down."

As soon as my feet hit the ground, I take off. I shrug at the confused expressions on my teammates' faces as I evade their congratulatory fist bumps. I spin and duck past the media and coaching staff.

"My bad!" I call out as I slip through a group of cheerleaders congregating near the door.

"Coming through!" I yell as I weave through fans lining the hallway.

I try to cut through a large group blocking my way. "Pardon me," I project.

At the sound of my voice, one girl shrieks and freezes in

my path. I spin to avoid a head-on collision but lose my footing and crash through the double doors, spilling out into the parking lot. Taking a second to collect myself, I wince as I press against my throbbing torso. As I limp-jog down the center aisle of cars, I scan for him in every direction. I hop up on the trunk of Cam's car to get a better look. Except for families trickling out of the gym and students passing by heading to the dorms, there's no sight of anyone else. My shoulders slump forward.

Damn!

"Congrats on the win!" Jim, a campus security guard, calls out as I head back inside.

"Thanks, man! Hey, I know this sounds wild, but did Sid King come through here?"

He frowns. "*The* Sid King, inventor of the Wonder Kid Dunk? At a college game?"

"Never mind," I mutter, slinking away.

"Sup, Alicia," I greet another security guard as we pass each other in the corridor.

"Wassup, Pretty Boy."

"I just saw the most insane car pass me on the way in," I overhear Alicia recounting to Jim.

I freeze in my tracks and whip around. "W-what kind of car? Did you see the driver?"

Alicia crinkles her eyebrows. "Uh, n-no. The windows were tinted. It was an emerald-green Aston. The engine's rumble was something fierce—like a bomber squadron circling overhead."

The hairs on the back of my neck stand up.

It *was* him! *I knew it!* If there's anyone who'd drive an Aston Martin, it's him. There's a video online with his sick car collection. Even his rentals are exotic.

"Thanks!" I shout as I race back to my teammates.

The rest of the night goes by in a blur of celebration—though nothing, not my winner's high, booze, or the gorgeous girls filling our dorm, comes close to topping the exhilaration of seeing Sid for a few seconds.

During my freshman year, I became the fifth player to win Big 12 Player of the Year and Big 12 Freshman of the Year in the same season. The awards are given to the most outstanding player in the Big 12 Conference, a group of ten, originally twelve, universities that compete at the NCAA Division I level.

The most recent player to win both in the same season was Sid. It, of course, led sports broadcasters to launch a comparison of us. The truth is, we couldn't be more different. For one, there hasn't been a player more hyped in the league than Sid, which, of course, created enormous pressure for him. The thing is, despite all the hype, Sid delivered. During his rookie professional season, he averaged twenty-two points, six assists, and seven rebounds. Stats that I've memorized and hope to beat one day. Named Rookie of the Year, his game has only improved with each passing season.

Where I'm lean and agile, Sid is pure muscle and a powerhouse on the court. He hits threes with ease and defends the rim effortlessly. It's hard to defend him without getting physical, which leads to him getting fouled often, sending him to the free-throw line every quarter. Off the court, he's a bachelor, successful investor, and activist. He dates around, always a famous supermodel or celebrity, most recently linked to Katrina, a mononymous, A-list actress.

People Magazine voted him the Sexiest Man Alive last year. There's a spread in the issue with him sitting down naked with only a basketball covering his groin. A picture of it damn near broke the internet. Ultra-defined muscles, ripped abs, high cheekbones, rich brown skin, and the most magnetic chestnut brown eyes. Half of the men covering his career either want to fuck or be him, but they'd eat their hearts before they'd ever admit it.

Separate from his nine-figure league contract, he's signed multi-million dollar endorsements and made it known that he plans to own a basketball team one day. As a vocal activist, he lends his voice and money to numerous causes. The dude's lived up to all the hype and then some. I haven't achieved anything remotely close. I've been rocking the same pair of worn-in black and gray Jordan 1 Retro sneakers all year. I drive Uncle Adam's ancient Toyota Camry around campus. The car conks out if I go above eighty miles per hour. I haven't funded or sat on boards for organizations making a difference in the world. I don't have five seasons of pro ball under my belt. It's bonkers for us even to be mentioned in the same sentence.

Personality-wise, I'm painted as poised, introverted, and haunted by the death of my parents, and it's not untrue. During my sophomore year, a sports profile was published on me by a reputable journalist. He described my ability to nail pull-up three-pointers from deep while in transition as some of the prettiest basketball seen in decades. My teammates started clowning me by calling me "Pretty Boy." The nickname quickly spread around campus. Once ladies got a hold of it, its meaning became more about my looks than my game.

While I'm most comfortable in a T-shirt and ripped skinny jeans, Sid rocks the latest runway fashion. He made headlines when he wore a version of a skort, a combination of a skirt and shorts, with a ripped tank revealing a pierced nipple, a skinny tie, and leather combat boots. His muscular hamstrings and calves were...memorable. Since then, there have been endless copycats of men in skorts, but none could pull it off quite like him. Coupled with his original style, he has an innate elegance you can't curate or copy.

I haven't been able to shake the wonder of seeing him at my

game. If I don't get drafted, I'll never find out why he was there. But there's so much more than that at stake. I need to become who I promised my parents I would. I need to make them proud. Nothing can ever matter more than honoring them and their sacrifices.

Chapter Two

To say it surprised anyone when I announced my plans to enter the NBA draft would be untrue. What *is* surprising is the fact analysts regard me as the consensus number one draft pick. It's rare for a college senior to be the top pick in the NBA. It's so rare—it hasn't happened in the last fifteen years. The belief is that the earlier a player enters the league, the sooner they can begin training at a high level to reach their potential. The older a player, the more prone they are to injury. It was important to my parents that I finished college. If they were alive, I would have negotiated entering the draft after my freshman year, which is more common. But I didn't have that choice. So, I stayed in school, trained hard, and worked my ass off on the court.

The LA Knights won the lottery and have the first pick, and that's the team I want to join. Nothing prepares you for draft day. Adam and I flew to Chicago to join nineteen other players invited to attend the Blue Room at the United Center. An invitation is a positive sign that you'll get picked in the draft's first round, but it isn't a guarantee. You drop to the second round if you're not picked in the first. Teams pay considerably less to second-round picks, at least initially, and often use them as pawns in franchise trade negotiations.

I can barely keep my protein shake down because my body is so out of whack from the nerves. For as long as I can remember, my only goal's been to make it to the league, become an elite player, and become the man who would make my parents proud. If I don't make the first draft round, I'll never be able to live with myself.

"I need a second, Unc," I say to Adam, gesturing for him to follow me. I find an empty stairwell and lean against the wall.

"Still sick?" He reaches inside his pocket and pulls out a pack of gum. "Here, chew on this."

"Thanks. My body can't figure out if it wants to barf or crap."

The sugary mint helps to wipe out the taste of the protein shake, settling the nausea a bit.

"You remember that Halloween when we went trick or treatin', and you ate so many of those red jelly beans you barfed up red goo all over my couch?"

I burst out laughing. "Don't remind me. I can't even look at them without being queasy."

"I still don't know how your mom knew you'd been sick when I dropped you off the next day." A distant awe settles into his features.

"She had a sixth sense for that kind of thing. Sometimes, Dad or I came home sick, and there'd already be soup on the stove. She'd always say—"

"I had a feeling you weren't feeling well," Adam interjects.

"Yeah, exactly!"

"When you were a toddler and had a stomach ache, she'd press your belly against her own to—as she put it—absorb your pain. I was skeptical at first, but it worked. You'd fall asleep in her arms and wake up feeling better."

I grin. "She used to tell me that story, but I'm not sure I ever believed it."

"Believe it! I saw it with my own eyes."

"She was a sorceress or something." I shake my head.

"A healer. When your grandpa Malcolm passed, I was so angry, I pushed everyone away. Rose showed up at the house one evening with a casserole and a bottle of Macallan. She didn't fear my rage. I'm not even sure she saw rage, only my pain. She poured us both a glass and before I knew it, she had me cracked open. We laughed together, recalling memories of Dad, and then we cried. She said that tears are the overflow of a brimming heart. I never forgot that."

It sounds like her. Memories transport me back to Brooklyn, where I hear Mom's ebullient laughter echoing throughout the kitchen.

I squeeze my eyes shut. The ache is sharp.

Not today...

I try to pluck it away, but like an invasive weed, the thought breaks through.

They exist only in memory.

And memories fade with time.

I looked it up once—athazagoraphobia—the fear of forgetting someone or being forgotten. They call it a social phobia. I call it an orphan's fear. The years have taught me it's futile fighting it, even if facing it means surrendering to a hollowing anguish.

"Let's see," Adam says, reeling me back. He braces my shoulders and meets my gaze. His eyes are glossy too. There's an immersive room inside of both of us where memories of Brooklyn project off the walls. We try to keep the door shut, but invisible tethers—a whiff of a scent or the echo of a baritone laugh—yank us inside. And when I'm in there, the world outside the room reduces to a distant memory. Yesterday, Bob

Marley's "Is This Love" hurled me from the airport cafe to our old living room, where Dad wrapped his arms around Mom's waist. Dad and Bob's voices intermingled as he and Mom rocked to the music. The memory almost brought me to my knees.

"Take a deep breath. You know, besides my drop-dead good looks, I have superpowers of my own."

I roll my eyes. "Is that right?"

"I think you got specks of dust or something in your eyes. They did a weird rolling thing." He smirks. "My superpower tells me that some of the greatest experiences of your life are yet to come, starting today."

His confidence is a lifeline.

"I hope so. Any chance your superpower can confirm the number of championship rings I'll cop?"

He grins. "You've been chasing rings since the first time you picked up a ball."

I chuckle. It's mostly true.

"At least four." He winks and pats my chest. "Now, what'd'ya say we get you drafted?"

ENTERING THE BLUE ROOM, I RECOGNIZE PLAYERS I'VE PLAYED against in college and others I've seen or read about on ESPN. I recognize a seven-foot-five international player who's a big deal in the UK. Dude's a beanstalk.

"Pretty Boy Ty." I hear as Adam and I make our way to our seats. I turn toward the voice and come face-to-face with Jeff Banks, arguably the best shooting guard Duke University has ever seen. Rocking a silver metallic suit, flashy as ever, he's six-foot-six and lanky with a head full of thick curls. He has a vertical labret piercing, big round eyes, and a boyish smile.

Analysts predict that Jeff will be picked in the top five of the first draft.

"If it isn't the Prince of Duke in the flesh." I extend my hand and pull him into a quick hug. His palms are clammy. "You nervous too?"

"Hell yeah, but 'Prince?'" He smirks. "I think you meant the God of Duke."

I throw my arm over Adam's shoulder. "Unc, meet the very humble Jeff Banks."

"Whoa, the resemblance is uncanny," Jeff says, glancing between us. "Pleasure to meet you, sir." He extends his hand to Adam.

I look a lot like my uncle, who looked like his older brother, my dad. I have his and dad's height, but Adam has way more muscle.

"Likewise. I saw one of your games against North Carolina. You crushed them," Adam recalls.

"Ah, back in February, yeah, that game was lit. I damn near ruptured my Achilles."

Adam grimaces. "Every balla's nightmare."

"Word." He nods at me. "I just wanted to wish you good luck. Remember, we earned our spot here, even though we're nervous. I'll find you later. Peace." He braces my shoulder, then he's off.

"Nice kid," Adam says as we watch him fade into the crowd.

"Yeah, but he has an ego larger than this arena. Weird combo." I shake my head, then lead the way to our seats.

On some level, I know that it's normal to be anxious on a day like today, but I didn't expect to feel...so much. My parents would have been crazy proud to be here today. The countless practices they drove me to through the years, the games attended, and the pep talks. This is as much their day as my own. The day sits heavily, and my wiring is off like I could blow a fuse at any moment. I hate the driver who cheated them out of being here. If they were, Dad would be crying happy tears. Mom would be, too, but in her reserved way. Uncle Adam is the best surrogate parent I could've hoped for, but it's still not the same. They've left a gaping hole in both of our lives.

"Catharine, Phil, it's good of you to make it," Adam greets my new agents from Preeminent Management. The agency's managed at least forty-five first-round draft picks and a slew of top players in the league.

"There's nowhere else we'd rather be," Catharine replies. Her knee-length dress, the color of red amaranth, looks expertly tailored. A thick black braid adorns her head like a halo.

"How are you holding up, Ty?" she asks, peering into my eyes.

"Is it obvious? I probably look like the green-faced vomit emoji," I joke.

"It's normal to be nervous," she says, patting my shoulders.

"It's true that everything changes today, and it's important to acknowledge this pivotal moment in your life. Yet, it's only one more step in an already stellar career," Phil says, with a trace of an Italian accent.

His warm smile reveals a perfect set of dimples. My gaze pans over his head of sleek black curls, deep-set brown eyes, and trim beard down to his white dress shirt, blue tie, and slate gray suit pants. His shirt is rolled up at the sleeves, balancing the otherwise crisp look. I spot his jacket draped over his chair. He's young, but he gives off old money. If I had to guess, I'd bet he already has enough dough to retire comfortably, but he works because he's good at it and loves it.

"You look fantastic, by the way. Those gorgeous eyes of yours sparkle against the dark blue," he says, winking while dusting something off my blazer.

"Thanks." I smile. It grows too wide, so I reel it in. I overdo it, and now I'm frowning, so I smile again, but it's even wider than before. *Okay, then.*

I nod and beeline to my seat next to Adam.

Players, agents, and family members pack the room. Besides commentary on the draft tomorrow, the second most covered topic will be everyone's drip. Some players are showing out tonight. I went for a monochromatic look with a navy-blue, Armani suit, matching blue button-up, and no tie, compliments of Preeminent Management. I spot Gene, a player from the University of North Carolina, wearing a silk, paisley suit with no shirt. Wait, there *is* a shirt, but it's see-through. An elaborate diamond choker thing sparkles from his neck. Gene's so comfortable in his skin that he rocks it as easily as a jersey and shorts. Tennyson, a player from the University of Kentucky, is dripped in hot pink and black polka dots. He's even dyed half of his afro a matching pink. The drip fits the personalities in the room to a T. I've only ever wanted to be known for my game. If I could skip all the PR engagements and interviews that come with the gig, I'd be the happiest athlete on earth. Unfortunately, that's not how it works. NBA players are supposed to be superstars, especially the great ones. The more exposure a player receives, the more it enhances the sport, so you're expected to seek opportunities to enhance your profile. The league is counting on it.

The buzz in the room reduces to a hush as Tom Jones, the league's commissioner, approaches the dais.

"And so it begins," Adam says, squeezing my hand. I zone out Tom's opening remarks, lean forward, and dip my head between my palms. I tell myself to breathe, but my stomach hangs from weathered suspension cables. Breathing risks sending it into free fall.

"With the first pick in the NBA Draft, the LA Knights draft Tyler Washington from—" The room erupts into applause and congratulatory shouts, drowning Tom out. I bet TV screens at home have cut to my alma mater, where my old teammates are celebrating. I imagined this moment a million times before, and in every version, I jump out of my seat in excitement and hug my family. So, I'm surprised that I am glued to my seat and flooded with more emotions than I ever cared to show in public. Memories of my parents flash through my mind, and the ache overwhelms me. *Stand up.* But instead, I cover my face in my hands and choke for a second, trying to breathe.

I'm swept up in an embrace by a teary-eyed Adam.

"You did it, kid. Congratulations! They'd be so proud of you. *I'm* so proud of you," he says, pressing his forehead to mine. How often I've felt anchored by his embrace when drowning in a sea of nightmares over the last few years.

"I don't know where I'd be without you." The raw honesty of that truth causes a prick behind my eyes. Without Adam, I'd have no one. God knows where I would be today. Despite his grief, he picked up where my parents left off and helped make today come true.

"As long as my heart beats, I'll always be here, kid," he says, squeezing my shoulders. The thought of Adam's heart not beating tugs the weathered suspension cables, and my stomach drops. I palm my stomach, causing Adam to wince as he realizes his poor choice of words. Forcing a small smile, I turn to hug Catharine and Phil, who both offer congratulations, and then I make my way to the stage.

Tom embraces me in a perfunctory hug.

"Congratulations, Ty. This is darn near historic. You should be very proud. I know you'll do great things in Los Angeles, and I'm sure your parents are watching over you with great pride today. " A southern drawl coats his voice.

I choke back tears and let out a shaky breath. "Thank you, sir. It's a pleasure to meet you. I'm honored to be granted the opportunity to play in the league."

We pose for a quick picture. As I leave the stage, Tom announces that Jeff will head to Indiana.

Good for him. It's what he wanted.

I excuse myself once back in my seat. I dap a few fellow players and accept their cheers of congratulations as I make my way to the restroom. Once there, I blow my nose and splash my face with cold water.

I reach for a paper towel as I peer at myself in the mirror. My mom's long brown lashes and hazel eyes stare back at me, but they are my dad's almond shape. I have my dad's coily brown hair, longer on top and faded on the sides. My mother's freckles dust over my dad's angular cheekbones. Having features from both of my parents makes me feel closer to them. I used to resent the moniker "Pretty Boy," which most people assume refers to my looks, until I realized that I am what's left of both of my parents. Besides Adam, I'm the last living trace of their love. I will only ever feel proud of that. I take a deep breath, dry my face, and head back to my seat.

After dinner, a couple of the guys try to drag me to the draft party, but I fall back, opting to turn in early.

"Go out and celebrate. Would it kill you to make friends?"

"I'm not here to make friends, Unc." I plunk myself in a plush armchair in the living room of the two-bedroom hotel suite the league put us in for the night.

"I worry about you. Ever since your parents died, you've closed yourself off." He grabs a couple water bottles from the mini fridge and tosses me one.

I shrug as I catch it. In high school, I learned the hard way that being popular and having friends aren't the same thing. My so-called friends were awkward as fuck when my parents died. They treated me like a pathetic sympathy case. Then, they acted like I was a burden when I was still grieving months later. Grief is loneliness and sadness on steroids.

"You don't need to worry about me. I'm good."

"It's my job to worry about you. Promise me you'll at least attempt to be friends with the guys in LA. It tears me up thinking of you holed up in your hotel or dorm after games like you were in college."

I grunt. "I celebrated with the team in college a few times, didn't I?"

"A few celebrations during four years of college...You're kind of proving my point. Promise me you'll make more of an attempt in the league."

I can't promise him that, nor can I lie to him. I'm better on my own. Meeting his gaze, I silently beg him not to push me on this.

He sighs. "They'd want you to be happy, kid."

My eyes sting as I climb to my feet and walk toward my room.

"I'm sure they'd want to be alive," I mutter as I shut the door.

Once I strip down to my T-shirt and briefs, I sink into the bed. Though my eyes are too heavy to read, I tuck my book next to me. Unlocking my phone, I scroll to my favorites and hit play on a compilation video of Sid's freak shots.

Sleep comes easily, whereas rest proves difficult.

I dream I am back in college. I turn in my philosophy paper and am headed to my dorm to pull an all-nighter for my calculus exam. I'm rounding the corner of the parking lot when I run smack into a crowd. There's a murmur of excitement as I push through to the front. My pulse quickens as an ochre-colored Aston Martin, with its gleaming, winged logo, comes into focus. I freeze in my tracks when I see who's leaning against the passenger door of the car.

Sid.

His face lights up when our gazes lock, activating all the nerves in my body. I glance past my shoulder to confirm he's beaming at me, and I notice that everyone's looking at me.

"Catch," he says.

My hand darts up and clasps the car keys. He winks and climbs into the front passenger seat. His gold watch gleams against the sun as he gestures for me to get in. I pop my faded hoodie up to hide from the gazillion camera phones aimed at me. Throwing my bag in the back seat, I climb behind the wheel. As soon as the car fires up, every- thing shifts. I'm hurtling down the highway at breakneck speed. I squeeze my eyes shut, then open them again and wince from the shooting pain between my eyes. When I glance over at the passenger seat, it's empty. My breath reeks and tastes like booze. I slam on the acceleration, desperate to reach my dorm, before I puke all over myself. I signal to exit, or at least I think I do. As soon as I switch lanes, a piercing car horn blasts through the car, and a blinding light explodes in my peripheral vision. There's a loud pop as my head smacks back, bouncing off the steering wheel. The road spins, gluing my head to the driver's side window. I press against the throbbing ache in my head, and my fingers sink into a wet gash. I lower my hand to eye level—it's coated in blood. Another blinding light catches my peripheral vision just as I smack full force into another car. An agonizing scream pierces my brain, causing me to release the steering wheel and plug my ears with my palms. My mother's powdery perfume wafts—"

"Hey, hey, wake up."

Jerking awake, I almost headbutt Adam, whose face hovers over my own.

I palm the hammering in my head. "W-what happened?"

My shirt is plastered to my skin, slick with sweat.

"You were screaming and..." Adam's voice trails off when I hold up a hand. A sharp twist in my stomach has me buckling over. I scramble out of bed, beelining for the wastebasket, and hurl.

I jolt from Adam's touch.

"Shh. It's okay." He rubs soft circles along my back.

My throat burns. The vile taste of sickness overwhelms my senses. I suck in air to calm the violent convulsions in my stomach. Scooting against the wall and tucking my knees against my chest, I dip my head between my legs. Just when I think things are returning to normal, the cries of horror from my nightmare —my mother's voice—blast through my head like a blow horn. I stab my palms against my ears and collapse into a fetal position. Spots of darkness spread from the outer edges of my vision as the walls close in. My voice is in there somewhere, yelling for it to stop. A blast of tiny needles pierces my head and chest, and in an instant the screams are gone.

"Tyler, hey, hey, you're okay." Adam's leaning over me, cradling my head. "You had a panic attack...and a nightmare, I think."

My teeth chatter. "C-cold."

"You were in shock. I grabbed the only thing I could find." He holds up an empty ice bucket.

"T-thanks," I grunt.

He studies me. "You still have the nightmares."

I wince. Technically, I didn't lie. I told him that everything was under control, which it is. So what if I have nightmares from time to time—it doesn't interrupt my game.

I swallow, grimacing from the ache in my throat. "Sometimes...randomly."

"Randomly, as in a couple of times a week? A month?" Concern drenches his voice. He will not let this go quickly.

"A few times a week," I mutter.

"Is it the same nightmare where you're the drunk driver that killed your parents?"

I nod.

"My God. It's been too long. Can I set up a session for you with Michael?"

He found Michael, a grief counselor, when my parents passed. I attended a few sessions before I called it quits. It was too hard to open up back then and not much has changed for me since.

I shake my head as I crawl to a sitting position and tuck my knees into my chest. "Nah. I'm good."

"Tyler, this isn't healthy. I can't force you to get help, but you need it. I love you, and seeing you like this is torture."

I rub my neck as a familiar gnawing creeps up—guilt. I don't want to hurt him, but I'm not a kid anymore. If I say I'm fine, then I'm fine.

"I love you too, and I need you to trust me. They're just nightmares. No need to stress yourself out."

As I climb to my feet, my legs ache like I ran twenty miles. I steel myself, not wanting to appear weak in front of him.

"I'm going to shower and get rid of this." I gesture to the soiled wastebasket.

"It's not just nightmares, though, is it? You've also refused to make friends or have a semblance of a social life. I know basketball has always meant everything to you, but something changed when your parents died. You don't play because it's fun anymore. You play like your life depends on it. No, that makes it sound healthier than what this is. You play like the game is more important than your life."

It is more important!

How the fuck wouldn't it be? I grit my jaw to keep from blowing my top. He'll never understand. How could he? His parents, my grandparents, died of old age. My parents were murdered trying to support my dreams. The least I can do is see that those dreams come true. The last thing I need is some head doctor poking around, twisting my shit up.

I screw my eyes shut. "Today was supposed to be a good day...maybe even a happy one."

"You trying to convince me or yourself of that?" he asks quietly.

The whole day was different from how I imagined it. After the sadness and anxiety passed, I've just been...low.

"Can we just let it go for now?"

He grunts. "Fine. Go shower. Don't think for a second that this conversation is over. Basketball will never be more important than your health. It's my job to remind you of that."

I turn and nod to the ice bucket. "Thanks."

He grunts.

I stand under the showerhead, letting the hot water wash away the sweat and stench of sickness. Rolling my neck and shoulders, I try to release the knots of tension pinching my nerves. I focus on the lines of grout lacing the shower tiles to block out the nightmare. The pained look on Adam's face sits stark in my memory. Then there's the familiar voice—*it would be so much easier to end it.*

Just. End. It.

I shake my head, pushing the thought away, and scramble for another that's tied to less pain.

Sid.

It wasn't all a nightmare. He smiled at me. For a moment, I was the most important person in his world. I wasn't myself. I was laughing gas. Weightless.

If the ghost of his smile has that kind of effect on me, I can't imagine what it'd feel like to know him. I shake my head at the thought.

Chapter Three

I t's been months since the NBA draft. I've heard crazy stories about rookie initiation duties in the NBA. The real thing isn't as bad as I imagined, at least on the Knights. Like any family or team, a culture exists. As a new member, you're expected to observe and learn about the team's culture without being too disruptive. I've learned in the locker room to talk less and let the vets dominate the conversation. Never be the first to leave the gym to show that you're willing to put in the work. Be careful to avoid any demonstrations of entitlement, or it'll be impossible to break that perception. Never be the first one in the shower. Locker rooms are small, so cleaning up after yourself is essential for everyone's sanity. On the road, we're expected to bring everyone snacks for the plane ride and post-game towels for the veteran players.

Our team is young this season. To help guide us, we have vets—Tevin, center and power forward, and Idris, shooting guard. They've been more big bros than anything. I overheard Idris pull aside a fellow rookie who had a hygiene issue. He explained no one wanted to hang around or guard a player that stinks, so he needed to shower and wear deodorant from now on. I was grateful. The other dude's odor made me sick. Tevin sent a fellow rookie back to the locker room to change his socks right before tonight's game. The rookie was wearing the signature brand of a competing player. I'm not sure what he was thinking.

I made my NBA debut tonight against the Los Angeles Royals, finishing with eleven points, and we secured a victory. Technically, it isn't my first debut since being drafted. I represented the Knights in the Las Vegas NBA Summer League this past summer, where thirty NBA teams, comprised of sophomores, rookies, and G League players, competed over nine days. We beat Milwaukee, and I posted fifteen points.

Tonight's win hits differently. I've been a fan of the Royals franchise since I was a kid, so it's surreal to be playing against the team in my debut. The Knights and the Royals share the same arena for home games. We may play for the same city, but we still compete ferociously.

Before I can escape the court, an interviewer approaches me. I know this is part of the gig, but I loathe it.

"Ty, Tim Bryant here, *LA Times*. How did it feel to play in your first NBA game?"

I repeat what I rehearsed on the way in this morning. "It's a chance of a lifetime to play with some of the best players in the league. I plan to keep learning, support my teammates, and work hard to enhance my game."

Looking at him, I remember the young kids at home who dream of being in the league one day, and I shift my gaze to the camera. I use the towel around my neck to soak up some of the sweat on my face.

"And we all can't wait to see the leaps that you'll make. It's known that you lost your parents tragically a few years ago. What would your parents say to you today if they were still alive?" Tim points the microphone back in my direction.

Being asked this question in almost every interview I've

been a part of used to choke me up, but I learned to have a canned response prepared to avoid thinking about the answer.

"I think they would be proud of me. They loved and supported me. Every shot that I make is in honor of them and their sacrifices."

"They sound like they were amazing and caring parents, Ty. Okay, last question. Earlier today, Sid "The Wonder Kid" King was asked if he was worried you'd beat his record by tallying at least twenty-seven points and nine rebounds before your tenth game as a rookie, here's his response." Tim's assistant passes him the clip already queued on a phone, then hits play.

A sweat-glistened, courtside Sid—who has just banked a win by the score displayed on the bottom of the screen—has his head dipped forward to hear the interviewer's question. His eyes light up. I take a deep breath to slow down my heartbeat. It isn't lost on me that there's a camera pointed at my face, and one bad reaction would spread like wildfire across the internet. Sid seems to think about the question before answering. Unlike me, he always seems comfortable in front of the camera, even when asked provocative questions.

"I have a response, but it's more advice. Yo, Ty, if you're out there watching, drown out the noise, man, and go hard in the paint this year. I remember the pressure of rookie year, having also been the first pick in the draft. You feel you have to elevate the team by yourself. Stay locked in, and stick to the basics of doing what you love. You've already come so far after facing a terrible loss. There are bright times ahead." He's slapped on the back by a teammate and turns to dap him. The clip ends.

Well damn, I wasn't sure what response to expect, bravado maybe. More seasoned players discourage comparison. They'd laugh in the face of a question like that on camera. I didn't expect thoughtful and solid advice. Also, he knows about my parents' accident?

Whaaat?

I'm a rookie out of college. It's expected that I know everything public about him since he's one of the best players in the league, but not vice versa. I think back to my game in college and how I wondered if I imagined seeing him, but now I'm not sure. I recall searching Google and social media platforms to confirm his whereabouts that night, but my search yielded zilch.

I formulate a response as Tim points the mic back to me.

"Wow, sound advice from one of the greatest players alive." I clear my throat. "I'm, uh, humbled and grateful."

Tim nods for me to continue.

"Uh, I plan to do just that—play the best ball and leave it all on the floor every night. Thanks, Tim. I gotta run."

"Appreciate it, Ty. Good game tonight." Tim turns to the camera to close out the segment.

I head to the locker room, grinning but also stunned. Sid knows of me. *Wild.*

Chapter Four

A few weeks later, I beat Sid's record in my ninth game. To commemorate the record break, ESPN arranged an interview between us. We're both allowed to ask each other whatever we want. It's supposed to come off as an organic and relaxed conversation between professionals. I spent the last week writing and rewriting questions I wanted to ask him, but then I finally gave up and decided to wing it. We're both flown into ESPN's office near Lincoln Center in New York City on a brisk day in early December.

First to arrive, I spend a few minutes thawing my bones. I change into an outfit curated for me—a cashmere, forest green sweater with gold speckles and dark blue, slim-fitting slacks. The studio's bumping hip-hop throwbacks, and I'm humming along between sips of lemon honey tea when Sid walks in. I hear his hearty laugh and rich voice before I see him. It's uncanny how familiar his voice is, though we've never met. Being a famous person is wild that way. I expect an entourage, but it appears he's arrived alone. He's rocking a burnt orange bubble coat, black beanie, gold-ish corduroys, and a black sweater. Wireless headphones hang from his neck along with a sleek gold chain.

Our gazes lock, and that lethal half-smile, half-smirk splits across his face.

All heads turn in his direction, and I'm grateful it isn't just me experiencing his magnetism.

I thought I'd feel small next to his towering presence, but I'm taller somehow.

Rare.

"Mr. Washington in the flesh," he says, voice buttery smooth like velvet.

"Hey, it's a pleasure to finally meet you," I reply.

His gaze scans over my face, leaving a trace of warmth in its trail.

His presence evokes a memory I haven't thought about in years. My mom used to convince me to meditate by bribing me with dessert. One time, she'd bribed me with homemade chocolate glazed doughnuts. We sat and meditated while the dough was doing something Mom called proofing. I swear an hour had passed when I peeked an eye open to check the time. Groaning, I saw that the long hand had only moved nine spaces forward. I stole a glance at Mom and did a double-take. She was glowing like the fireflies we searched for during evening strolls in the summertime. My neck tilted back as I watched the sunlight orbit around her like she was in the center of the galaxy. She sat so perfectly still that waves of calming energy wafted over me. I nearly jumped out of my skin when the kitchen timer went off. I thought only minutes had passed when time had leaped.

I asked her what she saw when she meditated. She imagined a utopia with crystal clear waters with healing properties so potent that a few minutes of soaking soothed all the aches from her body. Lilies, poppies, and lavender covered the land, but jasmine perfumed the air. Elephants and gentle wild cats roamed. A grand swing swept her up to an enchanted house at the summit of a mountain. Inside the house was a room with a large bed full of the fluffiest pillows and softest bedding. She had the best naps of her life there. Glass walls offered sweeping views of the land. She said it was the safest place in the universe where nothing bad could happen—*a land where her soul dwelled.*

I am strangely reminded of Mom's utopia, gazing into the depths of Sid's eyes.

"You know, most college nicknames are ridiculous, but yours tracks," he says.

The brimming, resonant tone of his voice passes through me like a gentle charge. I take a steadying breath. "Is that right?"

Wait, did he just say that I'm pretty? I accept the compliment instead of clarifying the true meaning of my moniker.

I wrap my hand around the hand he's extended and fall into the pull of his dap. As my chest rests against him, I absorb every bit of the five inches he has on me at six-foot-nine, and the bulk of his muscle mass. I imagine a full hug would be like a swaddle. I pull away from the hug, but not before I absorb his heavenly cologne. It's distinct.

"It's a pleasure to meet you too. Congratulations on breaking my record. I'm selfishly glad it was you. I think you bring something fresh to the game," he says, removing his coat and beanie. The sides of his fade are shaved in geometric patterns. Everything works on this guy. It's kind of ridiculous.

He thanks the wardrobe attendant standing by as he hands her his coat, scarf, and beanie, then retrieves his phone and a sheet of paper from his coat pocket. He asks her if keeping his corduroys is fine but switches to the sweater picked out. She asks who the designer is, and he explains the pants are by an up-and-coming designer out of Brooklyn.

She flicks long strands of hair off her shoulder, leans in, and says, "The Wonder Kid can do whatever he wants. I'd never tell." It's forward and flirtatious. He's used to or misses it because his only reply is, "Cool. Thank you."

He turns back to me and passes me his phone and paper to hold while he removes his sweatshirt. He's wearing a tight-fitting cotton tank underneath. My eyes graze the indent of his nipple ring as he throws the royal blue sweater over his head and takes in the fit.

He shrugs. "I think it works."

Of course it works.

"Good lookin' out," he says as he retrieves his phone and paper from me. The attendant takes his original sweater and departs.

He grabs a glass bottle of water from the table before we get started. Our chairs face each other roughly four feet apart, and there is a microphone overhead and one attached to us. We run a few sound and camera checks. Makeup is minimal for us. We go over the details and structure of the interview with the director. The structure is simple—we're the interviewers. Sid and I will take turns asking each other whatever we want. If there are questions we're uncomfortable answering, we can just say "Next question," and it'll be edited out. We'll both receive the final version for sign-off as our contract stipulates. We flip a coin to decide who will ask the first question, and Sid wins the toss. He opens up the paper he's placed on the side table, and I realize he's prepared questions. I rub my sweaty palms against my thighs, regretting my decision to wing it.

The camera rolls.

"Hello, people of the world, I'm Sid King, and this is Ty Washington, and like me, you can see he's awful pretty," he says, spot-on impersonating a famous boxer.

The room erupts into laughter, myself included.

Sid grins, a glint of mischief whirling in his eyes. "First and foremost, Ty"—he leans back, hooking an arm over his chair—

"congratulations again on tallying thirty points and eleven rebounds in your ninth game as a rookie. How does it feel to have made history in your first season in the league?"

His professional but relaxed interview style throws me for a second.

"Uh, thanks," I reply.

He nods for me to continue.

"It's great. I, uh, tend to focus on the next thing instead of spending too much time reflecting on the wins." This is a half-truth. What good are the wins if the people you love most aren't here to celebrate them?

"I can kinda relate to that. When you've lived in survival mode for most of your life, it's really hard to find comfort in achievement and wins. We're geared to move towards the next thing," he says, unhooking his arm from over the chair to lean forward slightly. "I sometimes think the act of reflection is for when I'm an old geezer, swaying in a rocking chair on my porch, looking back over my life. For now, I want to stay in the arena and reach new bounds."

"Me too. Though there is value in celebrating the wins in real-time with the people that matter most to you."

A knowing expression crawls across his face.

It's my turn to ask a question. "If you could have a career other than basketball, what would it be?" I pull down the hem of my pants around my ankle, wishing there was a pill for moments like this that could help me forget myself. I'm convinced there's an inverse relationship between joy and self-consciousness.

His eyebrows hike up. "That's a good question. I have so much energy. I can't imagine not training rigorously for a living. I mean, you know firsthand that to get to the league, you have to maintain a single-minded focus. I'd probably play soccer. What about you?"

"Formula 1 Racing," I answer without missing a beat.

"Word? Are you an adrenaline junky?" he asks, eyes wide.

"I think it's cool how present you have to be while racing, making super split-second decisions. Also, the whips are sick!"

He grins. "Imagine having that much horsepower at your fingertips."

I'm not sure he has to imagine. I've seen a segment once that featured his luxury car collection.

"I have a question," he says. "It's serious. Brace yourself."

I nod.

"Thanksgiving just passed, as you know. How'd you spend it, and where do you land on the age-old debate—pumpkin vs. sweet potato pie?"

I chuckle at the randomness of the question, causing him to laugh too.

"I woke up and went for a run, then I delivered food to families in need. My uncle is a firefighter with a tough schedule, so we didn't get a chance to spend it together this year."

A small frown etches away the remnants of his laughter. Maybe he understands the inherent loneliness of a holiday spent amongst strangers, though he doesn't seem likely to acknowledge it on camera. I can't help but wonder what this conversation could have been without cameras in the room.

"It's cool that you give back. What about the pie question?"

"Oh, 100% pumpkin. My mom's pie used to slap. Though peach or apple trumps pumpkin for me," I reply.

He holds his chest like it's wounded. "Nah, bruh! It's sweet potato all the way." He turns to the camera. "Viewers at home, take to social media and cast your vote. Let's solve this once and for all."

I bite back a smile. "How'd you spend yours?"

I imagine him laid out on a private beach somewhere like Bora Bora with a gorgeous supermodel or two, having epic sex under the night sky. Lazing like a king, he'd dine on exotic seafood fished from the South Pacific Ocean, prepared by a private chef.

"In my family, we have an age-old tradition where everyone comes over to my house to feast. It used to be hosted at my mom's house, but my crib is more fun. *No offense, Ma!* Well, the traditional part is that we turn Thanksgiving into an epic three-day sleepover where we eat leftovers, play board games, watch movies, and chill. Even if I have games, I'll try to fly back in time to catch some of it." A wildly cute grin lights up his face. It's the best thing I've seen in a while.

"Man, that honestly sounds amazing. I want a big family one day. I'd create similar traditions." My parents and I used to love cooking together during the holidays. Uncle Adam would sometimes join us by bringing a guy he was dating. It was everything. I had it so good.

"I see it for you. In the meantime, you're welcome to join mine. I get the sense you'd fit right in. Just a word of caution— my cousin Kieran cheats at Monopoly, so count your houses and stacks before getting up from the table."

"Thanks. I might take you up on that. I should warn you, I'm vicious about copping utilities, Boardwalk, and Park Place. Cross me, and I'll bankrupt you."

He laughs. "Yeah, you'll fit right in."

I reel back my smile. "I want to travel away from basketball for a bit. What's a book or movie that you read or watched recently that you really enjoyed?"

"You want to know something funny?" He hands me his paper. "Peep the third question."

"You typed this up?" I glance up and catch his nod in response. I grin, impressed with his preparation for the interview. "The question is, 'What's a book you've read that you found deeply enjoyable?'"

I hand back the paper. "You love reading too?"

"Ever since I was a kid." The heel of his foot drums against the floor. "To answer your question, I just read about a marathon runner and ex-marine who experienced childhood trauma." He shakes his head. "Tough read. He flailed for years from self-doubt and low self-esteem, but then he turned his life around. The mental fortitude this guy has, even to this day, is next level. I stayed up all night reading it."

"I love books that capture the resilience of a person. It can reach superhuman proportions. Remind me to cop the title from you."

He hums. "Whenever I'm wiped on the court and need gas I think of him, and I'm instantly recharged. What about you?"

"I'm re-reading *The Count of Monte Cristo* by Alexandre Dumas. I read it in high school, but it hits differently after all these years."

"How so?" His palms bracket the back of his head as he leans back for a stretch.

"Well, it's full of life lessons. The main character is this young dude who has everything going for him—love, a promotion that would raise him and his dad out of poverty, favor with his employer—then he's falsely imprisoned, and his life is turned upside down. It's apparently inspired by Alexandre's dad who was a prisoner of war at one point."

"Word? I read it in high school too, but I didn't know about his dad. Everyone in my class hated it and thought it was too long, but I dug it. I recall how unsatisfactory vengeance felt in the end, despite wanting everyone responsible for ol' boy's imprisonment to pay."

My face splits open into the widest grin.

"I remember thinking the key to happiness isn't getting what you desire necessarily, but when your desires align with what will bring you peace," he continues.

"Yes! Exactly!" I've gleaned from interviews over the years that he's smart, but the media overlooks his wisdom. I guess that's the shallow part of celebrity—it creates caricatures of its subjects. It's a shame it's virtually impossible to maintain anonymity and be a pro athlete. I'd pay anything for it.

"Something tells me if you've read it more than once, you've probably memorized a few lines."

"Ha. You aren't wrong. I almost got a quote from it tatted on me."

"Would you mind sharing it?" He asks, eyes eager and bursting with sunlight.

I may hate cameras and prefer solitude over company, but I'm always down to recite my favorite lines from books. I read a paraphrased version:

> *Life is a storm, my young friend. You will bask in the sunlight one moment, be shattered on the rocks the next...You must look into that storm and shout, 'Do your worst, for I will do mine!' Then the fates will know you as we know you."*

"Man!" He shakes his head. "I remember that. I read it and felt invincible. I walked through the hood like *I dare someone to try me!*" He sticks his chest out, making us both laugh. "I'd love to have that quote framed on my wall." A beat later, "I mean, you could cop a lot worse tats. My teammate has a tat that spells 'wanker' or something in Mandarin. He told people it meant 'highly gifted,' but someone called bullshit online." The crew's laughter mixes in with ours. "This interview may inspire readers old and young to read more of Dumas. He sounds like a swaggy dude."

My face hurts from grinning so much. I bite the inside of my cheek to try to reel it in. The internet is vicious—five minutes after the interview drops, someone will post a viral reel of me grinning like an idiot whenever he opens his mouth.

"What about you? Have any tats?" I ask. No visible ones, from what I can tell.

"Two. Copped 'em within months of each other a few years back." He lifts his sweater and tank and shows me a cursive sentence, emanating from his left underarm down his taut obliques.

Fuck, his abs have abs.

Focus.

"Carpe diem quam minimum credula postero," I read aloud.

"I recognize 'seize the day.' What does the rest mean?"

"Pluck the day, trusting as little as possible in the next one."

"Pluck the day?"

"Yeah, pluck the day as it is ripe. Here's the other one."

He twists his torso so that I can get a better view. The second tattoo is in the same spot but on the opposite side of his torso. His tats are concealed unless he's shirtless and raises his arm.

"Memento mori," I read aloud.

"Remember death or remember that you will die," he translates. "I wanted to burn into my consciousness that I only exist at this moment. Tomorrow is an illusion."

I study him. I sense that it's not just ink that's left a permanent imprint on him. I'd recognize grief anywhere. Why else would he use his body to memorialize death? I wonder who he's lost.

"What does existing in the moment mean for you?" I ask.

He adjusts his sweater back in place. "There's freedom in accepting the ephemeral nature of life. We spend so much time fearing the end. I choose to appreciate the current moment for what it is."

"I know what you mean." When I'm in the throes of depression, death seems most inviting, like a sweet release and a shot at a family reunion. "I don't remember whose turn it is to ask a question," I admit, clearing my throat.

I flick a glance at the crew. A half dozen pairs of eyes stare back at us. A wave of heat creeps over my neck and face.

The director signals for us to wrap it up.

I groan inwardly as I nod. "One last question from me, have you thought about life after basketball?"

He frowns as his gaze flicks over his watch. "Uh, yeah. I think about my legacy often. It was enough to be a talented basketball player when I was younger. While I love the game and am grateful to have the chance to play every day, when this is all over, I want to dedicate more time to the non-profit organizations I support. Man, I look at my young cousins and feel a deep sense of urgency to help make this world a more equitable place for them." The conviction in his voice tells me that this is important to him.

"That's honorable. As someone coming up a few years behind you, I have to admit that witnessing your passion for social justice influenced the athlete that I want to be and how I want to use my platform.'"

"Thanks. I'm humbled. We're so blessed to have the reach that we have. It's easy to take it for granted."

"I'm honored to sit down with you one-on-one," I confess.

"Same. It's official! We're best friends now."

I burst out laughing. "Should we cop bestie rings?"

"Fo' sho! I'll have my assistant call your assistant for your ring size."

"No need." I wave off the offer. "When I get sized for the championship ring, I'll have my assistant call your assistant."

"You're dreaming. Hey, did someone spike Ty's mug? I think he's drunk." He searches the room for answers, then scoots forward, picks up my mug, and sniffs. He screws his face up. "Moonshine."

The crew roars with laughter.

"Bruh, now everyone's gonna know about my bootleg basement distillery. You promised you wouldn't snitch!"

"My bad! Everyone at home, this appears to be"—he peers inside the mug again—"lemon tea." He winks at the camera. "The man's not drunk, just delusional. Everyone knows the Marvels are taking it all the way this year."

We're laughing when the director yells cut.

"Great interview, guys! Excellent chemistry, effortless flow."

"Thanks, Joaquin. That was fun," Sid replies.

Of course he remembers the director's name. I'm terrible with names.

We have our mics removed and our original clothes returned. After I get back from changing, I notice Sid's already wearing his coat.

He studies me. "There's a big difference between you and the freshmen who get drafted a year after college."

I nod, not sure what to say.

"Some of 'em have the mindset of a fourteen-year-old. I've never had the luxury of being that young. Here"—he hands me his phone—"put your digits in. Let's link up for a meal whenever we're in the same town. Or if you ever need any league advice, hit me up."

I thought the whole *let's be friends* thing was just a thing to say on camera, but I'm wondering if Sid says what he means. I take his phone. My hands tremble a little as I type in my info.

"Here you go." I hand the phone back to him and pull on my coat.

"That's tough," he says, gesturing to my Italian shearling leather aviator jacket.

"Thanks," I reply, staring down at it. "It was my dad's."

"Mmm." He slides his phone in his pocket. "Aight, well, I gotta run and catch my plane to the Chi."

"Ah, you play the Crows tomorrow. Good luck."

He smiles. "Thanks."

Neither one of us makes a move to separate. Our gazes lock and it's like that day in the gym all over again. The air around us sizzles like we're in a heatwave and not the dead of winter.

His gaze trails over my face, one suspended second after another until it reaches my lips where it stills.

An involuntary grin spreads across my face.

"Damn. Those dimples. I'm sure the ladies eat their hearts out," he says, voice sliding an octave.

A heat-generating vibration spreads up my spine and unfolds into a tingling massage. He could say the sky's blue in that velvety voice, and you'd think he was seducing you.

I shrug. "I'm married to the game right now."

His face crinkles like I told him it's summer out. "That can't be right. You have to make time for fun."

I release a drawn-out sigh. "I honestly wouldn't even know where to start."

"Oh, virgin?" he asks, raising his eyebrows. His phone rings, but he sends it to voicemail.

"Yeah—I mean, no! Definitely not. Not that there's anything wrong with a virgin. I just meant, well, you know how it is. People expect what they read about you. It doesn't help that our salaries are public. Hard to tell the gold diggers from the rest, and I've never been much for sleeping around. Even if it's casual, I only have the energy to hit up the same person. I refuse to lose focus on the game. I owe it to my parents..." I trail off.

For fuck's sake. Rambling—party of one!

When it comes to opening up, I'm that night-blooming flower that unfurls once a year on a full moon. Yet, an hour around him and I'm spread open, offering myself to feed his curiosity. And I can't tell if it's due to me being star-struck, his disarming magnetism, or something else.

"Yeah, but seeing the same person comes with 'the talk'... *Where is this going? Do you love me, yada yada?*"

"You prefer to keep things casual?" I ask.

"Not really. I haven't met anyone I could see myself laying down roots with. I am not opposed to—"

His phone rings again, interrupting his train of thought.

"Argh. I need to bounce, or I'll never hear the end of it from my coach. Hit me up."

No dap this time. His knuckles tap my chest, and then he's answering his phone and jogging out.

I watch as he disappears around the corner. I glance around the room and notice most of the equipment packed. The server is waiting for me to leave to pack up the refreshments. I thank the crew one final time, then head out to New Jersey to grab dinner with Adam. I realized after Sid left that I never received his number. It's probably for the best. Even if I had it, I'm not sure I'd have the courage to message him. I can't imagine him hitting me up. The guy probably has more friends than he knows what to do with.

But what if he calls?

The thought makes me jittery, but it's the kind of jitter that I don't hate entirely.

TWO WEEKS LATER, I'M SINKING INTO THE HOTEL COUCH AND kicking off my shoes when my phone vibrates. I don't recognize the number, but the second I glimpse the ESPN social media poll on sweet potato vs. pumpkin pie, I scoff and look around in disbelief. Sid King texts me randomly—*how is this my life?* Like the text is scheduled to delete itself in thirty seconds, I save his number with zero chill.

ME

It's in the bag for pumpkin. I put $100 on it.

Sweet potato is in the lead by a slim margin.

SID

Bet. Let's sweeten the pot. The loser busts a
move during their next game.

ME

Ugh. Literally anything else. I hate attention.

SID

So you know you're gonna lose then?

I'm being goaded, but that doesn't stop my fingers from firing back.

ME

Bring it

Wait, how do I know this is who I think it is?

I'm eighty percent confident it's Sid, but you never know.

I grin when bubbles appear, but it vanishes when they disappear a minute later.

Okay, I'm sixty percent confident I've been messaging Sid this entire time.

I click out of the message and reach for my book when my phone vibrates again. I snatch it up and hit play on a video. Sid's half smile, half smirk appears. He's wearing a cream sweatshirt, but the torso and shoulders are brushed with blue-gray watercolors.

"Hey you," he says, staring into the camera.

He flips the camera, and a row of Marvels' players comes into focus. Having just sat through team dinner myself, I recognize the setup.

"Yo! Pumpkin or sweet potato pie?" Sid calls out.

At least a dozen heads snap toward the camera, and a chorus of "pump-sweet-kin-tatoes" is shouted in its direction. The camera view flips back to Sid's face.

"We should've maybe rehearsed that. Looking forward to your dance skills." He winks, and then the video ends.

I drag my finger across the video bar until it's back at the beginning and hit pause over his face. I grin hard as I take him in.

Chapter Five

It's Christmas Eve, and we're in the final four minutes of an early game against the Phoenix Stars at home. We're down ten points. Coach lets me start at the top of each quarter, but he benched me for the last seven minutes to hydrate and rest. We held the lead for most of the game, but in the last five minutes, Craig, the Stars' point guard, scored two back-to-back shots. Then their center hit a very rare three-pointer and was fouled, sending him to the free-throw line and increasing our deficit to ten points.

"Ty, you're up!" Coach barks.

I jump up and execute a few hamstring curls while waiting to get injected back into the game. I shake away the fatigue from jolting awake at four in the morning with another nightmare. As soon as this game ends, I'm headed home to sleep through the next twenty-four hours.

It's our possession when I'm injected back into the game. I groan as Lucas, the Stars' power forward, moves to defend me.

"Your coach used to be a legend," he says, raising his elbow close to my nose. I swat his arm away and pivot, keeping him to my left. I dribble the ball and scan the court. Idris is in the perfect spot to hit a corner shot, except he's jammed up by their center.

"Look at him now, trusting the last minutes of the game to a rookie," Lucas spits. "The league has gotten soft. If you were my rook, I'd make you get down on your knees and—"

"Hey"—I hit a fast dribble, cutting him up, and sink a bucket—"Eat a dick." I glare at him as I run backward.

Fuck face.

The Stars attempt a corner three-pointer but miss.

Yes!

Idris drives the possession straight down the lane, but he's fouled mid-air and heads to the free-throw line. I bend forward to catch my breath. We trade high fives after both of his free throws stick.

As the Stars take possession, the crowd yells, "Dee-Fense!" Their energy is electrifying.

I spot an opening for an interception and steal possession from an irate Craig.

Candy from a baby.

I drive fast up the court to hit a corner shot, but I miss. Tevin grabs the rebound and lobs the ball back to me. I cut around Lucas and release another corner shot, falling backward.

Swoosh—it's clean!

The crowd goes wild. That shot was a beauty! It'll definitely make the final cut of the highlights reel.

We cut the deficit to two points, the score 112–110. The Stars call a timeout to stop our momentum, but it doesn't matter. We're taking this tonight. The crowd knows it, my teammates know it, and even the Stars know it!

The game resumes, and as expected, Craig takes possession of the ball and attempts a fast break, running upcourt. Only as he takes flight for a dunk, Tevin makes a clean block, smacking the ball right into my hands. Craig punches the air and yells at the refs. One glance at Tev and we burst out laughing.

I pass the ball to Idris, who gets jammed up and loses possession, causing a loose ball, but not for long. Our small forward, Hanson, grabs it and launches it to me. I catch it and shoot as the shot clock buzzer goes off. The ball barrels through the air and dives straight through the net.

Cash, baby!

The crowd explodes as the Stars call a timeout. I gesture for them to get louder, placing a hand to my ear and mouthing, *I can't hear you.* A wave of chants booms through the arena. "Good Knight! Good Knight!" A rallying cry for us to put the game to sleep. I throw my hands in the air, egging them on. Realizing now's as good a time as any to fulfill my end of the bet with Sid, I dip low and sway side to side.

The crowd goes ape!

I jump up, spin, and am about to hit a double Milly Rock when Kaleb backs into me, hitting a Reverse Running Man. I burst out laughing and join him, busting out the original Running Man. A thunder of cheers reverberates through the stadium. Bet fulfilled, I bow as Kaleb blows kisses at the crowd. Coach signals for us to get our asses over to the bench.

As we race over, I mentally pat myself on the back for not punking out. Sid won our bet by a slim margin. I'm still not convinced sweet potato pie is more popular than pumpkin, but a bet's a bet.

The arena falls silent when Craig hits a center two-pointer, bringing the Stars back in the lead with under thirty seconds left in the game.

Coach calls a timeout. We huddle to confirm our next strategy, only once the game resumes, our plan goes to hell when Tevin is double-teamed while in possession of the ball. Hanson creates a screen, freeing up Tevin to pass the ball to Idris. Idris drives it down the lane and lobs an insane alley-oop to me as

I'm in mid-air. I spin so my back's facing the rim and hit a flawless reverse dunk.

Game over!

The crowd combusts as our bench spills onto the court. I jump on Idris as we're swallowed up by our teammates. I rest a peace sign against my chest. The final score is 115–114.

After post-game interviews and our team meeting, most of my teammates rush out to travel home to be with loved ones for Christmas. I take my time getting dressed. Adam is on duty for the next few days. We plan to celebrate Christmas and the New Year together when he gets a break. I'm in desperate need of sleep. The nightmares are always bad this time of year, but this year takes the cake. They've jolted me awake almost every night this week, leaving me running on fumes. I shower and then dip into an ice bath before sitting in a compression suit.

I'm headed to my Porsche 911 GT3 RS when my phone vibrates. I don't recognize the number, but I pick up since I'm Adam's emergency contact. I try not to let my thoughts go there.

I clear my throat. "Hello?"

"So, you effortlessly hit reverse dunks and swishers from half-court, huh? That's how you roll?"

I exhale, knowing Adam's safe, then my face breaks into a wide grin.

"Liked that, did you?"

"It's hard to hate." I hear a smile coating Sid's husky voice. "And then you threw a dagger with a smooth Running Man."

I chuckle. "A bet's a bet. Did you catch in the 2nd quarter—"

"Your wild double hesi against Lucas? Saaaaavage. He went flyin' into the cameraman and lost a shoe. Why'd you do ol' boy like that?"

I can't help but laugh. "I can't stand that dude."

"No one in the league can! His team merely tolerates him. The refs are half-blind when it comes to him."

"Seriously. It's hella obvious. What's with that?"

"I think he'd be fouled out in the first quarter if they called him on every foul." He sighs because even discussing Lucas can make you feel exasperated.

"I'd be fine with that. Wait, didn't you and him get into it on the court last season?"

"Yeah. Not my finest moment. Dude was spouting some homophobic BS. He's lucky I only shoved him."

"What the fuck?" The thought makes my blood boil. I think of Adam, who's been out as long as I can remember. He's ten times the man Lucas will ever be.

"Great game, though! At least three of your shots will make highlights."

I grin. "Yeah, I know. Hey, what number is this? It's different from the one you texted me from."

"I'm calling from my house phone."

"House phone. That's old school."

"Yeah, only a handful of people have it. I need a break from my cell sometimes. Especially during the holidays when I want to chill with my fam and keep it low-key."

"I get that." I imagine with his popularity, his phone is always blowing up.

He falls silent, and for a second, I think the call got disconnected. Then he clears his throat. "So, any chance you're free tomorrow and want to celebrate Christmas with me? It'll be a chill affair—just me, my mom, my cousin, and a family friend. Both of them are like brothers to me. I usually have a game on Christmas, so we keep it low-key. By some stroke of luck, I'm off this year."

Whoa. Just like that, I'm invited into the private world of one of the most famous men on earth. I lean against the door of my car. Can't say I expected that at all. He loosely extended an invitation to celebrate the holidays with his family during our interview, but I didn't think he was for real. I really need sleep, but if the current jitters in my stomach are anything to go by, spending the day with Sid sounds pretty dope.

"Wow, uh, it's really nice of you to, uh, extend an invite."

"Oh, and your uncle is invited too. Adam is his name, right? The plane has more than enough room."

"Yeah, Adam's his—wait—you have a private plane? Who are you, Jay-Z?"

He chuckles. "My pilot, Nat's, on standby, ready to meet you at LAX."

"Honestly, I was planning to sleep through it this year since Adam has to work. I'd be honored."

He lets out a deep sigh. "Man, that ain't right. We can't have you sleeping through the best day of the year. I'm shooting you a text right now with the details. What time should the plane aim for?"

"Tonight? But Christmas is tomorrow."

"Bruh, Christmas starts at midnight. My mom has dinner on now, and the pies will be ready in a few hours. I just got back from picking up a tree. We're about to decorate it."

I grin. "Kinda late to buy a tree, isn't it?"

"Mad late. It was slim pickings, but Gladys will be the envy of the neighborhood when I'm done decorating her and the—"

"You named your tree Gladys?" I interject.

"Of course. It's part of the family now. The rest of the decorations were put up weeks ago, but I get way too much joy out of picking and decorating the tree to delegate it to anyone else. The last few weeks have been hectic between road games and publicity stuff."

"I always imagined it's busy business being you. Uh, what time is it?" I check the time on the phone. "I can be at LAX in four-ish hours. Cool?"

"Hold on a sec. I'll text Nat to leave now. It'll take her roughly five hours to get to you."

"That's perfect." I throw my bag in the back seat before climbing in. The call transfers to my car's speakers.

"Done. I'll text you the hangar details once I have them," he says.

While I am stoked to not spend another holiday alone, something is gnawing at me about the invite.

"Wait, Sid?"

"Yeah?"

"Why me? I mean, why are you inviting me?"

"We're friends, remember?"

"Seriously. I'm sure you have lots of friends."

The line goes silent.

"Are you there?" I ask.

I hear a deep sigh. "Yeah. I'm here," he says, voice low before the line goes silent again.

I'm about to tell him to forget I asked when he pipes up. "Listen, I love my teammates, but they're, uh, I don't know, kind of basic at times. I enjoyed our interview and your...vibe. I can't tell you the last time I had such an enjoyable conversation that wasn't centered on basketball, cars, or women. I also had a feeling that you might be spending the day alone."

My shoulders drop as I release a long breath. The truth is, I think about Sid and our interview every day. I've never met anyone who can both lower my guard and throw my body completely out of whack. I fidget in my seat as another question burns on my tongue. I'd like to know if any part of the invite was extended because of sympathy towards me because of my parents. I don't want his pity.

"Got it. Do you buy the media's portrayal of me as haunted, introverted, and lonely?"

"Hm. Introverted and serious, yes. Maybe a little lonely too. I mean, I understand you're focused on the game, but it helps to have someone when the day's through, even if temporarily. As for if you're haunted..." He sighs. "It isn't for me to say, but it's okay if you are. We're all haunted in some way—whether by the secrets we protect, the truths we deny, or the inexplicable ugliness life throws our way."

His words are a sunburst in the middle of my chest. It's not just that I'm seen. More miraculously, he makes me want to be seen. I want to ask what haunts him, but I decide to save the question for when we're alone in person.

"You're a wise one, eh?"

"There are those who have knowledge and those who have understanding."

"Oh, I see! We droppin' *Count of Monte Cristo* quotes casually now?"

He chuckles, and I can envision it clearly—mischievous eyes gleaming, slightly crinkled, lush lips spread in that sexy smirk, revealing the dimple on the left side of his face, straight pearly whites except for the one tooth on the lower right that's almost imperceptibly crooked.

"Busted. I'm re-reading it. You're driving?"

"Yep, I should run soon. Don't be jealous, but my friend is sending a private plane to transport me to Miami to celebrate Christmas with his family."

"Sounds like a dream of a friend."

I laugh. "Yeah, let's see if he still wants to be my friend when I wipe the floor with his team when we face off in a few weeks."

"Talking recklessly, youngblood. You sure you're fit to be driving?"

"Ha ha! I'll see you in a couple of hours, Wonder Kid."

"I'll be the one wearing the Santa hat, Pretty Boy."

"One could argue that we're both pretty." I cringe as soon as the words leave my mouth. *Where'd the hell that come from?*

"Huh. Can't say I've ever been called *pretty* before...*unreasonably handsome*, sure...a *smoke show*, many times. According to People Magazine, I'm the Sexiest Man Alive. Though to keep it a hunnit, they only confirmed what I've always known."

There's a humor in his voice that tells me he doesn't take any of what he just said seriously.

"Sexiest Man Alive, eh? I heard you can pay for that designation."

He scoffs. "Fuck off!"

"I'm hanging up before I am dis-invited."

He chuckles. "Never. Peace."

The line goes dead.

A few minutes later, I receive a text with the hangar details. I make a quick detour to pick up a few gifts for his family. My mom would turn over in her grave if I showed up empty-handed. I can't let my captain down.

Chapter Six

My first private plane experience, and I slept through most of it. After deplaning, Sid's driver waits in front of a black Escalade on the tarmac. I'm wearing shades and a beanie to fly below the radar, but it's unnecessary since I go directly from the plane to the car.

"Mr. Washington, it's a pleasure to meet you. My name is Leslie."

I catch a Caribbean accent.

I extend my hand. "What's up, Leslie? Nice to meet you too."

Leslie is stout, with a full head of salt and pepper hair. He has round eyes and cheeks dusted with freckles. He looks breezy, clad in linen pants and a button-down shirt. We exchange small talk. He tells me it's a fifteen-minute drive from Miami International Airport to Sid's house in Coconut Grove.

I, like millions of viewers, toured Sid's estate online in a segment where he was followed around answering seventy questions. It has eight bedrooms, nine bathrooms, a gourmet indoor and outdoor kitchen, both an infinity and one of those swanky architectural pools, a home theater, a large, detached garage for his luxury cars, a separate guest house, a basketball court, and a gym. As a rookie, I signed a four-year contract with the Knights for $47 million. I receive a base salary of $10 million in year one. Sid's house costs more than my entire year one salary.

Back in LA, I purchased a relatively modest five-bedroom, four-bathroom house in Topanga Canyon with views of the Santa Monica mountains. It's my sanctuary. The property has a pool and a home gym. It's a ten-minute drive to the beach. I've never been one for super lavish things, and I don't see the need to change that. My mom, who was a finance manager, always spoke about the opportunity cost of every dollar spent and the power of compound interest. She'd always say that true wealth is generational. I know I want kids one day, and I plan to grow my wealth for them.

I crack the window, eager to inhale the sea breeze. When we arrive at a tall gate, Leslie hovers a fob over a pad, and the gate opens. We drive up a windy path, and tall hedges conceal the view of the house.

"Wow!" I gasp when the house comes into view.

Leslie chuckles. Twinkling Christmas lights cover the hedges and facade of the house. Candy cane lights frame the windows, and two illuminated gigantic leaping stag reindeer line the entryway. Snow that has to be fake covers the lawn. A large green wreath with pinecones, holly berries, and a red bow mounts the door. Two marble columns frame the doorway, with the largest poinsettias I've ever seen sitting on top. My mom would have gasped if she saw their size. She loved them.

I'm so engrossed in Sid's decorations that I don't register climbing out of the car. Leslie refuses my help to carry my bags as we make our way to the front door. It's only when I am a few feet from the door that I see a tall gold and metallic nutcracker hidden between two tall hedges.

My jaw hangs. "Seriously!"

Leslie chuckles. "Mr. King is a big kid when it comes to Christmas. Don't let the man's ferocity on the court fool you." He gestures to the nutcracker. "It's made of polyresin and fiberglass, with over 200 LED lights. It's hand-painted. Imported from some far-off place."

"Wow, Sid's imagination is on Willy Wonka's level. This—all of this—is like something out of a catalog."

I spin around, taking it all in. In the far corner of the garden are a half dozen twinkling gingerbread decorations with green and white peppermint smocks, frosting hair, and a mix of crimson ties and bows. They're lined up along the exit path like they're waiting to bid guests farewell. I shake my head. Sid definitely has layers.

Leslie attempts to punch in a code to the door when it suddenly opens from the inside. An exquisite cologne permeates my senses as we peer up at a beaming Sid, looking merry in a Santa hat.

"You made it in good time," Sid says, pulling me into a bear hug.

Yup, hugging Sid feels like what I imagined—being swaddled.

"Thanks for inviting me," I reply as we release each other. Slow-release hugs could easily become our thing.

"Pardon me, sir." Leslie brushes past us with my bags.

Sid slides out of his way. "Thanks, Leslie."

I eye his sweater. I wouldn't say it's ugly, but it is very festive. He beams when he catches me staring.

"Peep this." He clicks a button under the sweater, and the embroidered tree lights up. "Dope, right?"

An adorable smile supplants his raw sexiness. How does a single face have such range?

"Very cool."

"Glad you like it. I have one for you."

I chuckle. "Of course you do. Man, your yard is like something out of a magazine or a storybook."

"Christmas is legit my favorite holiday. You know I've never lost a Christmas game? It's like ol' St. Nick has my back or something. Come in, come in." He steps to the side, allowing me entry.

I'm met with the sweet aroma of cinnamon and baked dough. "Wow...what's that?" I ask, sniffing the air.

He grins. "The pies just came out of the oven."

"Ah!" I pat my rumbling stomach. "Smells like a bakery in here."

"I can't take credit. My mom made a spread before she left. It's actually weird that she bounced. We think she might have a date or something. She usually stays over, but this year she made some excuse about wanting to sleep in her bed. We're not buying it."

"She's always private about her dates?"

He smirks. "She's Fort Knox with it. The woman has more secrets than the Pentagon."

I chuckle.

"So tonight, it's just us and my cousin Kieran and his best friend—who is also our childhood friend—Tommy."

Tension seeps out of my shoulders. I'm not big on being around large groups of people I don't know.

"Cool. I brought gifts for everyone. I had little time, so don't judge them harshly. Is anyone sober? I picked up a few bottles of aged Japanese whiskey. My dad was gifted a bottle once and loved it. I picked up a necklace for your mom, and well, for you, you'll have to wait and unwrap your gift later."

He flashes me a wide grin. "Thanks, man. My bad for the late invite. We were on the road until yesterday, and I lost track of time. I made a mental note to invite you after our interview in New York, but it somehow slipped my mind."

I wave it off. "It's all good. It's not like you didn't go all Batman, sending a plane to scoop me. Anyone sober?"

"Nah. Kieran and Tommy will love the whiskey."

I start to remove my shoes.

"I didn't even have to ask you," he says, tracking my movement.

"I grew up with the same rule. Before I forget"—I reach into my pocket—"here you go." I extend five twenty-dollar bills.

He grins. "Keep it. Watching you dance was reward enough."

"Glad you enjoyed it 'cause it'll never happen again."

"Never? Not even when you cop a ring?"

I arch my eyebrows. "*When*—I appreciate the vote of confidence."

"Keep playing the way you've been, and it'll happen. Come on," he says.

I trail him through the house, grinning hard.

"Whoa," I whisper as I freeze at the entrance of the family room, taken aback by the luxuriousness. There's a massive three-sided fireplace ablaze, casting a warm glow. The room alone is a quarter the size of my house. I shouldn't be surprised. Being Sid's height, you'd need the twelve-foot ceilings. There's an indoor-outdoor vibe to the room from the double-height, arched, black, French windows that look out over a manicured courtyard. A rustic, brass-colored, wagon wheel chandelier illuminates the room along with a tall Christmas tree—I'm talking at least nine feet—adorned in silver and gold ornaments. Gladys.

Ella Fitzgerald's "What Are You Doing New Year's Eve" emanates from a sleek Hi-Fi audio system setup, with shelves of vinyl records, elevating what is already an elegant space.

A comforting peace settles within me from feeling like I am exactly where I am supposed to be.

"Wrought iron," Sid says, watching me eye the light fixture.

I nod. Fancy digs.

"Kieran and Tommy, meet my friend Ty." Sid turns to the two men, who are busy putting the finishing touches on Gladys. Both of their heads turn toward us. A motley pair if ever there was one. The smaller of the pair saunters over to us first.

"Hey, handsome, I'm Kieran. We caught your game earlier. Mad skillz. Had us on the edge of our seats." He embraces me in a hug. There's only one way to describe Kieran—mesmerizing! Smooth, deep voice, silky golden-brown skin, and lean runner's build. He's rocking a Christmas sweater similar to Sid's but longer, like a sweater dress. Brown locs with golden highlights fastened and piled high with the sides shaved low and similar geometric patterns as Sid's. Piercings cover his right ear. Deep-set eyes the same chestnut color as Sid's but outlined in black ink. Red polish covers the fingernails of one hand, green on the other, and the tips are metallic gold.

"Thanks. Nice to meet you," I say as we separate. "Something about a Christmas Eve win makes it sweeter. Dope nails and piercings, by the way."

"Thanks." His smile is radiant as he turns and walks over to Sid. "I love him already," he whispers, loud enough for me to catch.

Sid hooks his arm around his shoulder. "Knew you would." Kieran, who's probably no more than 5 'II", is dwarfed by Sid's gigantic frame.

"Hey, I'm Tommy," the next member of the odd pair says, extending his hand.

Tommy looks like an offensive tackle in the NFL, stocky with bulging muscles. Black hair shaved in a low fade, a medium-length goatee, three decorative slashes through both eyebrows, and a suspicious stare. He's wearing Sid's version of the Christmas sweater with joggers.

"Hey, Tommy. Nice to meet you," I reply as we shake hands. I brace for a bruising handshake, but his grasp is gentle.

I hear a rumbling sound as the Ella record comes to an end. My gaze sweeps past Tommy towards the Christmas tree.

I gasp. "Wait! Is that what I think?"

Making its way from the back of the tree is a large-scale, electric train set. Since I was a kid, I've wanted one.

Sid and Kieran chuckle at my reaction.

"Yeah, and it has headlights and emits smoke. Come look up close," Tommy replies, leading the way.

We weave through two cast iron metal frame armchairs with cream cushions and matching ottomans. He presses a button on the remote control to pause the train's motion so that I can get a closer look. A large, textured area rug cushions my knees as I squat in front of Gladys. The "Jingle Bells" melody comes on after he presses another button, making my eyes go wide.

"Cool, man! I got to cop one of these."

"This set has over 50 pieces. Here, play around with it." He passes me the remote and I go to town, trying out all the settings. There's a button to reverse the train and another to light up each car with different colors.

I turn to wave goodbye to Leslie as he wishes us a Merry Christmas.

"Hold on," Sid says. He swipes a thick envelope from the Nordic-style coffee table adorned with spruce garland, pinecones, and lit candles. "Something for the family." He extends the envelope to Leslie.

Leslie holds up his hands in refusal. "You already gave me a gift for the family."

"Something more for the family then," Sid counters.

Leslie shakes his head. "Sir, you've given me more than enough."

"C'mon, Leslie, you know how stubborn Sid is. This will go on for hours. Take the gift," Kieran pleads with a light-hearted voice from one of the two cream-colored, L-shaped couches, where he's sitting cross-legged.

"Alright, then. Thank you. It's an honor to have been under your employment another year," Leslie says, voice earnest.

Sid shakes his hand. "The honor is all mine. Have a safe trip home, and give Taryn, Bernard, and Latoya my regards."

"Will do! Call if you need anything. You'd be saving me from my in-laws," Leslie replies, chuckling as he heads toward the door.

"Ty, I thought you were hungry. Wanna eat?" Sid asks.

I sigh and look at the train set that's now blowing red smoke. "Eat food or keep playing with the train set? Decisions, decisions," I whisper, causing laughter around the room.

"How about you make a plate and eat it in front of the train set?" Kieran offers.

"Genius!" I exclaim, climbing to my feet. "Word on the street is there's another one of those sweaters around here for me." I'm ready to become immersed in Christmas cheer.

"C'mon. Sweater, food, then train set," Sid lists.

I follow his muscular frame and ridiculously delicious scent up the stairs and to a second bedroom on the left.

"This is your room," he says.

I thought I'd be stuck out in the guest house. It's cool that Sid has me hunkered inside with his family. I recognize my bags on the dresser and a holiday sweater on the bed with a gift-wrapped box. I tour the room. There's a massive bed, a marble ensuite bathroom, and a fireplace.

I whistle. "Man, fancy digs...a family of four could fit comfortably." I nod to the bed.

"It's an Alaskan king."

I nod. I've never heard of it.

"This is dope." I gesture to a large painting hanging next to the bed. "I want to build an art collection one day, but I honestly wouldn't know where to start."

He moves to stand next to me. "Wanna know my secret? I only purchase art that makes me feel good. I skip all pretenses. I stand before a piece of art and observe it. I pay attention to what comes up for me, and if it's a feeling that I want to hold on to, I'll buy it. Take this piece. What do you feel looking at it?"

Hmm. I take in the indigo-colored night sky and feel relaxed in the way nightfall brings. I peer at the golden stained-glass windows, and I imagine that if I could press my forehead against the glass, I'd see a lavish ball underway in a grand marble hall. There'd be brandy and champagne flowing, uninhibited dancing, tuxedos, cigar smoke, and evening gowns. Words like opulence, joy, and celebration come to mind. It reminds me of something...it's on the tip of my tongue, but I can't reach it.

"It makes me feel fancy but kinda loose and free too," I say.

"That's good." He grins. "When I saw it for the first time, I thought of James Bond in a tuxedo, jacket off, sleeves rolled up, and tie loosened, sitting in a swanky bar sipping his martini, unwinding after some badass adventure. He's surrounded by gorgeous company."

"Vivid." I imagine Sid as James Bond. He'd sell out theaters.

"It's incredible where it takes your mind, isn't it?" he asks.

I steal a glance in his direction. My breath catches when our gazes lock.

A second passes, followed by another, and then another. Maybe it's the refraction of the incandescent lighting that leads to the discovery of brass specks punctuating his irises. The longer I stare, the more the ground shifts, and I free-fall into his depths.

"Mmm, like liquid gold," I mutter to myself.

"Hmm?" he asks, voice dark like night.

My words die in my throat and my pulse quickens.

What's the part of the brain that processes sensory experiences? I aced biology—I should know this. The somatic cortex? Whatever it's called, something about his energy sends mine into overdrive.

An audible rumble from my stomach rips through the air. His eyes go wide, and we burst out laughing.

He passes me the sweater from off of the bed. "Let's feed you before you pass out. Here."

I wipe my sweaty palms on my jeans before pulling off my shirt and throwing the sweater over my head. It's roomier than I wear.

"Huh, you're smaller than I thought," he observes, eyeing me like a tailor.

"Yeah, well, we aren't all giants. It's all good, though. I get paid to cut up giants."

"Oh, word? It's like that? Take care not to be crushed—"

My stomach rumbles again, interrupting his comeback.

"Christ! Let's feed you—"

"Wait, what's the gift?" I ask, nodding in its direction.

He rubs the back of his neck. "It's for you."

"You didn't know I'd be coming until a few hours ago."

"I picked it up a while ago after New York," he says.

Damn. His thoughtfulness renders me speechless.

"You good?" he asks.

"Y-yeah," I reply. I clear my throat. "Maybe a little light-headed from hunger."

"C'mon," he says, leading the way back downstairs.

I follow him into the gourmet kitchen. The spread is impressive. My gaze immediately locks in on the apple, peach, and pecan pies.

"Sheesh! These look mouthwatering."

"Thanks. They're vegan and free of gluten and refined sugar."

"I read about your clean diet. It's for real?"

He nods. "I eat organic meat. I avoid processed foods, sugars, and gluten. I limit dairy and alcohol. Man, I've unlocked so much energy since I switched to this diet last year."

"Sid insisted Aunt Lily make your favorite pies," Kieran says, joining us in the kitchen with Tommy trailing behind.

"Is that so?" I ask, directing the question to Sid. He leans against a wall, facing the three of us with his arms and long legs crossed elegantly.

"At the King's residence, we aim to provide exemplary service," he quips in a refined voice while sticking his nose up and straightening an imaginary bow tie.

Kieran snickers. He flashes Sid a face that says you're-so-full-of-it.

Sid shrugs. "It's true, troublemaker."

"Do you both live in Miami too?" I ask Tommy and Kieran as I help myself to a plate.

"We live in Brooklyn," Kieran replies.

"Oh yeah, which parts? I was born and raised in Brooklyn before I moved in with my uncle in New Jersey."

"A Brooklyn native. Your kind's becoming rare in our hood. We're in Fort Greene," Tommy answers.

I wonder if they live together.

"Thanks to this guy"—he says, gesturing to Sid—"we own a brownstone. I have the top floor unit, and Tommy has the bottom unit," Kieran adds as if reading my mind.

Tommy wraps Kieran up in a hug as Kieran leans his head against his chest. I wonder if they're a couple.

"Those two have been inseparable since high school. Neither one could keep a boyfriend for long because they refused to make space for anyone else," Sid says, eyeing them with a glint of amusement.

"Fuck those dudes," Tommy replies, making Kieran grin. He arches his forehead back, and Tommy kisses it without hesitation. I've seen married couples lack the closeness that they seem to share.

"Tommy is a science professor, and I'm an interior designer," Kieran offers.

"Chemistry, biology, earth science…" I rattle off.

"Chemistry," Tommy confirms.

I nod. "Dope. I had the best chemistry teacher in high school. It was one of my favorite classes."

Kieran snickers. "Said no one ever."

"K literally fell asleep when I tried to explain bonding and intermolecular forces once," Tommy says, shaking his head.

As if on cue, Kieran's knees buckle as he mock faints, sliding down Tommy's chest. "Just hearing the words intermolecular forces makes me drowsy," he jokes, making Sid and me laugh.

Tommy sighs, then lifts Kieran and anchors him against his chest to keep him vertical.

"I'm kidding! You know I think it's sexy that you're a nerd." Kieran turns his face to meet Tommy's gaze. Tommy crinkles his nose at him affectionately, then nestles it in Kieran's locs, closing his eyes like he's just inhaled the best scent in the world.

I can't imagine anyone smelling better than Sid.

"Get a room, you two!" Sid says.

"We have one," Tommy replies without lifting his nose.

The doorbell rings. Sid looks at Kieran, arching an eyebrow.

"Vincent wouldn't ring the bell," he says as he pulls up a live feed of the front gate on his phone.

"Vincent is Aunt Lily's driver," Kieran explains to me.

"Huh," Sid says.

"Who is it?" Kieran asks.

"Katrina. I wasn't expecting her."

"One of your girlfriends showing up unannounced in the middle of the night—shocker," Kieran says dryly.

"She's not my girlfriend. It's casual," Sid says to me.

I swallow a big bite of food and cough to clear my throat. "It's cool, ahem, with me. The more the merrier."

"Be right back," Sid says, and I watch him depart. It's strange, but I've enjoyed having his undivided attention. Maybe it's not strange—the guy is magnetic. How he's remained single this long is nothing short of a feat.

Kieran, Tommy, and I are bitching about the high-rise developments that have popped up all over Brooklyn when Sid returns embraced by Katrina, who is as gorgeous as she appears on the screen. She's dressed for a night out in a strapless, cherry-red tube dress. Diamond earrings sparkle from her ears, matching her dazzling smile. Her hair is swept up in a curly ponytail.

"You've met Tommy and Kieran. This is my friend Ty. He plays for—"

"The Knights, duh. You think I live under a rock?" Katrina teases as she floats over to me and plants a soft double-cheek kiss. Her perfume smells expensive and floral.

"Pleasure to meet you, Ty. If I knew you were here, I would have brought one of my single girlfriends."

I smile, but before I can reply, she adds, "Or single boyfriends?"

Kieran scoffs. "Oh my god! You're here for less than sixty seconds and you're already prying your way into the man's business."

"Geez! No one in this house cares." She continues spreading the love, sauntering over to him and Tommy for double-cheek kisses. "Everyone deserves someone warm to snuggle up with, don't they, baby?" she says, making her way back to Sid. She stands on her tiptoes and pulls his face down to meet her parted lips for a kiss. Sid looks a smidge bashful as she deepens the kiss and lets out a tiny moan. The increased sexual energy in the air is palpable.

"Who needs a room now?" Kieran asks.

Sid pulls away and cups her tiny waist to spin her around so that her back is leaning against his chest.

"That may be, but Ty is married to the game. He's the most focused rookie of his class," Sid says while wiping the lipstick from his lips.

"That's too bad. With features that gorgeous and a body that ripped, he could have a lover in every zip code," she says.

"Maybe we should stop objectifying and talking about Ty in the third person and move on," Tommy mutters.

Fighting embarrassment, I stuff my face with the last bite of food from my plate.

"Nice to meet you," I say belatedly. I nod to Sid. "The food was delicious. The lasagna is the best I've had."

"Yeah?" he grins. "Tell my mom that tomorrow. She'd love to hear it."

I nod.

"How about we move to the living room until you have room for pie?"

I pat my stomach. "Who says I don't have room for pie?"

I throw my plate in the dishwasher after Sid points me to a cabinet door. I grab a small dessert plate and cut a slice of both peach and apple pie.

"Holy cow! I think he could eat us under the table," Kieran tells Tommy and Sid.

"A dream. A gorgeous balla with a big appetite for home-cooked grub," Katrina says, staring at me like I'm dessert.

Sid shakes his head and grins. "You hungry, Kat?"

"That's an understatement," Kieran mutters, and I snicker.

"As if I could eat after seven p.m. with this waistline," she retorts, scanning the food.

"You'd be beautiful any size," Sid says in a way that tells me he's said this to her many times before.

Katrina cackles. "Tell Hollywood that." She reaches into the fridge for sparkling water.

By a unanimous vote, it's decided that we'll stream a new action movie in Sid's theater. We space out in the plush recliner seating. Sid takes the seat to my right, and Katrina sits next to him. Her head lies against his chest as she stretches her legs out over the adjacent seats. Once the lights are out and the movie starts, I get drowsy. I try to fight it, but then Sid passes around blankets, and between the warmth and my full belly, I'm out like a light.

I WAKE SUDDENLY AND FIND MYSELF ALONE. IT TAKES ME A minute to figure out where I am. I check my phone and see a text from Sid.

SID

You looked too peaceful to wake up. See you in the morning. Merry Christmas!

Removing the blanket, I stand and stretch. I'm all muzzy, like I'll crash again as soon as my head hits the pillow. I head toward the staircase, Gladys' lights illuminating my path. I wince at the familiar sharp pain in my right knee as I climb the steps. I'm always sore after a game.

When I reach the room two doors from my own, I hear Sid's voice. Two wall sconces are lit, casting a soft glow over his room. He's lying shirtless in bed with his eyes closed. I wonder if he's sleep-talking. I hear it again, a moan, his moan. The sudden awareness that I'm watching Sid get head hits me like a jolt.

"Fuck. I'm about to come," he grunts, pressing his head back into the pillow, revealing his strong Adam's apple. Katrina's head emerges from under the sheets, followed by the rest of her body clad in lace lingerie. My gaze trails over the sculpted domes of his pecs down to the ridges of his abs. "I need to grab a condom if you want to climb on. I'm close." He moves to rise, and I glimpse his cock pointing north. It glistens long and thick with a slight curve. My gaze flicks down to my growing erection.

What the fuck?

 I rip myself away.

Once inside my room, I lean against the door, pull out my cock and stroke it hard. Three strokes in, I'm biting my fist and releasing all over my hand and Sid's oaken floor. I come to the image of me taking Sid down my throat.

What the actual fuck?

Chapter Seven

My attempts to sleep the rest of the morning are unsuccessful. I end up jerking off twice more to images of me and Sid having sex. I've been bi-curious for a while now, but that can't be what this is. This feels way past curiosity. If he was in my bed right now...

I stare down at my erection and groan.

Yeah...this is something else entirely.

Last summer, I helped Adam set up an online dating profile, and by helped, I mean I set one up as he complained the whole time about preferring to meet guys the old-school way. I'd be lying if I said that I felt nothing as I scanned through profile after profile of ripped dudes. I replay all of my sexual encounters—which have all been with women. I enjoyed myself somewhat, but sex isn't something I crave the way my other friends do. It was just one more thing that made me feel different from them.

Just shy of nine o'clock in the morning, I shower, brush my teeth, and find the gym for a workout. Exercise always helps me get my head right. Dressed in basketball shorts and a T-shirt, I grab my phone and a towel from the bathroom and head down-stairs. I set the bag of gifts that I brought for Sid's family under the Christmas tree. Scanning Sid's record collection, I read the titles scrawled along the spine covers more easily in the morning light. I inherited my dad's vast collection, but Sid might have me beat. Jimi Hendrix records fill two shelves. I note to ask him about it.

I open the patio door and eye a structure that looks like it could be the gym.

As I slide the patio door closed, I hear, "You must be Ty!"

I swing around and find a kind-faced woman sitting regally at the head of the patio table. I recognize Sid's mom from TV. She's often in the crowd at his home games. Her salt and pepper locs are twisted intricately up in a bun. He shares her high cheekbones. A floral sundress and a carmine-colored, silk shawl are draped around her shoulders.

"Good morning. I am, indeed. You must be Ms. King." As I approach, I inhale a delicious scent of citrus, rose, and pepper. I see where Sid gets his taste for smelling amazing.

"Call me Lily, sweetheart. Come sit with me for a bit. How'd you sleep?" She places her book down on the table.

I smile and nod as I take a seat across from her.

How'd I sleep?

Oh, you know, I'm loving the idea of having sex with your son so much that I was up all night jerking off and freaking out.

"I fell asleep when we were in the theater. Out like a light."

"I know how that goes. I blame it on the plush blankets and super comfortable recliner seats."

I chuckle. "That might have something to do with it."

"Did you have enough to eat last night?" she asks.

"Maybe too much. I stuffed my face. Your lasagna is out of this world! The pies too."

Her face lights up. "That makes me so happy to hear. My

son is very excited to have made your acquaintance. He's been going on about how the peach and apple pies had to be perfect. As if I've ever made a bad pie! He called me after your interview and told me all about it. He said that he couldn't wait for me to meet you. When he told me yesterday that he'd forgotten to invite you, I almost pulled his ear like when he was a boy. He's only had one other friend that he's shown the same level of enthusiasm over."

A shadow flicks across her face. "He hates to talk about him, but I think it would be good for him."

I think back to our phone conversation yesterday when I wanted to ask Sid if he's haunted.

"I don't mean to pry, but is he no longer friends with that person?"

She opens up her mouth to answer, but her gaze sweeps past my shoulder.

I whip my head around at the sound of the patio door opening. Sid emerges wearing a tank top, shorts, and Christmas socks. His eyes are puffy.

I swallow roughly as the filthy images from the last few hours surface.

Fuck, it wasn't just in my head. *He really is that sexy.*

"Morning, baby, I was just getting to know our friend Ty here," Lily greets him.

Sid smiles at me as he kisses Lily on the cheek. My neck warms as I smile back at him.

"Morning, Ma. Why do I have the feeling you were revealing all of my secrets?"

"Of course not. We were just chatting about the best lasagna Ty has ever had." She winks at me.

"Good morning," he greets me as he sits beside me.

"Mornin'." I clear my throat. "Merry Christmas to you both."

"Merry Christmas," they reply in unison.

"Katrina's sleeping in?" I ask.

"She left. Had to catch an early flight to visit family."

"No G280 for her?"

"She already had a first-class ticket. I try not to bother the staff on holidays."

Lily peers at me, then Sid, then me again, and smiles to herself. I'd pay to know what she's thinking.

"Were you headed to the gym?" Sid asks, scanning my sneakers and clothes.

"Yeah."

"Mind if I join you? I'll change quickly," he says.

I shake my head. *So much for taking space to get my head right.*

"Ma, you need help with anything first?" he asks, standing up.

"No, thank you, dear. Chef Marcus dropped off the food not too long ago. I made brunch. It's keeping warm on the stove." She turns to me. "Sid insisted on hiring a chef to prepare Christmas dinner, even though I am perfectly capable of feeding my family."

"You deserve to rest, just like the rest of us. We've talked about this," he replies, his deep voice as gentle as the morning breeze.

"Fine. We're opening gifts after breakfast once Kieran and Tommy come down."

"Yes, ma'am," he agrees.

He turns to me. "Be right back."

"I'm going to make a fresh cup of tea. Pleasure to meet you, Ty!"

"Pleasure is mine, Ms. Kin—Lily," I correct myself.

She offers an amused smile before she departs.

I PUSH MYSELF HARD ON THE TREADMILL. I WANT THE ACHE TO BE intense enough to block out the fact that I caught myself checking out the imprint of Sid's cock through his gym shorts while we were warming up. I want to block out his delicious scent that's permeated every corner of the gym. I want to block out the grunts he's making right now on the pull-up bar. I increase the speed incrementally until I'm running max speed, covered in sweat. Even though I feel nauseated, I push through, only pulling back when my vision turns blurry. Lowering the incline, I gradually reduce the speed until I come to a full stop.

I turn around to find Sid watching me from his seat on the bench. Our gazes lock.

The way he's looking at me....

I can't be the only one impacted by the tension rippling through the air.

I break eye contact as I tilt my head up for a swig of water.

When he speaks, it's not what I expect. I don't know what I expected. He's straight, after all...I think.

"Can you spot me?" he asks, clearing his throat.

"Sure." I towel off, grab another swig of water, and make my way to the bench.

After a couple of sets, he pauses and peers up at me.

"I'm dead. My tank is running on E."

"Katrina kept you up most of the night?" I ask, feigning ignorance.

"I think it's all the excitement surrounding Christmas and the week of road games. I wore myself out."

"Ah. Well, as Coach would say 'Tough nuts!' Give me two more sets."

"No mercy." He chuckles. "You're cold."

I bite the side of my mouth to refocus my brain on the pain instead of Sid's grunting.

After he's done with his sets, we switch places. I regret it immediately. Having Sid's crotch right over my head does things to my out-of-whack body. My pulse speeds up as my semi-erection thickens. I quickly switch my thoughts to insects to calm down. It works.

I finish the sets, then confess that I'm kinda wiped too. He seems relieved. We stretch and then head back to the house. Once I'm back in my room, I climb in the shower. I imagine myself lying across the bench back in the gym, head turned as Sid feeds me his erection. My hand travels southward and wraps around my wet, aching cock. I close my eyes and stroke myself as I imagine the glide of Sid's cock against my tongue, my lips stretched taut as I suck him down. The sound of his husky moans from last night echoes through me. Stroking myself faster, my balls draw up. I bite my fist to stifle a moan as my release coats my chest. My legs tremble, and I lean against the shower wall.

My phone rings as I step out of the shower. I throw a towel around my waist and jog over to the nightstand to retrieve it.

"Hey, Unc, Merry Christmas!"

"Merry Christmas, kid! How are you spending the day? I hate that I can't be with you today. I have a gift for you."

"I have a gift for you too. Uh, I'm actually spending it with Sid King and his family out in Miami."

"Really? How'd that come about?" Adam asks, surprise coating his voice.

"We met during the interview in New York, remember? He called and invited me to spend the holiday with his fam."

"We spoke two days ago. You didn't mention it."

"He invited me yesterday. Said he meant to do it earlier, but he lost track of time. He apparently told his mom weeks ago because she made my favorite pies. Anyway, he sent his private plane to scoop me."

"Wow! You must have made some connection during the interview."

"It's my charm, Unc. I'm irresistible."

"You get that from me and your dad. The Washington men are notorious charmers."

We both laugh.

"Can I ask you a question?"

"You can ask me anything, you know that."

I clear my throat. "How'd you know you were gay?"

I think the question catches him by surprise because he's silent for a few beats.

"It's a long story, but I found out in my early twenties. Believe it or not, I was set to marry a woman. I knew it wasn't a right match all along, but for some idiotic reason, I proposed. Well, I'm not being fair. My girlfriend gave me an ultimatum and said she wouldn't keep being strung along. I didn't want to lose the friendship, so I proposed. I was miserable about it. Your dad pulled me aside a month before the wedding and asked me what I was doing. He said anyone with the gift of sight could tell I wasn't interested in being married to her. I told him I felt nothing other than platonic feelings toward women. He point-blank asked me if I was gay. I swear the question set off all sorts of lights in my brain. It's like I knew the answer the second he asked the question.

"I asked him, 'How can I be if I've never been with a man?'

"'Do you think there's a virgin alive today who could be straight?' he asked.

"I said, 'Of course.'

"'Dummy, you're a virgin when it comes to men. That doesn't mean you can't be gay,' he replied.

"I asked him if he thought differently of me.

"'You being gay makes more sense to me than you marrying

your girlfriend.' He told me who I love could never change the way he feels about me, and if anyone gave me flack, to tell them his big bro would kick their butts."

"He was always protective of you."

"He always had my back." He clears the scratch out of his voice. "I felt like the luckiest son of a bitch having him as my big brother. I still do."

"Yeah, I know what you mean. I felt the same way."

"You and your mom were his world. He was crazy about you."

It's nice to hear, but it hurts. "You're killing me."

"I'm sorry. I just don't want you to think for a second that you aren't loved. Now, why did you ask me about being gay?"

I almost say *no reason,* but I have a sneaking suspicion that if I don't tell Adam, I'll never tell anyone.

"I've been curious..."

"Curious?"

"Yeah, about what it would be like to be with a man."

"Ah. Would this have something to do with The Wonder Kid?"

"Maybe."

Adam's silent on the other end.

"Okay, fine, it's more than a maybe," I blurt out, making him chuckle. "It doesn't make sense. Sometimes our gazes lock, and it's so intense that my brain times out. We both like reading, and he seems endlessly curious, which is so attractive, and talking to him is the easiest thing in the world." I think about how mentioning *The Count of Monte Cristo* during the interview encouraged him to look into it. It's something I would do. "Then there's the physical attraction...fuck. It's like my body can't control itself when he's around. He looks at me like I'm this fascinating person that he wants to take apart and study."

Feeling dizzy from pacing around, I sit on the edge of the bed and rest my head in my hands.

"That definitely sounds like a lot more than a *maybe*, kid."

I release an exasperated sigh. "*But*, he's seeing this gorgeous actress who he claims it's just casual with. She popped up out of the blue last night, and they were all over each other. So, there's a very real chance it could all be one-sided. I'm not sure."

"Hmm. Well, okay, let's put Sid aside for a second. I promise we'll pick him back up soon. Have you felt anything romantic or sexual before for another man, or rather, how does it feel when you're with women?"

My shoulders relax as his voice does its calming thing. "It's okay, I guess. I mean, I've never gone crazy for it like other dudes."

"*It* meaning sex with women?" he asks.

"Yeah, and it's never felt intense enough for me to want to keep seeing them." Of the handful of women I've been with, Bianca, the girl I lost my virginity to, comes to mind. Brilliant, gorgeous, thick in all the right places. I was waiting for the train home one day when she approached me out of nowhere. I pretended it was normal for one of the baddest girls in school to strike up a conversation with me. Being on the basketball team had its perks, but she was *way* out of my league. For one, I was a junior, and she was a senior with a college boyfriend, or so I had thought. It turns out she'd broken up with him and was interested in me for a reason I never quite figured out.

Our first conversation was awkward as fuck. I almost pretended I left something at school just to escape it. I couldn't get past the fact she knew I existed. So I stood there like a dud —a monosyllabic dud. I was low-key relieved when the train arrived jam-packed because it meant we had to squeeze into different train cars. After that day, Bianca started appearing at my games, rooting for me louder than anyone except my parents. Then, one day, she said her parents wouldn't be home until late and invited me to her house. We hung out in her room, listening to music and pretending to do homework. She casually traced lines along my arm as we talked. I debated leaning in for a kiss when she beat me to it. It wasn't my first kiss, but it was the best I'd had. Things got hella awkward once clothes started coming off. I think she could tell I was a virgin, but she didn't make me feel weird about it. She took the lead, and it was over in less than two minutes.

I remember telling my dad about it later that night, after dinner, when he'd stopped by my room to chill. He sat on the floor, legs outstretched, facing my bed, and listened attentively. He asked me how I felt about having sex for the first time. I told him I didn't know. He said that not knowing was okay because it was a big step and that it takes time for us to make sense of the big things that happen to us sometimes. It wasn't the first time he and I talked about sex, but it felt different since I was no longer a virgin. He asked me if I wore a condom. I did. Then he asked me if I sat with Bianca afterward and if I asked her if she was okay. I did. We talked a lot that night about the responsibility that comes with having sex, like how it's important to keep the intimacy shared between two partners private. I remember thinking about how my loose-lipped teammates definitely didn't believe that. I don't know what I thought about sex before our conversation that night, but after, I felt like it wasn't something to be careless about. I guess that's why I didn't hop at every opportunity to hook up in college or even now. He told me Washington men love hard and how he had an entire plan to marry Mom and build a family, but she needed some convincing. She wanted to finish college first. She made it clear she wouldn't accept his proposal until graduation. I asked him when he proposed, and we laughed when he told me it was in the parking lot after her graduation ceremony. I told him I wanted to propose to a girl by twenty-five but wait until I was thirty to get married. I asked him if that was too young, and he said "For Washington men, no way."

"That's important to make note of. What about with men?" Adam asks, reeling me back in.

"Never...but it felt like a door opened in college. There were a few guys around campus I was kinda into, but it never felt safe to pursue. I didn't want to jeopardize my shot at making the league, and hooking up with women was just easier."

"I'm honestly relieved to hear that you dated at all. You never mentioned anyone."

I shrug. "Not really much to share."

"So the attraction that you feel for Sid is more intense than you've felt for any other man or woman, but you aren't sure if it's mutual. I have that right?"

"Yeah, fuck, it feels intense every time I'm around him," I groan. "It's indescribable."

"Do we know if he's straight or not?"

"He's only been with women publicly."

"That doesn't necessarily mean he's straight. Has he said or done anything to make you think he could feel the same way as you do?"

"That's the thing, it's hard to tell. It's not like I have a lot of friends to compare his behavior. He flew me out here to spend the holiday with his closest family. Asked his mom to make my favorite pies. I'm staring at a gift he picked up weeks ago for me after our interview in New York. But maybe I'm reading too much into it, and he's just a generous dude?"

"Possibly. What if he isn't straight? What would it mean for you?"

A coil of tension twists in my abdomen as the enormity of the question settles in. "God...I don't know." I scrub my hands over my face. "Maybe we could hook up casually? Does it need to be more than that?"

"Hmm," Adam hums quietly.

"What? You think I'm full of shit?"

"Hey, I didn't say that, but I have another question. How do you feel about possibly being queer?"

I sigh. *The million-dollar question.* "Real talk...kinda terrified. I only want to be known for being a great basketball player. If it got out that I'm not straight, I'd be reduced to being known as only *that gay player* on the Knights. Some dudes already talk crazy to get in my head, like that Lucas asshole I told you about. I can only imagine the bullshit I'd have to deal with on the daily."

"Yeah, it won't be easy, but that doesn't mean it isn't worthwhile."

I think about that. More athletes are coming out, though few of them look like me.

"On the flip side, I can't front, the idea of exploring this... *itch* that I have, especially with someone like Sid, feels..." God. How do I explain what I barely understand? "When he's near, something inside me comes online—parts that I didn't realize had switched off. Or maybe I did, but I moved on because I didn't know how to fix it. And there are new parts that I'm discovering."

"About yourself?"

"Yeah, and it's both exhilarating and terrifying." I've never experienced this intensity of desire for anyone. But it isn't just desire, is it? I sense that whatever this is—it's immense.

"I imagine that if we did this—if he felt the same..." I blow out a breath.

"It would be significant?"

"Yes...for me, at least."

"So, it would be more than scratching an itch. Is that part of what's terrifying?"

"Mm-hmm. That and being gay in the league."

"Wow...okay. Well, your parents would probably say what I will say—you deserve to be happy. I know basketball means the world to you. You don't have to choose. If it turns out you're not straight, you can still play basketball. If and when you decide to come out is your decision. It's bullshit, the idea that people have to run out of the closet as soon as they realize that they're not straight. You can take time to process, date privately, *and* be an amazing athlete. If and whenever you decide to come out publicly, I will be right by your side. You're young, kid. You have time to figure it all out. We'll talk about how to practice safe sex when you come home in a few days."

I know he's right. They would want me to do what's right for me. His advice has a way of opening windows and letting light into all of the suffocating and dark places that trip me up. "Thanks, Unc. But it's a little too late for the sex talk."

"I thought you hadn't been with men."

"I haven't."

"We'll talk about how you have sex with men safely, wise guy."

I laugh, and it feels so good. I've been low-key spiraling all morning. "Oh, yeah...duh."

"Now, on the matter of Sid, it sounds like there's chemistry between you two. Has he said anything to make you think he's homophobic?"

"No, actually, his cousin and childhood best friend are here and they're gay, I think. Sid seems cool with it, like really cool."

"That's good. Let's validate that you have feelings for him, even if we aren't sure about his feelings for you. Maybe he's someone you could confide in whenever you feel it's safe to do so."

"Yeah, maybe. How do I not act like a freak around him?"

"First, be kind to yourself. Liking someone or desiring them is nothing to be ashamed of. Also, any relationship worth its salt begins with friendship. You're just getting to know him. Maybe focus on that. Get to know him and allow him to get to know you. If there is more there, in my experience, it won't stay hidden for long."

I think about that. I do want to get to know him. Friendship doesn't sound bad. Maybe if I got laid, it'd take the edge off. It's been months since I've fucked anyone. Maybe I'm just horny.

"Thanks. I know literally putting out fires is your passion, but you could be a therapist."

"Expect my invoice in the mail," he says, chuckling.

"I still want to buy you a bigger house and a tricked-out whip."

"I don't need any of that, kid. I'm already a super proud uncle."

"Uh-huh."

"It's true. My break is over. I gotta run. See you in a few days."

"Stay safe, please. I know it's your job, but try not to run into burning buildings unless you like, really, *really* have to," I plead.

"Heard. I love you."

"I love you too."

I take a deep breath after we hang up. Every time we speak, I can't shake the gut-twisting ache that it might be the last time.

I throw on briefs and a T-shirt and lie down, closing my eyes. Friendship doesn't seem so hard. I can do this.

A couple of minutes later, there's a knock on the door.

"Yo!"

"It's open," I respond.

One glance at Sid's very fitted velvet Christmas-themed onesie and I burst out laughing.

"Dig it?" he asks, with a sexy grin. He sets down the gift that I brought for him and then struts around in a circle, hitting one ridiculous pose after another.

When I see the "naughty elf" written across the butt flap, I howl with laughter. The butt area, double cargo pockets, and elbows are lined with buffalo plaid. There's a large, fuzzy, white pom-pom attached to the apex of his hood.

How did they make a Christmas-themed onesie for a dude

that big? I have to suck in air to stop my stomach from cramping.

Are those buttons along the butt flap? I have many questions.

Buttons that start low down his chest, below his nipples, fasten the whole thing. They end right above his groin area. He flexes his muscles, causing the velvet over his groin to shift, outlining his dick, and my cock stirs.

Damn.

The more the fabric shifts, highlighting the swell and ripple of muscles, the more my erection grows. It's kinda obscene how sexy he looks. I stifle a groan when he spins one last time, and one button on the butt flap unsnaps, revealing a sliver of skin. I covertly place a pillow over my lap.

"Um, one question. Was it custom-made?" I pipe up, needing a distraction.

His jaw drops. "How'd you know? Kieran gifted it to me. He ordered it for me from a guy out in San Francisco. Copped one for Tommy too, but on his butt it reads 'I'm so good Santa came twice.'" He chuckles, then bends down and picks up the gift I brought him. By some miracle, the buttons remain snapped in place.

"Were you napping?"

I nod. "Power nap."

"Cool. I'll let you get back to it, but I want you to open your gift."

"I can come downstairs, and we can open them together with your family," I offer, then regret it since I'm still rocking an erection.

"All good. I know you're resting. Open yours first."

"No, you first. Remember, if I had more time, I would have put more thought into it."

"Whatever it is, it'll be great," he says as he rips open the wrapping paper, starting with the two triangular flaps and then the middle seam.

"It's a picture frame," he says. He flips it over so that it's right side up. As he reads the quote, I watch his sexy grin spread into a bright smile.

"You remember I said I wanted a copy framed on my wall?"

I grin back. "Yep." I wasn't sure he would remember telling me he wanted a framed copy of the unabbreviated quote from *The Count of Monte Cristo* I read out loud during our interview.

"It's perfect," he says, meeting my gaze.

"You can replace the frame if bronze ain't your thing. Options were limited."

"Nah, it's perfect. Seriously." He hugs it against his chest.

"Glad you like it."

"Open yours!" He passes me the gift from the nightstand, chewing on his lip.

"You wrapped this?" I ask.

He nods.

"I can tell." The wrap job is professional.

"Is that a compliment?"

I grin in response. I rip apart the paper and peer at a leather-bound book set. I flip to the cover and see *The Count of Monte Cristo* embossed in gold lettering.

"Wait, are these–?"

"First edition in English," he confirms.

"No way! These cost a mint!"

He waves that off. "The accent on the cover is made of 22-karat gold."

As I stare at him in disbelief, his grin widens at my reaction.

I scan the first few lines of the first chapter, trailing my finger over the cover and smelling the pages.

"Wow, okay, do you need some time alone with it?" he jokes.

"It's a truly thoughtful gift. Are you sure you don't want to keep it for yourself?"

"You dig Dumas and the story so much that you thought about getting it tattooed. It belongs to you."

I grin and stand to hug him, grateful I don't have a tenting situation in my pants.

He wraps me up in his cocoon embrace. Tension seeps out of me as his strong arms wrap around my back.

I hold on a few seconds longer than I would have yesterday. I start to feel self-conscious about it until I realize he's holding on too.

I pull away, then punch his arm.

"Ow! What was that for?"

"Inviting me at the last minute. I am usually an excellent gift giver."

He scoffs and hugs the frame against his chest. "How dare you speak poorly of my gift!"

"Can I ask you a question?"

He nods.

"What did you get Katrina?"

"Uh," he squints, thinking about it. "My assistant sent over a handbag or necklace."

"Did your assistant pick out my gift too?"

He shakes his head. "Why?"

I shrug. "Thank you for the gift. I love it."

He pumps his fist in victory, and I can't help but grin. "You want to get back to your nap or join us for some bowling?"

"You have a bowling alley?" I ask, wide-eyed.

He nods. "I need to give you a proper tour before you leave."

"I'm down to bowl."

"Tommy is a pro. Prepare your ego. He never scores less than 270." He shakes his head.

"I'm still stuck on you having a bowling alley in your house," I remark as I pull sweats on from my bag.

"Is this cool, or should I throw on something nicer?"

"Nah, you're good," he confirms, scanning my body.

"I'm hungry. Have you eaten?"

"Not yet. Let's grab a plate on the way," he says.

He leads the way out, and my eyes devour the muscles of his back and ass. I tuck myself under the waistband of my briefs. I groan inwardly when I realize I have to watch him bowl in that onesie. Whatever confidence I felt on the call with Adam is non-existent now.

Chapter Eight

We watched Brooklyn beat Boston after a couple of hours of bowling. Brooklyn's star power forward, Salem Jones, is a beast when defending the rim. His block on the last possession secured the victory for Brooklyn. We played Monopoly and traded stories. Sid wasn't lying. Kieran is definitely a cheater, but he only steals from Sid. Considering Sid bought more properties on the board than the rest of us, including Boardwalk, I can't say I felt bad for him.

I shared stories about my parents and Adam. I learned Sid was protective of Kieran growing up. There was no shortage of homophobic bullies. Kieran moved in with Lily and Sid during his junior year of high school because his mom kicked him out for being gay. Tommy entered the picture during Kieran's senior year after transferring from another school. They bonded immediately. No one dared to mess with Kieran once he and Tommy became inseparable. Tommy's size was a major deterrent, and his temper toward bullies didn't hurt either.

"I have to head out pretty early in the morning," I say to Sid, who's lying against the opposite armrest of the living room couch, hands behind his head, gazing at me through heavy eyelids. It's after midnight and everyone else retired for the night. We just put down the PS5 remotes after I beat him in Madden NFL three times in a row.

"What time? I'll text the pilot now," Sid asks, reaching for his phone.

"Six. Got practice in the morning." I pull out my phone to set an alarm.

"That's brutal." He tosses his phone on the table and leans back, but then suddenly pops up again. "Be right back."

I watch him disappear toward the kitchen. He returns a few minutes later, throws back a handful of pills, and swallows them down with a glass of water.

"What's that?"

"Supplements," he answers after swallowing.

"Like what?"

"Vitamins…fish oil, probiotics, prebiotics, and adaptogens. Want?" he offers.

I shake my head. "I'm good."

"Helps with energy, immunity, and stuff, y'know?" He tosses more water back. "Thanks for coming through and spending Christmas with me and the fam."

"I had fun. Thanks for having me. I'm gonna dream about your mom's lasagna for a while."

His smile stretches into a yawn.

"Ready to sleep?"

"Got a few more minutes in me," he says, settling into the couch.

"I've been meaning to ask, do you find it hard to sleep after an evening game too?"

"Fo-sho. Sometimes I don't get to sleep until the sun is up."

I nod. "Same."

"I'm big on power naps. I try to sleep when I can."

I hardly ever nap if I can help it. Less chance of a nightmare.

"My turn," he says. "What's surprised you most about being in the NBA?"

I think about it. Practices are more intense, and it's different playing against All-Stars, but I kinda expected that. "Honestly, the travel, man. Forty-one away games. Managing jet lag, time zones, and temperatures. It's grueling."

He grins. "It takes some getting used to. Sleep as much as you can. It's the quickest way to recover. Do you meditate?"

I shrug. "I've tried. It never sticks."

"I use an app and try to commit to a ten to fifteen-minute meditation a few times daily. It makes a difference." He picks up his phone and a minute later, my phone vibrates with a text with an invite to join his family account.

"Try it on the plane tomorrow. It works, man."

I'm realizing there's more to staying in top shape than I thought. Considering what I'll need to put my body through each season, I need to step my game up.

"Thanks! I feel like I owe you." His generosity is next level.

"Come on, that's whack. You still haven't accepted we're friends then."

It's kind of true. I don't trust easily. But even more, Sid's damn near a legend. His friendship can't be this easy.

"It's all good. You'll see."

I meet his gaze. "I appreciate it...you know?"

He nods. "I know."

I relax into the couch, leaning my head back. We fall into a companionable silence.

"Is the game still as fun for you as it was in the beginning?"

He opens his mouth to speak but then closes it again.

I quirk my eyebrows. "It isn't?" Maybe he isn't as giddy as Christmas Sid, but whenever a ball is in his hand, he looks damn near close.

"Here's the thing. I've loved basketball for as long as I can remember. Besides being a fan of the game, it helps me mentally."

I quirk my eyebrows, gesturing for him to continue.

"You know those games when you're down a shit ton of points from missed shots, sloppy turnovers, and a weak defense? I mean, you spend everything in the bank and have zilch to show for it? And the only way to turn the tide is to reach deep. You tap into a force. Like you're attempting plays you've never tried before. You're way out there on the edge. And somehow, the shit works!"

I think back to a couple of games in college. That force...or energy is infectious. Suddenly, everyone's fired up, and before we knew it, it was the final buzzer, and we went from getting blown out to being crowned the champ. It's indescribable.

"Yeah...I see from that grin that you know exactly what I'm talking about. Those are the moments that make it all worth it. If your only goal is to make money and gain celebrity, you'll find it difficult to play at a high level season after season. I've learned to be consistent in how I train, eat, sleep, and recover. It goes a long way toward keeping me locked in. And I don't have a ring yet."

"I can't imagine tiring of chasing rings. All of that makes sense, but man, I hate being in front of the camera. How do you always look so comfortable in interviews?"

He laughs. "I've seen you in interviews. You do better than you think."

I scoff. "I don't know about that."

"You're smart to be wary of it, though. My advice is to always say less where the media is concerned. When asked provocative questions, I get off on giving the most boring answer I can think of. If you're looking for a sensational clip, it ain't coming from me."

"Your advice to me when asked about the media's comparison of us. Was that real?"

"Hell yeah." His face turns serious. "You even have to ask?"

I shake my head. "I hate that they compare us. I mean, you're one of the best in the league. I'm in my first year. Our style is completely different. Let us be us."

"I get it, though," he says, scratching his arm. "You bring something special to the league. Your explosive offensive power, tight handles, and ability to focus and get in the paint is an unexpected combo from a rookie. They were just as excited when I joined."

That makes me scoff. "The excitement over you joining the league was stratospheric. Let's not pretend it was remotely close to the buzz I received."

He shakes his head. "It was a circus, is what it was. That shit's fake as fuck. You can't let fame or flattery validate you or feed your self-esteem. I keep my circle tight, and it's full of people who aren't afraid to tell me the truth. Too many people will blow smoke up your ass to get something from you." He straightens up. "Can I tell you something I haven't really admitted out loud?"

I nod. "Of course."

"I wish I had stayed in college like you for a few more years. I think talent and hard work can make you a great athlete, but you need other skills if you want to be more than that. I was faced with a fuck ton of money that my family needed ASAP, so I did what I had to, but I enjoy learning, as corny as that sounds."

"It's not corny at all. I get it. I can't front. I only stayed because I'd promised my parents that I would. They wanted me to get a degree. They stressed it all the time." My parents may have been more excited about me graduating than going pro. "When they passed, I inherited enough dough to put me through college. I was always jealous of dudes like you who entered the draft a year after college. I was fiending to go the one-and-done route."

He shakes his head. "You did it the right way, though most dudes might disagree with me. They only see the cheddar." He sighs. "What was it like to graduate?"

I shrug. Adam was excited for me to walk, but I wasn't into it. I looked around at my stoked classmates and their tearful families and couldn't relate. There's a framed picture of me in my cap and gown hanging in Adam's house. Every time I'm there, I want to set fire to it. He might be relieved that it's gone. A blank wall has to be better than staring at an empty person every day.

"I walked for Adam. He wouldn't let me skip it. And for my parents. I know it isn't the same, but you can hire private instructors to teach you that stuff. And there are books."

"I have. Everything from how to be a better public speaker, business writing, and basic finance. I was never comfortable having people in suits think for me."

That doesn't surprise me...not with a brain that curious. "That's dope, man."

"Thanks." After a beat, he asks, "Why basketball for you?"

"I suppose the reasons have changed. I've wanted to ball for as long as I can remember. Besides Adam, it's probably the most honest relationship that I have. Then my parents died, and my reasons changed."

"Oh yeah? How so?"

I shuffle to sit upright. "They died trying to get to my game. They sacrificed a lot through the years to help me go pro. Money, time, energy. I need to honor them by making their sacrifices worth it. I can't fumble this."

His lips part slightly, but he stops short of speaking. He brackets his arms over his head.

"What?" I ask, fidgeting under the intensity of his stare.

"I won't pretend to fathom a loss like the one you experienced. But...it's just a lot of pressure to put on yourself. You graduated for them. You're chasing rings for them...I guess I'm just wondering what *you* want out of life."

"Chasing rings is what I want. I just said—"

"You just said that you do it to honor your parents."

"Yeah, I did, but..." Tension stiffens my shoulders as I stare at the ceiling, trying to make sense of my jumbled thoughts. Ball's taken on a different meaning, yes, but it's the one area of my life that's been consistent, and consistency isn't a small thing for me. Has joining the league lived up to everything I thought it would be? Does it bring me happiness beyond my imagination? No, but the kid who spent hours believing that it would died five winters ago with my parents. I'd be lying if I didn't admit that sometimes I feel like an imposter living out his dreams.

I scrub my hands across my face. "I still ball for me."

He hums.

I clear my throat. "I've been meaning to confirm something. My game in college. You were there?" Now's as good a time as any to ask the question I've been curious about for months. To my surprise, he grins.

"I wondered when you'd bring that up. Yeah, I, uh, came to see you."

I curtain off my grin with my hand. "Why?"

"I caught one of your games on TV and wanted to see you play in person."

"What did you think?" I rush out.

He doesn't answer right away, and I immediately wish I could reel back the question.

"I didn't mean to put you on—"

"You remember the first time you went to a basketball game?" he asks.

"Uh...yeah, Madison Square Garden. I was seven or eight. It was me, my dad, and Adam. The Royals were in town." I grin when I recall how ferociously the Choppers fought to defend our city. "Lightning Jack slammed down an insane buzzer-beater that almost blew the roof off of the arena." Dad and Adam balanced me between each of their shoulders as we lost it, cheering for Jack and the rest of the team. "It was peak, bro." My knee bounces, recalling how wired I was for days after.

"Lightning Jack! Wow, man's a legend. I met him last year at the ESPYs. He's the nicest dude."

Huh. Maybe meeting your heroes isn't always a bad thing. The grin slips from my face when it hits me that he changed the subject instead of answering my question. He probably thought I sucked that night. It wasn't a blowout win, but we fought hard.

I rub my neck. "What about your first game?"

"My mom took me for my sixth birthday. She'd been saving up for a long time. I'd experienced nothing like it. The players were giants. At one point, I even wondered if they were gods. The excitement in the arena...my entire body felt like a beating heart. Even my skin had a pulse." He shakes his head. "It was the purest form of euphoria. I've been chasing that feeling ever since. I catch strains of it from time to time, but nothing has ever come close." He clears his throat. "That's until the night I saw you play. My palms, my throat, and the blood under my skin vibrated. You ran—no—you commanded the court like the sky would fall if your team missed a play. No one wanted it more than you. You were exceptional."

Damn.

A tickle in my throat expands, walling off words. The impact of his statement, the strength of his gaze, it's enough to pull me under. All I can muster is a nod in response. I lean my head back and stare at the Christmas tree lights reflected off the ceiling. I'd wager the blush spreading up my neck and face burns brighter than the tree.

"You got emotional when your teammates lifted you in the air after the game?" he asks, breaking the silence.

I hug my knees into my chest. "Er, you caught that?"

He nods. "You don't have to talk about it if it makes you uncomfortable."

"It's, uh, kinda dumb. I searched the bleachers for my parents. For a moment, I forgot they were gone."

I ignore the ache that rests below the surface and concentrate on plotting the angles of the ceiling shapes reflected by the tree lights.

Sid remains silent, but his penetrating stare is loud.

I'm afraid that if I meet his gaze, I'll see pity. It's late and I'm tired...too tired to hold in whatever needs out. After an interminable silence, I muster the courage to turn my head and meet his gaze.

His brows pinch, and there's an overcast where his eyes usually gleam.

I wave it off. "It's all good, man."

"You don't have to do that. At least not with me."

I shake my head and look away. Too much kindness.

"I can't. If I don't swallow it down..." I trail off, raising a seawall behind my eyes to prevent the flood of emotions from breaking through.

"How have you worked through your grief?"

I shrug. "After my parents died, I kinda fell apart. I'd go to school but check out. My teachers passed me out of sympathy or something. I'd head straight home and climb into bed until the next morning. I lost my appetite. On some level, I think I wanted to waste away so that I could join them. It went on that way for months. Adam found a grief counselor for me, and he kinda helped."

He shifts to sit upright. "Does it still feel raw?"

"It's weird. It's always there hiding behind a memory. Now and then, I'm that kid in high school, and I can't get out of bed for days."

"That sounds like depression, Ty."

"Maybe." I shrug. "It just is."

His eyebrows draw together. "Can you describe what it feels like for you?"

"Depression?"

He nods.

I have to think about it before I can answer.

"It's kinda like my brain is off of its track."

He nods for me to continue.

"I can't muster the strength to give a shit about anything or anyone. Something as simple as brushing my teeth feels insurmountable. It's like I'm stuck in a daze with a single thought. And it's not that I'm necessarily sad. It's just that everything seems hollow. Like everyone is playing a game that I have no interest in participating in. It's all numbing, except it isn't, I guess. I mean, it's more that I'm numb. It takes over—" I scrub my hands over my face and drag out a breath.

No matter how many words I use, they're all woefully insufficient. How do you describe being stripped—locked off—from everything that feels good? I could use words like desolate, bleak, and grim, but would Sid understand? Maybe he would shiver for a second before his brain jumps in and reminds him of all the good in the world. But if his brain is like mine, it would stay offline, infected by a parasite that streams the same message every second of every day—Just. End. It.

"Everything?" he asks.

I give him a questioning look.

He leans slightly toward me. "You said that it takes over everything?"

I nod. "But it's kinda fucked because I'm the only one that knows it's there. And it takes even me forever to realize it. One minute I'm fine, then blink"—I snap my fingers—"and my place in the world is wrong. I'll try to shake it off, but days pass before I realize I've only sunk deeper."

"God, that sounds rough." He rubs at his lips, lost in thought. "What helps you climb out?"

Adam used to help, but his concern and love felt heavy, deepening the gap between where I was and what was normal. I prefer to get through it on my own.

"It just has to pass."

"Have you thought about therapy?"

"Nah, I don't need it."

"I see a therapist," he says. His lips turn up slightly. "Does it surprise you? Living in this world…"

I press my lips together. In all of the ways that I imagined Sid, I can't say that I imagined him in therapy. I guess even I'm guilty of forgetting there's a man behind the celebrity. "What do you go for? Is it helpful?"

"I lost my best friend in high school. I was having recurring nightmares about him, and it was affecting my game. We've also covered a lot of other things—anger, imposter syndrome, and my father's abandonment. Honestly, people go to therapy for different reasons. You don't need to hit some kind of secret trauma threshold before it's okay to go. You can go because you want to improve your life."

How is he this open? It's difficult for me to be vulnerable. I learned when my parents passed that the world moves on quickly when bad things happen to other people, and they expect you to move on too. I learned how to bury my grief, and one of the unintended effects is that it's become harder for me to open up.

"I'm sorry you lost your best friend."

"Thanks. It was a crazy period in my life. You know, being an athlete is as much about mental health as it is physical health. If you go through periods of depression, you should have a therapist in your corner to help you through it. We all need help. Will you consider talking to one?"

"My uncle has been begging me to see one for a minute and now you. I guess I should give it a shot."

"For real?"

I nod. "Yeah, maybe."

"I'm here too. Hit me up."

"The anniversary of my parent's death is coming up in early February."

"Oh yeah?"

"Adam and I usually visit their graves and then have lunch together."

"Every year?"

I nod.

He hums. "Sounds like a great way to remember them."

We fall back into a companionable silence.

"So, you take supplements, eat clean, meditate, and see a therapist. I'm impressed," I confess.

"It's just how I'm wired. I like to feel good," he says.

And look and smell good too.

"Want to watch something?" I ask.

"Sure, as long as it's a Christmas movie."

"You *really* love Christmas," I say, grinning.

He smiles. "Since day one."

"How did you get past security?"

He arches his head. "Huh?"

"At my college game."

"Oh, there was an older guy at the front. He promised he wouldn't make a big deal about me being there in exchange for a selfie and autograph."

"Slight curve to his back, thick glasses?" I ask, describing Jim.

"Yeah, why?"

I chuckle. "Damn. He's good. I asked him if he saw you and he looked at me like I had three heads."

I SWEAR BARELY AN HOUR HAS PASSED WHEN MY ALARM WAKES ME up. I groan as I reach to silence it. Sid groans too.

"Sorry," I grunt. I sit up bleary-eyed and get my bearings. I gaze over at Sid. An arm covers his face.

I take in his onesie and smile.

We slept together on the couch and even though we didn't touch each other, something about it still feels...perfect.

"I'm going to shower and head out," I whisper as he stirs.

"Aight, Leslie should be here any minute to take you to the airport."

"Thanks. You do think of it all," I say with a yawn.

He stretches and tries to sit up but falls back down.

Adorable.

"Stay there."

I stand up and stretch. His sleepy gaze tracks my movements. I lean over to hug him goodbye.

"Christ, you smell amazing," I whisper. Without thinking, I nuzzle my nose in his neck. I stiffen, realizing how weird that was, but then he chuckles. The rasp of his morning laugh goes straight to my dick. Luckily, when I pull away, his eyes are closed again. I quickly adjust my semi-erection.

"You don't snore," he says.

"Good to know," I say, swiping up my phone.

"You got a boner."

"Word?" I ask, not surprised.

"No bullshit," he confirms, grinning.

"When did you fall asleep?"

His heavy-lidded eyes peel open, gazing up at me. I don't think it's meant to look as sexy as it does. But damn if it doesn't make heat rise up my back.

"Not long after you. I got up in the middle of the night to piss. That's when I saw it."

I groan and cover my face with my hands.

Wait...he got up to use the restroom, then returned to sleep on the couch next to me instead of his bed? Why?

"It's nothing to be embarrassed about. You should be proud. Bet the ladies are pleased."

I'm not prepared for Sid commenting on my dick size at the crack of dawn on, like, three and a half hours of sleep.

"Yeah, ladies," I mutter while bending forward to get a kink out of my back.

He raises one eyebrow. "Or men?"

Fuck. I'm really not prepared for this.

"Married to the game right now. Remember?"

He hums.

I remain silent. Silence is good.

"You know, if you weren't str..."

His voice trails off as our heads swivel toward the approaching footsteps. Leslie emerges, looking bright-eyed.

"Morning, gents! Mr. Washington, ready to go?"

"Morning, Leslie. Give me fifteen minutes? Need to get cleaned up and pack real quick."

"Take your time," Leslie replies.

Before I head upstairs, I glance back at Sid and find him watching me.

"How was Christmas?" I hear him ask Leslie as I run up the stairs.

I rush to get myself together, intent on not being late to practice. As I leave my bedroom with my bags in hand, Sid emerges from his room looking fresh-faced.

"Here, give me one of those," he says, retrieving one of my bags.

Leslie meets us at the bottom of the staircase and takes the bags out to the car.

"Sorry to have woken you up so early."

"It's all good. I'll probably read until I crash. I don't have practice for a few hours."

"Good luck against New York later," I bid him.

"Thanks. Not sure I need it," he jokes. Their roster is weak this season. "Good luck against Cleveland."

"Thanks. Tell your family I said goodbye. I enjoyed spending time with them."

"You'll see them again," he says in his prescient way.

I grin at that. We stand facing each other for a few more seconds.

"Well...peace then," I say, slipping my hands in my pockets.

"Yeah," he replies, leaning in slightly, or maybe it's my imagination. "Have a safe flight." He steps back to let me pass.

I climb into the back seat and turn to glance at the house. Sid's leaning against his front door, arms and legs crossed, watching me. The sun highlights the incline of his cheekbone and the blade of his jaw. His sexy gaze is penetrating as he nibbles on his bottom lip.

Fuck my life.

He's such a wet dream.

He's my dream.

I shake the thought from my head.

My dream has always been and can only ever be, chasing rings.

Still, I can't peel my eyes away until he disappears behind the hedges. I'm sure his PR team is worth every penny, but there's something indescribable about meeting him in real life that you just have to experience for yourself. He possesses a nourishing warmth that seeps into my bones and reminds me of what it's like to be untethered from grief.

L ATER THAT NIGHT, MY PHONE BUZZES WHEN I'M BACK AT HOME. I pick it up and grin when I see his name. Opening the text, I find a picture of me sleeping on the couch from last night. It's a good shot. It looks like sleep is kind to me. Something about him keeping a picture of me on his phone makes me grin like an idiot. Another message pops up.

SID

Thanks for sleeping with me, Pretty Boy

My jaw drops. This is flirting. It has to be flirting. I almost screenshot it and send it to Adam for confirmation, but I tell myself to chill.

ME

The pleasure was mine

I slap my forehead for not stealing a picture of him in his onesie. Though I'm not sure I need it. Some things are impossible for a man to forget.

SID

Playing basketball, opening presents, watching movies, stretching, sleeping, interviewing...

ME

?

SID

All the things you look pretty doing

I shoot back an eye roll emoji.

SID

I hear I smell good in the morning

Fishing for compliments, are we?

ME

It's infuriating

SID

I think you meant irresistible

I grin hard.

ME

Congrats on the W. I watched the highlights.

SID

Thanks. I watched your highlights too. 32 points. You were amazing even w/o the W.

ME

I only care about the Ws

SID

You'll get 'em

ME

I'm exhausted. I don't recommend playing on four hours of sleep.

SID

Me too, though the night company was worth it

ME

Yeah? Mine was aight

SID

You slept with the sexiest man alive. You call that aight?

My jaw is officially on the mattress.

"This is flirting!" I yell into the air.

ME

> I said what I said. Though technically, I slept next to arguably the sexiest man alive. I'd think I'd remember if I slept with him.

Argh! I throw the phone across the mattress. That was way too forward. Fuuuuck. I ignore the phone when it buzzes. I turn off the lights and stare into the dark. The phone buzzes again. After an exhausting two-minute mental battle, I flick the light back on and scramble for the phone with zero chill.

SID

> It would be unforgettable.

Damn...I bet.

> Night, Pretty Boy

ME

> Night, Wonder Kid

I turn off the lights and jerk off for what feels like the zillionth time in the last forty-eight hours.

Chapter Nine

I t's been three weeks since Christmas and I'm back in Miami. This time with my teammates for a Tuesday evening game against the Marvels. It's the first time Sid and I will face off. A fact that the media has run into the ground all week. Despite my efforts to drown it out, you'd have to live on another planet without access to a phone, television, or laptop to ignore it entirely. At the hotel gym, I noticed both my face and Sid's plastered on treadmill screens tuned in to NBA TV. Ignoring my better judgment, I flip to the channel and catch Hal Patchett, a sports commentator, sharing his assessment:

"...ferocious, they don't call him the Wonder Kid for nothing. On the flip side, with the wisdom and poise you'd expect from a veteran, Ty's explosive offensive power and speed make it difficult for larger opponents to contain him. He's known to scramble defenses. His long and mid-range shooting is steadily improving. This season, he's shooting 41.5% on shots from forty feet, a percentage not too far from some of the best point guards in the league. Let's face it, there's no stopping him! Even if you consider the rare night when Ty's shooting percentage is low, the stats show that the Knights always score more

when he's on the floor. He influences the game whether he takes shots or not. His ability to get hot in the third quarter requires him to be defended until the final buzzer. Knowledge is power and the Knights have learned to create specific plays to take advantage of Ty's influence. Viewers may be familiar with the term "hockey assist," which refers to a pass that leads to a pass that leads to a basket. Ty's hockey assists rank third highest in the league. Defensively, there's room for Ty to grow, but he already shows promise. Take this clip from their last game against Milwaukee. Ty, with possession of the ball, cuts to the wing. He is double-teamed by the defense—"

I turn off the screen and return to drowning out the noise. If we lose the game tonight, Hal will do a 180 and eviscerate me during tomorrow's segment. I remember all that matters is my efforts and that of my teammates, not the critics. Never the critics.

We're staying at the Four Seasons Hotel. For everyone else, the day started at a half-past eight for breakfast. I'm not as lucky as the rest of the team. A nightmare ripped me awake at four a.m. My feet got tangled when I tried to reach the wastebasket, and I ended up painting the hotel carpet with regurgitated grilled chicken and potatoes that I had for dinner. I'm grateful to the front desk clerk who discreetly arranged for me to switch rooms. I was wide awake after I showered, so I hit the gym to sweat out the damn-near-crippling anxiety coursing through me. I can't wait for this game to be over so that the press can move on.

After breakfast, we're transported the two miles to FTX Arena for a shootaround where we practice taking shots from various positions around the court. I roll my neck back and forth before dribbling and releasing a center three-pointer. It spins around the rim before tumbling through the net. I catch another ball and release it again, this time from the left corner. The tension seeps out of me. Few things are as relaxing as a ball in my hands.

Idris and I are tapped to answer questions from the media. When asked the highly anticipated question, "What's your thought process as you prepare to face arguably one of the best players in the league, Sid King, for the first time tonight?"

I answer, "For me, it's business as usual. I play the best that I can in every game, regardless of who we're playing. We know what we came here to do tonight, and we're focused on seeing that it gets done."

What my answer omits is that I've been studying Sid's game. I've observed that he is strongest when he has the ball. He's unstoppable when it comes to isolation plays. However, ISO plays are predictable, so we have plays designed to counter them. He's decent with catch-and-shoot shots, but I'm better. Our ability to keep the ball moving until we find an open teammate is one of the reasons we have the second-highest field goal percentage and lead in assists this season. We've seen the Marvels struggle to defend teams with good ball and player movement. If we stay locked in, we have a solid chance of clinching a W tonight.

After the shootaround, we head back to the hotel for lunch. I toss the food around on my plate as I pretend to listen to Tevin's animated recount of last night's hookup. After about my fifth yawn, I call it quits and head back to my room for a quick nap. I spent over an hour trying to turn off my brain and sleep, so it's way too soon when my alarm goes off. We're transported back to the arena at a quarter past four. We warm up on a non-game court. After, we crowd around the locker room for our pre-game meeting.

Before I know it, it's game time. I throw on my noise-canceling headphones, then pop the hood on the Knights sweatshirt that I'm rocking over my jersey. The arena is buzzing with Marvels fans. I scan a few blue Knights jerseys in a sea of white, red, and yellow Marvels jerseys. I drown everything out except rapper King D's voice booming from my headphones as

I warm up. In between shots, I spot Sid practicing a flawless left-handed layup. Like me, he's ambidextrous. Whatever feelings I've developed for him are left off of the court. I plan to play the best ball I can tonight. Every shot, every game, is for *them*. I can't let them down.

I'm bouncing on my heels as I catch a pass from an assistant coach and charge the rim to post a floater. While a part of me is anxious for it to be over, I've been looking forward to this match-up since joining the NBA. Every aspiring player thinks about the day they'll face off against All-Star players. I wondered what a match-up against Sid would feel like years ago when he entered the NBA, and now I am about to find out.

After team intros, we change out of our warm-up gear and meet at mid-court for tipoff. The referee blows his whistle and tosses the ball above the heads of the opposing centers, Tevin and Kristian. Kristian taps the ball toward Sid, giving the Marvels the first possession.

Here we go!

As expected, the Marvels make a play to isolate Sid, who is being defended by Harry, our forward. Sid backdowns Harry and attempts a shot while falling away from the basket, but Tevin blocks the shot.

Hell yeah!

They better have something else in their arsenal or we'll put this game to bed quickly! Kaleb, our power forward, passes the ball to Idris, who attempts a three-point corner shot but misses. Sid then knocks down a three-point pull-up jump shot with the accuracy of a sharpshooter.

Damn!

Tevin feeds me the ball as Kevin moves in to defend me. I feint a shot, sending Kevin tumbling past me, and clearing my path to sink a jump shot.

They really think one guy can contain me!

Sid follows up by driving to the rim and slams a dunk.

Our gazes lock, and he smirks.

"Ball!" I yell to Kaleb, who lobs it to me from across the court. Boris, a center for the Marvels, reaches in to steal possession.

Seriously! Their strategy is to put up the slowest dude on their team—possibly in the league—to defend me?

Just to fuck with him, I run a series of fast dribble combinations between my legs, crossing over behind my back, and reversing as I let the shot clock wind down. Every time he reaches in, it's too slow, and the ball's already switched over. With six seconds left on the clock, I sidestep him and charge to the rim. I slice through two Marvels' players as I take flight. Just as I release the ball over the rim, a hand comes out of nowhere, smacking it away with a thunderous force.

The crowd goes wild as I hiss, "What the fuck!"

I land slightly off balance, staggering forward to break my fall.

I whip around and find Sid towering over me.

"Welcome to Miami," he says with a wink before he races backward up-court.

I clench my jaw and glare at him.

Message received.

He knocks down a swift three-pointer despite Kaleb's aggressive defense. On our next possession, Kaleb passes me the ball as Sid damn near pushes his own teammate out of the way to defend me. Tevin tries to free me up by attempting a screen, but Sid shoulders him, sending him flying. The crowd goes wild, seeing us play one-on-one for the first time, and our teammates pander to them by staying back. Spinning, I give Sid my back to create space. I try to shake him by dribbling left, cutting right, then left again, but he's one step ahead. I guess I'm not the only one who studies their opponents' moves. I turn and he's right on top of me, blocking any opening for a shot. He's relentless. My speed against his bulk—I know I can shake him. I turn and dribble right, and he follows. I sidestep him, feinting right but going left, but he remains rooted in place, not falling for it. When I glimpse the shot clock, there are four seconds left. I change speed and dart left, creating a sliver of an opening. Charging off of my back foot, I race like hell to the rim. Sid on my six, I spin to evade Justin and charge into the air. I release the ball a split second before the shot clock goes off. It ricochets off of the backboard and spins around the rim. I drop into a half crouch and whip around to face the net, just as the ball swoops through the basket.

"Hell yeah!" I bark, beating my chest.

The Marvels call a time-out.

I turn to face Sid, whose expression is neutral.

"Thanks for the dance," I quip, returning the wink.

His lips curl up slightly. Before he can reply, Idris barrels into me, bumping me with his broad chest, shouting, "That's how you fucking do it, Rook!"

Both teams continue to battle like it's the playoffs. In the fourth quarter, Sid hits a crossover dribble and drives through three of our defenders to float it in with his left hand, bringing the Marvels into the lead, 76–75. Fuck, that play was tough...and hot. His corded muscles and explosive drive powered through three bodies like they were featherweight. If he ever quit basketball, he'd do damage as a linebacker in the NFL. It's damn near impossible to take that much contact without committing an offensive foul, but he has a certain finesse.

Wait—why the hell am I fanboying? I shake it off and get back into the game.

Justin fouls Idris attempting a layup. He makes one of the two free throws. We trade high fives. We'll take whatever points we can get.

Justin misses the next shot. Double-teamed, I lose possession of the ball. I scramble to retake possession, cutting Sid off, and release a mid-range fadeaway jump shot.

Cash!

Sid responds by banking in a two-point jump shot. It's feeling like a tennis match.

The arena is vibrating. The crowd is louder than I've ever heard in my life.

Harry and I move in to double-team Sid, but Harry gets jammed when Justin blocks his path, creating a screen. Locking eyes with Sid, I reach in to steal possession just as he pushes the ball through his legs. I squat low, ready to counter any possible drive. He fakes left, but I stay rooted in place. He crosses the ball behind his back and pushes off like he's about to hit a jump shot. I jump to block him, but his feet never leave the floor. He spins and takes off. I smack my head for falling for his jump fake!

Stupid, stupid, stupid.

I charge after him, but Kristian intercepts me. I waste no time shaking him, but I'm still too slow. Sid flies through the air and whips out an insane between-the-legs, left-handed dunk. The fucker hangs off of the rim in a grand *fuck you* gesture, and the crowd goes ape.

God! When he gets this hot, he's unstoppable.

Coach calls another time-out. The Marvels are in the lead with a score of 86–82.

Sid flashes a cocky grin to Justin when he slings an arm around his shoulder and slaps his chest. So fucking smug. I don't want to just win—I want to demolish the Marvels. I'm aching to wipe that cocky grin off of his face. I want to send their crowd slinking home full of regret for backing a team of fucking losers. The thought makes me grin. If we take this game, I'll hit up whatever club Tev and Idris drag me to and celebrate until I pass out.

The game resumes and it's an all-out war. We go toe-to-toe until it's the second to last possession of the fourth quarter and we're down two points. I rub my hands on my jersey and swipe my face against my arm to clear the sweat from my eyes. I catch the pass from Idris just as Sid moves in to guard me.

"Hey, what's the name of that cologne you wear?"

"What?" he asks, elbowing me while reaching in for a steal.

"The one from Christmas." I evade his reach and cross the ball between my legs.

"You tryna get in my head?"

"Come on. Tell me." I turn slightly and feint a pass to Idris.

"Why?" he asks, not falling for my fakeout.

"I can't get it out of my head"—I scan for an open look—"It's like silk sheets, leather"—I tilt away, pulling the ball out of reach as he swipes for it—"the forest after the rain"—I swat his hand off of my jersey—"campfire."

He grins but schools it a second later when I try to charge past him.

"So you love it?" he asks, squatting low to block my path.

"Regrettably." I shake my head. "Though there's one thing that I like more."

"Yeah, what's that?" He attempts another steal as I flick a glance at the shot clock, but my reflexes protect the ball. I jut forward like I'm going to charge to the rim, but in a split second, change directions, step back, then release a quick jump shot.

I know it's good the second it leaves my hand.

"Winnin'." I jet backward with a shit-eating grin, relishing the pinched expression that flits across his face.

Get used to losing, fucker!

I tie the game with one possession left for the quarter at 97 points.

"Lock in!" Idris yells as we move into defensive positions. Tevin and Kaleb, two of our biggest defenders, cover Sid. Winning the game comes down to our defense over the next twenty-four seconds. It doesn't matter if we played well and gave it everything we got tonight. We need to close this out, then the next game, and the one after that, to win championships...*to honor them.*

The ref blows the whistle, starting the final game clock. Idris, guarding Kevin, smacks the ball out of his hand. They both dive to grab possession, but Idris is a smidge too slow. Kevin flips over and launches the ball to Justin. I abandon defending Kristian to cover a wide-open Justin, but I'm too late. He catches the ball and releases a corner three-pointer. We're all frozen in place watching the ball hurtling toward the net. Justin groans and holds his head—the arc is too high. I'm about to fist the air when Sid soars through the air out of nowhere, catches the rebound, and slams it in.

Noooooo! I clutch my head.

The sound of the game clock going off hits like a water cannon, and I stumble backward in disbelief. Justin barrels straight toward a victorious Sid who is being swallowed by his teammates. The home crowd chants "MVP" at Sid despite the award not being decided for months.

How the fuck did he do it with two seconds left?

"You played well, Rook. You win some and lose some," Idris says, patting my back. "Come on." He nudges me toward the locker room. My feet drag like they're tethered to concrete blocks. I block out the butt pats and head knocks. An acidic burn courses through my stomach. I'm supposed to honor them, and I can't even secure a win in the last twenty seconds of a game.

Chest slumped forward, I mutter my way through the post-game interview, grateful when the moderator announces that it's the final question.

"Ty, Jana from *Miami Sports*, you posted thirty-five points tonight, including a dagger in the second to last play of the fourth quarter. There's been a lot of hype this week as you and Sid prepared to face off for the first time. Many people feel you've already demonstrated equal, if not greater, promise than he did in his rookie year. How do you feel it went tonight?"

I unclench my jaw. "It was a battle. While we did a great job moving the ball, we struggled defending the basket. The Marvels are a formidable team and definitely made it a challenging game. I don't think anyone comes into this arena without bringing their A-game. We will learn from today's loss and come back stronger next time. Thanks, everyone."

I push my chair back and tuck my head as I beeline straight for the door, desperate to be alone.

Chapter Ten

If I got to Justin sooner, I'd have had him. I could have stolen possession and—

Idris smacks my chest. "Yo, you good? Don't sweat it, man. Pussy and vodka will lift your head up."

We have a break before our game in San Antonio, so a few of the guys are hitting up South Beach to dull the sting of our loss with booze.

"I'm good. Have fun though," I grumble, tossing my food around the plate.

He sighs. "Don't go dark, bro. Hit me up if you change your mind."

I grunt and push back my chair.

Despite a hot shower and cryotherapy, each step toward the practice court sends shooting pain from the arch of my feet to my lower back. I gave tonight's game everything in my chamber, and all I have to show for it is an L and a sore body. I spend twenty minutes practicing mid-range shots before a passing assistant coach offers to run drills with me for the next hour. Once back in my room, I take another shower, pop two mela-tonin, and peel open the book Sid recommended about the ex-marine. Midnight rolls around and I'm wide awake. Having restarted the same chapter many times, I give up reading. I pull up Sid's post-game interview. He's dressed for a night out in a rust-colored, fitted hat, a sapphire blue button-down with the sleeves rolled up, and blue jeans.

"Sid, Liam from ESPN, thirty-seven points posted, including the game-winning buzzer beater. What deciding factor do you attribute to tonight's win?"

He opens his mouth but covers it as he tilts away from the mic and sneezes.

"Thanks," he says as he's handed a tissue. "Pardon me." He leans back, eyes shuddering closed, and sneezes again. He shakes his head, then tilts forward toward the mic. "Everyone locked in." He scans the paper in front of him. "Justin banked a triple-double, and Kevin and Kristian scored over eighteen points a piece. We defended the ball well. We've been working hard to reduce our unforced turnovers, and it showed tonight."

"What do you think of the Knights' performance?" a reporter asks.

"I think they moved the ball, made big plays. It was a close game."

"Sid, Rachel from Sports Broadcast, great game. Much has been written about your face off against the Knights' rookie, Ty Washington. How do you feel about the endless comparisons of his game against your rookie performance?"

Ugh. Enough with this shit already.

"Look, I think we're two different players with completely different styles. That being said, a rookie who consistently banks over thirty points per game—I mean, tonight alone, he banked thirty-five points, twelve rebounds, and ten assists—you can't love the game and not get excited about those stats. He's tenacious, bold, and calm under pressure. When you love to compete at a high level, players like Ty keep the game interesting." He grins. "I had fun tonight."

I smile reluctantly. How'd he memorize my stats that fast?

"Sid, over here, what's your mindset heading on the road to face off against Toronto?"

"We know what we need to do and have full faith that we'll make our best effort to improve both our offense and—"

A call from the last person I expected to hear from interrupts the video. I wipe my face, pat down my hair, then freeze. *What am I doing?* He can't see me.

I crunch up to a sitting position and accept the call. "This a prank?"

"Why would this be a prank?" Sid asks. If midnight had a voice, it would sound like his. Husky, dark, mysterious.

I clear my throat. "Calling to gloat? I half expected you to be out celebrating."

"Nah, winning's a normal occurrence for us."

I picture the cocky smirk on his face and see red. "Fuck off. Let me hit you back the day after nev—"

"Wait—" He chuckles. "What are you up to? I knew you'd be up."

I huff out a breath. "Popped melatonin hours ago but no luck."

"Come over."

"What?" I scoff. "For what?"

"Why not? You don't fly out until tomorrow, and I don't leave for Toronto until later in the afternoon."

Why not?

Why not!

Oh, I don't know. Maybe because I've been suppressing the urge to punch something since leaving the court where I lost to you, jackass. Maybe because I'm trying to shake the feeling that someone pulled my shorts down in front of twenty thousand people. I keep telling myself that this game was like any other, but it wasn't—not really. The media morphed it into a spectacle when I just wanted to ball—and win. Maybe because the invitation is causing my stomach to rearrange itself.

I scrub my hand over my face.

"You still there?"

"Unfortunately," I grumble, and the fucker chuckles.

I shake my head, already regretting what I'm about to say next.

"Text me your address." I hang up.

The text with his address comes in, and I jump up to change. I throw on jeans, a T-shirt, a beanie, and shades. I slide my phone and wallet into my jeans and lace up my Jordans.

I ask the cabbie to let me out a few blocks from his house. Except for an older man walking his dog, the streets are empty. I text him when I arrive, and I'm immediately buzzed in. My hamstrings burn as I make my way up the long, windy driveway.

Sid leans against his door in light gray sweats, a black T-shirt, and socks. Hands in his pockets, eyes gleaming, though rimmed red with exhaustion. "Thanks for coming."

I shrug and slide my hands into my pockets, matching his posture. "Your house is more comfortable than the hotel room."

"Uh-huh," he says with a wry smile, stepping back to allow me entry. I somehow overlooked the missing holiday decor until now. The house is dimly lit.

"This place doesn't feel massive with just you in it?"

He waits for me as I kneel to remove my shoes. "I have you tonight," he replies.

My gaze snaps up to meet his, searching for a sign that he meant for it to sound as seductive as I heard it. His expression is neutral. Fuck, I can't read him.

"You know what I mean," I grumble.

"Honestly, I am rarely alone."

I think of Katrina and all the other women he's been linked with and swallow hard.

"Yeah, I've seen the pictures."

"Wait, I didn't mean it like that. My mom is here more than me. Kieran and Tommy fly out often. They have their own set of keys. Not to mention, my teammates are always rolling through."

I nod and shrug.

This thing between us, whatever it is, is slippery, and I don't have the energy to tread it carefully.

"Help yourself to anything in the kitchen." His gaze hasn't left my face since the driveway, and for some reason, it's easier to look everywhere but him.

"You hate losing, don't you?"

I shrug. "Doesn't everyone?"

"Yeah, I suppose. But you, like, really hate it. You played well. It's not easy going up against the greatest to ever do it."

"Oh, fuck off," I fire back, wanting to knock that shit-eating grin off of his face.

His head snaps back like he's been slapped. "Such ugly words out of that pretty mouth."

So corny. I shake my head despite the dumb grin breaking out on my face.

"So much fire," he mutters.

"What?" I squint at him.

"You come off chill and unaffected, but deep inside, a wild-fire rages...I saw it tonight."

"What is this? You're analyzing me now?"

"Just trying to figure you out."

"Why?" I ask, crossing my arms across my chest.

He opens his mouth but hesitates.

"Careful."

His brows pinch together. "W-what?"

"All of that thinking looks painful."

He grins. It's shy at first, but then his confident smirk reappears. "I like this side of you. Remind me to beat you more—"

"You know what..." I lunge for him. He steps back, a mix of shock and amusement on his face.

"Hey now," he says, raising his hands. "This ain't the way to beat the best—"

I growl and lunge for him again, but he spins on his heels and bolts.

He leaves a trail of laughter as I chase him up the steps.

"Fifty bills you can't catch me," he taunts as we face off in his bedroom. "I could be blindfolded, and you still couldn't catch me."

I look away, feigning disinterest, before charging toward him. He tucks his knees and hops up on the bed, landing in a squat.

"Hey, hey, wait—hold up," he says, laughing and stepping back.

"Take it back," I grit out.

"I would if I could. It's just I like this side of you too—"

I growl and charge for him again, aiming for his knees, but the fucker jumps off the bed and lands in a deep squat before shuffling his feet side to side like he's running an agility drill. I swipe my arm out to catch the hem of his T-shirt, but the glint of a bronze frame catches my eye. Big mistake! The fucker executes a surprise attack by jumping on the bed and straddling my back before I can flip over.

"Get off of me, dickhead," I fume. My heart pounds against my chest as his muscular thighs bracket my torso.

Lips brushed against my ear, he whispers, "You want to touch a winner so bad—go ahead."

Heat coils up my back and neck as his scent invades every inch of my body. This close, his voice sounds strained, almost hoarse.

I try to buck him off of me, but he's way above my weight class. "I'm gonna annihilate you the next time we face off, you smug, dumb-smelling troll."

He chuckles. I'm a squirrel threatening a lion. "You can smell me anytime you want," he rasps, causing an involuntary shiver down my spine.

Then my dick stiffens.

Traitorous fucking body.

A mix of rage, arousal, and confusion erupts. I clench my fists and howl into his comforter, part growl, part yell.

"Mmm. Better...yes?" he says softly before climbing off and lying beside me with his arms behind his head.

My throat aches as I unclench his comforter, but the rest of my body melts into his mattress. I rest my head against my arms and turn my head to face him.

Seconds pass of us staring at each other. I hate how much I love his face right now.

"You hung my gift." I nod toward the bronze picture frame.

"Told you I would," he replies, staring into my eyes.

I ignore the heat spreading through my chest and tell myself not to read too much into it.

"You hungry?"

I yawn and shake my head.

"Me neither. Want to watch a movie?"

"Sure."

"Cool. Pick the movie. I'm gonna grab us water." He jumps off the bed and throws me the remote.

I scan the room and double back to the bottle of cologne on top of his dresser. I pad over and bring it to my nose. *This is it.* I read the label...*notes of sandalwood, Balsam of Peru, leather, and musk.* I spritz some into the air. It's amazing, but it's missing something.

I return the bottle to the dresser and lie back down. I stare at the dancing flames of his fireplace, forgetting to look for a movie when he returns.

"Need something to change into?"

"I'm sleeping in here?"

He shrugs. "Yeah, why not? It'll be more comfortable than when we fell asleep on the couch on Christmas."

He removes his shirt, revealing his tats, nipple ring, and chiseled abs. My gaze trails down to the V-shaped muscular grooves of his Adonis belt.

Fuck! I can't sleep next to him. The day's been torture enough.

"T-that's how you sleep?"

He looks down at his chest. "Yeah. I feel trapped otherwise."

"Cool," I reply, dragging out the word.

Those abs. Fuck me.

His gaze falls to my lower lip, tugged between my teeth. He nods and I remember he asked a question.

"Uh, yeah. Can I borrow an old T-shirt?"

He tosses one to me.

I drop my jeans and pull off my shirt. I raise his tee over my head and pause. My eyes close, inhaling its scent. It's *him*—the scent that's missing from the cologne.

I think the move goes unnoticed, but when my head emerges through the neck of the shirt, his lips are turned slightly upward.

We climb under the covers. His bed is so wide, you could fit another person between us.

"Congrats on the win or whatever," I say, turning to face him.

"So salty." He smirks. "Thanks. You made us work for it. I'm not usually this exhausted after a game."

And that's all we say about basketball.

We talk about our travel experiences. I have a single stamp on my passport. I vacationed in Paris with my parents right before my freshman year of high school. I recall the Eiffel Tower lit up at night against the blue sky. We also lost hours inside of the Louvre. Mom and I fell in love with an old bookstore with quotes from books written on the walls. There was a wall of portraits of famous authors like James Baldwin, Maya Angelou, and Virginia Woolf. There were beds tucked all over the two stories. A placard explained that tens of thousands of people have slept there, and in exchange for lodging, they're asked to make the bed in the morning, read a book, and help out in the store. I loved that place. We ate at the same bakery every day, making our way through the menu, and sat in an idyllic garden. Sid's passport has way more stamps. He shared stories about vacations in the Caribbean, Bali, and Brazil.

After over an hour of talking, my eyes are heavy from exhaustion, and Sid's yawned at least a half dozen times. Deciding to stop fighting it, we cut off the unwatched TV and call it a night. Shuffling closer toward the edge of the bed, I face away from him and pull the covers over my head. I think I might doze off any second, but close to an hour later, I'm still awake.

"Come here," Sid's gravelly voice commands.

Startled, my head whips in his direction. He has the covers lifted, inviting me into his arms.

I search his face to see if he's serious. He tilts his head, gesturing for me to come. I'm sure I'll overthink it tomorrow, but I scoot over, and he wraps me up in his arms. I take a deep breath to slow the rapid drumming in my chest. His massive chest is warm and, god, he smells amazing. I relax into his embrace, letting the weight of my head rest against his pecs. I scoot back a little, hoping my dick stays soft. The rise and fall of his chest lulls me to sleep.

I'm ripped awake. My first thought is that a low-magnitude earthquake caused the bed to tremble. Are there even earthquakes in Miami? I follow the sound of a soft murmur to a trembling Sid.

My face is wet as I lift it from his chest.

"Hey, hey," I whisper, reaching over to tap his shoulder. My hand snaps back from the feverish heat of his sweaty skin.

I reach over him to turn on his nightstand lamp. He's shivering and murmuring something with his eyes closed.

I place my palm against his forehead. He's burning up. Racing to the bathroom, I wet a towel with cold water. Then I search inside his medicine cabinet and retrieve a bottle of acetaminophen. If it's in his cabinet, it probably means he's not allergic to it. I run downstairs to fill a bowl with ice, race back upstairs, and wrap the cold towel around a couple of ice cubes. I dab the cold towel against his skin, starting from his forehead. He jerks awake and shudders.

"Hey, it's okay. You have a fever, I think," I whisper.

He groans.

"Can you sit up for a second?"

He winces at the question and falls back against his pillow. His eyes shudder closed. For a second, I think he's fallen back asleep, but then he mumbles, "It hurts."

"I know, but we need to get you medicine."

He sluggishly arches up enough to rest on the side of his elbow.

"Open up. It's acetaminophen." I slide two pills in and tilt the glass of water to his mouth. He takes a sip, and his head falls back to his pillow. I pick the cloth back up and dab along his face, neck, and chest. Eyes closed, he whines but doesn't seem to have enough energy to stop me. I hate the cold, too, when I'm sick, but it works. I continue down his chest, having to reach under the covers to get to his lower body. His legs are so hot that all of the ice melts and the cloth is warm when I pull it away. I toss it around in the ice water before continuing.

When his teeth chatter, I give him a break. He'll need fluids and something bland to eat when he wakes up to take painkillers. I run downstairs to take inventory of the fridge. It's thankfully stocked. I chop up veggies and peeled ginger and throw it all in a pot with water to boil. My mom used to include the stems of parsley and mushrooms, so I do the same. I cover it and let it do its thing. I'm grateful for all of the times I helped my mom cook. She made it clear that she didn't want to live in a house with men who didn't know how to cook or clean up after themselves.

He's still asleep when I pop back upstairs to check on him. Once the soup is done, I dab him down with the ice cloth one more time before I climb into bed next to him. I check my phone. It's a little after three in the morning. I yawn, turn to face him, and find him shivering. I do what I always want when I'm sick—I shuffle over and pull him into my arms, drawing his back against my chest.

After a few minutes, the shivering stops.

He's so warm in my arms that I reach over for the cold cloth and spread it against his forehead to help reduce his temperature.

I WAKE UP A FEW HOURS LATER. HE'S STILL KNOCKED OUT, EXCEPT now I'm splayed on my back, and his face is against my chest. I reach up and press my palm against his forehead. He's still warm but not as hot.

He stirs at my touch.

I freeze, not wanting to wake him, but his eyes flutter open after a beat.

"Hey, how are you feeling?"

His head darts up, and wide eyes meet mine. "What hap..." His voice trails off as he presses his palm against his throat.

"It hurts?"

He nods. "Hell."

"Warm salt water should help," I say as I slide out from under him. He groans as his head falls into the spot I just vacated.

I return with a mug of warm salt water.

"Come on." I help him out of bed. He sways a little once on his feet, so I wrap my arm around his waist to anchor him.

"Legs…everything hurts," he mutters.

"Gargle with this, and then you can climb back into bed. Let it sit in the back of your throat for a few seconds."

He grunts as we move toward the bathroom. I leave him leaning against the sink, brushing his teeth when I run back downstairs to heat the broth and squeeze oranges until I have a cup filled with juice. I hear the shower running when I return upstairs.

I search his room for fresh sheets and come up empty, but I find some in a hallway closet. I'm finishing changing the sheets when he emerges a few minutes later with a towel around his waist and steam billowing from the bathroom.

"Drink both down," I say, pointing to the glass and bowl on the nightstand.

He stares at the bowl. "You made it?" he asks, his voice even hoarser than before.

"Yeah, figured you'd need something when you wake up. Painkillers on an empty stomach aren't good. And you need fluids."

"Thank you."

I wave him off. "It's all good. You'd do the same for me."

"I would, but still, thank you."

"How do you feel?"

"Like shit. It would have been worse if you weren't here." He stares at the bowl of soup. "I dreamed that I was doused in ice-cold Gatorade after winning a championship."

"Were you in the NFL?" I joke. It's not really a tradition in the league.

"Nah. We beat Boston."

"You should've known it was a dream if Boston made it to the Finals." Their roster this season is weak.

He grins. "Word."

"Have an extra toothbrush?"

"Yeah, under the sink."

He's in bed when I return, clad in sweats and a T-shirt.

"Can't taste anything, but I'm sure it's delicious," he says as he raises the bowl of soup to his mouth.

"Probably for the best. It's pretty much vegetables, ginger, water, and sea salt. Want toast with it?"

"I'm good. I'm going to drink this down, take more painkillers, and sleep."

I nod and am about to climb in next to him when I realize he probably wants to be alone to rest.

"You need anything before I dip? There's a pot on the stove." I gesture to the soup.

He shakes his head as he swallows. "You have to leave now, or can you chill for a bit? I can have Leslie drop you back."

I nod. "Yeah, I have time."

"Cool. Light hurts. Mind messaging him from my phone? The code is 7525."

"I got you."

I freeze, seeing the notifications of unread texts. Bypassing them, I shoot Leslie a message. I go to hand him back his phone but then stop. "Anyone else you need me to hit up?"

"Yeah. I need to call out sick. Can you text my GM, Brian? His name is—"

"Brian G. Found it. I got you." I pen a short message and hit send. "You got messages from Katrina, Tara, and someone named Lottie."

"Thanks." He tosses the phone on the nightstand.

"You know how you got sick?" I ask as I settle in next to him.

"Justin. The dude's always sniffling. The team's been dropping like flies for weeks. I thought I was in the clear."

"Damn. You have supplements to help?"

"Yeah. I'll take 'em later," he says as he closes his eyes and burrows under the covers.

"Nah, attack fast and early. Where are they?"

Following his instructions, I retrieve them from a cabinet that rivals the Whole Foods supplement aisle. No wonder it took him so long to drop. He takes care of himself. When I return with his supplements and a bowl of cereal for me, he's asleep. I eat, set an alarm so I'm on the road by ten thirty, and then climb in next to him. I watch the fire until I drift back asleep.

I GROAN AND REACH FOR MY ALARM ONCE IT GOES OFF. SID'S ARM is wrapped around my torso, and his leg is nestled between mine. Damn, it feels good to be a little spoon. I reach back and press my palm against his forehead. He's warmer than normal but cooler than before.

"Wish you could stay," he says. His hoarse, husky, sleepy voice makes me shiver and rut against him.

I bite my lip and stifle a groan. "I wish I could too. How are you feeling? I think your fever broke."

"Yeah? I've felt better."

I start to disentangle myself. "I'll bring you more soup and juice before I leave."

"Wait, one more minute," he pleads, drawing me closer to him.

I nod. I want to burrow under someone warm when I'm sick too.

The birdsong and Sid's soft, congested breathing fills the quiet.

Ten minutes pass before I muster the strength to disentangle myself and climb out of bed. I bring him a fresh bowl of hot soup, a glass of water, and juice. He insists on walking me out once I'm dressed.

I'm putting on my shoes in the foyer when he asks, "Next week is the anniversary of your parents' passing, right?" His comforter is caped around his shoulders, and a tissue is stuffed up his nose. He's still the most gorgeous person I've ever seen in my life.

I nod. It's cool that he remembered. I've been thinking a lot about it, mostly to prepare myself.

"If you need to talk, I'm here."

I blow out a breath. "Thanks. That means a lot. It's rough, but visiting their graves helps."

"Makes sense. It's a kind of ritual. What's the name of the cemetery that they're buried in?"

Our heads turn toward the door at the sound of tires crunching gravel.

"Uh, Evergreen Memorial. Why?"

"Curious," he replies.

"Thanks for inviting me over. I haven't slept that well in years. I've been missing out sleeping alone."

A shadow dims his face. "You're welcome here anytime."

I nod. I'm not sure how often I'll have the chance with our schedules.

"Aight, I should go before I'm late." I open the door and startle at the sight of Lily standing on the other side with her key in hand. Equally startled, her face transforms into a wide grin once recognition sets in.

"Ty! What a wonderful surprise. It's good to see you again."

"Hi, Lily!" I bend forward and accept her hug. "It's great to see you too."

"Told you I'm rarely alone," Sid says. "I caught Justin's bug," he says to his mom. "Ty's helped nurse me back to health."

"Really?" She rolls up on her tiptoes to cradle his jaw.

He grins and shoos her hand away. "She still thinks I'm five."

She pats his cheeks affectionately. "Wait until you're a parent, you'll see. They're always your baby." She rolls back to stand flat and slips out of her shoes. "I'm making soup."

"Ty beat you to it."

Lily arches an eyebrow and glances at me. "Is that right?"

"Yeah, luckily, he can't taste anything. It's pretty bland."

"I was right about you," she says, climbing back to her tiptoes to kiss my cheek.

I grin as she turns and walks into the house.

"I'll make lemon honey tea and look for medicine," she tells Sid.

Sid palms my shoulder. "Sorry, man. You're stuck with us now. Once Lily King loves you, you'll never escape. I hope you like cable knit sweaters and socks."

I grin. "Can't ever have too many mom types in your life."

We both turn to the sound of Leslie pulling into the driveway.

I turn to give Sid a dap, but he pulls me into a hug. "Thanks again."

"No doubt. Rest up."

As we pull away, I tell myself not to turn back, but I cave right before the hedges block my view. I grin at the sight of Sid leaning against his door, gazing at the retreating car.

Chapter Eleven

I fly into Newark Airport on a red-eye on the day of my parents' death anniversary and cab over to Adam's house in New Jersey. With the NBA's hectic schedule, I won't always be able to fly in on the actual anniversary, but I'll always make my way the minute I get a break. I'm grateful that it worked out this year. Adam and I need this. The door opens from the inside as I turn my key into the lock. A handsome, tall man with pale brown eyes, jet-black curls, freckles, and dusky skin peers back at me. He's pulling his coat over a fleece sweater.

"Hey," I greet him.

"Hi, Ty, I'm Ishan."

I shake the hand that he extends.

"Your uncle is still, er, in bed. I work at the fire station," he says, rubbing his neck.

Damn, Unc! You still got it.

"Nice to meet you, Ishan. Are you leaving on my account?" I lean back against the door frame as he slides past.

"I'd much prefer to stay and get to know you, but my shift

starts in half an hour. I hope to get the chance next time you're in town."

He looks up at my uncle's window.

"I'm crazy about your uncle," he says, beaming.

I've always known my uncle was a catch. Setting up his dating profile solidified it. His phone blew up in the first couple of hours. His schedule makes it hard for him to settle down. Dating another firefighter makes sense.

"I look forward to it," I reply.

"See ya later," he bids as he turns towards his car.

I dust the snow off my boots on the doormat, then enter the house.

The familiar scent of cedar fills my nostrils. Home.

Adam is awake when I exit the shower.

"Hey! You made it," he says, rubbing his eyes.

"Morning, Unc. It's good to be home." I envelop him in a hug.

"The house hasn't been the same since you left." He kisses me on the cheek.

"I'll visit more. You know I'd kill for you to live in LA, but you love your job too much."

"You'll see a lot more of me when I retire. By then, who knows what city you'll be in. I'm too old to schlep around."

"Uh huh, and a certain Ishan has nothing to do with it?" I tease.

His face breaks out into a boyish grin. "Met him on your way in?"

I nod. "He treats you well?"

His nod and 100-watt smile tell me everything I need to know. He likes this one.

"I'm going to get dressed and make us breakfast. I want to hear more about him."

"We'll catch up after the cemetery. Let's eat quickly and

head over. Morning is the best time there," he says as he disappears into the bathroom.

I put on a pot of coffee and make us cinnamon raisin oatmeal with chopped up fruit. We eat quickly, making small talk about the changes in the neighborhood. Then, we pile into Adam's Ford Explorer and head to the cemetery.

"Six years, man. It feels like yesterday," he remarks, shaking his head.

I sigh. "Seriously. It still hurts like hell some days."

He squeezes my hand. "I know, kid. I have questions for the big one upstairs when I reach the pearly gates. Have you thought any more about seeing a therapist?"

"Maybe. Sid also thinks I should see one."

He steals a glance at me. "Oh yeah? I started seeing one when Mitch passed. Between him and your parents, I needed a lifeline."

Mitch, Adam's best friend and fellow firefighter, lost his life saving a kid from a burning building. The kid lost his life too. It was horrific.

"Yeah? How has it been for you?" I wonder why he's never mentioned it before.

"Hard at first to open up, but it's like any practice. You get out what you put in. I look forward to my weekly sessions. I had a breakthrough recently. I evidently sabotage my relationships because of how risky my job is."

"Huh. I just thought you were picky."

"It's some of that too. But yeah, find a therapist you like. Many offer free consultations. Try a few before deciding. Between your grief and nightmares, I think it could help. You know, being an athlete is as much mental as physical."

"Sid said the same thing."

"Huh. I like the Wonder Kid even more. Any update on that front?"

We pull into the parking lot of the cemetery.

I let out an exasperated sigh. "Yes...no...ugh. Maybe. I'll tell you over lunch."

Adam chuckles and pats my back.

We grab flowers from a shop across from the cemetery and then make our way to their plots. I used to come here often. The grief counselor I saw when my parents passed said it might help to sit and talk to them. In its way, it did help to dull the ache when it was almost unbearable.

We reach their plots and discover two enormous bouquets of white lilies and roses placed on each grave.

"This you?" I ask Adam.

The look on his face tells me he's just as surprised as I am.

"Let's see if there's a card." He leans down, searches the arrangement, and fishes one out.

He reads it, then gazes up at me with arched eyebrows. "Well, I'll be damned. Your Sid is a thoughtful guy." He hands me the card.

The hairs on the back of my neck stand up.

"My Sid?" I flip the card over and read the handwritten note.

"Dear Mr. and Mrs. Washington, I pray for your souls to rest in eternal peace. Those who are loved live on in the hearts of those who hold them dear. Though it feels like I've known him for a lifetime, I've only known your son for a short while, but it's clear he loves you deeply. It's said that true friendship is rare. Then, I shall count my blessings daily and cherish the friendship that I have with your son, who I imagine is a reflection of all of your light and love. May peace be upon you.

A friend of your son,

Sidney King."

The world dissolves into a blur.

Adam removes his glove and swipes his hand across my cheek. "I know, right? What a special heart that one has."

God, if there was ever a time when someone could point to

a moment and say "And that's when I knew for sure that I was falling for him," this moment would take the cake.

I pocket the card and wipe my face. I lay the bouquets that I purchased next to Sid's.

Adam hands me a tissue. "You go first."

I nod and take a deep breath.

"Mom and Dad, I pray for your souls to continue to rest in peace." I clear my throat. "The other day, I was thinking about our trip to Paris. It was a spring day, brimming with beauty. Flowers were in ultra bloom, birds were crooning like you, Dad, and the breeze was warm. We spread out a picnic blanket in Luxembourg Gardens. Mom and I were lying in your arms. Paris felt like a planet away from Brooklyn that afternoon. You could feel the joy emanating from us a mile away. Then, Dad, you said in your gentle way: *Mark Twain said that "The two most important days in your life are the day you are born and the day you find out why." I've always known my why. It's to love you both. I'm the happiest man alive.* You brought Mom to tears, and I hated seeing Mom cry, so I started crying too. Mom kissed you, then pulled me close, kissed my cheek and blew a raspberry on my neck. It was her way of saying she was alright. I looked up and saw tears in your eyes. We were a mess. We started laughing as Mom pulled out tissues and started cleaning us up. That memory is one of my most prized possessions. Thank you for the deep love and care that you've shown me. There wasn't a day under your roof that I didn't feel loved. I know I say it every year, but really, Unc has done an amazing job picking up where you left off. You would be proud of the father he's become. I hope you're proud of the choices that I've made."

I wipe my eyes. I turn to Adam, whose turn it is to speak, but he's crying. I pull him into a hug, and we ground each other for a few minutes. "Oh," I say, turning back to the graves, "I'm most likely gay, and I'm pretty sure I'm falling in love with Sid."

Adam rubs my back. "Morris"—he wipes his nose—"you

were my guardian angel. I still feel your protective presence. Rose, you were the sister I always wanted. You somehow brought our family closer together. There was always a place for me in your home. I miss you both so much that it hurts to my bones. I'm so proud of our boy, Tyler. He's everything you wanted him to be and then some. He's sensitive, thoughtful, and warm-hearted. He's wicked smart and tenacious. I pray for his continued healing and that he may be brave in opening his heart to friendship and love, though I think he's making good progress there." He rubs the back of my neck. "He and I keep each other rooted to this earth, and though I'd give anything to have you back, I'm honored to have raised your boy with all the love in my heart. Rest easy, beloved."

"God," I sigh, looking up at the blurry sky. Adam hands me another tissue, and I blow my nose again.

We finish the hour exchanging memories and watching other families remember their loved ones.

"Tell me about Ishan," I ask after I order a curry shrimp roti, and Adam orders jerk chicken and yams with rice and peas. We meandered over to our favorite restaurant for lunch after the cemetery.

"Sure. He joined the fire station last year from Hoboken. You know I avoid younger guys, but man, he was persistent. At one point, Tom pulled me aside and said, 'Just give the guy a shot before his distracted lovesick eyes get us killed.'" Tom's Adam's second oldest colleague after Mitch.

"Dude has it that bad? My unc got game!"

"If by game, you mean avoidance and ambivalence, sure. I agreed to one date. And, well, that was three months ago. We've been getting hot and heavy ever since."

"He's what, five years younger?"

"Six."

I wave it off. "We speak every week. Why the secrecy?" We're usually an open book with each other.

"No secrecy. I just needed to know for myself first."

"What's he like?"

"He's—different. The other day I got hit with a splintered plank on my way out of that abandoned building on Fourth."

I stiffen. "What happ—" The words die in my throat.

Don't go there.

He's fine.

Fuck.

"Now, wait a minute, don't you start. I was fine, with barely any damage. Just a bit of back soreness. The doctor cleared me after a couple of days of bed rest."

I swallow, but my throat is lodged.

I can't lose him.

"Tyler, breathe!"

I'd have no one if I lost him.

My chest is pounding.

I won't be alone because I won't stay. I made a promise ages ago. Fire takes him, water takes me. God knows. It'll be easy. The beach near my house is always empty before sunrise. I mean it. There'd be nothing left for me here.

"Breathe!" Adam orders, rubbing my back.

I duck my head between my elbows.

"You're not breathing, kid!"

I suck in air and release it.

"Again," he says. "Focus on my voice or the rise and fall of your breathing, Ty."

I latch on to his voice.

"I'm right here, kid." He leans down so that our foreheads touch. "You see me? I'm fine."

I take him in. He's right in front of me, bones, uncharred skin, pumping heart and all.

He's fine.

"I can't—it's not—I can't control it," I mutter.

"I know. Anxiety is high today. I should have been careful with my words. Just breathe for me."

I sit up, grateful that we're in a back booth and I'm facing a wall.

"When it gets intense like that, I want you to try something. It's a technique to ground yourself. Acknowledge five things you see around you. Four things you can touch, three things you hear, two things you can smell, and one thing you can taste. Let's try it now. Name five things you see."

I clear my throat and look around: "Coffee, uh, food, you, tables, coats, you."

"Very good. What are four things you can touch?"

I scrub my hands over my eyes.

"Come on, kid. What are four things you can touch?"

"Er, my hair...this table, uh, you, the fork."

Why didn't the hospital call me? I'm his emergency contact.

"Perfect. What are three things that you hear?"

I swallow to push down the thickness in my throat. "Uh, your voice, forks scraping plates, chatter, cars. They should have called me. Why didn't the fire department call me?"

He breaks eye contact and stares at his coffee.

"You told them not to?"

"I'm sorry. I didn't want you to worry. I was fine."

"That's not fair. You promised. Am I still your emergency contact?"

"Of course. Who else?" he asks, meeting my gaze.

"I can't always control how I react, but you can't keep stuff like this from me. It's fucked up."

"I know. I'm sorry. Everyone at the fire department, Tom

and Ishan, they all know to call you if ever...they know. Don't worry."

I nod and wipe my eyes.

Adam pats my hand. "Two things you smell."

"Coffee and chicken."

"And one thing you taste."

"Ginger beer," I reply, raising my glass for a sip.

"Good job. It takes only a minute or two, but it injects you back into the present when your mind is off track," he says.

I close my eyes and take a deep breath. I'm drained, but my heart is beating normally again.

"How'd you learn it?"

"Therapy. I'm slowly building a toolkit of techniques. I can teach you other ones too."

I nod. "Please."

I head to the bathroom to throw cold water on my face.

"Continue telling me about Ishan," I say when I return.

He swallows a sip of his coffee and nods. "Sure. At the end of his 24-hour shift, he brought over groceries, hot and cold bandages, and those word search puzzles I like. He made soup and spent his break by my side, tending to me. His family is from Bangalore. He's second-generation Indian American."

"Sounds like a good dude. You think it could be serious?"

"I do," he answers, trying to fight back a grin.

I chuckle. "Cool. I look forward to getting to know him when I'm back. I'm happy for you."

"Thanks. You know I need your seal of approval. I can't be with anyone who messes this up," he says, gesturing between us.

"You deserve to be happy. I won't let anyone mess us up."

"Tell me about you and Sid," he says in a hushed voice. I tighten my hoodie over my head and peer around at the surrounding tables. Everyone seems lost in their own world.

Our food arrives then. My stomach rumbles at the sight of Adam's chicken. God, I've missed Caribbean food.

I bite into my roti and moan. This has to be God's food.

I swallow a large bite and chase it down with water. "We slept together twice. No sex. Just fell asleep together. Though last time, we were wrapped around each other all night, mostly because he was sick, I think. The chemistry is intense between us." My knee bounces under the table. "I think he's bi...maybe...and I'm pretty sure he thinks I'm gay or at least bi. It's just confusing as fuck, because I need to focus on my game. I already feel a lot for him, and it's distracting. You know how hard I need to work and focus. I can't see where it goes."

"Hmph. Sorry, kiddo. Love doesn't give two shits about your plans. By the sound of things, there's strong emotional intimacy budding between you two. It's a beautiful thing, really, being able to share emotional intimacy with another man. It has nothing to do with sex. I can't tell you how many times a conversation or a hug helped me or one of my friends on the brink of a mental breakdown. For what it's worth, you can have a career and a partner. They aren't mutually exclusive. I don't believe for a second that having a partner will hurt your game. Especially a partner in the NBA who understands the grueling schedule and training required."

I try to imagine what a relationship with someone like Sid would look like, but I come up blank. I've never met anyone like him. He's mature and smart. So fucking sexy. His voice alone...fuck. Being with him would consume me, and that's terrifying.

"Maybe. I can't think about having a partner right now. Not to mention, there's also the matter of Sid dating casually. I don't think he'd even want to commit to one person." I'd never ask him to.

"Then keep it casual. What's the rush? Be friends and focus

on your game. It can be whatever you want. You're young, for Christ's sake. Allow yourself to have a little fun. You deserve it."

"How come when you say it, it makes absolute sense, but things get all jumbled in my head?"

"It's easy to be the rational one when you're not the person wrestling with doubts," he says, patting my hand.

"True dat." I stare at his chicken. "Want to switch plates?"

"Heavens, yes! Your roti looks insane."

I chuckle as we trade.

"Fucking hell," I moan when the first bite of chicken and yams hits my tongue. "Almost as good as your food," I say after swallowing.

"Jerk maybe, but I have yet to make a roti this buttery and flaky."

"Yours is pretty close." I swallow another bite of food. "Just say the word, and I'll invest in your restaurant."

"Anything to get me out of being a firefighter, eh?" He laughs.

"You knock me for trying?"

"No, I guess I can't," he says, resting his palm over my hand.

After lunch, I hang with him back at the house for a few hours before I catch my flight back to LA.

I TEXT SID WHEN I'M IN BED THAT NIGHT.

ME

Thanks for the flowers. It meant a lot.

I place my phone down as it buzzes. I expect a text, but he's FaceTiming me.

I grin into the camera. "Hi."

His handsome face smiles back. "How are you?"

"Alright. My Uncle Adam and I lost it so much we could've probably used an IV drip this morning. It's always hard going there."

"Damn. I wish I could've been there with you both. We had a game in Portland."

I hate crying in front of other people, but for some reason, the idea of Sid being there doesn't bother me. I think that says more about him than me.

"Hotel Monaco?"

He nods.

"Seriously, thanks for the note and the flowers. You didn't have to."

"Wish I could do more for you."

I shake my head. "You do enough. I need to step my friendship up."

"It's not a competition. I've enjoyed getting to know you," he says.

"I've enjoyed getting to know you too, the real you."

He grins.

It still blows my mind that I can say anything to garner such a sexy smile from him.

"I didn't have a chance to check the highlights. How was the game?" I ask.

"Thirty-five points, we won, 128-114."

"Congrats, damn, when's the last time you scored less than thirty?"

His brows bunch as he gazes up at the ceiling. "Honestly, not sure." He flexes his arm behind his head as he leans back against the headboard.

While he's staring away, my gaze trails the bulge of his triceps.

I school my face back to neutral when he stares back at me.

"I like watching you nibble on your lip," he confesses.

Fuck, that's a new kind of honesty for him. If only he knew that I nibble on my lip because he's delicious.

"Yeah?" My voice comes out low and dark.

He hums, staring at my bottom lip as I roll it under my tongue to wet it.

"Why is your shirt on? I thought you slept without it."

"It'll come off soon," he replies, a glint of mischief in his eyes.

"Expecting company?" As soon as the question leaves my mouth, I regret it. Why ask questions I don't want the answer to?

He shakes his head. "I was hoping to stay on with you to hear about your day."

I turn the camera away, unable to hide the grin that splits across my face.

"Hold on. Let me connect our call from my laptop," I mutter.

"Cool. I'm already set up on my iPad."

I dim the lights and set up the laptop on the pillow next to me. Sid's shirt is off when I return.

I take him in. I could spend years tasting every inch of him. My cock thickens at the thought.

"Care to share what you're thinking right now?" he asks.

If his sexy smirk is anything to go by, I'm sure he knows. *He has to know.*

"Wish I could, but it's the kinda thing that's better shown."

He nods. "Will you show it to me?"

There's the mischief.

"I want to. Whether it'll happen or not..."

"It'll happen," he says.

I chuckle and look away. *His big dick energy is next level.*

"I'd like to try something with you if you're game?"

"Sure," I reply, adjusting my semi off camera.

"I have a feeling you relived the memory of your parents' deaths today."

"Yeah." Can't say I saw that coming.

"Thought that might be the case. Painful memories come with heavy emotions. Meditation is a way to clear them out. Can I guide us through a quick meditation?"

I swallow roughly and nod. It's unnerving that he thought about me and what I might need today.

He studies me. "I wish I could hug you."

"Me too," I reply, but it comes out gruff.

"This will feel as good, if not better, than a hug. Get comfortable. The only goal is to try to stay present. Thinking about the future causes anxiety. Thinking about the past binds us to old memories and feelings. Our power is in the present."

I nod, then stack the pillows up against the headboard for support.

"Close your eyes or focus on an object or space in front of you. I'm gonna close mine."

My heavy eyes close.

"We're going to start by taking a few natural breaths. Breathing always reminds me that I'm alive."

I nod, even though he probably can't see me. I roll my shoulders and stretch out my back.

"No biggie if your mind wanders. Just try to return your thoughts. It helps to focus on the feel of your stomach expanding and contracting."

"Okay," I reply. My mind flashes back to a young kid at the cemetery. He arrived with an older woman, but she stood back to give him space. His shoulders trembled as he kneeled on the grass. His grief looked fresh, and I wonder if he—

"Let go of any thoughts that come up and return to focusing on your breath," Sid says.

I sigh. "The struggle is real."

"You're doing great."

He leads us through a breathing exercise that's similar to the one that I used to do with my mom. I follow his verbal cues to inhale through my nose for five seconds, hold my breath for seven seconds, and then exhale through my mouth for nine seconds, ending with a hold at the bottom of the exhale before repeating.

My mind wanders constantly. But now and then, I zero in on my breath entering and leaving my body, and for those quiet seconds, the heaviness of the day lifts. Imagine if a person could be perpetually present-minded. Now, that's a dope super-hero power. They would always be in—

"Keep releasing the thoughts that come up," Sid says.

I let out a deep exhale and return to the swell of oxygen, expanding my abdomen with every inhale, then the slight discomfort of holding it inside of me, chased by euphoria when I expel it and my chest decompresses.

"We're gonna move on to an exercise that helps you release tension in your body. When I call out a body part, I want you to inhale and then hold your breath like we've been doing. Except this time, when you hold your breath, I want you to squeeze the body part and hold the tension until I tell you to release it, and if it's awkward to squeeze, then just visualize yourself squeezing it. When I ask you to release it, match your exhale with the release."

I repeat the steps in my head. *Inhale, squeeze, hold, exhale on his command.* "Sounds easy enough."

Starting with the toes of my left foot, we gradually travel up my legs to the top of my head. For the moments that I'm able to focus, tension seeps out of my body, unknotting my stomach, expanding my chest, loosening my throat, dropping my shoulders, and dulling the ache behind my eyes.

We close out with a few deep breaths set at our own pace, ending together with one deep breath. Sid surprises me when he chants "om" in an exhalation, and his deep voice sends a vibration down my chest and legs. I asked my mom once why she chanted *om*. She said sounds have a way of healing us and that *om* is one of the oldest and most sacred of sounds. I smile, thinking about how much she'd like Sid.

I open my eyes and am sucked into the intensified colors of my room. Sid's eyes are outlined with gold ink. I can't help but beam, matching his brilliant smile.

"That was dope," I confess. "My brain wandered like mad, though."

"You look lighter...You were carrying a lot."

I nod. "That last exercise...Man, I had knots everywhere. I had no idea."

"I read once that we consume something like thirty-four gigabytes of data and information a day," he says, leaning back against his headboard. "That's like 100,000 words. Our brains are so full. How the hell are we supposed to know what's happening in our body?"

I scoff. "100,000 words! That's wild."

"Yeah, it's like a 300-page book or something. It's why I dig meditation. A few seconds of quiet goes a long way, or else I'm stuck in my head."

"Man, your voice is soothing. You should record a session for that app you sent me."

He grins. "It's not a bad idea."

"Should we try to sleep?" I ask around a yawn, even though I'm not ready to hang up yet.

"Soon. If you're up for it, tell me about your parents," he says, adjusting the iPad to climb under the covers.

I get comfortable, too, and adjust my laptop to face my pillow.

"Uh, my dad's name was Morris, and my mom's Rose. My dad was my best friend. He'd do this thing every morning where he'd ask me..."

And so it went. We talked for a little under an hour before

Sid fell asleep. Sleeping meant hanging up, so I fought it, staring at his sleeping face until I drifted off.

HAVING FORGOTTEN TO CLOSE THE BLINDS, THE BRIGHT SUN wakes me in the morning. I reach my arms over my head and stretch. So this is what a nightmare-less night of uninterrupted sleep feels like. I notice the laptop screen is dark. I click the mouse pad, and my heart jigs when Sid appears partially off-camera getting dressed.

"You didn't hang up," I say, my voice raspy as I wipe the sleep from my eyes and mouth. I reach for the glass of water next to my bed and take a sip.

"Why would I?" he replies. The smoky timbre of his morning voice washes over me. It's like pure sex.

He's clad in only gray briefs and a lapis blue-colored pullover sweater. I can't decide what turns me on more, his high muscular ass or the prominent outline of his cock.

"Getting ready to hit the road?" I ask, fondling my morning wood under the covers.

"Yeah, we're about to fly to Utah." He disappears from view and comes back wearing black skinny jeans.

I watch as he sprays cologne. My stomach tingles imagining his delicious scent.

Quietly watching him get ready and then pack, I check my phone for messages.

When I turn back, he's throwing on a wool car coat in grey herringbone and a dark grey fisherman beanie. The beanie accentuates the angular lines of his high cheekbones.

His face fills the screen as he picks up the iPad.

He's so handsome, it's stunning.

His eyes gaze over my face as if he's committing it to memory.

He hums.

I'm sure I'm blushing. I clear my throat. "Have a safe flight. Good luck against Utah."

He nods. "Thanks. Who's coming to your town later?"

"Portland, actually."

"I dare you to put up more points than me," he challenges.

"Bet. I'll put up more shots and assists. Though I'll have home-court advantage, so I'm not sure it's fair."

"We'll call it fair. Good luck."

We linger a breath longer before I hang up.

Later that evening, I posted thirty-eight points and nine assists, three more than Sid.

Chapter Twelve

I t's the Saturday night of the NBA All-Star Weekend. Fortunately for me, it's being hosted in Los Angeles this year. A series of exhibition games and musical and charitable events is leading up to the All-Star Game tomorrow night. The weekend attracts the hottest hip-hop, R&B, and pop performers.

Yesterday, I participated in a basketball exhibition game called the Fresh Stars Challenge. Twenty-eight players, a mix of rookies, sophomores, and players from the G-League, were selected to take part. We were drafted into four teams and coached by a mix of current and retired basketball players. The first to reach eighty points, my team won. I averaged a rookie-best of eighteen points and was crowned MVP. Today, I participated in the Skillz Challenge competition to test ball-handling, passing, and shooting ability. One of three rookies representing Team Rooks, we made it to the final contest but lost by four seconds during the half-court shot round.

It's a quarter past midnight now, and traffic is at a crawl as I pull up to King D's mansion party. He's an OG rapper who throws notorious A-list parties. A sea of luxury cars wait their turn for valet service. I wring my hands, balancing the steering wheel with my knees. If I don't get laid soon, I'm gonna explode. This is the longest period I've gone without fucking. I keep reminding myself of that to counter the strong urge to pop a U-turn and head home. Well, that and Idris using his veteran card to coerce me into coming. He rolled his chair over to me in the locker room last week and said, "I added you to King D's guest list this weekend."

"Nah, I'm good. I fucking hate parties," I replied.

He shook his head. "This ain't a party, my yute. Parties are for children. It's an adult experience. I'm pulling rank. You gotta come. You've never been out with us. Basketball ain't just ball, bro. Team bonding matters."

I heard Adam's voice, reminding me to live a little. The guys probably think I'm a cornball for never clubbing and opting to do my own thing after road games.

My eyes clenched shut, and I huffed out a pained breath. "Fine."

He grinned and shoved my shoulder. "What have you heard about the event?"

I shrugged. "They get wild...uh, and mad celebrities attend." I tracked my brain for other details, but I came up blank.

He snapped his fingers, "A-ha! Everyone knows that shit gets wild, but if you ask for details, motherfuckers clam up. Know why?"

I shook my head.

"NDA, bruh. Nobody gets past the threshold without signing one. You can keep your phone, but pictures aren't allowed. I've seen A-list celebrities ejected like they're garbage just for posing for a selfie. I'm talking hemmed up by the collar."

I chuckled.

"Invites are hard to come by. Only legends, bad bitches, and the ultra-famous make it in."

"So, how'd you get me on the list?" I asked, under no impression that I was included in any of those groups. Not yet, at least.

He cocked his head and looked at me like I just dunked in the wrong net. "Bruh, find me a rapper who doesn't want to be a balla. You still don't have a sense of your clout in this town, do you?"

I shrugged.

"I forget what it's like to be a rook. Life before endless pussy, free designer drip, and last-minute reservations anywhere you want," he said, gazing off.

"Anything else I need to know about the par–adult experience?" I asked, interrupting his trek down an undoubtedly filthy memory lane.

His eyes drilled into me. "You tryna make me catch a case? I signed an NDA. King D is ruthless, bro. He sues and bans motherfuckers for life. I'll tell you this, though—come with an open mind. Whatever your vice, you'll find it there. I mean, like, let your imagination go wild, man." As he kicked off the base of my chair and floated back to his station, thoughts of Sid sprang to mind.

I pull up to the front of the mansion and hand the valet my keys. Idris, Tevin, and Malik are already here somewhere, based on our group text. I make my way inside after I'm confirmed to be on the guest list and sign the electronic NDA. Rihanna is booming from the speakers, making my body tremble with the bass. The ground floor is jam-packed with barely clad, sweaty, dancing bodies squeezed together. Strobe lights dancing off of shoulders, hands, and faces illuminate the floor. I recognize a few players, including Kristian, Sid's teammate. I haven't spoken with Sid since the anniversary of my parents' passing two weeks back. We've traded a few texts here and there. A part of me is itching for the opportunity to leave the party with him tonight. Then there's the other part of me that's honestly afraid to cross that line. What I feel for him is so intense it scares the shit out of me. I'm barely in control when I'm around him, and control is the only thing holding my shit together. The best thing I can do for myself and everyone else is to keep my head down and ball.

I recognize a famous football player right as he snorts a line of something off of the coffee table. I head to the bar to get a drink. My roommate in college kept alcohol stocked in our closet. He'd make all sorts of hipster cocktails like reimagined Manhattans and ones with mezcal, Lapsang souchong tea, and all types of bitters I'd never heard of. I'd hated mezcal the first time I'd tried it, or so I thought. By the second glass, it had grown on me. I rarely drink during the basketball season, but if I have any chance of getting laid tonight, I need to loosen up. The situation couldn't work more in my favor. With everyone signing an NDA, my chances of finding another guy to fuck discreetly couldn't be better. I can't just hop on a dating app and fuck a regular guy without risking getting blackmailed or outed. I roll out the tension in my shoulders as I slide into a newly vacated spot at the bar and order a Mezcal Manhattan.

After grabbing my drink, I make my way to the pool area. A firm hand clasps my shoulder, and I spin around to face Tevin. He's shirtless, wearing orange swim trunks. I almost miss the red, curly-haired, model-looking woman holding his hand. The music drowns his voice out, so I tilt my head closer to him.

"...get lost with this baddie. Malik and Idris are upstairs."

"Good lookin'," I yell back. I glance between him and the woman. "Have fun."

The pool is full of bodies, some intertwined and making out, with lots of topless people swimming around. This party could easily become an epic orgy. I'm about to turn and search for Malik and Idris when I notice a few Marvels players in the lounge area next to the pool. Palm trees block my view, so I venture closer. Justin's lap is full of a woman with her face nestled between his chin and neck. He's slowly massaging her round breasts. My gaze pans right to Boris—I think that's Boris —the Marvels' center. He's making out with a woman straddling his lap. His hand travels down her back and disappears under her skirt.

A bead of sweat slides down my back.

I zero in on another lounge area, partially concealed at the end of the row. I press forward to get a better view. Not watching where I'm going, I almost smack into a security guard who flashes me a dubious look. I nod as I step around him. When I gaze back to the lounge area, my muscles tighten as I take in a shirtless Sid in red swim trunks. The gold chain resting against his oiled bare chest gleams. *Damn, he looks good.* Thoughts of him woke me up hard this morning.

I recognize the woman sitting next to him, Stacy, one of the hottest pop singers out right now. Clad in a lavender-colored two-piece swimsuit, she presses her mouth against Sid's ear, apparently sharing something funny because his head tilts back with laughter. They look cozy and annoyingly hot together.

A cold burn freezes my hand. I stare down and release the death grip on my glass. Of course he's already linked for the night. As if sensing someone watching, he dips his chin forward, and his gaze roams the area. I spin on my heels and walk back inside the house. I throw back my drink and head for the staircase. Once I reach the second floor, I realize there are at least two more levels and at least ten rooms full of people to look through. By the time I've searched the third room, I think I've seen it all. The first room had at least a half-dozen people going at it like bunnies—gay, straight, you name it. I've seen more drugs here than a DEA evidence lockup. I figure I'll run into my teammates eventually, so I head to the nearby bar for another drink. As I'm waiting my turn, I scan the crowd at the bar, and I immediately recognize the man standing next to me —Wilhelm Burton—an actor starring in a fictional drama series about a loyal leader of a lawless motorcycle gang. Despite the missing tattoos, he looks as sexy and rugged as his character. His medium-length blond hair is up in a bun, and he has a neat beard, blue-green eyes, and peach lips. He's wearing dark blue, ripped jeans and a tight-fitting, nude-colored T-shirt that highlights his muscles. The bartender interrupts my shameless gawking to take my order. I order another Mezcal Manhattan.

"Make that two," Wilhelm says.

I gaze in his direction as he turns his body to face me.

"Imagine running into Ty Washington at a party," he says.

I quirk my eyebrows. I don't think I'll ever get used to being a recognizable person.

"Same could be said about Wilhelm Burton," I reply. He nods. As someone much more famous, he's not surprised I recognize him.

"Call me Will. I saw you play in Miami a few weeks back. It was a great game. You literally cut up one of the greatest players the game's ever seen. I thought you had him there for a moment," he says, grinning.

"Thanks. We worked hard, but they outplayed us. What were you doing in Miami?"

"I was being photographed for a Louis Vuitton campaign."

I nod as the bartender delivers our drinks. I'm about to tell him to enjoy his night when he says, "I'm heading back up to the rooftop lounge." He signals for me to join him.

"What's on the rooftop?" I ask.

"Epic views," he says with a wickedly sexy grin.

The rooftop is less crowded. Khruangbin's "A Calf Born in Winter" blares from the speakers. A pool sits in the center of the lounge, but the real thing to take in is the 360-degree view. One side of the rooftop overlooks the boundless Pacific Ocean with the lucent, full moon reflected off of the water. The opposite side overlooks the mountains.

"Malibu at night is one of my favorite places in the world," he says, facing me.

"I live close by but don't take advantage of it enough."

"An ex I dated lives in Malibu. I've spent a lot of time here. I was sadder about losing the view of the beach than the actual breakup."

I chuckle. "Couldn't negotiate sharing the space with her?"

He studies me, something shifting in his gaze. "He—" he says, hesitating before continuing, "—owned the house."

Oh, shit.

I fight a grin. "That's a bummer. Ocean views aren't cheap to come by," I say, straightening my spine.

"Pardon my forwardness, but your dating life seems top secret," he says. "I looked you up after your game in Miami."

I raise my eyebrows. "No secret. I don't date. I'm focused on my game."

He leans closer to me and lowers his voice. "That's respectable...but hypothetically, *if* you dated, would I have a shot?"

I grin at his boldness. It's hot as fuck. This kinda thing never happens to me. I've heard stories about ballas being propositioned by celebrities. It's one thing to hear about it, but it's another thing for it to happen in real life.

Fuck, I could really use a distraction from Sid. And I mean, I *did* prep.

Standing this close to me with his chiseled features and rugged swag...

I clear my throat. "I don't date, but I'd be game tonight."

His face lights up. "Definitely interested." He throws his drink back. "We could leave now if you wanted."

His urgency goes straight to my dick, and I'm glad it's dark out or else I'd be worried about a tenting situation.

I thumb my ear. "Uh, I kinda need to admit something. I've never been with a man before. Not sure if you want someone more exp—"

"All good. I'm happy to take the lead. It'd be my honor to be your first," he says, and his sincerity slackens some of the tension in my shoulders.

He sets down his empty glass on the table next to us.

If anyone told me it'd be this easy to hook up with a guy, I'd have secretly wished they were right while laughing in their face. Idris warned me that anything was possible tonight.

"Here, give me your number," he says as he hands over his phone.

Once I type it in and hand it back to him, he calls my phone so I have his number. I notice a few messages on my phone, but when I unlock it, I sense we're being watched, so I scan the rooftop. At first glance, I don't notice anyone looking our way, but then I see a flash of red in my periphery. There's a column obscuring my line of sight. I step back to get a better look and spot Sid—now clad in a V-neck T-shirt—talking to an actress who stars in a mega superhero movie. He's nodding in response but staring directly at Will and me.

I shoot him a nod.

He gives me an intense look that I can't decipher, so I quirk my eyebrows at him.

He continues staring at me while crossing his arms in front of his chest.

"Let's head down. I can leave first and meet you at your place," Will offers.

I whip my head back around to face him. "Sounds good."

"After you," he directs me.

I lead the way towards the exit.

Halfway down the steps, I hear, "Ty, hold up."

I halt, causing Will to collide with me. I turn, reaching out an arm to steady us both.

I look at Sid, then Will, and feel a little awkward.

"Give me a sec. I'll be right back," I tell Will.

"Meet you outside? I need to find a restroom real quick," he whispers.

I nod as he brushes past me.

Sid nods for me to follow him as he heads down the steps past me. When we reach the quietest level, he turns down an empty corridor and faces me.

"You didn't get my text?" he asks, leaning his arm against the wall.

"What text?" I pull out my phone and see Will's missed call from a moment ago.

SID

You're here! Where'd you go?

"My bad, I didn't see your message until now. See." I show him my phone.

"Why didn't you come over when you saw me by the pool downstairs?"

Ugh. He spotted me lurking. I suppress a groan. "I didn't want to cock-block you."

"So if I'm talking to someone, I have to be trying to fuck them?"

"Nah. It just seemed intimate between you two, so I wanted to give you space."

"We're both board members for a grassroots organization focused on criminal justice reform. There's never been anything more than that between us."

"Oh, that's dope...I meant no offense." Tension emanates from him in waves. "What's up? You good?"

"Yeah. I just thought if we'd ever see each other out at an event, we'd chill together after everything, you know?" He crosses his arms over his chest again.

My chest tightens, staring into his gorgeous eyes that almost look hurt.

"I do want to chill with you, but if you're on a date or whatever, I'll give you space. That's all that was."

"There's the reputation of me as a playboy, and there's the real me. I thought you knew the difference."

"Wait," I reply, getting pissed off. "What am I missing? You have dated a series of actresses, models, and singers. Have you not?"

He shifts his weight. "Yes, but—"

"Okay then," I interrupt. "What am I supposed to think when I see you with a gorgeous, barely dressed singer sitting in a corner alone, laughing, as she whispers some shit in your ear? Is it far-fetched that I'd think you were on a date or about to hook up?" I cringe. I sound like a jealous lover, and I hate it.

"Fair. The next time you see me out, at least say what's up instead of acting like we're strangers."

"Got it." I fire back.

I stare off past his shoulder, ignoring the heat of his gaze.

The growing silence is heavy, but the pull to be next to him is strong. I'd stand here with him all night if Will wasn't waiting for me.

I release a heavy sigh. "I got to bounce." I hope he hears the remorse in my voice.

His voice is low when he replies, "Congrats on making MVP yesterday." The pinch between his brows relaxes.

"Thanks. Good luck with All-Stars tomorrow," I reply, softening my tone. He's the Eastern Conference captain, drafted for a third year in a row.

We stare at each other. The intensity of his gaze, which I'm certain mirrors my own, leads to an aching swell in my chest. Will it ever feel less galvanic between us? Even when I'm aggravated, god, I want him. All of my reservations about crossing the line seem insignificant right now. Whatever's buzzing between us is metamorphic. His piercing gaze, the force field of energy bouncing between us, his scent—fuck.

Why does he have to be so sexy? It's too much. If he made a move, there's no way I could resist him. It'd be impossible. Reason is frail and at odds with the fire raging through my body for him.

His hand, concealed by the wall we're leaning against, embraces mine, and my breath catches in my throat. His thumb rubs soft circles in the area between my thumb and index finger. My eyes shudder closed as a ball of heat rolls down my spine.

"Where are you going with that actor guy?" he asks, barely above a whisper.

I gaze at our embrace and feel almost hypnotized by the heat generated with every rotation of his thumb. My lips part as I meet his gaze.

"Home," I say, my breath shaky from his touch.

He pulls his hand away, and something twists inside of me at the masked look of hurt on his face. My hand, no longer mine to restrain, pulls his hand back and traces soft circles in his palm. His Adam's apple bobs, signaling that he feels it too.

His gaze flicks past me just as I hear, "Hey, handsome. I thought that was you."

My head spins around at the sound of my agent, Phil's, voice.

I reluctantly release Sid's hand.

"Hey—Phil, what are you doing here?"

"You kidding? This is the only place to be. I should probably pay King D a commission for the amount of new business this event brings me every year."

I grin. The dude is a workaholic. "Have you met Sid?" I ask, flicking a quick gaze at Sid.

"I haven't had the pleasure. It's nice to meet you. I'm a ginormous fan," Phil says, extending a hand.

"Nice to meet you," Sid replies, shaking his hand with a tight smile.

Maybe I should have lied when he asked me where I was going with Will, but I didn't want to lie to him.

"I'm surprised to see you here. I can't get you to attend any of these events," Phil says, patting my shoulder.

"Yeah, I didn't have a choice. Team vets made it clear that if I decline another invite, I'd be in the doghouse," I joke. I glance at Sid and follow his gaze to Phil's hand resting on my shoulder. I inch closer toward him, forcing Phil's hand to drop.

My arm brushes the rippling muscle of Sid's chest, and I'm not sure whose breath shudders first.

I clear my throat. "It's good to see you. Good luck tonight," I tell Phil, hoping he gets the hint.

Sid shifts his gaze toward the opposite end of the corridor, and I immediately long to have it back, focused on me. Then his fingers interlace with mine. I bite the inside of my lip to keep from reacting as he rubs circles across my concealed palm.

"Thanks. Oh, I almost forgot. Nike wants you for their new campaign."

My jaw drops. "Word?" I didn't think I'd land a Nike endorsement for a few more years.

"Yep. I'll call you on Monday with the details. Nice to meet you, Sid."

"Likewise," Sid replies.

Phil turns and heads toward the staircase.

"Is he your type?" Sid asks, releasing a deep breath.

"Who? Phil?" I ask, meeting his gaze.

"I meant the actor guy...but him too?"

I glance around. "I don't know if I have a type. He'll be my first with a guy. Things kinda changed for me a couple of months ago."

"What happened a couple of months ago?"

I catch a slight tremble in his voice.

You happened is on the tip of my tongue. I'm tired of holding back from whatever this is. It's time I put my cards on the table.

I lean in. "I was staying at my friend's house for Christmas, and I fell asleep in his home cinema. As I was heading to my bedroom in the middle of the night, I saw him getting head from his fr—casual lover and it hit me—I wanted to be the one fucking him."

His eyes go wide.

My phone vibrates. It's the same area code as the number I just scanned for Will.

I groan. "Fuck. I'm sorry. I have to go."

A storm of emotions crosses his face.

I turn to walk away, but he doesn't release my hand.

"I didn't take you for a cock-blocker," I joke, but it lands flat.

"Cock-blocker?" he repeats, eyebrows creased, spelling confusion. He steps forward, dipping his face so close that heat races across my cheeks. His lips brush against my ear. "Who said that standing here with me means you won't get fucked tonight?"

"W-what?" I stammer.

Does he mean what I think he means? I tilt my head back, searching his eyes for an answer. I mean, that was direct, wasn't it?

I'm stunned...

The penetrating look and the raw sexual energy emanating from him are confirmation.

"Take *me* home," he says—no, commands.

This is really happening.

Tingling heat spreads through my entire body.

My phone rings again, jolting me out of my head. I pick up without breaking eye contact.

"Hey." I can barely hear Will over the noise on his end. I turn up the volume. I feel bad for leading him on, then flaking, but gazing up at Sid, I know with absolute certainty that I'm making the right choice. "My bad, I ran into my—friend, and he, uh, needs a place to stay tonight. I'm sorry. I need to fall back."

Will does a poor job of masking his disappointment. He asks if he can hit me up when he's back in town in two weeks.

"Uh, sure," I reply. A part of me hopes that this thing between Sid and me isn't a one-night thing. Another voice tells me it has to be—there's no room for distractions in my life.

Sid's eyebrows are raised after I hang up, but he doesn't say anything except, "Let's go."

Before we make it to our cars, he's stopped a handful of times by A-list celebrities that I recognize. I give him space and make my way to the valet. I text him my address, then hop in my car. While waiting to pull out, I catch him jogging out of the house. His gaze pans right, then left, searching for me.

Look at your phone.

As if he heard me, he reaches into his pocket and fishes it out. A few seconds later, the widest grin spreads across his face. He races over to the valet and tosses him his ticket.

Chapter Thirteen

When I finally reach my place, an eternity later, Sid pulls into my driveway behind me.

I hop out and turn to watch his sexy, muscular frame climb out of a rental Lamborghini, looking like a wet dream. I've wanted this for months, and now that it's about to happen, I'm buzzing. My fingers tremble as I open an app to unlock my door. Sid steps behind me, wraps his fingers around my waist, and presses me against his chest.

"Fuck," I whisper, shuddering from his molten touch. He reaches past me and turns the doorknob.

"Can I get you—"

He spins me around and swallows my words with his mouth. I moan as his warm tongue slides against mine. He tastes like the cinnamon mints that he chews. Our mouths suck, lick, and swallow each other's moans. My legs tremble as he backs me against the door, his hands digging into the waist of my jeans. As far as first kisses go, holy fuck, it's better than anything I've imagined.

He pulls away. "God, I've wanted to taste you since the first time I met you," he pants, nibbling on my bottom lip.

My eyes widen. "The interview?"

He hums.

I wasn't off about our chemistry.

His warm tongue licks over my neck, and my fingers dig into the corded muscles of his back as I arch my neck to him. He bites down on a tendon, causing a sting, before he kisses and licks the spot soothingly. His thigh rubs against my rock-hard length as I catch his bottom lip with my own, ravenous to taste him again. I'm covered in his intoxicating scent, and it's heady how much I love smelling him on my skin.

He pulls my shirt over my head as I untie the drawstring of his swim trunks. We get turned around, and his back hits the door as I pull down his trunks, and his engorged cock springs free. It's even more impressive up close. *Fuck!* Thank goodness I've been training for my first time with plugs, a dildo, and a shit ton of lube. I step back to take it in.

"You're so fucking sexy." My mouth waters. "I've never wanted to give head more in my life."

He gives me a sexy-as-sin smirk that makes my blood pulse.

Needing him naked, I lift his shirt up over his head. I zero in on his nipple ring, and I want it in my mouth as badly as I need my next breath. He moans and leans back against the door for support as I lick across his nipple with the tip of my tongue, then tug on the ring gently with my teeth. I spit in my hand, then stroke his glistening cock.

"Wait, don't want to come yet," he grits.

I ease off his nipple, trailing my tongue over his tats as I continue stroking him slowly. My dick is at full mast as I stare at the pre-cum glistening on his head.

He pants. "How are you so good at this?"

The question makes me grin. "I've had time to think about —" I brush a kiss against his sexy lips as I continue to stroke him. "Mmmm. I've had time to think about all the ways I want to taste, suck, and fucking explore every inch of you."

I swallow up his moan, sucking his tongue, bobbing to match the languid strokes of my hand on his cock. His fingers dig into my hips, then he tenses, and his warm release jets out, covering my hand.

He grunts. "Damn—that hit without warning."

That was so fucking hot.

"When were you last tested?" I ask.

"Last week. I'm cleared. I haven't been with anyone since, and I always use a condom."

I gaze into his eyes as I slowly suck his cum off of my fingers.

"Fuccck." My eyes roll closed. "How can you taste better than I imagined?"

I moan as I dip my finger down to his tip and circle it in his cum, bringing it to my mouth for another taste.

He cups the back of my neck and kisses me roughly, licking into my mouth. The velvet timbre of his moan goes straight to my aching cock. As he unbuckles my jeans, I brace against him, peeling off my shoes and tossing aside my jeans. Taking out my cock, he applies firm pressure and long strokes.

"How'd I know your dick would be pretty too," he says, glancing down at it. "Where's the shower?"

"Second door on the right."

He sucks on my neck as I guide us there. His hardening cock presses against my back.

Of course, it bounces back quickly.

"Will you fit?"

It takes him a second to realize what I'm asking. "You definitely want me inside of you tonight?"

I tense up. I know some guys aren't into it, but in most of my fantasies, I imagined him penetrating me.

"It's okay if it isn't your thing."

He spins us so that I'm pinned against the wall and tilts my chin up. "Hold up. I'm dying to be inside of you. It's just that tonight isn't about me. It's your first time. It should be about what you want. You set the pace."

"I want it with you."

He grins, then brushes a kiss against my lips. "Cool. We'll go slowly and spend time opening you up." He trails from the crease of my mouth down to my neck with kisses.

"Come on." I push off the wall and steer us to the bathroom. "I've been using a dildo and plug to train, and I'm in the clear too. I was tested months ago and haven't hooked up with anyone since. I'm on PrEP."

"Months. Damn. That's hard to believe. You're smokin'. I already know I'm going to want to live buried inside of you," he says, mouth pressed against my ear.

"Fuck, you can't say shit like that," I groan, rutting against him.

He grunts. "It's true."

I turn the faucet on in the shower. He wraps an arm around my waist and presses my back against his chest. The other hand reaches around and takes my cock as he applies firm, deep strokes. His hard cock ruts between the globes of my ass, and my orgasm erupts hard.

"God, Sid," I moan as I push back against him, deepening the friction between us. He strokes me through my orgasm.

"I plan to make you come over and over, baby," he whispers. He sucks on my earlobes. The steam from the shower, the term of endearment, and his touch everywhere leave me dizzy. His tight embrace is the only thing holding me up.

I catch my breath as he reaches over my shoulder to pump body wash into his hands. His large hands are smooth as he rubs the soap over my chest in circles, and I melt under his touch. He resumes sucking on my neck as he soaps me down.

"You're gonna leave a hickey," I say, rutting against his erection. The warmth of his mouth, the sharp sting, then the soothing swipe of his tongue feels so damn good. The idea of him marking me makes my dick pulse back to life, despite never wanting to be possessed by a person before.

He groans. "My bad. You're right." He tries to pull away, but I reach my hand up to apply pressure to the back of his head.

"I want it. Don't stop." I moan when he kisses the spot tenderly.

"Honestly, the thought of seeing you in interviews with my hickey on your neck...fuck." His hard length slides between the globes of my ass. "What is it about you that makes me possessive, like a caveman?"

"Fuck. Shut up, or I'm gonna come again," I groan as I rock back against him. The smoky timbre of his voice sends a heat wave through my body.

"I need inside of you."

I step forward and grab an extra washcloth for him. He quickly lathers his body all over, and I follow suit.

Getting out first, I towel off and hand him one.

He steps out and towers over me. Backing me up against the wall, he pulls my lower lip between his teeth before his tongue enters my mouth for another scorching kiss. When he wraps the towel around his waist, his erection tents the cotton. His hands caress my ass, grasping each cheek firmly and then softly. "I got so hard on Christmas watching you on the treadmill. Your ass in those thin shorts—damn."

Wait, what! We could have fucked then?

"Me? Listening to your grunts on the pull-up bar drove me crazy. As soon as I returned to the room, I had to rub one out," I confess.

He grins. "That's wild. I rubbed one out, too, after the gym that morning."

I groan. That's so hot. "You fucking killed me in that onesie."

He chuckles.

I shake my head. "No mercy. And you wonder why I had a boner in my sleep."

"Mmm, it worked, didn't it?"

I reach inside his towel and stroke his erection. "Yeah, it did. Let's go."

He wets a fresh washcloth before I lead him into my bedroom.

"Wow," he exclaims, pulling my back against his chest. We take in the floor-to-ceiling view of the lush greenery and mountains. "It reminds me of a villa I rented off-season last year in Bali."

"Yeah? The views are one reason I was sold on the place. It feels remote here."

I walk over to the nightstand, retrieve condoms and lube, and toss them on the bed. I turn to face him, and our gazes lock like the first time at the end of my college game. I drink him in. He's so beautiful. I'll never forget this night for as long as I live.

He prowls over, and I gasp when he drops to his knees. Kissing the tip of my cock, his tongue licks up my pre-cum. A moan rips out of me when he sucks me deep into his mouth, the suction so intense. It's been months since I've gotten head, and it's never felt as good as this.

"Sid," I hiss as his tongue massages my head, then he sucks me back down to my base and pulls back up, over and over again. His tongue trails down to suck on my balls, causing my knees to tremble.

"God," I moan as my fingers dig into his shoulders.

He pulls off of me again. "Get in bed," he orders, licking his lips.

I crawl into the middle of the bed. Sid right behind me, he grasps my waist. "Ohhh," I moan as his tongue licks a warm strip across my rim.

He grunts. "You're fucking gorgeous. I couldn't resist." Flipping me to my back, he resumes giving me the best head of my life. The tip of his tongue teases the underside of my shaft over my frenulum, causing my back to arch off the bed as he licks up another stream of pre-cum. His eyes close as he doubles down and deep-throats me, humming around my cock.

I'm levitating from the pleasure ripping through my body. I fill up with air, then draw out an exhale that turns into a moan as he resumes taking me down his throat. My eyes pop open when his tongue trails down to my hole. Warm circles tease my rim, and then he sucks as he jerks me off. I've never been rimmed before, but damn, it's heaven. I fist the sheets to keep from thrusting my ass deeper into his mouth. He moans as his tongue attempts to penetrate my hole. He pulls back and his lubed finger rubs across my rim.

"Is this okay?" he asks.

"Yeah...I'm nervous," I confess. It's one thing to use toys where I control the pace. It's another thing to be penetrated by someone else for the first time.

"We'll go slowly. Tell me to stop or tap my arm if anything feels uncomfortable."

I nod as my body relaxes, sensing it's in safe hands.

He lowers his mouth and I close my eyes as his tongue applies firm pressure and slowly breaches me. My legs part wider for him. I reach down, massaging his head.

My legs quiver as he licks and sucks my hole, the flat tip of his tongue offering a distinct, penetrating sensation. I'm moaning and gasping his name over and over like a chant. It feels so unbelievably intimate that I might have clammed up if it were anyone other than him.

He pulls his mouth back and begins to insert his lubed finger.

I tense up.

He stills. "Take a deep breath."

Crawling up my body, he envelops my mouth in a kiss as he strokes my erection. When he sucks on my bottom lip, then bites it, I moan from the sting. His eyes resemble black ink as he watches me writhing and moaning.

On my next inhale, he slowly inserts his finger. He makes slow circles, helping my muscles stretch and relax.

"Mmm, you feel unbelievable," he rasps, kissing softly against my lips.

He moves down my body again and takes my cock into his mouth while his finger fucks me.

I moan. "Feels s'good."

He adds a second lubed finger and curves up while deepening his penetration.

Between the warmth of his mouth sucking me down and the stroke of his fingers, I feel the pull of an orgasm.

"Wait—shit, I'm close."

Slowly withdrawing his fingers, he crawls up my body, kissing along the way, spending time licking and sucking my erect nipples. Retrieving a condom, he tries to tear it open, but his fingers slip. He wipes his lubed fingers on the washcloth that he brought from the bathroom. He really does think of it all.

"I'm going to prep you some more first," he says, voice raspy with need. He starts to roll on the condom.

"Wait—I want to give you head." My mouth salivates, staring at his glistening cock.

"I'm too close," he says.

Damn. "Before you leave this bed…"

"Mmm," he hums as his heated gaze rests on my lips while he sheathes himself with the condom. "It's my favorite way to be woken up," he says as he slicks the condom with a generous amount of lube.

The idea of waking Sid up with head…damn. I reach down and stroke myself.

"That turns you on?" He zeroes in on my erection as my slit glistens with pre-cum. "Going down on me when I sleep?"

"Yeah," I grunt, stroking myself.

"Fuck...that's hot. Have me anytime."

He climbs back onto the bed and sucks me down again.

"Ngh—s'good," I sputter. Inserting a finger again, he slowly builds up to three. His fingers curve in a come-hither motion, gently pulsing. He gradually increases the pressure, massaging my prostate over and over until the pleasure is blinding. My back arches off the bed and my eyes tear up. "Yes, mmm, fuck," I cry, never ever wanting him to stop.

"Fuck. I'm going to come just from the sounds coming out of you." He reaches down with his free hand and squeezes the base of his shaft as he laps up my pre-cum.

"I'm close," I pant.

He pulls off of me and lines his cock up to my rim, rubbing his tip over my hole back and forth.

"Push out when I enter you." Damn if his authoritative voice doesn't go straight to my balls. "And breathe."

I didn't realize I was holding my breath. I mean, he's not small.

He freezes. "Hey, we don't have to go further today. We can take our time and work up to it."

No way in hell am I backing out. I want this.

"I've been dreaming about this for months. I'm stretched. Come on."

"Are you sure?" he asks.

I take a deep breath. "Yeah, get in me. I'm ready."

He grins. "Take another deep breath in, then exhale through your mouth."

When I start to exhale and push out, he guides his head in slowly.

"Oh, fuck," I hiss from the pressure as he breaches the first muscle ring while continuing to stroke my cock.

"Come here," he says as he pulls out. He leans forward, covering me, and brushes a tender kiss against my lips. Our kiss deepens as he sucks on my tongue in a possessive way that has me opening up for him in every way possible. He penetrates me again. After a combination of kissing, stroking my cock, and moving slowly, he's fully seated inside of me. We're both sweaty. He pauses and nods. I nod back.

He slowly draws back and then rolls his hips until he bottoms out.

"So tight," he drawls. At the same time, my eyes roll closed, and I choke out, "God, Sid!" It feels so much more intense than the toys that I've used.

He continues to stroke me slowly, biting his lip as his heated gaze trails over my face.

"Feel okay?" he asks, voice strained.

I moan in response. I'm still getting used to his size, though each stroke feels more pleasurable. His earthy scent, the sandalwood from my body wash, mixed with the heady scent of our sex, makes me dazed with rapture. It fully settles in that it's him inside of me.

"Kiss me," I plead.

He moans as he licks my tongue and sucks it into his mouth. He adjusts the angle on the next drive, and I buck from a sharp sensation. All of my nerve endings are fired up. I barely recognize the guttural sounds bubbling out of me as my eyes fill up.

He stills and places soft kisses on the sides of my eyes where my tears have pooled. He trails kisses over my forehead, dimples, nose, and chin. "I can stop," he whispers as he kisses my lips.

"No, I want you. So good. Keep going."

"Are you sure?"

I answer by clenching and pushing down to deepen his penetration.

"Ahhh, fuck," he moans, biting his bottom lip. "Don't move, or I'll come," he warns.

He grounds himself by staring out of the window for a few seconds before he resumes slowly tunneling in and out of me.

He pulls my legs up, folding me in half as he speeds up the pace of his thrusts. Each of his deep strokes massages my prostate, causing tremors throughout my body, building in its heat and intensity. I moan his name as I dig my fingers into his back.

His sexy penetrating gaze bores into me. "Look at you, taking me so well."

There are no words for the euphoria seeping into every cell of my body. Primal moans blanket every exhale.

He pumps my cock as he thrusts into me with powerful strokes.

My entire body starts to spasm, the intensity all-encompassing. The pleasure swells and swells. My eyes roll to the back of my head and my lower back levitates off the bed.

"Fuck," I bellow as tremor after tremor courses through my body until there's just white space...echoes of silence.

"Mmmm, your first prostate orga—fuck, you're clenching my dick hard."

I can't control the tremors coursing through me. Each roll of his hips sends more waves throughout my body, sending a shooting sensation behind my eyes.

What the ever-loving fuck is a prostate orgasm? How is my dick still hard?

"Fuck," I pant. "I've never..." My brain wipes out as he pulls out and slams back in. "Fuuck."

"Hmm?" He's fucked the words out of me, and by the mischievous smile on his face, he knows it.

He changes angles and strokes me slower, deepening his reach.

Sex has never, ever felt like this. How does a person even learn how to fuck someone this well? Is it all instinct? Loads of experience?

I cling to him, relishing in the slide of our heated, sweaty bodies.

He swipes up the pre-cum glistening on the tip of my cock and sucks it into his mouth.

Why is that so hot?

I pull his neck down, wanting a taste of his tongue.

"I won't last much longer," he warns, nibbling on my lip.

He jerks me off as his cock continues to hit my prostate. I'm so close my balls draw up, and my hands lower down his back to massage the globes of his muscular ass, savoring the firmness. *How'd I ever think I was straight?* Corded muscles, Sid's heady scent, large, strong hands stroking me, and a gorgeous thick and long cock rubbing my prostate is my body's idea of nirvana. I suck on my finger and move it towards his hole.

"Okay?"

When he nods, I graze the pucker of his hole, using my saliva to massage the rim. I apply a little pressure to finger him deeper, barely penetrating the ring of muscle. It's enough sensation to drive him wild. His eyes roll into the back of his head as his thrusts become wild and jerky.

"Mmm...argh...Ty," he cries out. His abs contract as he fucks me deep and wild. Forehead pressed against mine, I swear his eyes are on fire as his hooded gaze bores into me, spreading a feverish heat everywhere. I love seeing him unfettered like this. His thrusts become slower, milking his release into the condom.

I whine when he pulls out, feeling empty. Too empty.

His chest heaves as he falls onto his elbows, planted on each side of my thighs, and catches his breath.

"I—fuck—mmm—I got you. One sec," he pants. He takes another minute to catch his breath before placing kisses on my steel cock. He fingers me and then takes me into his mouth again, gagging as I hit the back of his throat.

"Sid," I moan as my toes curl. I'm too close to last.

He sucks me down, and the delicious gurgling sounds send me over. "I'm about to come," I warn.

He massages my balls as he pulls off my dick with a pop before swallowing me back down.

"Oh, fuck," I groan, arching up, pushing deeper into his mouth as my orgasm shoots down his throat.

Our panting breaths and racing hearts fill the room. He collapses on his back next to me.

If I never make a good decision again, I can revel in knowing that choosing Sid, the god of sex, to take my anal virginity is the best decision I ever made. I can't believe I almost had my first time with someone else. Of course it had to be him.

He turns to face me and throws an arm over my stomach. I'm nodding off when he whispers, "Baby, wake up. We should clean up."

I smile inwardly. I love that he's still calling me "baby" after sex.

I remember Adam's hygiene advice when he gave me the sex talk on New Year's Eve.

"I'll crawl," I groan.

He chuckles. "We'll hold each other up. Come on."

Once in the bathroom, he dispenses with the condom. We climb into the shower and clean ourselves, too blissed for words. When I get out, I towel off and then pass Sid an extra toothbrush from the cabinet. We use my double sink to brush simultaneously. I coat the fresh scratches on his back with ointment. My skin feels dry. I pump lotion into my hand, but he swipes it up and massages it into my skin. As he rubs the lotion onto my back, I turn my face and tilt my chin up to place a soft kiss on his lips.

He presses me against his chest and deepens the kiss. We pull apart, and I return the favor and massage lotion into his skin.

"Do you feel sore?" he asks.

I feel like I've been fucked, and I love it. I'm not sure if sore is the right word.

"Maybe a little," I reply as we head back into the bedroom.

"Help yourself to anything in my drawers or closet."

He nods, rummages inside, and pulls on cotton shorts, opting to go commando. The easy access to his cock and the way the shorts hug him tight makes my mouth water.

"I've worked up an appetite," he says.

"Me too. Want something quick like cereal?" I offer.

"Perfect."

I wrap my arm around his waist, and he slings his arm over my shoulders. I lead him to the kitchen, where we make ourselves a bowl of cereal.

He peers into my fridge and cabinets. "You eat pretty healthy."

"I want to be the best. I have to eat well."

He gazes at me.

"Can I ask you something?" I ask as we take adjacent seats on the island bar stools with our knees touching.

He nods while scooping up a bite of cereal.

"You knew your way around in there. I'm not the first guy you've been with?"

There's no way that was Sid's first time with a man.

A turbulent expression passes over his face, and I put down my spoon, bracing for his response.

"Remember I mentioned my best friend in high school who died? He was my first. Well, we were each other's. We were together for a while before he passed."

"Oh. And you haven't been with a man since?"

He shakes his head.

Interesting.

"I know I bottomed tonight, but I think I'd like to top, too, at some point," I say, assuming we'll do this again. I'd love to bring to life some fantasies that have replayed over and over in my head over the last few months.

"Cool. I'm vers," he says.

Hell yes. Best news ever.

"How do you identify?" I ask.

"I'm bi. I've learned through therapy that sexuality isn't always as simple as falling into one label or category. I'm bi, for sure. But there's usually an emotional bond coupled with my attraction to men. It's like I'm bi and demisexual. I know people expect you to fit in one label, but I think sexuality can be way more complex than that."

I grin inwardly. I feel emotionally connected to him too.

"I get that. We're constantly changing and discovering more about ourselves. I've never felt for women anything remotely close to whatever is between us."

He grins and rubs my thigh. My eyes roll closed from the heat of his touch.

I clear my throat. "What happened to your best friend? If you don't mind my asking."

He tenses. "He killed himself."

Fuck. I reach across to massage the back of his neck.

"I'm so sorry."

He stares into his bowl, and for a naked second, despair crosses his face, but it disappears as soon as it arrives. Given the timing, the death of his best friend would explain his tattoos.

A beat passes, then he embraces my hand and lifts it to his mouth for a gentle kiss. "Listen, I want to tell you about him. It brings up a lot for me, and I need my head right for tomorrow's game."

I nod. "I'm here whenever you're ready. Let's finish up and get some sleep." I down the rest of the cereal, then leave the kitchen to activate the security system. I'm, of course, curious about Sid's ex, but I know firsthand grief's interminable touch.

The residual, emotional pain from recounting a tragedy can linger for minutes, hours, or days.

We climb into bed, both exchanging yawns. Sid pulls me into an embrace with my head against his chest, and I listen to the thrum of his heartbeat as I doze off.

I climb back into bed quietly after using the restroom in the middle of the night. Sid is on his back, lightly snoring, his arm covering part of his face. His ripped chest expands and contracts with each breath. I feel my erection growing just looking at him. It's unreal having him in my bed. Life's fucking wild.

Kneeling, I reach for the drawstring of his shorts. I gently pull his cock out and wrap my mouth around him. His sleepy, husky moan fills the room. It's my first time sucking cock, but I'm so hungry for him. I lick the tip of his head while slowly stroking his hardening shaft.

"Mmm," he moans and widens his legs to give me more access. I suck him slowly, making popping noises. I gag fast and pull off before sliding back down and gagging again. I relax my throat as I suck him deeper. His pre-cum coats my tongue, and I drink it down, moaning from the heady taste.

He gently touches the back of my neck, coaxing me down his shaft. I wrap my hand over him, signaling he shouldn't hold back. I bob up and down, eliciting insanely hot moans. Our gazes lock and my balls draw up. I rut against the sheets, desperate for friction.

"Pass the lube and a condom," he commands.

"Fuck, your voice," I groan as I reach for both and hand them to him. I thought his voice was sexy before. It's orgasmic when he's sleepy and horny.

He rips open the wrapper, and then slides the condom on, coating it with lots of lube.

"Climb on top," he says, reaching for my waist.

"I wanted to taste you a little longer," I whine as I straddle him.

His cock twitches against my rim.

Cupping my face, he pulls me into a spine-tingling kiss.

"I'm so fucking lucky," he whispers against my lips once we separate.

I grin at him, but it turns into a moan when he inserts a lubed finger and curves it slowly, driving in and out.

"Your mouth felt amazing. I'm just desperate to feel you again before I come."

"Is that 'fill' with an 'i' or 'feel' with two 'e's'?" I grit out.

His brain is still half asleep, and he thinks about it for a beat. "Both," he says, inserting another finger.

My forehead against his, our gazes remain locked as I moan from the stroke of his fingers.

I start to roll my hips, fucking his hand. "I'm ready."

"I don't want you to be sore," he says, fingering me deeper.

"Sid," I moan as he curves in, lighting me up. His gaze brushes every inch of my face with a mix of raw desire and wonder. My head shoots back as my balls draw up, but he reaches down with his free hand and squeezes the base of my cock.

He lifts and then lowers me onto his cock. We moan as I slide down his length. I hold at the bottom to adjust to his size then nod for him to continue.

"Oh, damn," I moan, leaning forward to brace myself. Grasping the back of my neck, he pulls me into a kiss. He fucks me slowly...rolling his hips as our tongues tangle and our mouths drink our moans.

My back arches as I gyrate in slow circles on his cock. Our kiss turns wet, sloppy, and desperate. His eyes squeeze closed as his head presses back into the pillow. The only warning before he cups my ass and deepens his thrusts.

"Sid," I rasp as he slides against my prostate.

"God, you're so tight." He moans. "I love how you feel."

He sucks on the same spot on my neck again, and the sting unleashes a toe-curling moan that draws up my orgasm. I squeeze my base and pull my neck back, not ready to come yet.

Staring into the depths of his eyes while I take him...I've never had this. He holds my hips and pushes me down, deepening his reach as he drives into me. His iron abs contract doing most of the work.

I cry out in ecstasy as my vision turns cloudy.

"You're beautiful," he says, as tears slip from the corners of my eyes. His eyes hold a storm of emotions too.

I close my eyes and let my head fall back as I ride him.

"No, no, let me see you," he whispers.

I can't. I don't know what's happening to me or why this is so intense.

"Please, baby." His soft plea squeezes my chest, and I muster the courage to meet his gaze.

"I want to see you," he says, slowing his thrusts.

"What are you doing to me?" I whisper, quickly wiping my eyes.

"I could ask the same thing," he says, voice shaky. "I'm close...fuck. I want to stay in you all night."

I moan at the thought of him resting his dick inside of me when we sleep as I bend down to kiss his cheekbones.

Fucking me slowly with the roll of his hips, he reaches for my cock and strokes me.

Oh, god! "I'm coming," I grit out as a deep toe-curling moan rocks through me.

"Me too," he huffs as he grasps my hips and pounds harder, reaching somehow deeper inside of me.

A cacophony of expletives echoes into the morning as we both fall apart and orgasm together.

I collapse on top of him, nestling my face in the crook of his neck.

He massages my back, running his hands up and down absentmindedly.

"That was perfect," he pants.

"S'perfect," I mutter.

When I start to climb off of him, he holds my waist and pulls me down so that our foreheads are touching.

I stare into his eyes, and hidden doors not meant to be uncovered rattle as he peers back with a trembling intensity—almost like he could love what he sees. I close my eyes and brush my forehead against his. He tilts up and nibbles on my bottom lip. He's obsessed with it.

"I hate how empty I feel after," I whine when he slowly slides out of me.

He sucks his thumb in his mouth, then massages my rim.

"I definitely want to live buried inside of you." His deep, soothing voice makes my stomach flutter.

"Me aside, I know you're like the best balla on the planet, but living inside of me might be your true calling."

He chuckles. "I think you're right."

SID'S PHONE WAKES US UP. I RECOGNIZE THE RINGTONE "Bluebird" by Alexis Ffrench. I push up slightly to free his hand. He retrieves his phone. I lie back down and wipe the sleep from my face.

"Mind if I get this? It's Kieran on FaceTime." His gravelly voice sends a zing of heat up my spine.

I shake my head as I yawn. I figure he'll climb out of bed and take the call from a different room, but he sits up and answers.

"What's good, Cuz?" He stares into the camera, wipes his eyes, and then takes a drink from the glass of water on the nightstand. After he places it down, he massages soft circles across my chest.

"Good mornin' All-Star Captain! I wake you? I thought you'd be up already," Kieran greets him.

"Had a late night."

"Looks like a fun one. Your lip is bruised."

I snicker quietly. *Sorry, not sorry.*

Sid chuckles and throws the covers over my body. "Yeah, blame this one," he says, pointing the screen toward me.

Kieran's rubbing a rose-pink face mask over his skin but freezes as recognition settles in. His eyes go wide.

I expand my self-view. The first thing I notice is how ravaged I look. My lip is bruised too. The morning light highlights the gold of my irises, but my eyes are rimmed red and puffy.

"Shit, my neck!" I exclaim, zeroing in on the purple bruise.

Sid massages the area gently with a proud smirk on his face. That smirk goes straight to my dick.

"Hello, handsome. Looks like you had a fun night too. Tommy! You owe me $50! I told you!" Keiran yells off camera.

"Hi, Kieran. Wait, what did you two bet on?"

"Love, the two of you could light up the Empire State Building with the electricity coursing between you. Also, my cousin couldn't stop talking about yo–."

"Okay, enough out of you!" Sid says, stealing the phone.

"Fine. I'm just calling to wish you good luck on your game later today. Are you still coming to New York next month?" Kieran asks.

"I appreciate it. The game should be fun. A lot of the guys showing out. And yes, I'll be there."

"Okay. Call me later. Good to see you, Ty! If you don't end up marrying Sid, marry me and Tommy! No one should look that gorgeous in the morn–."

"Bye," Sid interrupts, hanging up the phone.

"I think I like him more than you," I tease.

"Is that so?" he asks, pulling my back against his chest so we're spooning. He reaches into my boxers and strokes my cock.

"What about now?" he teases back.

I remain silent, pretending to be unsure, but a moan erupts from me when he presses against my slit.

"Mmm, love that sound." He kisses my cheek as he strokes me firmly.

I moan, feeling all the blood rush from my brain southward, and roll to my back.

He trails kisses down to my nipple. My eyes roll closed as the warmth of his tongue flicks back and forth. He alternates sucking and nibbling on it creating the perfect mix of pain and pleasure. I fall apart and fuck his hand.

Lifting my arm, his tongue swipes across my pit. I jolt from the intensity of the sensation, and prickles of heat shoot all over my body. He sniffs, licks, and sucks on my pit as his hand strokes me fast and rough. I bite my bottom lip and grunt as my orgasm crests.

"What about now?" he says, popping off of me. "Still like another man more than me?"

I groan from the loss of contact.

"Hmm?" he asks, trailing the flat of his tongue across my nipple. He tugs it between his teeth, causing a sting, which he soothes with the massage of his tongue. When he wraps his hand back around my erection, I'm done.

"S'you—only you," I babble as my abs contract, and I explode. Jets of cum cover my chest as he strokes and licks me until I'm spent.

Chest heaving, I turn and gaze at him. "Fu-ck."

I stare down at my erect nipples.

"Give me time—I'll learn all of your spots." He lifts my

hand and brushes a kiss against the inside of my wrist, sending a tingle down my back into my toes.

Pits, nipples, wrists, bottoming...fuck. Who am I?

I reach for his erection, but he covers my hand.

"Turn to your side."

I nod and turn my back to him. Angling my head back, I watch him pour lube over his shaft.

His dick glides between my thighs as he takes hold of my waist. "I love your ass," he moans against my ear. "It's so fucking perfect."

I moan when he clasps the front of my neck, turns my face, and licks into my mouth.

I suck on his tongue and squeeze my thighs as he thrusts his hard length back and forth.

"You know how you like to be woken up with head?" I ask, releasing his tongue.

He grunts.

"I want to wake up with your cock inside of me."

His eyes dim to dark orbs as his thrusts become jerky. "When?"

"Whenever you want." Every cell in my body lights up at the idea of being woken up on Sid's cock.

"Fuck, that's...ungh."

I shiver from his smoky grunts against my ear. His thrusts quicken, his pre-cum leaving a slick trail between my thighs. The velvet brush of his skin builds heat with every roll of his hips. I reach behind and clasp the globe of his ass, pressing him closer as I squeeze my thighs tighter, choking his dick.

"Mmm," he moans as his breath becomes choppy. He anchors me against his chest and stills with a low grunt as his warm release fills the crook of my thighs. "Damn," he pants, resting his forehead against my shoulder blades.

"It's settled then—I wake you up with head whenever I

want, and you wake me up with your cock whenever you want?"

He grunts. "Fuck yeah. What about head? Can I wake—"

"Yeah," I rush out, making him grin.

WE'RE STILL IN BED, WRAPPED UP IN EACH OTHER, WHEN HE ASKS, "Are you coming to watch the game later?"

"Yeah. It's my first All-Star Game as a pro. And I guess seeing you play can't hurt."

"Uh-huh," he says, grinning.

"How the fuck do I explain this hickey?"

"Just tell them I gave it to you," he says, kissing it.

"Like they'd believe me. You're a notorious ladies' man."

"Yet, if I could skip the game and stay right here with you, I would," he says.

"Smooth. There's no All-Star Game without the Wonder Kid, Captain. I plan to earn a spot on the team next year. Give you real competition."

"I look forward to it," he says, sucking my earlobe. I close my eyes and savor the warmth of his mouth.

Hunger eventually forces us out of bed. We brush our teeth and head to the kitchen.

"Oh, I'm definitely sore," I say, wincing as we make our way to the kitchen.

"Shit, was I too rough?" he asks, embracing my hips.

"It didn't feel rough. I mean, I can't imagine your cock not leaving me a little sore."

"Sorry," he says, kissing my neck. "Let's eat, then I'll run you a bath. I'll pick up fiber supplements. Also, use a damp tissue to wipe until the soreness goes away. Drink lots of water today. We can also ice your rim."

"Why lots of water?"

"Helps soften...you know," he says, nodding toward the bathroom.

"Oh." I nod, turning to face him. "Iced rim sounds kinky."

He laughs.

I lean my face up to capture his mouth. He kisses me back like he owns my mouth in a way that's becoming dangerously familiar.

I play with the barbell of his nipple ring. He moans, then moves to nibble and kiss his favorite spot on my neck. I wrap my arms around his back, wanting to feel him closer.

God, how is it like this?

I knew it could be good if we got together, but I never could have imagined it would be this good.

"I can't seem to stay soft around you," he says, pulling away.

"We need to eat if we want to keep fucking like rabbits." I pull him toward the kitchen.

He pauses and stares out the living room window. "The views in this house! Dayuum."

The morning sun reflects off of the wildflower-covered mountains. The house sits high up, secluded with no other property in view. It's easy to feel like you're the only one in the world here.

He scans the bookshelf. He smiles when he sees the set of first edition *The Count of Monte Cristo* books he gifted me for Christmas. I had a custom floating shelf built for the set.

"We both have something of each other in our homes," I say.

He grins as he scans the titles on my bookshelf.

"You like James Baldwin." He observes the full shelf of Baldwin's books.

"Yeah, I have about as many Baldwin books as you have Hendrix records. Have you read that one?"

He shakes his head as he scans the first page.

"Borrow it. It's one of my favorites of his."

"Thanks," he says, his voice drifting.

"Food first, then go secure a W, then you can read," I order, pulling him towards the kitchen.

As he gets ready to head back to his hotel to get dressed and ready for the game, a hug goodbye turns into a make-out session with me plastered against the door.

"Go before you are late," I say as I fondle his dick.

He sighs. "I can't." His tongue swipes across my neck.

"This hickey is noticeable from Mars. You done marking me yet?"

"I'll switch to the other side and give that spot a break," he says, breath warm against my neck, making me shiver.

He groans when I slip from under him.

"I won't let you be late. Go and post at least forty points."

"That's a given," he retorts.

He tries to pull me into an embrace again, but I swat his hand away.

"Fine. I guess I'll go be great," he whines. "Oh. Before you agree to the Nike deal, hit me up with the details. Happy to weigh in."

"Yeah?" I reply. His endorsement earnings have shattered records. It'd be clutch to get his perspective. "Still being generous even after we fucked, eh?"

"Don't let the big dick and killer looks fool you. I'm a good guy," he quips, winking. He dips his face to kiss me, nibbling on my lip.

He studies me and it feels as intimate as anything we've done. He shakes his head.

"You should go while you still can." My voice comes out hoarse.

"Don't tempt me," he says, opening the door and walking backward.

I remain glued to the door watching him climb into his whip and drive away.

It hits me that we didn't plan to see each other again. I know he keeps things casual, but I can't see myself fucking anyone else anytime soon.

I shrug off the unsettling twinge of uncertainty. At least I'll see him at the game later. I strip off my clothes and climb into the bath that he ran for me before he left. When I climb back into bed to nap, his scent all over the sheets gets me hard. I stroke myself as scenes from our night flicker through my mind. It doesn't take long for me to come and drift into a peaceful slumber.

Chapter Fourteen

The high number of A-list celebrities in the building for the All-Star Game is wild. The air buzzes with electricity. Despite the buzz, all the players on the floor are ballin' like it's a pickup game amongst friends. The league has received criticism over the years because of the game's relaxed style. It's more of an exhibition match for high-caliber players to show off their offensive abilities with minimal defense. The league even increased the winners' prize to $150,000 per player, whereas the losing team receives $30,000. The prize is supposed to incentivize players to take the game more seriously. It hasn't really worked, but it's still entertaining to watch.

The two team captains are voted from the Eastern and Western Conferences and build their teams by selecting a mix of players from an All-Star pool. The pool includes ten conference starters elected by votes from fans, players, and the media. Fourteen reserve players are also selected. The game is employing a new competitive format this year. The first three quarters begin with a zero score for both teams and last twelve minutes. The winning team of each quarter is the team that scores the most points. The game clock is turned off at the start of the fourth quarter, and a final target score is set. The target score is the leading team's cumulative score of the first three quarters, plus twenty-five points added. The first team to reach the final target score wins the game.

When I reached my seat, Idris, Malik, and Harry grilled me about the hickey on my neck. I shrugged and said real men don't fuck and tell. My dad taught me that. Still, they insisted. Thank God for Sid's insane between-the-legs dunk in the second quarter that finally distracted them.

It's the fourth quarter, and Sid's already posted thirty-eight points, the most of any player, and his team is four points away from reaching the target score of 158. Seven points away from a win, the opposing team's point guard lands a backhanded dunk that does little to wow the crowd.

Sid takes possession of the ball and points to Justin. Our heads swivel in Justin's direction, eager to see what Sid has up his sleeve. He races up court at full speed, heading straight toward Justin, and just when I think he's going to barrel into him, he soars through the air. At the last second, he spreads his legs, clearing Justin's head, and slams the ball through the net with a one-handed dunk.

The crowd goes fucking ape. Justin's over six feet! My jaw is on the floor as Idris and Harry clutch their heads. Sid places a hand over his heart and then races down the court, something I've never seen him do after scoring. The play brings his total field goals to forty and his team two points away from a win. Then, the center for Minnesota catches a lob and completes a corner three-pointer.

Sid takes possession of the ball. This could be the winning shot. He fakes a shot and lobs it to a point guard who plays for the Bay Area Hawks. The point guard is at least fifty feet out from the net. What the hell is Sid thinking? The point guard bounces back even further, crosses the ball between his legs, and releases it from deep downtown. My eyes bulge as the ball soars through the air.

Malik starts to yell, "Air bal—" but swallows his words as the ball crashes straight through the net, clinching the win for Sid's team. The crowd erupts, myself included. I have to restrain myself from cheering too hard. Given the media's attention on us, I know they'd run with my fanboying for Sid.

"Captain Wonder Kid strikes again," Malik says with admiration.

"He's a beast," Idris replies.

I just nod and grin.

Sid is presented with the All-Star MVP Trophy during the winner's ceremony. He smiles as he raises it over his head, muscles flexing. He looks badass. A champion's champion.

My skin prickles, recalling the pleasure of those strong hands and the warmth of his sexy, smiling mouth. As the ceremony comes to an end, Sid scans the sea of people chanting his name. My heart rate ticks up as his gaze pans closer and closer to where I'm seated. Our gazes lock, and a tingling warmth courses through my body. I want to mouth *congratulations,* but there are cameras everywhere. I hold his gaze until he turns away, smiling. He daps players and the coaching staff before he retreats to the locker room. I'm about to turn to Idris when Katrina emerges from the entrance of the tunnel. Sid steps to the side to hug her. As he's pulling away, she reaches up and plants a kiss on his lips.

Oof! She wraps her arms around his waist as he pulls his head back. It's done so smoothly that I can't tell if it was a natural end to the kiss or if he broke it intentionally. The cameras eat up their exchange.

My heart is racing, and my stomach feels like it's been pumped with cement. So, this is what being one of Sid's casual lovers feels like. I palm my gut-punched stomach as Harry asks if I want to roll with him to an after-party. I stammer something about being wiped and needing to head home. He studies me, and I think he's going to call bullshit but says, "Rest up, bruh. You don't look so great."

Yeah, I'm a fucking idiot. I conflated hot sex with something more meaningful.

While the regular season doesn't resume until Thursday, I know I'll need a few days to get my head right. Or a lifetime. Who am I kidding? I have it bad for Sid.

I duck my head and slip out of the arena, pausing for some autographs. Then, I stop by my local grocery store to pick up dinner. I get a text from Tevin when I get home. It's a link to a slideshow of celebrity photos from the All-Star Game. The media's speed never ceases to amaze me. I click on it, and my pulse quickens when my photo fills the screen. There are two— one of me watching the game and one of my hickey zoomed in.

I read the caption.

> *Knights Pretty Boy Ty should change his name to Lothario after being seen spotting a gigantic hickey and bruised lip during Sunday's All-Star Game. We wonder who's the lucky lady."*

I thumb down the text. As far as the press goes, it's pretty harmless. I scroll down and groan at a photo of Katrina's frame pressed against Sid's body after the game. My brain immediately replays her mouth wrapped around his cock on Christmas.

Fuck me. Why did I have to watch them?

My regret and I toss the phone on the counter. After I put dinner on, I leave the kitchen to change into sweats, opting to go shirtless. I set up to eat in the living room, turning to ESPN, where they're playing game highlights. Seeing Sid on the screen makes me think about him sleeping with Katrina tonight. My stomach roils. I push the thoughts out of my head, turn off the TV, and take my dinner to the patio to finish. I'm exhausted by the time I take the first bite. This is why I refuse to date. I hate distractions. I need to be focused on my game. Feeling over this day, I make my wake to my room, drop my sweats, and climb under the covers. The same scent that made me orgasm earlier makes me miserable and lonely now, so I drag myself out of bed and rip the sheets off.

I'm finished putting clean sheets on the bed when the doorbell rings. I pull up the camera feed on my phone and freeze—Sid's standing at my front door with two duffel bags. I'm flooded with conflicting emotions. My ears are pounding even as my thumb stabs the buzzer on my phone to grant him entry, and I move towards the foyer.

I'm in too deep.

The second our gazes latch, he drops his bags and envelops me in a hug. Every cell in my body relaxes into him as he dips his head and crushes his lips against mine. I moan as his tongue pierces my lips, demanding entry. He presses the small of my lower back closer to him. I kiss along his lips, jaw, and cheeks.

How is it possible for me to have missed him this much when I saw him only a couple of hours ago?

"How are you here right now?" I ask.

He rips a moan from me when he suctions my neck hard, then licks over the area before kissing it gently.

"I couldn't get here fast enough. I sped through interviews, tossed champagne back with the team, and then ran to the hotel to grab my bags. Mind if I stay here with you? Both of us having a few days off is too good an opportunity to pass up." His dark, raspy voice fuels the ache of my erection as his feverish kisses glide over my dimples and freckles.

He wants to stay with me for a few days. Fuck, yes.

I groan when his fingers slide past my drawstring and take hold of my cock.

But what about after?

I rut against him, desperate for friction.

What are we and where does Katrina fit in?

I need answers.

"Wait—" I say, voice hoarse, my thoughts warring between my brain and dick.

He stiffens. The light in his eyes flickers, and I hate that I caused it.

"I have to admit something."

"Okay," he replies, releasing me.

"I saw you and Katrina after the game."

"That was—"

"Just hear me out. I know casual is easy for you, and I guess it's been for me too. I don't understand why it feels so intense between us, but it does. I've fought hard to get to the league and need to focus on my game. You know what I have to do for my parents. I can't get sidetracked, and just seeing you with Katrina kinda fucked me up. I'm not cut out to be a part of your rotation of—"

"Whoa, hold up. Nothing happened between me and Katrina tonight. I hugged her, and she congratulated me on the win. Yes, she kissed me at the game, but I pulled away. She asked if we could hang out after, and I told her I had plans. I plan to meet up with her later to explain that we can't hook up anymore. I didn't want to be an asshole in front of cameras. I promise. It really has been casual between us."

I have so many questions, but the one that rolls off my tongue surprises me. "Will she be hurt?"

"It's not like that. She's always been straight up with me about seeing other people. When we meet up, it's always to hook up. I don't get the sense she's emotionally invested in me. Her being at the game tonight wasn't for me. It was part of a press tour for her movie. When I told her we couldn't link tonight, she didn't bat an eye. I told you Kat and I were casual. I wouldn't lie to you."

I don't know why I ignored him every time he said it. Maybe it's a sign I should probably work on the whole not trusting people thing.

"For the record," he continues, "this isn't casual for me. I might not have been clear last night. It's not casual for me when I experience this kind of connection with someone. I've only ever had that once, but it's not because I didn't want it."

"What are you saying, exactly?" I ask, wrapping my arms around my chest.

"Damn, you're stubborn...I'm saying I want you to myself."

My jaw hangs open. "Want how?"

"Like me and you, committed."

His words hit like a dust storm, completely blinding me.

"Commit how? Like exclusively hook up?"

"Not just hook up, all of it, and yes, exclusively," he says with so much conviction, it unsettles me. "I don't share."

"How?" I scoff. "You're like the most famous athlete on the planet right now. If we came out, our careers would be a sideshow."

I can see my name plastered in headlines any time he's mentioned. I've never wanted his fame. It's surprising he can even fuck in private, considering the way the media rides his dick. They obsess over everyone he dates, and they'd pry into my life too. Every time we'd face off, idiots would question the legitimacy of the win or loss. They'd insinuate that we threw the game for each other. It'd be harder than ever to keep my head down and focus on chasing rings. I'd lose focus and maybe even my place in the league. My parents' deaths would have been in vain.

Holy fuck!

I can't—we can't do this.

And how the fuck is he so confident about me? He can have

anyone. The thought of him being with anyone else...seeing him with Katrina was a sledgehammer to my stomach. If we were to do this, it would be terrifying how much our relationship would consume me. I can't choose him over my career. I have to see things through for my parents. Even if...fuck. I rub the sharp ache in my chest. Even if it means passing up the opportunity to be with the first person I've fallen in love with.

Christ!

How'd I allow myself to be so stupid? I can't be in love. It'd ruin everything I need to do. I need to grind and be selfish.

I clasp my stomach to keep it from collapsing. The more I try to breathe, the more air seeps out. I clasp a hand over my strangled sternum and turn away from him, trying to stave off the alarm I'm choking.

"W-what's happening?"

I bend forward, gasping for air. My palms clam up as sweat trickles down my back.

"Breathe, baby! Can you speak?" His voice trembles as he bolts to kneel in front of me. I wheeze as I shake my head.

"Should I call an ambulance?" He reaches for his phone. The idea of an ambulance showing up deepens my panic. I lurch forward, knocking his phone out of his hand, and shake my head again.

"Okay. No ambulance. Breathe. Just like this." He sucks in a breath and exhales slowly.

I can't. There's no air.

I clench my eyes shut and dig the heel of my palm into my sternum, trying to unknot the tightness.

I hear Adam's voice though the memory is hazy. Was it five things you can see or five things you can feel? I take a guess, unpeeling my eyes and searching the room for five things I can see—Sid, books, fuck...the room starts to spin.

I clench my eyes shut, but the room spins in the darkness, so I open them again.

...duffel bags, bulb, door.

Sid says something, but it's drowned out as I search for four things I can feel. I touch my chest and the wall, kneel, and then the hardwood floor and the rug. As I inhale the scent of Sid's cologne, a streak of air pierces through the tightness in my chest. I draw another breath, focusing on his scent, then another, until my chest expands with air. I tilt back until I'm sitting on the floor and bury my head in my hands. My skin is slick with sweat.

"Baby..." He kneels in front of me. "Was that a panic attack?" His voice is gentle and thick with worry. I'm mortified he's seeing me like this. I stare at the spot on the floor where my tears have pooled. I nod, keeping my gaze pointed to the floor.

"Do they happen often?"

I nod again.

"How can I help?"

You can't. No one can.

I clear my throat. "It's over."

The stinging shame and embarrassment, on the other hand, are mushrooming. I want to crawl into a dark hole and stay there until the shame passes in a hundred years. And the exhaustion. I could sleep for a month, and it probably wouldn't be enough.

"I just need to sleep. You should go celebrate with you—"

"No," he interjects. His fingertips graze the underside of my chin. I fight the urge to clench my eyes shut as my gaze crawls to meet his. I'm not sure what I expected to find, but it wasn't the watery eyes staring back at me.

"I want to see all of you, remember?"

I reach up and wipe the tears from his face. "I'm sorry...I scared you."

He shakes his head. "I scared you first by saying I wanted you for myself. I'm sorry."

"I want you too." The words fly out of my mouth.

God, I'm so confused. My heart wants one thing, but my brain tells me to run fast and stick to the plan.

"It's just you're famous as fuck, and I'm private. I plan to fly below the radar for as long as I can. I got freaked out when I thought about what it would mean for us to be together publicly," I admit.

He leans back to sit on the floor as his outstretched legs bracket my thighs. "It's incredible. The first person in my adult life I want to go all in for doesn't want any part of my fame." He shakes his head. "You don't know how many people I've had to cut out because that's all they want from me."

"If I were with you, it'd be just for you."

He nods. "I know. I knew that from the jump. I don't care about fame. I work hard to keep my public image focused on ball and the issues I care about."

"I want the same thing."

"I don't want to push you, but we could make this work," he says, reaching for my hand. "My family already knows I'm bi. I see myself coming out publicly later. We can be together but keep our relationship out of the public eye."

How? For one, we live in separate states. Could we really make long distance work? Also, how would we explain our being seen together publicly? We can't hide behind closed doors all the time. As I gaze into his soulful eyes and absorb the swell of emotions that make me want to hold on to him and never let go, figuring out the details seems less important.

I release a heavy sigh. "Okay."

"Okay?" His eyes widen with hope.

"Okay."

"Okay, as in we're doing this? You're mine?" he asks, a shy grin peeking through.

I grin. "I'm yours."

He pulls me into his lap, and we grin at each other like idiots.

"I'm yours too...only yours," he says, sending a flare of heat up my spine. He leans in to kiss me, and I deepen it, drawing a low moan from him.

"I have nightmares and panic attacks sometimes," I admit once we pull apart.

His forehead creases. "When did they start?"

"After my parents died."

"What can I do to help when they happen?"

I shrug. "You kinda did it already by reminding me to breathe. Adam does the same. You saw me scanning the room and touching random stuff earlier. It's a technique he taught me."

"I can do that. We can take this at your pace, but there's nothing you can't tell me."

Does that extend to my doubts? Only one way to find out.

"Uh, are you sure you want to be exclusive? It's not for everyone."

"Yes. I'm not a guy who would make a decision like this half-heartedly. I've been single for a long time for a reason. I know what I want, and I say what I mean. Despite what they say about me, I've always wanted to build a life with someone." Admittedly, I'm guilty of believing most of what I read about him. "Lately, hooking up with people without a real connection has felt empty. What I felt last night. Fuck. I didn't realize how starved I was for it. You and I travel more than 40,000 miles a year each season. We won't see each other nearly as much as we want. I don't want to waste time," he continues.

I think back to my teammates in college who dreamt of making it to the league, copping luxury cars, and fucking their way through Hollywood, just like him. It'll take me a minute to replace that image of him with the man before me.

"This is new for me. I'm yours. There's no question about it. I just need a minute to accept that we're doing this," I say.

"You mean you need time to accept that I'm yours?"

I nod.

"You'll see. I'd never give you a reason to doubt it."

I cock an eyebrow. "And casual lovers kissing you at games?"

"Never again. I get the feeling my gorgeous boyfriend wouldn't like it."

"Facts," I fire back.

He grins, buries his face in my neck, and kisses his favorite spot. "Hey"—he levels his gaze with mine—"I thought the victor got the spoils. You didn't congratulate me."

He's right. I forgot everything and saw red after seeing him with Katrina. "My bad. Congratulations, champ. You were phenomenal—forty-one points, six rebounds, three assists, two blocks, and a steal. Sealed the W and earned MVP!"

His face lights up with astonishment, signaling he clearly doesn't get how deep I'm in for him.

"Thank you," he says, grinning. "Did you catch my message to you when I scored the forty points you commanded?"

"Your hand over your heart?"

"You saw it." His soft smile tugs at my chest.

"I did. Damn, that's sweet." I lean in to kiss him again. He tucks his knees in like he's moving to stand. I start to climb off of him when he wraps an arm around my waist, anchoring me in place.

"Wrap your arms around my neck."

I scoff. "There's no way." He's strong, but there's no way he can peel us both off of the floor.

He holds me by the waist and in one swift move, I'm tilted backward as he climbs to a kneeling position. I chuckle nervously as I hook my arms around his neck. He takes a deep breath, and then I'm tilted back again as he jumps to a squatting position.

"You were saying," he says as he stands upright.

I groan. "And now I'm hard."

He walks us toward the bedroom.

"There's a photo online covering my hickey," I tell him as he kisses the spot.

"Word? Seeing it on you at the game did it for me. I've officially devolved into a caveman."

Possessive Sid turns me on...all the fucking way. "Come sex me up, Captain."

"No. Not until you're healed. You said you were sore earlier."

"Noooo," I protest.

"Oh, that reminds me. I stopped to pick up fiber supplements on the way here."

"You're gonna spoil me."

"Duh," he replies. "I'm hungry. Can we order grub?"

"I cooked."

"Word?" He changes directions, navigating us toward the kitchen.

"Hey." He stares into my eyes. "When that actor calls, tell him to fuck off. Better yet, pass me the phone, and I'll tell him."

"What act—oh, Will? Wait, I wanted to leave the party with you. I was only going to fuck him to get you out of my system." It sounds corny now that I've said it out loud.

He halts and pins me against the hallway wall for leverage.

"I'm honored to have been your first with a man. I know you can be with anyone you want, but the thought of him touching you makes me..." His eyes narrow, his jaw ticks, and oh my god, there's something wrong with me. I'm rock hard. Possessive Sid turns me the fuck on. I rut my cock against his stomach.

"I have a secret," I whisper into his ear. "When I woke up hard yesterday, I was dreaming about you. I fucked myself with a dildo, wishing you were inside of me. When I'm alone in my hotel room on the road, I imagine myself down on my knees, taking you down my throat. And when I stroke myself—" His eyes darken as he squeezes my ass, grinding me against him. "I imagine my dick sinking into you. When I come all over my chest, it's your name that I gasp into the pillow."

"Damn." He balances me with one hand and adjusts his erection. "I was right about you."

I send him a questioning look.

"I knew you had a filthy side. I can tell our sexting is gonna be off the chains."

I scoff. "You knew I have a filthy side? How?"

"You play ball like you're incredible at fucking. So sexy."

I suck my teeth. *That's not a thing.*

"And the way you eye fucked the shit out of me on Christmas...it was feral."

I burst out laughing. "Did you have to wear the onesie all day?"

He grins. "I regret nothing."

"C'mon, let's feed you so I can eat too," I say.

"You didn't eat yet?" he asks as he adjusts himself again.

"I'm not hungry for food, sexy man."

"Ah, you want my cum." He licks over my hickey and steers us to the kitchen. "We're meditating before bed by the way," he says.

"Yeah...had a feeling that was coming."

BEING WITH SID FOR THE LAST TWO DAYS HAS BEEN PURE BLISS. I can't believe it's already our last night together. We fell into a rhythm of cooking together, reading, exercising, and long drives along the Pacific Coast Highway. We woke up early yesterday and drove to an ultra-secluded spot on the beach to watch the sunrise. And, of course, there's been lots of delicious sex. We're insatiable for each other. We carry lube and condoms with us everywhere. A set of bench presses in my gym turned into me riding Sid reverse cowboy position.

Sid loves Southern California and said that he could see himself living here. It's too compelling of an idea.

I'm lying in his arms on my living room couch savoring the last few hours together. We're both quiet, listening to the crackle of cherry wood in the fireplace.

"I think I'm ready to talk about my first boyfriend and best friend growing up," he says, breaking the quiet.

My heartbeat kicks up knowing the story ends in tragedy.

I take a steadying breath.

I place a kiss on his chest and tuck in closer to him. "Tell me," I reply softly.

"His name was Paul. He and his dad moved to my block when I was in middle school. We immediately took to each other. His mother left when he was five to start a family with a new guy she'd been having an affair with. We bonded over both having deadbeat parents. He was super talented, with both brains and athleticism. He loved football the way I love basketball. Man, he had an extraordinary memory and could easily recall things that he learned. I always wanted to be smart like him. He needed to understand how a thing worked and would relentlessly seek answers, whereas I would shrug and be cool with leaving it a mystery.

"We often spent nights at each other's houses, talking late, playing video games, and dreaming about being in the NFL and NBA. Something shifted between us during my sophomore year of high school. It was like one day we both turned around and realized the other person was attractive. Or maybe it was the way girls started looking at us that made us really look at one another. We had both dated randomly, but we were like Kieran and Tommy in that our friendship was always more important than the girls we dated. One day, he slept over at my house. Until then, he'd flirt with me here and there, but I didn't think too much of it. He was flirtatious by nature, or so I thought. He came over pretty upset, I remember. His dad drank a lot and would often pick fights. He was verbally abusive and sometimes things would get physical. My mom was working a night shift, so we had the place to ourselves. Paul was too upset to tell me about the fight. I tried to distract him by offering to play video games, but he wasn't in the mood.

"I'll never forget the look that swept over his face when he turned to me and said: *Nobody wants me. I sometimes think it would be better if I was dead.* His tone was flat like he'd thought of the simplest solution for how he'd felt. I didn't realize how much he meant to me until he planted the idea of his death in my mind. It made me sick. Paul saw panic spread across my face and raced over to me. He said he was just bullshitting and didn't mean it.

"I was freaked out because I knew he had meant it. I remember feeling ashamed of the tears stinging my eyes.

"He kept asking me to say something, but I was too choked to speak.

"A part of me knew that once Paul had put an idea in his head, he was relentless about making it happen. At that moment, something cracked between us. I said once in therapy that it was the illusion that we were on the same path. I always thought we were in sync about believing in a future where we would both go pro and live the lives of our wildest dreams. With a few words, I realized it was a lie.

"I asked him to promise that he would never leave me. He looked at me in a far-off way and promised. Then, he wiped my eyes. He was bigger than me—he kind of had Tommy's build. He had these big ol' ears that stuck out and gave him a distinct look and deep-set eyes that told you he was intelligent before he opened his mouth. Growing into his looks, his size, athleticism, and smarts made him sought after.

"After he promised he wouldn't leave me, we hugged, and I held him crazy tight, afraid that if I released him, he'd disappear.

"I pulled back and held his face. I wanted to show him how much I loved him, so I kissed him. A quick peck on his lips. My eyes went wide when I realized what I had done, what I had admitted. But then he kissed me back and things progressed quickly.

"That's how we became boyfriends. The next few months were solid. We were best friends at school and couldn't keep off each other once we got home. The idea of coming out seemed crazy. Homophobia was in the air in our neighborhood. Two guys couldn't hug or show any affection without declaring 'no homo' or 'pause.' It was toxic as hell. In a way, I've never seen Paul happier or sadder. It was like knowing that he was gay was the most depressing thing to learn about himself, thanks to his homophobic father. Yet, behind closed doors, he didn't hold back with me. I knew that he loved me. What we had was pure and honest, even if the world around us told us otherwise."

"How did you feel about learning that you had romantic feelings for him?" I interject as I raise my face to kiss his chin while rubbing soft circles over his chest.

He kisses my forehead in return before answering. "Paul was all that mattered. I didn't care what anyone else thought. I knew it wasn't safe for us to be out. That was confirmed later on during my senior year when I had to fight bullies off of Kieran. But I knew that I wouldn't live in my hood forever. I also knew that my mom wasn't homophobic, and we would still be good if I came out, a security that Paul didn't have."

"I'm glad you had your mom. The idea of you having a dad like Paul's makes me want to rage."

"Me too. I told him we would be set once I was drafted. By then, I had a sense that if I kept playing at a high level, I would make the draft. Paul was too practical to dream with me. The same curiosity I loved about him could also make him see things too black and white. He couldn't fathom a Black NBA or NFL player being out in the league. He thought we'd be closeted our entire lives, so he became depressed and eventually started pulling away. His dad saw us kissing once and lost it on him. I pulled his dad off him, absorbing some of his blows. His dad forbade me from stepping foot in their house ever again."

"What the fuck?" I clench my fists. "No kid deserves that."

"Yeah, his dad was vicious. We confessed everything to my mom that night. She told Paul he could stay with us, but he was too convinced he was a burden to accept. She lifted Paul's chin and told him there was nothing wrong with our love and that she was proud of us for following our hearts. The three of us stayed up late that night eating and talking.

"That night was one of the best nights of my life. Being able to tell someone I love about us felt unreal. Even Paul's black and blue eyes were bright as we laughed with Mom. I wasn't naive. I knew one good night couldn't undo the insidious toll of his father's abuse or his mom's abandonment. His grades steadily declined as his fighting with his dad worsened, and he started skipping school and football practice. He ghosted me. I sometimes saw him in the stands at my games, but he'd leave before the end. The last time I saw him, I confronted him during halftime at one of my games. I followed him outside and asked him, more yelled at him, to explain why he'd been ghosting me. He just kept saying that he loved me and would never truly leave me. I remember shaking him and asking him to stop hurting us. To hold it together a little longer. There were a few people around, but I didn't care. I needed him to see the carnage of his apathy. He pushed me off of him and I flew backward, hitting my head against the wall. I knew he regretted it the minute he did it. It didn't even hurt. It just sounded bad.

"His eyes grew wide, shocked by what he had done.

"I told him I was okay and reached for him, but he evaded my grasp.

"*I love you, and I'm sorry* were the last words he said to me.

"My assistant coach came outside and yelled for me to get back to the game.

"After, I ran home to talk to him. When I reached the block, I saw an ambulance driving away and a crowd in front of Paul's house. I ran to my mom, who was leaning against our fence sobbing. Her face told me everything I needed to know.

"When we got to the hospital, Paul was already gone. He had overdosed on pills. His dad didn't find him in time."

"I'm so sorry," I say. I raise my head from Sid's chest, and his shirt is soaked with my tears.

I pull off my T-shirt and wipe his face.

"I remember when I asked if you thought I was haunted, and you said something like people are haunted by the ugliness life throws their way. You were talking from experience," I recount.

He nods. "Very few times in my life have I felt violent, but when I saw Paul's dad the next morning, I lost it. The men on the block had to pull me off of him. I am not proud of it. He didn't even block my blows.

"I couldn't bring myself to go to Paul's funeral. I was too angry at him, but I went to the cemetery and watched him lowered into the ground from afar.

"The next few weeks were a nightmare. I watched old girl-friends who meant nothing to him cry around the school, feigning heartbreak—meanwhile, I was eviscerated. I woke up upset every night. I thought I'd be swallowed by the black hole of his absence. A few months later, Kieran came to live with us. He was in bad shape too, having been thrown out for being gay. Feeling broken together helped us feel less broken somehow. Then the bullies came for him. Protecting him gave me purpose. Having someone else I could share my memories of Paul with, not just as a friend but as my boyfriend, helped."

I shake my head. Life makes no sense. It brings people in need together while taking those we need from us.

"I can tell it's hard on you to go back there. Thank you for telling me."

"Not as deep, but it still cuts," he says. He nestles me deeper into his arms. "I could see him in the NFL one day. I still can sometimes when I watch a game."

"The world is a joyless, purposeless, and dark place when you're depressed. You couldn't have saved him."

"I know. I eventually realized that I couldn't, but it still gutted me."

I nod. "It would have gutted me too."

"I know that there are other Pauls out there. It's why I support LGBTQIA suicide prevention organizations."

"Yeah?" In everything I've read about him over the years, it never came up.

He nods. "It isn't as public as my criminal justice reform work. Hey, look at me." His voice sounds raw.

I tilt my gaze up.

"Promise me that you will seriously consider seeing a therapist."

I stiffen from being caught off guard. How did this suddenly become about me?

"I'm not Paul."

"I know you aren't, but I can tell you're struggling."

I move to sit up. "Everyone struggles. I'm good."

He stares at me like I'm splintered, and I hate it. "Let's get you help for the anxiety attacks and nightmares."

I don't need help. Why doesn't anyone think that I'm capable of handling my shit? I shake my head and shift my gaze to the floor.

"Hey...look at me."

"Let's just drop it," I say, crossing my arms across my chest.

"Hey...look at me," he pleads. The deep but gentle pitch of his voice softens my resolve. I drag my head up to meet his gaze.

"You're not alone anymore. I know you can take care of yourself. That's not what this is."

"Then what is it? I already feel corny for having an attack in front of you."

"Corny..." He shakes his head and shifts to sit upright. "Ty, you're one of the smartest, most capable, not to mention sexiest people I know. And I know some sexy mofos," he jokes.

I bite down on the inside of my lip to hold back a grin. I sense a "but" coming.

"You're dope without even trying to be. I'd never think to use the word 'corny' in the same sentence with you." He scoots closer to me. My shoulders drop, inhaling his addictive scent and melting from the warmth of his mouth on my neck. My body is so greedy for him. I'm never more aware of my skin than when his lips brush against it.

"But you've also been through a lot, and that takes its toll, and it's not always easy to make sense of it by yourself. I think talking to someone trained to help would be good for you. I'll drop it for now, but think about it."

I know there's some truth to what he's saying, but I'm not ready. I just want to focus on my game this season. If it were any other topic, I'd be touched that he cares so much, but this one irks me for some reason. I've been taking care of myself for a while now.

"Okay," I grunt.

"You're so sexy when you're angry."

I turn my face to kiss him. He deepens the kiss, exploring my mouth in a way that rarely ends with us still clothed.

We end up grabbing lube and frotting until we orgasm, and then we fall asleep, spent, clinging to each other.

Chapter Fifteen

I t's been three months since Sid and I became official, and damn, it's been amazing. I get all the hype surrounding the honeymoon phase. We haven't been able to spend as much time together as I crave, with our teams competing in the playoffs. The precious time we're together usually results in us spent and naked, wrapped up around each other. We traded keys to each other's places to slip in and out as our schedules permit.

I worked my ass off and feel good about my regular season performance. I averaged twenty-one points, six rebounds, and five assists per game, beating the stats of all other rookies, though Jeff Banks—my friend from my college days—came in a close second. You'd think joining a league with veterans and All-Stars would humble him, but he still shows out every night like he's back at Duke.

In early April, I won the NBA Rookie of the Year Award, an annual award given to the top rookie of the regular season. The winner is selected by a panel of American and Canadian broadcasters and sportswriters who cast first, second, and third place votes. The votes are worth different points, and the player with the highest total points wins the award. To celebrate, Sid surprised me with a getaway to Mo'orea, where he booked us a remote villa. Tommy and Kieran joined us. When the four of us weren't in the ocean, Sid and I were holed up in our room. We had both gotten tested before the trip so we could stop using condoms. We made love like there was no tomorrow, having been separated for weeks, grinding to finish the regular season.

Now the playoffs are almost over. It began with sixteen teams, the eight best from the NBA's East and West conferences. The winner of each conference progresses to the NBA Finals Championship Series to compete to become the Finals champions. It's what we all compete for, season after season. Not only does the championship team win a trophy, but a gold ring encrusted with diamonds is awarded to the team's players, coaches, and members of the executive front office. The ring is a valuable symbol of a team's victory.

Both the Knights and the Marvels advanced to the playoffs given our high rankings, but the Bay Area Hawks defeated my team in game five of the semi-finals. While we fought hard, it was a long shot for us to take it with both Tevin and Malik out for the series with injuries. Sid's team made it to the Finals for a matchup against the San Antonio Finches. In game four, Sid posted a whopping fifty-two points with eight rebounds and seven assists, banking half of the Marvels' fourth-quarter points.

Tonight's game is the sixth of the series, and Sid could take it all. The Marvels lead the series with three wins to the Finches' two. Everyone is confident that the series will go to game seven as San Antonio is unlikely to go down without a fight, not to mention they have home-court advantage. I'm not stupid enough to count Sid out. If anyone could get it done tonight, it's him.

The Marvels came out strong, moving the ball well, creating open looks, and fighting hard to defend the basket. In the first half alone, they banked fifty-nine points. The Finches defended their home well, too, which is why there's less than a minute left on the game clock, and the Marvels are down one point.

Sid passes the ball to Justin, who has a wide-open shot. Justin jumps and releases the ball, falling backward. The second he releases it, I can tell it's too strong. I grab my temples as the ball ricochets off the rim. I expect the Finches to catch the rebound, but Sid flies in out of nowhere and slams it in with a left-handed dunk.

"Yes!" I yell, fisting the air.

The Finches take possession and post a layup despite the Marvels' defensive maneuvers. The Marvels are down a point again when Sid catches the ball and posts a two-pointer.

That's it, babe! I clap. *Just like that!*

The Finches point guard is wide fucking open and takes possession of the ball. He's about to release a corner three when he's fouled by Kristian, the Marvels' power forward.

"Nooooo, Kristian! You idiot!" I yell. Their point guard makes two of the three free throws, bringing San Antonio back in the lead by one point.

Fuck! I clasp my head.

It's the last possession…

"End it here, Sid! C'mon!" I bark at the television.

Sid takes the next possession.

This is it…

He dribbles left and hesitates as their point guard advances on him. He cuts right, crossing the ball behind his back.

I suck in a breath as he almost gets jammed up when their center pushes in and attempts a steal.

Eleven seconds left on the clock…

Sid's quick! He cuts the ball between his legs, then spins left, barely shaking their center, who is on his heels.

Ay! Watch your back!

He glances over his shoulder like he hears me before gluing his eyes on the rim.

I pace the room, trying to figure out his next move.

The crowd screams for the Finches to defend their turf when Sid hits a crossover and charges forward.

Every muscle in my body is strung tight. "What are you doing, babe?" He'll have to power through a row of men to get even remotely close to the rim.

I hunch down and palm the sides of my head as I weigh his options. He can't bum-rush their defense without committing a foul, but he could go for a mid-range shot. I follow his gaze, and that's when I see it!

Sid slices through an opening between the Finches' shooting guard and power forward, who, expecting a charge, plant themselves in place.

Fools!

He explodes off of his back foot and soars through the air. Back arched, he draws his balled arm back behind his head like a taut bowstring. With a kind of superhuman control over his body, he spins 360 degrees and catapults his arm forward, slamming the ball through the rim and beating the game clock by a sliver of a second!

Oh. My. God!

My mouth hangs open.

He did it!

He fucking did it!

I almost don't believe it until the camera pans to the scorers' table, and Pat James, a veteran TV announcer, falls out of his chair and shrieks for a replay of Sid's meta-human spin and poster dunk that has to go down as one of the most incredible shots in the history of the game.

I lose my shit, shadowboxing the air, jumping up and down on the couch until my throat aches from howling. I knew he could get it done.

I knew it!

A tearful Sid appears on the screen, wrapped up in an embrace by Lily, Kieran, and Tommy, the four of them forming a tight circle. I pull the collar of my T-shirt up to wipe my eyes. They're surrounded by a frenzy of players, families, and the press. Confetti and balloons rain down, littering the floor.

My phone rings, startling me. I send Tevin to voicemail. I skipped his watch party to watch the game at home alone because I knew I'd be emotional if the Marvels won. More emotional than I could explain to my teammates.

Katharine Thurgood from ESPN approaches Sid for an interview, but Justin intervenes, pulling Sid into a tight embrace, and they tearfully exchange words.

"Sid, could you describe what this moment feels like?" Katharine asks him once he's back in front of the camera.

My pulse races, staring at the intelligent, kind-hearted, and hard-working man on the screen. I think about his journey to this point—the grief and heartbreak from Paul's death, and fighting his way here through sheer talent, effort, and determination. This moment isn't about winning a championship or copping a ring. It's about a lifetime of resilience and hard work. He worked his ass off to get here. Considering his press commitments, I doubt I'll see him over the next few days, but I can't wait to tell him I'm so proud of him.

"This was a tough win, and it came down to the wire, but somehow, I got an open look and made it to the rim on that last play." He stares up at the sky, shaking his head. "I love this team. I spent the last five years pouring my blood, sweat, and heart into this game." His voice breaks. "It's been a difficult road to get here. I just kept my head down and worked hard. MIAMI, THIS IS FOR YOU!"

Katharine's in the middle of asking another question when Sid's pulled away by the Marvels' general manager.

"Hold on!" Sid says, turning back to the camera. "To my

family at home watching"—he places his hand on his heart, his signal to me—"god, I wish you were here. I love you, and I can't wait to celebrate with you. I'm bringing this trophy home to you." He sniffs as a fresh set of tears tumble down his gorgeous face.

My vision turns blurry. I've wanted to tell him I love him for a while now, but I've chickened out every time. I've never done this before. I don't know how soon is too soon to say the words. And now he's said them first in front of the entire world like a goddamn boss. I rub the pang in my chest. I'd give anything to be with him right now. I've never wanted for us to be out more than at this moment. I shoot him a quick congratulations text, saving what I want to say to him when I see him.

When I look back at the screen, I huff out a laugh as Kristian sneaks behind Sid and drains a giant cup of something icy over his head. Sid's mouth drops open, and then he laughs as he tilts his head to the side, shaking water from his ears. He whips his wet towel at a laughing Kristian, who darts out of the way before it makes contact.

During the awards ceremony, Sid is crowned the Finals MVP. I join the crowd chanting "MVP!" as Sid raises the trophy over his head. There are more Marvels fans in the crowd than I thought. The team congregates for pictures with the championship trophy, and then the festivities continue back in the locker room, where they don goggles and spray each other with champagne. Sid, double-fisting bottles, chases after his coach. Justin joins in but almost loses it on the slippery floor. Bursting with laughter, their coach throws up his hands in surrender once he's cornered and gets showered with bubbly.

After the broadcast ends, I'm buzzing with energy, and the quiet of the house is depressing. I grab my headphones, throw on my running shoes, and go for a run.

The cool night air kisses my skin as I take in the open stretch of road—not a person or car in sight. Sid got a ring! I grin as joy swells in my chest. "Woohoo!'" I yell, tilting back my head. As a long-time fan, I would've been rooting for Sid tonight even if we'd never met. But damn, the jubilation is something else entirely now that I know him—now that I'm in love with him. He keeps inspiring me. I'm more determined than ever to work hard so that one day soon, it's me raising a trophy over my head.

After my run, I shower, down a protein shake, and then climb into bed. I scroll through social media clips of the Marvels' after-party. In one clip, I glimpse Sid clad in a white T-shirt, championship-fitted hat, and ripped jeans, rapping with King D on stage. In another, he has an unlit cigar in his mouth, head bent forward, listening to his coach. He's surrounded by bottle service waitresses clad in his jerseys—worn as crop tops —bootie shorts, and garters.

For fuck's sake, the thirst is real.

I close the app and throw my phone on the charger.

I'M JOLTED AWAKE BY A THUMPING SOUND.

I listen for noise, but I'm met with only the sound of my breathing, so I shrug it off as most likely an animal brushing against the house. Living surrounded by mountains, I've seen everything from bears, mountain lions, coyotes, and snakes.

I check my phone and groan when I realize it's only 5:23 a.m. I see a missed call and text from two hours ago from Sid and grin.

SID

I love you so fucking much

I start to text him back when I hear the thumping again, followed by steps approaching my bedroom door. Before I can react, Sid tiptoes in, showered, with a towel around his waist. He freezes when he sees that I'm awake.

My mouth drops open. "You're home?" I kick back the sheets and launch myself at him. "I didn't think I'd see you for days!"

He catches me and laughs. "You thought I could stay away from you when I'm off work?" He kisses his favorite spot on my neck. "Figured instead of missing you all night, I'd dip and come home."

"I wanted to be with you too." I brush a kiss against his lips. "Congratulations, champ. You copped a ring and closed out an off-the-charts season! I'm so proud of you!" I press my forehead against his.

"Thanks, baby. It's surreal. I've dreamed about this forever, and now that it's here..." He shakes his head as his eyes well up. "It's better than what I dreamed."

"You've earned this. This win symbolizes your resilience, determination, and hard work." I wipe away his tears. "Hold on for a second. I got you something." I slide down to my feet and walk to the dresser.

His eyes widen as I hand him the jewelry box. "W-what if I lost?"

I shake my head. "It never crossed my mind."

He studies me, and his eyes well up.

"It's nothing," I say, even as my eyes start to fill. I nod towards the box. "Open it."

He dips down and kisses my forehead before wiping his eyes and removing the box's lid. "Whoa...No way!" His wide-eyed gaze flicks to me. "How?"

I wink. "It's a secret. You like it?"

He blows out air, then swipes a hand over his mouth as he stares in awe at the gold and sapphire crystal Patek Phillipe watch with an alligator band. "Baby, this is my dream watch!"

I grin and mentally pat myself on the back. I saw the stunning watch bookmarked when I was using his iPad. When he made it to the Finals, I started brainstorming gift ideas, and this one popped into my head. I checked his watch drawer to confirm he didn't have it already, and from there, everything went smoothly.

"Flip it."

He turns the watch over and smiles at the engraving: *Sid King, Finals Champ, MVP, Legend.*

I also included the two-digit year.

He thumbs over the writing. "You really believed I could pull it off."

"It was your time." I reach for the watch, unclasp it, and slide it onto his wrist. Once fastened, we gaze at it, and it's gorgeous. I stare into his eyes. "You're a worthy champion. Congratulations."

As our tears flow together, he pulls me into a kiss that has us both pulsing.

"Lie down." I drop my briefs and pull off my T-shirt as he removes his towel, revealing his thickened length.

I reignite the fireplace and retrieve lube from the nightstand.

Crawling on top of him, I lick along his bottom lip slowly. He tries to capture my tongue in his mouth, but I pull away.

"I'm in charge tonight, MVP. Allow the victor his spoils."

I lick the side of his neck, then move down to his nipples and tug them with my teeth softly. I suck hard, then lick soothingly. He moans when I raise his arms, trail my tongue over his pits, and continue down his sculpted abs. I bury my nose in his groomed hair before licking across the tip of his cock and sucking him down, spending extra time on his head, eliciting hoarse moans and curses.

He groans when I pull off of him and reach into my toy drawer and retrieve a cock ring and dildo.

His puffy, half-lidded eyes, sexy smirk, and wet, engorged cock make my dick leak.

What a vision. I'm the luckiest man in the world.

I climb back on the bed and lap up his pre-cum before working my way down until his head fills my throat.

His head falls back, digging into the pillow. "Fuuuuck, you give the best head, baby."

I grin inwardly. I've had a lot of practice with him.

I use my hands to stroke him as my tongue trails down to his crease.

I apply slow licks across his rim in circular motions. He writhes and sputters curses and delicious moans. He fucks my hand as I penetrate him with my tongue, oscillating between licking and sucking. His legs are trembling when I replace my tongue with a lubed finger, penetrating his tight ring of muscle. He feels unbelievable, making my dick scream for attention. I ignore it, adding a second finger, working up to a third.

"Ahh, I'm gonna come," he warns me.

I pull back, lube up my cock and roll on the vibrator ring. I turn it on to the lowest setting, not wanting him to come too soon.

I stroke my cock a few times, staring into penetrating eyes dilated from ecstasy, and then I enter him. The vibration of the ring has us both moaning.

"Damn, you feel amazing."

He whimpers, teetering on the edge of orgasm.

I activate all of my muscles as I channel my strength into thrusting slowly. The only thing holding me back from coming is his euphoric moans. I love that shit. He fists the sheets as he comes apart from the pleasure of every stroke hitting his prostate. The vibration extends the tremors wracking through him. No one else gets to see him like this. It's fucking intoxicating.

"I can't—Christ—fuck," he cries out.

"Not yet." I use my free hand to grab lube to start fingering myself open. "My hard cock—ungh"—I bite my bottom lip hard to stop myself from coming—"was made for your tight hole. You feel fucking unbelievable. We fit perfectly, baby. Hold on for me a little longer."

His eyes roll closed, and his forehead glistens with sweat. I swipe up the pre-cum beading on his slit and suck it into my mouth.

I pull out of him and climb up his large frame.

He punches the sheet in protest, making me grin and dip down for a kiss, drinking in his moans. We kiss sloppily as he ruts against my pelvis, desperate for friction. The vibrator intensifies the sensation of his touch.

"I've never been fucked by a championship MVP," I whisper against his mouth.

His eyes widen when I straddle him and slowly sink down on his cock.

"Holy fuck!" he groans, gripping my hips as he grinds up into me.

Damn, he's deep. My head falls forward as he bites, then sucks his favorite spot on my neck while my ass swallows his cock over and over.

"Sid!" I shriek when he squeezes the globes of my ass and thrusts hard.

"Hmm?" he rasps, a lazy grin on his face.

I remember who's in charge tonight and lean back and grab the dildo. I roll on the vibrating ring and turn it to the highest setting. His eyes widen as I press it against his rim and push it in, slowly penetrating and riding him at the same pace. Two penetrations in, his abs contract, and his eyes roll closed.

I clench around him and fuck him deep with the dildo. "Come for me."

He tenses, and a hoarse "Bab-arghh-fuck," rips out of him as he fills me with his orgasm.

I'm on the edge myself as I take what I need and fuck myself on his cock.

The tips of his fingers wrap around my balls, and my vision wipes out.

"Ngh, Sid," I wail as I come hard. I'm bent over, catching my breath, when he swipes my cum off of his chest and sucks it into his mouth. He misses a strip, and I lick it up before I collapse against him.

After a few deep breaths, he nestles around me so that we're spooning.

"I love you too," I whisper, turning my face to kiss his lips.

He grins and tucks me closer to him.

Chapter Sixteen

J olted awake, I stab the heel of my palm against my sternum to trap the gurgling acid. The pressure punches its way up, dragging last night's dinner. Lurching to the side of the bed, I grab the wastebasket. As I fall back to my pillow, I pull in air and listen to the fading echoes of my mother's shriek. I fist the comforter to keep from palming my forehead like countless times before. There won't be blood. This is real life.

I stare out the window and darkness stares back. I reach for my phone and groan. It's only twelve minutes past four in the morning. There are two missed calls, a voicemail, and an unread text. I read the text first and grin.

A tinge of unease worms around my inflamed stomach. Tonight's our last together before Sid heads to Vegas for the Olympics training camp. It's no surprise he was selected to join the twelve-member U.S. Olympic Men's Basketball Team to represent the U.S. in Barcelona next month. It's been a crazy few weeks for him since winning the championship. Nonstop interviews and appearances on television, podcasts, everywhere.

I hit play on Adam's voicemail.

"Kiddo, I regret that when you get this message, I'd have already reached the ripe age of sixty-eight. You may be wondering how the heck I can age twenty-four years in a single day. Well, it's funny you ask. I thought the same when I woke up and saw today's date. I scratched my head and thought, well, now, how can that be? It was just yesterday that I was holding you in my arms, parading you around the firehouse as you gurgled up spit bubbles and pissed all over my uniform. The only answer I've come up with is that we've fallen victim to a wicked time warp.

Cripes!

Happy Birthday, son! It's a blessing to watch you grow up. They'd be so proud of you. I'm crazy proud of you. Ishan wishes you a Happy Birthday too. He said he's gonna make you a grand birthday cake when you come next month, strawberries and all. Look out for our gift in the mail. I couldn't love you more, kid. Call me before time leaps again, and you're fifty!"

I chuckle as I hit the call button, but then I remember the time and hang up. If I call now, Adam would guess I'm up because I had a nightmare, and he'll be all over me about seeing a therapist. I drop the phone on the mattress, climb out of bed, and grab the wastebasket. I can sleep on the flight later.

"Fuck, that burns," I groan.

Before I can slam the shot glass down, Kaleb refills it again.

I wave him off. "I'm good!"

"Nah, you ain't. But you will be after you toss back a few more of these bad boys." I hitch forward as he slaps me on the back.

"Ay!" Idris nods at me. "No brooding tonight, homie. We put up with your dark and stormy shit all season. It's your birthday, aight! We'd have failed you if you ain't lit before the night's out."

"Y'all suck," I grumble as I toss back three more shots.

"Datta boy. Give that a few minutes to kick in." Tevin rubs his palms together as a long-legged woman saunters past our table. "Ass for days," he mutters in a daze. "I'm fittin' to make rounds," he announces.

"Fuck me!" Malik taps my arm. "How are we supposed to choose one?" I trail his gaze to a stripper twerking in a diamond-studded thong and glass platform heels.

"Who said we have to choose one?" Tevin asks, eyebrows arched. "The night's young, my dude."

I shake my head. *At least, I think I shake it.* My body feels a hundred degrees warmer than five minutes ago. I can't really feel it. I palm my face to see if it's still there.

Of all the ways I imagined spending my twenty-fourth birthday, I can't say I saw this. The guys bugged me for weeks about hitting up a club, but I wanted to celebrate it with Sid, especially since it was our last night together, so I turned them down. Then Sid came up with the idea to accept their offer and hit up a club in Miami. The guys dug it. Clubbing in Miami during our off-season was too good to pass up, especially at the coveted mega-club Twelve.

Kaleb passes around bottles of water. When I reach for one, he pulls it back. "You loose yet?"

"Why? Trying to cop a lap dance?" I bend over and attempt a twerk that's probably all hips, no ass.

His eyes go wide, and then he bursts out laughing. "Fuck

yeah! That's what I'm talkin' bout." He throws his arm around me and presses the bottle of water against my chest.

My lips are rubbery as I gulp it down, but thankfully, Tevin passes around chewing gum, and the spearmint helps with my cottonmouth. Besides my chest burning like I swallowed fire, I feel good, really good. My heart thumps to the rhythm of the bass as I close my eyes and rap along to Jay-Z.

I hope Sid's here soon. I need to fuck or be fucked, both preferably. I'm being lifted off the ground by the bass when a heavy arm drapes over my shoulder.

"Mobbin' out," Idris yells into my ear before he joins me, rapping and picking up every other bar. If the goal is to amp me up, it's working.

"Ay-yo, Pretty Boy can spit." Kaleb smacks Malik's chest and nods at me.

Malik grins. "He's loose alright."

Tevin, the ultimate hype man, wields a bottle of champagne in one hand like a mic and then slides behind a woman dancing at a nearby table for a slow grind to the outro.

"I'm out," I yell, gaze lasered to the dance floor. Except for Kaleb, the rest of the guys hang back to rack up lap dances. Ten feet on the dance floor, I'm sandwiched between some of the most absurdly beautiful women I've ever seen. One woman strings her arms around my neck as she moves in close for a dance. Her hand starts to roam my pecs and trails further and further down south. I extricate myself, but when I turn, I crash right into another woman. My hands bracket her hips as I stumble back from the force of her ass rotating in slow circles against my crotch. I close my eyes and ride the beat, imagining giving Sid a naked lap dance later.

I lose myself to the music, dancing with every woman that pushes in. I peer over at Kaleb, and he's dancing low with a woman damn near straddling his lap. I spot Malik, Tevin, and Idris dancing close by. I scan the floor for the hundredth time, hoping to see Sid. I texted him when we arrived, but he didn't hit me back. He planned to roll up, pretend it was a coincidence, and we turn up together.

I cringe at the drag of long nails snaking over my crotch, and I'm peeling myself away when I overhear Kaleb yell, "Yo, s'that Wonder Kid?"

I follow his gaze to the second floor and beam when I spot Sid leaning over the balcony, gazing right at me. He raises his glass to us. My whole body lights up as I wave for him to join us.

"Y'all friends?" Kaleb asks, more yells over the music.

Shit. I subdue my smile. "We did that interview thing once, remember? I wonder what he's doing here," I yell, rubbing my sweaty neck.

The crowd parts for Sid as he approaches. A sea of camera phones point in his direction. He's a wet dream. Iron abs and Adonis belt on full display as he rocks an unbuttoned crisp linen shirt and dark gray trouser shorts that hug his muscular thighs to perfection. The watch I gifted him glimmers against his wrist. I glimpse his nipple barbell and avert my gaze to stop myself from drooling. Except when I turn to my teammates, they're awe-struck too. Sid daps Idris and Tevin, the vets first. Tevin yells to Sid that we're in town celebrating my birthday. Sid's eyes widen with surprise as his gaze shifts to me. His acting is award-worthy.

"Happy Birthday, Pretty Boy," he says, offering me a dap. I zero in on his sumptuous lips and chestnut eyes.

"Thanks," I reply, biting back a grin.

"I'd offer to buy you a drink, but you look a few steps ahead." His gaze sweeps over my face, and I catch a flicker of desire.

"Yeah, we had shots of—" For the life of me, I can't remember what we drank.

"Vodka," Malik says.

"Lookie, lookie, at what we have here, Knights in our town,"

Justin says as he pulls up next to Sid and leans his elbow on his shoulder. "Y'all wanted to party with the champs?"

"Nah, it's Pretty Boy's birthday here. We should give them a proper Miami welcome," Sid says, gaze glued to me.

"How about we take them to Ivy's?" Justin replies.

"What's that?" Tevin asks.

"It's next level, bro. Trust me. The ladies are—" he kisses the tips of his fingers—"thicc and wild as fuck. We'll send Pretty Boy here straight to the balla's room."

I swallow a groan. The idea of being gyrated on by anyone other than the smokeshow in front of me isn't how I want to spend the night.

"That sounds perfect. Let's roll. Birthday boy rides with me," Sid commands. "I brought out the Porsche, or else I'd take more of you."

"The 911 Turbo S?" Harry asks, wide-eyed.

Sid raises his eyebrows. "How'd you kno–?"

"Saw your car collection on YouTube."

"Ah." Sid nods.

"Aight, so the rest of y'all roll with me." Justin turns and leads the way out. He signals to a few other Marvels players that it's time to bounce.

The valet brings the car around, and I climb in.

"Yo," Malik says, "our birthday boy must be far gone climbing into that sexy whip like he owns it."

I wince. The first time I saw it, I whistled and told Sid that if the Porsche was a man, he'd have competition. I begged him to drive it, and he tossed me the keys. That was a more appropriate reaction than the unfazed way that I just climbed in.

I turn to Sid for help. He snickers, leans past me, and shouts, "I might have to feed the birthday boy to sober him up a little."

With that, he revs up and takes off. The minute we're out of sight, I take in my fill of him.

"Fuck, you look hot. Tell me we're going home," I plead, massaging his pierced nipple, then trailing my fingers over his abs to his crotch. My mouth waters as his cock thickens.

"I look hot?" He scoffs. "What are you wearing?" He wets his bottom lip as he scans my body.

I traded in my skinny jeans and T-shirt for a sleeveless knit slate gray Chanel vest, a pair of Gucci pleated slacks, and Duke + Dexter loafers. A muted version of the white gold chain that Sid is rocking hangs from my neck.

"Like it?" I ask.

He hums. "You're gonna see how much I like it."

I grin. "I thought you were feeding me first."

He arches an eyebrow. "I never said I was feeding you food."

Fuck. "Keep looking at me like that, and I'll come all over the leather," I warn.

He flashes me a filthy grin. "Wouldn't be the first time."

"Mmm." I recall all the hot sex we've had in his cars. A bolt of heat courses up my spine. Between the fire fanning between us and the vodka coursing through my system, a reckless abandon hums through my veins. I've longed to be near him all night. I lean my head back on the headrest and unzip my pants. I close my eyes, reach inside of my fly, pull out my hardening dick, and start stroking myself. I pause and reach into the center console for the lube.

Without taking his eyes off the road, he reaches over and thumbs my slit, drawing out a moan. I try to fuck up into his hand.

"Don't come." He sucks his thumb into his mouth. "That load is mine."

I whimper as he releases my dick, and I slowly stroke myself until I reach the edge. Then I pull off, preferring to come down his throat.

My eyes narrow when the car pulls into a marina. A stunning mix of yachts and superyachts bob against the glinting water. "Where are we?" I ask, tucking myself away.

Sid grins and commands the car's virtual assistant to dial Justin. He rubs the back of my neck.

"Yo," Justin answers.

"Yo! I'mma fall back tonight. I just got hit up by a baddie who's in town." Sid winks at me.

"Fuckin' stud. I thought you said you were done dating... focusing on your game and shit. Which one is it this time? That Atlanta hottie from last year, the Brazilian, the triplets—"

I quirk an eyebrow at Sid. I could never bring myself to ask for his body count, but damn, I wonder.

"Or the French shawty with the crazy rac—"

"Ay!" Sid cuts in, grimacing. "That's all in the past. You don't know 'em."

"You owe me a hundred bills. Didn't I call it? Dating hiatus, my ass. She better be smokin' if you're skipping Ivy's."

Sid stares at me. "I'm in love with this one, man. Ain't nothin' for me at Ivy's."

Justin cackles. "You in love...good one. Pretty Boy still comin' thru?"

"Nah, he's lit," he says, massaging his favorite spot on my neck. "Gonna sleep it off."

"Aight. I'll let his boys know. Peace. Don't forget to strap and flush that shit after."

Sid shakes his head. "Peace."

"Triplets? French shawty? Who am I? Brooklyn Baddie?" I chide as soon as the line goes dead.

He grimaces. "You gonna skip the part where I said I'm off the market and in love?"

"I don't recall that at all," I lie, unbuckling my seatbelt and staring out the window. "What are we doing here?"

"C'mon," he says, sliding out of the car.

I follow his trail toward the docks, my curiosity doubling with each step.

"Bab—Sid"—I catch myself despite being the only two people around—"you rented us a yacht for the night!"

"Rent?" His face scrunches up. "Why would I rent something I own?"

I freeze. "You own a yacht?"

He nods.

My voice plunges to a low yell. "We've been dating for how long, and you didn't think to disclose that you own a—"

"Whoa, whoa! I disclosed it. Remember when you rode me in the back of the Aston, and you said that you could now cross fucking in a car off of your bucket list, and I said the plane and the yacht's next, and you laughed?"

My jaw drops. "That was your way of telling me you own a fucking yacht? How?"

He shrugs. "I thought it was clear."

I throw my arms up. "In what universe is that clear?"

"Listen, no one likes the dude who won't shut up about his yacht. It's corny. I'll admit, I could have been less subtle."

I scoff. "You think." I peer down the line of beaming vessels. "Which one is it, Bruce Wayne?"

I've seen a million interviews with him, and never once was a yacht featured.

"How'd you know it's modeled after the—"

Jogging away, I pass a cream and brass-colored yacht that's too classic and boring for Sid's taste. There's a purple and orange one that you'd need to be on acid to appreciate.

"Hold up," Sid says, on my heels as I zip past a row of similar classic styles. I race around the corner and freeze, causing Sid to barrel into me. He wraps his arm around my waist to break my fall.

"No fucking way!" I gaze up at the behemoth black vessel gleaming with a titanium trim.

"Sick! How'd you know it was this one?"

I glare at him. "You mean, besides the big dick energy radiating from it?"

He grins. "Meet Vengeance or V for short."

I shake my head. "You own a yacht."

He owns a yacht.

But it's not just a yacht—it's the Batmobile of yachts.

"C'mon. It's just us tonight, but the captain will be here late morning to take us out. I haven't been out in months. You like jet-skiing?"

"Never been." My eyes take in every inch of the vessel as I trail him through a side gate.

"I'll show you how. You're gonna love it." He leads me through a powered side door.

"Let me give you a tour. V's a tri-deck, meaning there are—"

"Three levels," I finish. "Damn, this is tight." I take in a sweeping grand room with redwood—or maybe mahogany—walls and wide windows overlooking the water. "Is this the living room?"

He nods. "Main salon." He pushes on a polished wood panel, and a fridge door opens. He hands me a glass bottle of chilled water and retrieves one for himself. My head feels like it's gonna explode. Who's hushed about owning something like this!

The center of the room has two plush, tufted, cognac-colored couches and a pair of matching leather armchairs. A circular, brass-beamed, glass table sits in the center. An enclosed glass bookshelf, full of leather-bound books I'm itching to touch, is off to the side. Curved glass with brass-finished wall sconces emit a soft glow over the space.

Damn...I don't even smoke, but this is so swank I want to fire up a cigar and kick my feet up.

I turn to Sid—the heat of his gaze beckoning me. "It's official, you made it."

He lets out a breathy chuckle. "You like it?"

I scoff. "I can't believe you're humble about this. There's a lifetime's worth of bragging rights here."

He grins. "C'mon, more to see."

I follow him past a pillar separating the living room from a formal dining area with a long, polished, wooden table and at least a dozen chairs. The detailing on the wall is exquisite. It reminds me of liquid gunmetal, and I can't resist tracing my fingers along it.

"An Italian company modeled the design after naval vessels. The hull, decking, and superstructure are all made of aluminum. There are five staterooms—"

"Sorry, my yacht vernacular is rusty. Staterooms?"

He chuckles and pulls me against his chest. "My bad. It's like a cabin or hotel room." He brushes a kiss against my neck. "Let's get you oriented. Straight ahead to the left is the galley kitchen and crew quarters. Straight ahead to the right is our suite." He taps on the wall to the right of us, and a door opens. "This is one of the day heads—bathrooms—equipped with a toilet, vanity, and bidet." I whistle, taking in the brass finishes. He spins us around so that we're facing a spiral staircase. "Downstairs are four guest rooms, two of which are VIP. Upstairs is the sky lounge, captain's bridge and quarters, and aft deck—basically the rear of the yacht. The glass side door here" —he points to the door near the dining room—"leads to the front of the yacht—the bow. There are sun pads and wrap-around seating. I'll give you a proper tour, but first—"

"I want to see our bedroom." I pull him in the direction that he pointed to.

"Not that one," he says as I turn a doorknob. "That's a laundry room."

"This place has a laundry room!"

"Yeah, one here and one in the crew quarters. This way to our room." Double doors open into a spacious room with a massive bed. I pause and remove my shoes, and he follows suit.

"Silk sheets?" I ask, quirking my eyebrow.

"Regulates the temperature," he says. "Smirk now, but wait until I have you laid out across them. I'll have to drag you out of bed."

My dick perks up at the thought. The room has massive windows, a flat-screen TV mounted to the wall, and an armchair and desk. I nod toward the staircase. "What's down there?"

"Our bathroom," he replies. "There's an infrared sauna."

I grin. Of course there is. I check out the walk-in closet to the left and zero in on two plush robes. I rub my face against one and moan.

"You said it's just us tonight, right? No captain or crew?"

He nods.

"Hold this," I hand him the water bottle, then strip out of my clothes, but before I can reach for the robe, his muscular arm wraps around my waist, pressing my back against his chest. His tongue stripes across my neck.

"Mmm," I moan as he sucks on my hickey.

Reaching around, he strokes my growing erection. "Turn around," he orders, voice rough and low.

I turn and groan as he licks into my mouth. I suck on his tongue and try to climb up his body, but I only get one leg hooked around him. As I lean against the wall for support, he lowers to his knees in one fluid motion. I hiss when he laps up my pre-cum. Rocking my hips, I plunge myself into his mouth. My knees tremble from the warm slide and suction.

"Sometimes I can't believe that you're mine," I whisper as I trace his sexy lips stretched taut around me.

"Hmm?" His tongue trails down to my balls, making my legs tremble.

"The thirst—Christ—s'good"—I palm the back of his head

as he sucks me down—"at the club—ngh, fuuuck." My toes curl as he pops off, spits on my dick, and licks across my slit before sucking it back down. I trace his gorgeous cheekbones. "Why me?"

He freezes, then pulls off my cock and stares up at me, eyebrows pinched. "What?"

I replay my words and wince. "Shh," I whisper.

"Baby."

I make a whiny noise, dropping my head back as my face flares with embarrassment.

"Oh fuck," I moan when his tongue glides along the underside of my cock.

He pops off of me. "We're not done with this conversation," he says before sucking on my head.

"Mm-hmm," I moan, caressing the back of his head. I surrender and let him take me apart. Once my gaze travels up from his stretched lips to his gorgeous, fiery eyes, I rupture. Delirious from his husky grunts, I fuck his face until I'm spent. He places a soft kiss against my dick before he climbs to his feet.

When I reach for his zipper, he pulls back and cups the back of my neck, dusting kisses from my chin down to the side of my neck. "You don't know why I'm with you?" I arch my neck and trail my fingers along his nipple and down his abs. He presses his forehead to mine. "Talk to me, baby. Where is this coming from?"

I stiffen. Damn vodka's revealing my insecurities. "Uh, everywhere...I have eyes. I see the way women look at you. Men too. You could be swimming in pussy and ass."

He shakes his head. "Nah. None of that's real. You know that. They want their idea of me. You actually see m—"

"You don't have to say that."

"Wait, let me finish," he says, brushing a kiss against my

lips. "You're everything I want in a partner. I've never been this happy with anyone. How could you doubt it?"

"I know that you love me. I just don't always get…"

"What do you mean?" he asks, eyebrows bunched. He's staring at me like I'm speaking in a foreign tongue.

I huff. "Why am I the one that you fell in love with?"

"I could ask you the same thing," he fires back.

I scoff. He's so unbelievably lovable.

He arches his eyebrow. "Okay," he says with a slow nod. He presses his lips against my ear. "I love you because you're you." A spiral of heat coils from my ear down to my toes. He presses closer to me. "I love your intellect and wisdom. I want to explore inside of that expansive brain all day. You're terrified of opening your heart up, yet you manage to love with every inch of it. You're sexy as fuck, like goddamn!" he barks, making me laugh. "And you're my best friend."

I tilt back to meet his gaze. "You're my best friend too."

"I know." He brushes a kiss against my lips. "Even though you avoid the media, well people in general"—he grins—"doesn't mean I don't see how people interact with you. How desperately they try to get past your walls. I don't know how I got through, but I count myself lucky that you let me in."

It wasn't really a choice. I couldn't keep him out if I tried.

"Even though I try every day, I'll never know all of your depths. And because of that, I'll always know humility with you. Sometimes, I fear I've met you too late, and we'll never have enough time."

My eyes sting as I nod. I carry the same fear. Even if we live to a hundred, it won't be enough time together.

"It's also low-key comforting that you're oblivious to people flirting with you. You have no radar for it— none."

"Nobody flirts with me," I retort as I pull on the robe.

He cackles against my neck.

I scan my memory for times when he might've noticed

someone flirting with me, and I come up blank. I stare at our fingers intertwined and gaze at my initials monogrammed on the robe. I grin. "Smooth."

He reaches into a drawer and pulls out matching monogrammed slippers. I slip them on along with the robe. "That's it. I'm never leaving this yacht."

He traces the outline of my lips. "Thought you had rings to cop, trophies to win?"

"Pfft. Paltry dreams."

He grins. "Just like that, V's turned you into a man of leisure?"

"That was your plan all along, wasn't it? Have V seduce me, so that I retire early? Who'd demolish your records if I'm retired?"

He winks. His fingers trail the rims of my eyes, and his smile recedes. "Another nightmare?"

I look away. "Yeah."

"Baby, we've got to get you to thera–"

I huff out a breath. "Can we not fight about this today? Today's been amazing..." My birthday hasn't been remotely good in years.

His chest caves as he releases a heavy sigh. "Fine. I'll drop it. Just for today. C'mon," he says, clasping my hand and leading the way.

"Why are there so many?" I ask, peering around the kitchen equipped with stainless steel everything, from the island to the walls of refrigerators, dishwashers, and Wolf ovens.

"V can accommodate a party guest list of a few hundred. Grab a drink. I had a fridge stocked earlier today."

"So this is how the rich do it." I hop up on the bare island and spread my legs. "You're taking me here?"

His gaze trails down my body. "Mmm. I want to feed you first." He reaches into his shorts to adjust his erection, then moves to the sink to wash his hands.

"We're cooking?"

"I had the restaurant brought to us," he says, flicking the off switch and pulling out a tray of food from a stainless-steel device that looks like a cross between a microwave and a toaster oven.

I slide off the island and peel back the cover.

"Whoa! Is that miso cod?"

He hums, embracing me from behind.

"And yellowtail collar? Wait a minute, is this from—"

"Yep," he says.

"How?" I ask, staring at him wide-eyed. I mentioned a few weeks ago that I'm dying to dine at an upscale and renowned Japanese-Peruvian restaurant here in Miami. The restaurant has a strict no-takeout policy. It's part of their ethos—something about the menu being a tasting experience enjoyed in-house blah blah. It's fucking pretentious, but the food's so damn delicious that everyone deals with it. The restaurant attracts celebrities, so paparazzi camp out in front. Sid's been several times, but I haven't since we generally avoid being seen together in public. I sneak in and out whenever I'm in Miami to see him.

He smirks. "Seriously?"

I shake my head. He's cocky about this but not owning a yacht.

I hop back up on the island. "God, you're a dream. How will I ever be able to date after you?"

He glares at me. "You know something I don't? Why are you thinking about dating after me?" Standing between my legs, he begins gathering the perfect bite.

"Holy fuck!" My eyes roll closed the second the buttery, salty, sweet flavors hit my palette.

"Yeah?" he asks.

I nod. "Oh, yeah."

I jump down and move to the sink to wash my hands. He holds the plate away from me when I return with a fork.

"Answer me," he demands.

My stomach grumbles in protest. "I'm not. I'm in love with you. It's just you've set the bar high—like skyscraper high."

He returns the plate to the island. "You know one of the things I love about *The Three Musketeers*?"

I dig into the food. "The adventure and camaraderie?"

"The honor duels," he answers before accepting my bite.

"That's rando—oh, you'd duel a guy for me?"

He feeds me a bite. "Damn straight!"

I chuckle, almost choking on my food. He pats my back and hands me a glass of water.

"My heart is composed of muscle, blood, and love for you, D'Artagnan," I choke out.

He drops his fork. "Hold up! I'm way more Athos than D'Artagnan!"

I think about it. Who could refute his noble air? "My bad. You're right."

I brush a quick kiss against his grinning mouth. "You know what I just realized?"

He arches his brows.

"We can probably run with us being seen in public at the club...make it seem like our friendship started tonight." We've been trying to figure out a way to show the media that we're friends so that it won't raise eyebrows when we're seen in public together. This could work.

"We *were* surrounded by teammates," he says, picking his fork back up.

"Yeah, you could post something casually wishing me a happy birthday. I bet the media will take it from there."

"Bet."

I don't realize I'm shaking until his hand settles over my knee. "Go piss!"

I shake my head. "It's too good. I can't abandon it," I whine, savoring another bite.

He chuckles. "It'll be here when you get back. Look, I'm putting down my fork until you return."

The half-liter worth of shots that I chugged have expanded my bladder like a taut water balloon. My entire body trembles as I reach for one more bite.

Sid grunts. "That's it!"

The next thing I know, I'm upside down, my nose buried in his back, dangling from his shoulder as he strides toward the bathroom. I squirm and laugh so hard that I snort, making us both laugh.

I get a whiff of his cologne and take a huge sniff of his back, making him squirm and slap my butt. I'm planted upright in front of the toilet. Holding on to him, the blood rushes from my head. I salute him and spin to take care of business.

I'm bounding back into the kitchen when I hear the flicker of a lighter. My face splits into the goofiest grin when I spot the swarm of candles, but I freeze when I take in the cake.

The night he fell sick, I told him about my trip to Paris. How my parents and I fell in love with the desserts from a tiny bakery tucked off of the beaten path in the Marais district. We ended each day of our trip with a visit to the bakery. Sid asked if I remembered the dessert that I loved best. I had, of course. It was an opera cake. My parents picked one up on my birthday every year after our trip. I admitted that I haven't been able to bring myself to eat it since they passed away.

"Together," he says, extending his hand.

I stand in place and stare at him.

He offers it so faithfully—*together*. An answer to an unspoken prayer. How could a solitary word promise such companionship? Does he sense the birthdays I've spent drowning in misery, feeling utterly alone?

I walk into his outstretched arms, and we stare into the fire, watching the candle wax transform by its own flame.

I close my eyes and wish that we spend the rest of our days together and no matter the storms, each year finds us closer, happier, and more in love than the last.

"Together," I whisper, and with a single rush of our breath, we blow out the candles.

Wisps of smoke scent the air like incense burned as an offering.

Sid hands me the first slice. I consider it before I take a bite. Ganache and buttercream. My eyes flutter closed.

A boy laughs in Paris. Suffused with boundless optimism, he tells his parents that when he's rich, they'll visit all the great bakeries of the world.

I miss him. I kind of felt like him tonight.

As I swallow the coffee almond sponge, I hear Mom and Dad singing Stevie Wonder's "Happy Birthday." I take a steadying breath. I'll miss them forever.

Sid wipes my eyes, and I recall a memory created only moments ago—his beautiful face illuminated by the candle-light. Hand outstretched, offering a grace I'll never forget as long as I live. He gave me the strength to do what I couldn't for years—visit the past and come away with a sense of peace.

Chapter Seventeen

When we're done eating, I'm ready to melt into a couch. We make our way up to the sky lounge. We're so far away from the world as I gaze out at the black-silk ocean. Sid hits a switch, and the glass turns frosty, giving us privacy. Before I can crash into the couch, he pulls me into his chest.

"I've watched women feel you up all night. It's my turn." The tips of his fingers bracket the side of my neck and tilt my face up for a kiss. My mouth is pliant as he sucks on my bottom lip before swiping his tongue inside. He massages my nipple between his thumb and index finger, sending shivers up my spine.

"Of course. All night—ah—" I moan as the tip of his tongue circles the side of my neck. My head falls back against his chest.

"Hmm?"

"I looked for you. I wanted to dance with you." I turn my face and pepper kisses across his Adam's apple.

He pulls out his phone. A sultry song fills the room.

"Yes," I hiss, melting against him.

I remove my robe, needing the hard plains of his chest

against my back. His hand cups the front of my neck as we tongue fuck each other. I grind against him along to the beat. He presses against me, his hips matching my rhythm. His tongue licks across my lips. The metal of his necklace creates goosebumps at the base of my neck.

"Why are you so sexy? I couldn't take my eyes off of you when you were on the dance floor," he whispers against my ear. "I didn't trust myself to come near you."

Why does it turn me on so much to know he was watching me? I clasp his hand and glide it over my erection. "What would you have done?"

He grunts. "I wanted to bend you over a table, slide down your pants and briefs, and feast on you in front of everyone until you were slick and trembling for me."

I whimper at the thought and roll my hips, trying to fuck his hand.

"Then I'd feed in my dick inch by inch."

I moan as he rubs his thumb across my leaking slit. I reach behind and massage his erection over his shorts.

"You'd fuck me hard?"

"Punishing."

"Mmm." My back arches as I grind against him.

"After I come inside of you, I'd turn you over, suck you down, then feed you your cum. I'd have carried you out with my fingers plugging your hole to keep my cum inside."

I moan and dip lower, rutting against him, and he is right there with me, grinding forward to the music. We both moan when his teeth clamp down on the side of my neck, and his fingers dig into my hips. I turn and nibble on his nipples before lowering to my knees and unbuckling his shorts. Gazing up into his half-lidded eyes, I cup his balls, lifting slightly, then stroking downwards. My mouth waters as his leaking tip bobs toward my mouth. He hisses when my tongue licks over the tip of his head, and my eyes roll closed, savoring his taste.

Everyone talks about the love hormone, dopamine, and the feel-good hormone, oxytocin, released during an orgasm, but what about the sensation that fires up the center of my brain when the first drop of his salty, sweet, metallic pre-cum hits my tongue? A consuming hunger builds from my core. I drag the tip of my tongue back and forth over his slit, lapping up every drop. Staring into his searing eyes, I choke myself on his cock. I pull off with a gasp, then suck him back down. I lick down his shaft while my fingers continue to massage his taint, pressing gently, then firmly.

"Ty," he moans, head falling back, muscular legs trembling. "Baby, pull off if you want me to fuck you."

My watery eyes meet his gaze, and my fingers dig into his thighs as his head fills my throat. I reach down and massage his heavy balls.

"Holy fuck," he cries as his hamstrings hit the back of the couch. I stroke myself with my free hand. Every stroke pulls the chain of a plug, holding back my release. I stroke myself harder, whimpering around his cock. He moans from the vibration and starts to thrust into my mouth. My eyes sting and shudder closed as he slides against my throat. My orgasm swells from the slick sounds of mouth and flesh mixed with his deep voice falling apart.

Oh fuck! I can't—fuck.

I pull off of him and clamp down on my bottom lip as the intensity of my release shoots an explosion of white speckles behind my eyes. I groan when he rubs his dick across my lips, then bends forward and licks off his pre-cum. Chest heaving, I whimper as he sucks on my tongue and clasps the back of my neck in the possessive way that ignites every cell in my body. I use my cum as a lubricant to stroke his shaft. I pull away from the kiss and tilt forward, smearing his leaking head all over my lips. He moans when I rub my nose into his base, obsessed with his scent.

I open my mouth and clasp the globes of his ass as I suction him deeper into my mouth.

He pistons, releasing delicious moans and grunts, and then his abs clench. "Baby, ungh, fuck," he babbles.

The intensity of his gaze sends ripples of heat up my spine. I rub on his taint, and his head drops back as a primal sound rips out of him. A moan from the base of my neck gurgles up as my throat is pumped full of his cum. My eyes roll closed as I swallow every drop.

He shivers when I brush a kiss against his tip. I grin and brush another, swiping my tongue across for a final taste. His legs tremble, and he slides down to the floor until his back hits the rug. Panting, he pulls me against his chest and closes his eyes. I reach for a throw pillow and tuck it under his head as he dozes off. I settle my ear against his chest, fish my phone out of my robe pocket, and scroll through social media. I'm not surprised to see images of Sid from the club trending. His ripped body and gorgeous face should be sculpted in stone for posterity. I read an obscene number of thirsty comments—so many wet tongue, eggplant, and peach emojis. Damn!

I glance up at his peaceful face and grin. *Mine.*

The Knights' social media account posted a reel of me doing the Running Man, making me grin. There are thousands of comments from people wishing me a "Happy Birthday." I scroll through wild-looking reels of me at the club, sandwiched between groping women. My face warms thinking about Sid watching that shit. In my defense, I look hella faded.

I shake my head and close out the app. I stare up at the purple-blue sky until I drift off. I fall asleep wondering if birthday wishes are like prayers in that sometimes they come true.

I WHIMPER AS SID'S LUBED FINGERS ENTER ME, AND SOFT KISSES pepper my neck. I melt into the pillow, realizing I'm dreaming until my eyes shoot open, and I gasp as his cock slides inside of me.

"Sid," I hiss.

He groans in my ear, sending a bolt of heat down my spine. "Hmm?"

I fist the sheets and moan as he fucks me deep, massaging my prostate on every drive. "You feel incredible," he rasps.

My eyes sting as he makes love to me. I don't know why, but I'm most sensitive in the morning.

I whisper, "I love you," as he thrusts deeper and deeper inside of me.

He kisses my tear-stained face and whispers, "I love you too. Always." Pulling me closer, he reaches his arm around to stroke me. Whenever I sob when we make love, he never lasts long. We fall apart when we reach the impossibly tender place that only our lovemaking can traverse. The tether that's forged through every stroke, every teardrop, every orgasm feels sacred and everlasting. I know we cannot possess another person, but Sid is mine, and I am his forever. I feel it in the marrow of my bones, the tendons of my heart, the core of my soul.

"Come with me," he whispers. We're so intricately fine-tuned that the minute he sucks in a deep breath signaling his release, my own ruptures from me, and I clench around him as my body shudders. He bites into my neck as he moans out in ecstasy. His heart races against my back as he strokes me through my release. I'm out of my body, drifting with the sea breeze as I drift back to sleep.

AFTER A MORNING OF JET SKIING, SWIMMING, AND WATCHING MY favorite F1 driver win the Miami Grand Prix on TV, Sid's driving us to my birthday gift. We stopped at his house on the way to swap the Porsche for the Bentley Bentayga and change into fresh clothes. His lips are ironclad as he rudely ignores my guesses on where we're headed, however practical or outlandish they might be. I was told to eat a light breakfast this morning. Though that doesn't tell me much.

We pull up to Hard Rock Stadium, and I see signs for the Miami International Autodrome.

I flash him a confused grin. "What are we doing here? The race was this morning."

"I know. I watched it with you." He hands the keys to the valet and gestures for me to wait as he steps away to make a call. *Odd.*

With the phone to his ear, he signals for me to follow him, and I trail him through the lot. As we reach a gate, a woman approaches from our left, waving a phone at him. He waves back and hangs up the call as she gestures for us to follow her. He turns to me and shrugs as we trail her through a corridor to a suite of lounges protected by an army of security guards. A couple of the guards do a double take. I'm glad videos of us at the club trended, and Sid posted a happy birthday message to me earlier. It gives us cover.

"Please wait in here," the woman says, directing us into a private room.

"What's going on?" I ask Sid once we're alone.

He pulls me into a quick kiss instead of answering me.

I look around for cameras. "What was that for?"

"I can't kiss my sexy boyfriend during his birthday weekend?"

"Of course you..." The door opens, and in walks none other than the champ and my favorite F1 driver, Archie Jefferson.

"Shut up," I scoff, backing away and covering my mouth.

No way!

No fucking way!

Sid chuckles at my reaction.

"What's good, man? I told you he was a genuine fan," Sid says, dapping Archie, who's in jeans and a long-sleeved shirt with sponsorship logos plastered across it.

"My bruv, good to see you!" Archie says. The sides of his hair are shaved low, and intricate cornrows are braided down the center. I stare into his warm, hooded eyes and shake my head. This isn't real.

"I hear it's your birthday, Ty. I'm a fan of yours, both of yours, actually," he says. "Epic Miami game between you two. Don't tell him"—he gestures to Sid—"but I was rooting for you."

His smile is radiant.

I've forgotten words.

I'm meeting Archie Jefferson!

The Archie Jefferson!

"I think we broke him," Sid says, laughing.

I try to pull it together.

"How? Fuuck! How?" I direct that blubber to Sid.

"I met Archie my second year in the league."

And you kept it a secret! I want to blurt out.

"That's right. It was at a gala or something, innit?" Archie recalls.

His skin glows like there's a lantern bobbing inside of him. He has a boyish grin and a mix of bad-boy swag and charm. He's smaller than I thought, but what's there is fit.

I force myself to pull it together. "Ahem. Okay." I think my brain is partly back online. "It's, uh, nice to meet you." *Nice? That's the understatement of the year!* He opens his arms for a hug while I awkwardly hold out my hand, extending a handshake. I drop my hand and accept the hug.

"Looks like a vampire went at your neck." He points to my hickey.

"Yeah, er, I—"

"He had a wild birthday. You know how we do," Sid says, saving me from an awkward loss of words.

"Ivy's?" Archie asks.

I nod, afraid I'll give away that I was lying if I speak.

"I'll never forget Sadie as long as I live," Archie reminisces. "Ready to go?"

"What?" I turn to Sid.

"Oh, yes, that. Your birthday gift—Archie's agreed to take you on the track for a spin."

My jaw drops. "Deadass?"

"You should see your face!" Archie says, grinning. "I promise to make our time unforgettable! Let's roll." He turns toward the door.

I turn to Sid and mouth, *Seriously?*

He laughs and mouths, *Happy Birthday!*

I mouth, *I love you!*

He grins and blows me a kiss.

I kneel when we reach the tracks and touch the rubber skid marks.

Surreal.

A car pulls up next to us. "This is our ride," Archie says, handing me a helmet and pulling on his own.

I whistle at the half-million-dollar car! "McLaren 720S Spider Luxury."

"I'm impressed. Have you driven in one before?"

"Nope. Even if I had, I bet it's a different experience with you at the wheel."

"Let's hope I don't disappoint," he says as we pile in.

He reaches over to help me figure out the seat adjustment for my height.

"Ready?" he asks once we're buckled up.

"Hell yeah!"

He revs up the car. "Hold on to the grab handle."

I brace for take-off, but instead of flying forward, we jolt back in reverse.

He shakes his head. "My days. Not this again."

"What's the matter?"

"I sometimes forget how to drive after a race. The adrenaline muddles up my brain."

"Oh, damn. That's rough."

He closes his eyes. "Left pedal to brake, right pedal to accelerate. You got this, Archibald."

Christ! He doesn't even recall the basics. He tenses, keeping his eyes closed, and takes a deep breath.

"Hey, Archie, it's okay, man. Meeting you made my day! We don't need—"

My words die in my throat as he covers his eyes with his hands, and the air grows thick with awkwardness.

I reach over to pat his shoulder but hesitate, my hand hovering mid-air.

Then, all of a sudden, I hear a snicker...or was it a sniffle?

His chest shakes, and then I hear it again.

I quirk my eyebrows. "Are you laugh—"

He explodes with laughter.

My eyes widen. "What the hell, man?" I scoff. "I thought you were serious."

That makes him double over, and I burst out laughing. "What's so fun—"

"I'm sorry," he splutters. "Your face." He shakes his head. "So concerned."

"It sounded plausible," I retort in my defense.

"Not for me," he says, wiping his eyes. "I'm an even better driver after a race." He revs up the car again. "Hold tight, Pretty Boy."

That's the only warning before I'm plastered to the seat by the G-force as we accelerate to a criminal speed. A rush slams into me when he executes the first turn, and my stomach drops.

"Fuck yeah! Let's go!" I bark, making Archie laugh as he shifts and commands the steering wheel with mesmerizing expertise.

"You're a proper adrenaline junky. That's usually the point where people start praying to their god."

I chuckle. "Nah, I feel alive!"

The right side of my body hits the door as we take the next corner. We hurtle through the air, ratcheting up my pulse. Watching Archie execute one shift after another in a controlled manner slides my brain into a stupor. Controlled movements make no sense at this speed.

"This is wild!" I shout as adrenaline laces my blood.

His smile is wicked as he presses down on the acceleration. If I thought we were going fast before, it's nothing compared to this. A force twice my weight presses against my chest.

"Faster!" I command, and Archie's whole face lights up. His unfettered joy reminds me of a kid playing with their favorite toy, albeit a $500K one. Or maybe his toy is speed, and the car is only an instrument. His elation kinda reminds me of Sid's joy at Christmastime.

"That was the first lap. We'll pick it up for the next one."

By the time his words land, he's already slamming on the accelerator.

"Holy fuck!" I yell as he swerves through a corner. The screeching tires sound like they're being pushed to the limit. My eyes snap closed, then open, then closed again.

"Oh fuck, we're gonna flip!" I bark as the left side of the car lifts off the ground.

"Whoa," Archie yells. "We're drifffffting!"

My eyes shoot open to find the world transformed into a dizzying blur. I stab a glance at Archie, and he grins cheek to cheek.

He decelerates and makes a series of maneuvers, righting us back on track.

"How about we give you a ride fit for a king and lose the traction control?"

"Uh, w-what?" I'm no expert, but I know traction control helps prevent skidding when driving around curves and sharp turns.

"It's turned off! I got you, though, I promise," he says, patting my arm.

The car swerves hard as we approach the first curve.

"We're dead!" I yell as I cover my eyes with my free hand.

Archie laughs. "Don't go into the light."

All of a sudden, the car thumps like we hit a body.

"Whooooaaaaaaa," he says, voice shaky. I glance over, and his smile vanishes.

"What the fuck was..."

My words die in my throat as the car skids out of control and the road becomes a streak of white light. Archie executes a fast series of micro-shifts using the pedals and the steering wheel. I clamp my eyes shut when none of his maneuvers seem to work. My heart kicks through my chest wall as screeching tires and blood rush through my ears. Every muscle in my body stiffens as I brace for impact. Loud warning sirens fire off in my brain, flooding it with a chaotic cocktail of fear, courage, and a reluctant surrender to whatever happens next.

Memories with Sid from the last few months—his face lit with laughter—*our falling*—surfaces a certitude. No matter how this ends, I am undoubtedly the luckiest man on the planet for experiencing a love like ours.

A deathly silence wipes out the teeth-chattering screeching, and for a second, I wonder if my brain's offering me peace in my final moments, but then I hear, "Open your eyes, young king."

I creak one eye open, and my jaw drops.

"How the fuck..." I palm the sides of my helmet as I look out at the track. I gawk at Archie, who's completely calm.

"It was a close one," he says, pretending to wipe sweat from his forehead.

I stare at him in disbelief.

He grins. "I told you I've got you."

I shake my head, wipe my eyes, and clench, then unclench the hand that had a death grip on the handle. "Fuck, man. Thought we were cooked for a minute."

He chuckles. "What's your favorite dessert?"

"Uh." I tilt my head. "Peach pie. Yours?"

"Doughnuts."

Ah, fuck. I walked right into that.

"Time for scrummy doughnuts for the birthday boy!"

He throws the rear of the car into rotation around the front set of wheels, creating a doughnut skid-mark pattern on the track. The windows are draped in dense smoke as we spiral in dizzying circles. I've done doughnuts before, but never at this maniacal speed. Turning to me, he belts out the "Happy Birthday" song, and I burst out laughing. He sounds terrible, though his lack of fucks is endearing. He rolls down the windows and brings it home, belting his wicked heart out. A couple of mechanics on the sidelines shout and clap for him.

"Had fun?" he asks, shifting to face me.

"Seriously! Can't you tell? I aged a decade, but it was exhilarating. I can't believe you do that for work." I'm covered from head to toe in sweat, and my throat aches from screaming and now laughing.

"Best job in the world," he says, grinning.

I remove my helmet.

He pulls out his phone and pulls up his social media profile. "Mind a birthday post?"

"Go for it."

He scans my face. "You look great."

I nod. "You too."

He unbuckles his seat belt, shifts a little closer to me, and starts to record. "Beautiful people, join me in wishing my bruv Ty a happy birthday! Like an F1 pro, he survived a wild ride that ended in delectable birthday doughnuts! Ty, want to say anything to the people?"

I ignore the camera and face him. "Thanks for the ride, man! That was unforgettable. I'm not sure if I'll have dreams or nightmares tonight. But I'm convinced you're the best driver in the world."

"Thanks, bruv! Next time I'm in LA, I'll swing by, and you can teach me how to shoot one of those insane half-court shots."

"Bet," I agree, grinning.

He reaches over and hugs me with his free arm.

He throws up deuces at the camera and stops recording.

As he waves out the window, I dip my head to see who he's waving to and spot Sid sitting in the stands. I wave him over. My legs feel like jelly when we climb out of the car. I hold on to the hood for a few seconds to get my bearings, and then I pull out my phone and snap a picture of the whip. It's a beauty! Archie asks a mechanic to take a picture of the three of us in front of it. I glimpse the shot. I'm standing in the middle with Sid and Archie on both sides. I'm framing this one for my mantle at home.

"Thanks, bro! I owe you one," Sid says to Archie.

"It was my pleasure. Ty already promised to teach me how to shoot a long-range shot. We're good." Archie says, hugging Sid.

"HOW WAS IT?" SID ASKS AS WE WALK TO THE CAR.

"That was the best birthday surprise of my life."

"Yeah?" He grins. "Love to hear it."

"Thank you, baby." I meet his gaze and fill him in on the experience, including the doughnuts and reel that we recorded.

"Ow!" he exclaims when I punch his arm.

"You let me talk your ear off about him while you knew him personally the whole time!"

He grins. "The minute you flashed your heart-shaped eyes for him, my brain got to work. It would have dampened the surprise if I told you I knew him."

I lean in and nudge his arm. "I only have heart-shaped eyes for you. I had starry eyes for him. Besides you, big shot, I never meet celebrities. Well, just Wilhelm...from All-Star—"

"Who?" he asks, saucily.

I pat his back. "No one."

He smirks. "Smart man."

"Think we have time for a quickie? Y'know...adrenaline plus my sexy as fuck boyfriend pulling off the surprise of a life-time," I ask as we're fastening our seatbelts.

Sid revs up the car and starts to pull out of the lot. "Is that right? If I step on it, we might have enough time to 69."

I relax back into the seat. "We have tinted windows."

"What, here?" Sid asks, scanning the deserted lot.

"Mm-hmm. Pull over up there." I point to the corner of the lot shaded by trees and unbuckle my jeans.

"Fuck," he replies, tracking my movement. He pulls into the spot and turns off the car. "Get in the back."

"Ow!" I exclaim with a chuckle when he bites my ass as I climb into the back seat.

He grabs the lube and scans the lot one more time before he climbs next to me. I pull down his zipper and reach into the fly of his briefs.

"How do you wan—oh, fuck." His head falls back when I lick across his tip. I wrap my mouth around his dick and slowly sink down on his cock until he's filling my throat. He leaves for training camp as soon as we get home, so this is the last time I'll taste him for weeks. I moan when his lubed finger circles my rim, then slides inside, relishing the burn from this morning's fuck. When his breath turns choppy like he's about to blow, I pop off and straddle him. Tugging his bottom lip between my teeth, I lower myself on his cock.

"Oh, fuck!" I moan as his eyes shudder closed. I hold for a few seconds before I start fucking myself on him. His hands grasp my ass as I ride him. His half-lidded eyes are so fucking sexy I have to look away, or I won't last long. I brush a kiss against his ear. "What am I—ungh—fuck, so deep." I gasp against his ear as he grinds his hips up, skewering me.

He groans when I pull off of him and flip around so that he can watch my ass swallow his dick. I ride him slowly, shuddering every time he fills me to the hilt. "Fuck, baby," I mutter. "Who's gonna wake me up on their big dick if—"

His hand clasps around my throat, and I'm pulled back against his broad chest. He licks into my ear. "What do you mean 'who'? This is my hole." He grabs my hip with his free hand and drives into me hard. "No one fucking touches it but me. You hear me?"

"Yes," I hiss. "Fuck, Sid."

He grunts and squeezes my throat, restricting air, and a euphoria washes over me.

"That's your dick inside of you. Feel it?"

Fuuuuck.

"Do you feel it?" he asks, dropping his hand from my neck to my dick and pumping me hard.

"Yesss," I pant, my eyes rolling closed.

"Mmm. No one touches it but you."

"It's fucking mine," I grit out.

"All yours. When I get back from Spain, I'm gonna bend you over and fuck my tight hole until you pass out, and even then —"

"Ngh," my balls draw up as I turn my face and moan into his neck.

"—I won't stop."

"Sid!" I gasp as my climax sends me hurtling over the edge. My body shudders and spasms as he stills with a grunt and comes inside of me. He sucks on my neck hard, like he's trying to permanently mark me as his. I clasp the back of his neck, sinking his teeth in deeper, reveling in the pain.

I'm boneless as I melt against him and catch my breath.

After he licks up my cum covering his hand, I turn and brush a kiss against his lips. It deepens when I taste myself on him.

"God, I'm gonna miss you," he pants after we pull away. My eyes shift to meet his at the sound of his strained voice. The sincerity in his eyes hits me square in the chest.

"I'll miss you too, baby. We'll talk every day?"

"Of course. Promise me you'll take care of yourself. Tell me if you have a panic—"

"Shh. Don't worry. I'll be fine."

"Just tell me. Okay?"

"Yeah."

"No secrets, Ty."

I nod and go to move, but he wraps his arms around my chest, anchoring me in place, and rocks into me, sending tremors throughout my body. "Not yet," he whispers, still softening. He kisses my cheek. "Are you okay? Was I too rough?" he asks, rubbing the front of my throat.

"You were perfect." I rest against his chest and close my eyes, relishing these last few moments together.

I groan when he finally slips out of me.

"Bend forward," he says.

"Why?" I ask, obeying him. "Ohh...ungh," I moan when his warm tongue drags across my rim. He sucks my hole and laps up his cum. My head drops forward when he grabs my hips and sticks his tongue in deep, feasting on me until I'm empty.

"S'hot," I pant.

"I taste delicious inside of you."

The thought makes my dick twitch. If he wasn't pressed for time, I'd go another round.

After we get dressed and pull out of the lot, he clears his throat. "Hey, I need to, uh, talk to you about something."

"O-okay," I say, caught off guard by his serious tone.

"I've made up my mind about what I'm about to tell you, and I feel pretty strongly about it, but it affects us both, so I want to hear your thoughts. I value your opinion, and I love you, and since we're a team, I want to—"

"Unless it's your intention to freak me out, spit it out," I blurt, rubbing my sweaty palms on my thighs.

"It's good news...I hope." He squeezes my hand. "I've been in talks with the Royals about a trade. They made me an epic offer, including a buyout with the Marvels. You know that I've dreamt of playing for Los Angeles since I was a kid, and I accomplished what I set out for in Miami."

My head jerks back. I can't believe what I'm hearing. Sid's been the face of the Marvels for the last five years. It's hard to think of Miami and not imagine him here.

But—and it's a ginormous but—if he moved to Los Angeles, we'd live in the same city. We could come home to each other whenever we have home games. It's what I've dreamt about since we started dating.

"Are you okay? Breathe, baby," he says, balancing the

steering wheel with his left hand and taking my hand with his right.

I grin inwardly. He thinks I'm on the edge of a panic attack. Archie's wicked sense of humor must have rubbed off on me because I make a split-second decision to fuck with him.

"You want to move to LA to play for the Royals next season because you've dreamed about playing for them since you were a kid, and you're done with Miami?"

"Yeah, and they're offering me an obscene amount of money," he adds.

I nod, then shrug. "It's your decision. Whatever you decide, I'll support you."

"That's it?"

"Yeah, I'll always support you," I say dryly, patting his shoulder.

"Okay...cool." His shoulders slump as he turns back to the road. "Thanks. I guess."

I stare out the window and drum my fingers against the door as we fall into an awkward silence for the rest of the drive.

When we reach his house, I steal a glance at him, and he looks so glum. Ugh, I hate it.

When he holds the front door open for me, I cave.

"OH MY GOD! YOU'RE MOVING TO LOS ANGELES!" I yell as I launch myself at him.

His eyes widen as he huffs out a laugh. "I thought you were upset."

"I was just messing with you. This is the best fucking news ever, baby! Are you for real?"

"Yeah. Things will move swiftly once I'm back from Barcelona."

My mouth gapes open. This is really happening. "You could stay with me—" I pause. "Sorry. What am I saying? That probably wouldn't make any sense, and you probably want your own place."

"Actually...I was thinking, we keep your place for appearances but look for a place of our own?"

"You want to live together?"

"I'd love to live with you." His brow furrows. "But we don't have to if it's too much or too fast for you."

The last time he proposed us taking a step forward by being exclusive, it resulted in me on my knees having a panic attack. I understand his cautiousness, but we've come a long way since then, and fuck...the idea of coming home to him during our hectic seasons seems too good to pass up.

"It's not too much for me. I'd love to live with you," I reply.

"Word?" he asks.

I nod and brush a kiss against his smiling lips. "Best birthday ever."

THIRTY MINUTES LATER, HE'S PACKED AND HEADING TO THE airport. I rub the ache in my sternum as I watch him drive away. His move to LA can't come soon enough.

I head back to the hotel to meet the guys, who I find in various stages of a hangover. They blew a small fortune at Ivy's, but by the look of things, they had fun, so I guess it was money well spent. Sid sends us back to LA on his plane. His pilot, Nat, knows the score on us and subtly winks at me when we board. All of Sid's staff have signed non-disclosure agreements to ensure our privacy.

Archie's reel goes viral and blows up my feed with happy birthday messages. I feel like the cool kid at school, recounting the ride to the guys. I had to throw in a few false details like Sid inviting me at the last minute. I hate lying to them, but I want to protect Sid and me for as long as possible.

Chapter Eighteen

"Back to paradise," Tevin says, gazing out the window as Nat taxies us into LAX.

I'm jittery from sitting too long. "Think I'll hit a trail after I get in."

Tevin yawns. "I'm dead, bro. Fuckin' Justin pushed his whiskey hard last night. I wouldn't be surprised if there's a case already waiting for us when we get home. Dude's a hustla. His shit's smooth, though. I can't front. Said somethin' about aging it in Spanish oak. Got a money maker on his hands. I knew better than to mix it with vodka." He winces. "Fuck it. I'm making today a cheat day. I'm craving pepperoni pizza, enchiladas, the Big Mek from—"

"You mean Big Mac?" I interrupt as I turn my phone off of airplane mode.

"Nah, bruh, Big Mek."

I bunch my eyebrows.

His jaw drops. "You're wildin'. You never had the Big Mek?"

I shake my head.

He grabs his phone, types in something, and slides it over.

I stare at his screen, taking in the double-decker cheese-burger spilling over with toppings and condiments. "Beast."

"You know how you always tellin' us about your uncle's Caribbean food? I got five hundred on this beating that."

I shake my head. "You fittin' to lose your money then."

"I'll put a rack on it. Look at it, bruh! And it tastes better than it looks. The cows were slain on a full moon or some shit." He leans forward in his chair. "Let me set the scene. Imagine two seasoned patties, juicy in the middle and seared to perfection on the outside. You dig?"

I nod.

"The juices from the burger get their freak on with the gooiest small batch of American cheese you've ever had. Add thin rings of pickles and caramelized onions, 'cause why the fuck not? Garlic aioli rains down from the heavens. Go on, lick your lips—you know you want to."

I shrug. "Sounds like a regular cheeseburger to me."

"I'm not finished. A red wine sauce infused with shallots, herbs, and wait for it...foie gras tops it off." He kisses his fingers. "Slide that thick, juicy baddie between a buttery brioche bun and boom!" He flicks his fingers against his temple.

I chuckle. "Aight. I'm intrigued. Only way to know it ain't hype is to try it myself. My next cheat day's on Friday."

He nods. "Say less. I got you. Prepare for your life to change —and your belly to expand. Wear sweats."

"Bet."

"Y'all want to train at my place tomorrow?" Idris asks from two rows behind us.

"I'm game," I answer, twisting in his direction.

"Can't. I traded the wife a spa getaway in exchange for this trip. Unless I can come through with my little terrors? Before you agree, I should forewarn you that Benji is going through a streaking phase. He threw a tantrum when I stopped him from stripping down in Target last week," Kaleb says, making us laugh.

"Little dude's a free soul. Bring 'em through," Idris says. He climbs to his feet and tilts his pelvis forward to stretch his back.

"I'm down, but only if it's after eleven. Y'all kill me with that crack of dawn shit," Malik says as he tucks himself deeper into the chair.

Idris sighs. "Someone tell this youngin' that greatness means getting off yo' ass and gettin' after it."

"Youngin', listen to the vet. Peep Sid. Dude won a championship, and he's right back at training for the Olympics during the offseason," Kaleb jumps in.

I grin. It is pretty badass, even if I miss him already.

"Do we need to pull up your airball compilation on YouTube?" Kaleb jokes.

"That's cold, bro. How you gonna reduce the kid to his failures?" Tevin pipes in.

Malik upnods to Tevin. "Thanks for havin' my back."

"He ain't lying tho. I'm just sayin', I'd get up at dawn if my field goal percentage was under forty percent," Tevin retorts, causing an eruption of laughter.

Malik shakes his head. "Et tu, Brute?" He jumps to his feet and lifts his chin. "Which one of y'all tough enough to say it to my face?"

He spins, turning his back on Kaleb, who sneaks up behind him and puts him in a full Nelson hold, forcing his hands straight up in the air. "What was that, youngin'?"

"Ohh, snap!" Tevin says dramatically, covering his mouth. Can always count on Tev to instigate.

"Money's on K!" Idris throws out.

I'm about to tell Malik my money's on him, but I'm distracted when my phone vibrates. I hit accept just as Malik counterattacks with a swift side-step. He tucks his leg behind

Kaleb's and drops his front knee, sending Kaleb crashing into the seats in front of him, breaking his hold.

"Don't break Sid's plane!" I yell.

The guys roar with laughter as Malik fist punches the air and bounces on his heels like a heavyweight champ.

"I want a rematch," Kaleb says, rubbing his lower back.

I shake my head. "Hey, Unc! You'd never believe who I— wait, hold on—" I can barely hear him over the ruckus. I move toward the front of the plane. "My bad—"

I stiffen once I register that the voice on the other end isn't Adam's.

"Ishan? Everything o—"

I suck in a breath as I hear the words—*Adam, cardiac arrest, hospital.*

This can't be real.

I squeeze my eyes shut and push out a strangled breath. I try to speak but I choke. Clearing my throat, I manage to rasp, "Alive?"

"The paramedics on the scene resuscitated him, but he's in surgery. I don't know if he'll..." Ishan muffles a sob, and it pierces my chest. "I don't understand. He was right there on my six. Our unit was one of the first to exit the building. I heard a weird sound, and when I looked back, he was lying on the ground. And we couldn't..." His voice catches.

My vision turns blurry as I imagine Adam losing consciousness.

"...he didn't have a pulse," he continues.

I crumple, sliding down the wall to the floor and squeezing my eyes shut to stop the cabin from spinning.

"A-are you still there?"

"Yeah..." I croak. "I'm on my way. Send me the information, please."

"I'll send it now."

"Ishan, wait, do whatever it takes to keep him alive. Insist on the best doctors. His insurance is irrelevant. I'll pay anything. Please. Make sure they resuscitate him if necessary. Keep him alive by any means. Please. Don't let them fuck up."

"Of course. I love him."

"I know. Thank you for being there with him. I'm on my way."

After I hang up, my phone buzzes. Seeing Adam's name makes me lightheaded. My fingers tremble as I read the hospital details.

IT'S A QUARTER PAST FOUR O'CLOCK IN THE MORNING WHEN I enter the hospital. Thank God for Sid's plane and Nat, who willingly offered to transport me to Teterboro Airport in New Jersey. Despite my attempts to shake them, the guys hung back with me while the plane refueled. Nat and I were back in the air in under an hour.

When the plane walls started to close in, I spent the better part of the flight repeatedly muttering five things I saw around me, four things that I could touch, three things that I could hear, two things that I could smell, and one thing that I could taste.

I called Ishan back as soon as the plane landed. I tried to stand, but my knees buckled as the phone rang out. A familiar swarm of unrest had me bolting to the restroom, where I puked up the measly coffee I managed to get down. I flushed the toilet and rinsed out my mouth with Sid's mouthwash.

I step off of the elevator and into a sea of firefighters. I'm pulled into a hug by Tom, Adam's best friend.

His eyes are swollen and red. "The son of a bitch scared all of us. He's got the heart of a lion. If anyone could pull through a cardiac arrest, it's him," he says, embracing my shoulder.

"Thanks. I—" I twist my head when a hand pats my back.

"Ty, whatever you need, and I mean anything, you let us know. That's our brother in there." Adam's boss, Chief Johnson, grasps my hand. "Thank you," I reply, shaking her hand. "It means a lot, you all being here."

She nods. "Go ahead. I bet you're desperate to go to him."

I nod and brush past her.

I find Adam's room with Tom's help. When I enter, I freeze. There are at least a half dozen cords and tubes inserted into him. I cover my mouth as a sob rips from my chest. There's a machine with zig-zag lines that I recognize from television. Whenever its alarm goes off, it's never good.

Ishan's head whips up. "Hey, hey! It's okay. He's okay," he says, releasing Adam's hand and darting over to me. "I just called you back. Surgery was successful. He hasn't woken up yet, but the surgeon said that's normal. He should wake up in the next couple of hours."

I shake my head as I suck in air, and hot tears pour down my face.

"He's okay. He's going to live," Ishan repeats.

I retreat, shaking my head. He's not okay. There's a tube sticking out of his mouth. His face looks swollen. He's stiff. If it wasn't for the plastic bulb thing expanding on every breath, he'd seem...dead. My back hits a wall.

A brick is lodged behind my breastbone, and it hurts to breathe.

Please God, not him. You've taken so much from me.

Ishan's lips are moving, but my thoughts drown him out.

Five things to hear...

The beeping does a stuttering thing, and my legs give out. I kneel and bracket my head between my arms, rocking in place.

My phone buzzes, and I drop it as I cup my hands over my mouth and wheeze, trying to unblock my throat.

Five things....

Beeping. Beeping...

I squeeze my eyes shut.

Five things...

Three graves...I'll visit three graves every year if he doesn't make it.

Five things I see.

Tubes, fucking tubes, machines, Adam's dying.

If fire takes him, water takes me.

I swear it, God.

I press on my chest bone and suck in air.

Somewhere in the recesses of my memory I hear Adam, "Ty, breathe!"

I suck in another breath, pushing past the ache. Then another, then another, until the ghastly thing lodged in my chest doesn't hurt so much.

A thumb slides under my chin. I peel my eyes open and meet Ishan's gaze as he kneels in front of me.

"He's alive," he says, nodding around a sad smile and wet eyes. "He's alive," he repeats with a mix of desperation and hope.

"H-he's alive," I whisper, more for him than me.

"Baby—"

My eyebrows bunch as I track the familiar voice to my phone in Ishan's hand.

"He was calling...I thought he could help," Ishan says, handing it to me.

"Baby, talk to me."

"S-Sid?"

"Yes, I'm here. Are you okay?"

I take him off of speakerphone.

"Sid," I sob into the phone quietly, too choked again to speak.

"I'm so sorry this is happening. Ishan said Adam's going to pull through, baby," he says gently.

"I know but…"

"It's terrifying."

"Yeah." I wipe my eyes. "He has tubes…" I can barely get the words out before my throat closes back up.

"The tubes are reinforcements. They're just helping to ensure everything is working as it should."

"I don't know," I choke out. "Why did he drop?"

"Let's find out. Put me on speaker."

I pull the phone away from my ear and hit the speaker button.

"Okay," I croak.

"Ishan, you think you can grab the surgeon or doctor on duty and ask them to come and explain to us what happened?" Sid asks.

Ishan nods and wipes his eyes. "The surgeon was waiting for you. Since I'm not next of kin or listed as an emergency contact, they wouldn't disclose any real details until you arrived."

I nod. "Thanks."

As he retreats toward the door, it opens.

"I was just coming to find you. Adam's nephew, Tyler, is here," Ishan says to a tall woman in scrubs and a white coat and a man in blue scrubs trailing behind her.

"One of the firefighters beat you to the punch," the woman says. "Hello, you must be Tyler. Nice to meet you. I'm Dr. Rivers, the Head of Cardiology. I performed the surgery on your uncle. This is Nurse Ford. He's our best. He'll take excellent care of Mr. Washington."

I climb to my feet and then shake both of their hands. Nurse Ford leaves us to check on Adam.

Clearing my throat, I try to muster the energy to collect my thoughts, but when I open my mouth, my voice cracks with emotion.

"Could you—" I clear my throat again, but it doesn't help. I zero in on the machine beeping across the room.

"Hi, Dr. Rivers. I'm David, Ty's best friend. Today's been a really rough day for him. We have a couple of questions. Ty and Ishan, I'll take notes of everything said and send it over," Sid says, using his middle name.

"Thanks...David," Ishan replies.

"You want to go first?" Ishan asks, inviting me to ask the first question. "Or David?" he adds.

The beeping machine stutters again, and my eyes dart to Adam. No one else seems concerned by the noise. A dozen questions flooded my brain on the plane, but now I'm struggling to think of one.

"Could you walk us through the surgery performed, the probable cause of the attack, and the process of recovery?" Sid asks, saving me from choking again.

I slump against the wall.

"Sure. Mr. Washington is very lucky. According to the paramedics, he went into cardiac arrest after exiting a four-alarm blaze..."

I make a mental note to look up what cardiac arrest means.

"He was immediately treated by the—"

"Is cardiac arrest like a heart attack?" Sid asks.

"Not quite. Cardiac arrest occurs when the heart suddenly stops pumping, preventing blood from flowing to the brain and other vital organs. It's caused by certain types of arrhythmias, basically irregular heart rhythms, that prevent the heart from pumping blood. If not treated within minutes, they're often fatal."

My eyes flood as I stare up at the ceiling and breathe out a sigh of relief.

"Tests revealed that Mr. Washington has coronary artery disease. It's most likely what triggered the cardiac event yesterday. As for the cause of the disease, research indicates that high levels of occupational stress, such as heat stress, frequent activation of the body's fight-or-flight response, and exposure to chemicals, smoke, soot, and other inhaled pollutants, all contribute to heart problems for firefighters."

"So it's common among firefighters?" Sid asks.

"Er—let me put it this way. Research shows that the risk of a cardiac event increases the longer a firefighter stays on the job. If a heart attack occurs, often as a result of severe coronary artery disease, it can trigger ventricular fibrillation and sudden cardiac arrest. Mr. Sharma mentioned that your uncle recently complained about feeling a heaviness in his chest, resulting in him needing to lie down."

I turn to Ishan. "When?"

His eyes well up. "Last week. We thought it was acid reflux," he says, regret etched all over his face.

I grasp his shoulder and pull him into a hug. He presses his forehead against my chest and sobs.

Dr. Rivers gives us a minute, offering a sympathetic grin.

"It's not your fault," I whisper. He nods and wipes his eyes with the tissues Nurse Ford passes out.

"Is the disease fatal?" I ask, finding my voice.

"I'll be straight with you. Your uncle is lucky to be alive, thanks to the quick intervention of the paramedics. Most people who experience cardiac arrest do not survive. For survivors, there is a risk of brain injury, neurological dysfunction, neurocognitive deficits..."

Brain injury.

I gaze over at Adam, wondering if it's still him in there. Will he recognize me, Ishan, or even himself? Since my parents' deaths, I've feared losing my memories of them. I've feared losing Adam. I never imagined I could lose him this way.

Sid's voice reels me back into the conversation. "How will we know if Adam suffered a brain impairment?"

Dr. Rivers raises her voice slightly to be heard over the

phone. "When a cardiac arrest is treated very quickly, a person may recover with no signs of injury. Others may have mild to severe damage. When Mr. Washington wakes up, we'll monitor him for signs—severe memory loss, loss of muscle control, and impaired speech, amongst other things. Keep in mind, if present, some symptoms may improve over time, so there isn't immediate cause for alarm. The best way to help Mr. Washington is to try to remain calm and patient."

"Can you tell us about the surgery performed and the road to recovery?" Ishan asks.

"Sure. We performed a less invasive procedure called an off-pump coronary artery bypass graft surgery. We take an artery or vein from one part of the body and use it to bypass a blocked coronary artery. The surgery restores normal blood flow to the patient's heart. Instead of the traditional…"

What if he loses his ability to walk? I'll have a ramp installed in his house. I'll hire a home nurse for him. I'll hire one anyway.

I can try to transfer to a basketball team on the East Coast so that I'm closer to him.

I wonder if he needs one of those heart monitor things. I'll look up the best one money can buy. I wonder if they have app-controlled ones that alert family members if there's an attack.

Maybe I should buy him a house close to the best hospital.

"…Recovery in the hospital can take up to a week if everything goes according to plan. Mr. Washington must attend our specialized postoperative rehabilitation and prevention program. In addition to monitored exercise, there's an education component that will teach him about the lifestyle changes required to aid in risk reduction and prevention of future cardiac events."

Thanks, Doctor. Si—David, caught most of that?" Ishan asks.

"Yep," Sid replies.

"Thanks," Ishan says, leaning against the wall.

"Doc, could you describe the level of pain Adam will be in after surgery?" Sid asks.

"Sure, we expect Mr. Washington…"

The machine beeps again, and my head snaps to Adam.

"What are the wires coming out of him?" I blurt out.

Dr. Rivers gestures with her hand. "Come closer. I'll show you."

I follow her to Adam, and my stomach twists at seeing the tube protruding from his throat. The doctor explains that it's there to help him breathe.

*Drains, pacing wires, arterial pressure lines…*I can't keep up with it all. My head aches.

After the doctor and nurse leave, Ishan returns to holding Adam's hand, and I step into the hallway to talk to Sid.

"Thanks for taking the lead. Ishan and I were…" My voice trails off.

"We're partners, baby—you don't have to thank me. I feel bad that I'm not there with you. I'll ask for a leave or pull out —"

"Nah…no way. I'll see you in a few weeks when you get home."

He's already done enough, and competing in the Olympics is important to him. I just need a night of rest, then I should be able to pull it together. "Focus on practice. Just hit me up when you can."

"Of course. That goes without saying. When's the last time you slept or ate?" He asks.

I haven't slept since in his arms. Feels like forever ago.

"Miami. Isn't it like after one in the morning for you?"

"I got worried when you didn't respond to my earlier messages. I checked in with Nat to make sure y'all landed safely, and she told me about Adam."

"She's good in emergencies. She agreed to fly me out here without any hesitation."

"She's the best. Plus, everyone on my staff knows to give you whatever you need. The plane is yours whenever."

I'm not sure I'll ever get used to his thorough generosity.

"I missed half of what the doctor said," I admit.

"That's okay. I caught most of it. I'll send all of the information when we get off. Sounds like the surgery was less intense than the traditional method."

That's information I should have paid attention to. "How so?"

"It didn't require Adam's heart to be stopped, and instead of cutting down the middle of his chest, they made an incision between his ribs. His recovery time will be faster."

I shake my head. I completely missed all of that.

I tip my head back and close my eyes. "Baby...I love you."

The thought of going through this without him feels impossible.

"I love you too. I'd do anything for you. I'll try to help in ways I think would be useful, but don't hesitate to tell me what you need." His deep voice relaxes some of the knots of tension in my shoulders. "What do you need right now?"

Your arms...for Adam to wake up...for him to remember me...for his heart to function normally.

"I'll tell you when I know. I'm gonna head back inside," I reply.

"Call or text and let me know when he wakes up?"

"Yeah...definitely."

"What's the name of the hospital?"

"Saint Mary's. ICU department."

"Okay. I'll research the top cardiology rehab programs in New Jersey to find the best one for him."

"I can do it tomorrow. Get some rest. I'll feel bad if you're distracted from training."

"Not helping would be distracting for me."

He's helped plenty already.

"Ty, wake up."

I jolt awake, causing an acidic burn to shoot up my chest.

"What's happening?" I ask, staring between Ishan and Adam.

"He just stirred. I think he's waking up," Ishan says.

We hover over Adam, searching for movement.

"I swear, he just moved," Ishan says, a desperate tinge in his voice.

Ishan's watch lights up, and I scan that it's a couple minutes past ten in the morning.

I nod. "Adam, can you hear us?"

He doesn't move an inch.

Then, a minute or so later, his eyes begin to move.

My gaze darts to Ishan, who nods, confirming that I didn't imagine it.

"Hey, Unc...it's Ty. Ishan and I are here with you," I say gently.

We wait for a response...or any sign that he's heard me.

Ishan looks at me and frowns.

"Maybe he's—" Ishan starts but freezes when Adam groans.

"I'll get the nurse," he says, darting out of the room.

"Ishan is getting the nurse, but I'm here with you," I say, taking his hand.

He groans again as his eyes slowly crack open. He winces.

My eyes well up as his gaze searches my face. I wipe them quickly, remembering Dr. Rivers' advice to appear calm. He looks so confused. His eyes droop closed again.

Ishan returns with Nurse Ford on his trail.

Ishan and I stand back as he observes Adam and checks his

vitals. The nurse tries to elicit a response from Adam, but he's out cold.

"He's pretty heavily sedated, so it may take him a while to become fully conscious. Everything looks good here. I'll be back to check on him in thirty minutes. If you need anything, just push this button right here," he says, gesturing to a button on the inside arm of Adam's bed frame.

Ishan and I settle back down into our chairs. I retrieve my phone from the floor where it's charging and see missed calls from Sid, his mom Lily, and cousin Kieran, and a few texts from my teammates checking in.

I listen to Sid and Lily's voicemails—both checking in for an update. A few seconds into Kieran's voicemail, I jump to my feet.

"I'll be right back," I tell Ishan.

He nods, keeping his eyes glued on Adam.

I head down the corridor and make a left turn. When I enter the waiting room, a bunch of heads turn in my direction. The room seems less crowded now that Adam's co-workers are gone.

A young kid pats an older man's arm and then points to me.

Ugh. This is the last place I want to be recognized.

I'm about to double back to Adam's room when I hear, "Ty."

I whip around and am immediately sandwiched in a hug by Tommy and Kieran.

"We came as soon as Sid called. We brought food and toiletries for you and your uncle's boyfriend...Ishan, right?" Kieran asks as we pull away.

"Thanks...yeah, that's his name. I appreciate it. We haven't eaten."

"Roasted chicken, mashed potatoes, and greens. Vegetable pot pie and some water, cold brew, and juices," Tommy says, handing me the bag and clasping my shoulder with his free hand.

"Wow. Thanks." My stomach rumbles as I peer into the bag.

"Can we get you anything? You or Ishan need a change of clothes?" Kieran asks.

"I'm good. I have a duffel with me, and Adam's bathroom has a shower, but let me check with Ishan. You sure you have time?"

"Of course. Go ahead and ask him. We'll be here," Tommy says.

Ishan makes a quick list of things that he needs and where to find them. Even though Ishan recently moved in, the list is ninety percent stuff for Adam. His shaving kit, loose-fitting clothes, laptop to watch movies, puzzles, pillows, and linen to make Adam more comfortable. I read through the list with gratitude for Ishan being in our lives. During times like this, the quality of people in your life matters more than anything. My chest pangs, thinking of Sid. God, I miss him. How's it only been a day?

BY THE TIME KIERAN AND TOMMY RETURN WITH THE LIST OF items and more food, I've cleaned up and changed into fresh clothes. I grab a quick coffee with them in the hospital diner. When I return to Adam's room, Ishan's in the shower. I drop into the chair and rub my eyes, desperate for the caffeine to kick in. I pull out my phone to text Sid when Adam groans. I fly out of my seat.

His eyes are finally open. "You're awake," I say, more to myself than to him.

He raises his hand. His movement is sluggish.

"Wait, there are tubes," I say, reaching for his hand. He gestures to the tube in his throat.

"It's to help you breathe. The doctor said it'll come out once you're awake and they've had a chance to check you. I'll push the button to call the nurse."

His eyes flood as he tightens his grip on my hand.

"It's okay. You're going to be okay. The nurse is on his way." I try my best to sound confident despite my voice breaking.

Ishan emerges from the restroom.

"He's awake. I pushed the button for the nurse."

The nurse walks in just as Ishan jets around to the other side of Adam.

Adam's eyes widen when he sees Ishan.

He recognizes us...I think.

"His eyes are open," I tell Nurse Ford.

"That's great!" he replies. I try to release Adam's hand to swap places with the nurse, but he doesn't let me go.

"Mr. Washington, my name is Rob. I am your nurse. You are in the Intensive Care Unit at St. Mary's Hospital. Today is Monday, July 2nd. You went into cardiac arrest, but you are stable and recovering."

"Can you squeeze your nephew's hand if you're in pain, Mr. Washington?"

He tightens his grip on my hand.

I nod to the nurse.

"Okay, we'll take care of that right now. You're doing great."

"I'm going to let go of your hand so that he can check your vitals. I'll be right here," I tell him.

He releases my hand slowly.

After the nurse confirms everything looks fine, he ups Adam's pain medicine.

Adam comes in and out of consciousness over the next two hours. When he's finally wide-eyed and awake, the on-call physician runs a series of tests, then confirms it's safe to begin removing his breathing tube. A thin tube is then fitted into his nostrils for oxygen intake support.

I hang back while the doctor moves Adam to an upright

position and walks him through a couple of breathing exercises. He informs us that the medical team will stop in frequently to monitor Adam over the next few hours.

"I'm so glad you're awake. You scared the shit out of me," Ishan says, kissing Adam's forehead.

His voice is so hoarse we barely hear his reply. "Sorry."

His brows furrow when I approach his bed. I'm still not a hundred percent confident that he recognizes me.

"Hi. I'm Ty—Tyler," I say awkwardly.

He reaches his arm out and cups the back of my neck. Not wanting the tubes in his hand to detach, I tilt my head down toward him. He applies light pressure until my forehead is pressed against his. My vision turns blurry as he rubs my neck like he usually does to calm me down...like my dad used to.

He remembers me.

"S'okay," he rasps.

I wipe my eyes and kiss the side of his forehead before letting out a sigh of relief.

Chapter Nineteen

In early August, I return home. A wave of fatigue hits as I lock the door and drop my duffles and pile of mail. The last few weeks were more grueling than I'd anticipated. Adam was discharged from the hospital a week after surgery. Ishan and I tag-teamed taking care of him, ensuring he made it to rehab and stayed on top of his medicine. True to his word, Sid found a state-of-the-art cardiac rehab program less than forty minutes from Adam's house in New Jersey.

As for the patient himself, some days were harder than others. For one, his recovery was more painful than any of us imagined. He slept a lot, being hopped up on painkillers. Being diagnosed with coronary artery disease meant a forced early retirement from the fire department, which he took pretty hard. I'm not sure if it's helpful or hurtful for him to watch Ishan leave for work. He became sullen after visits from his old colleagues. An abrupt end to a decades-long career comes with its share of grief. It was hard seeing him down every day.

Before I left, I interviewed and hired a home attendant and cleaning staff and set him up with a high-end meal prep service. But knowing him and his need to be self-sufficient, he's probably going to get rid of everyone once he's back on his feet.

I thought I'd spend the offseason training, but tending to Adam didn't leave much time. I got into a rhythm of waking up early to hit a local gym. I had a fifty-inch portable basketball hoop delivered to the house and spent whatever free time I had practicing shooting in the backyard. Now that I'm home, I plan to make up for lost time.

But first, I need rest.

I push off the door and pull out my phone to call Sid. I read on the plane that we beat Spain by seven points. I get his voicemail.

"Hey babe, congrats on the win. I can't wait to hear about it. I just got home. Thanks for sending Nat to swoop me. I'm wiped. I'll probably crash soon. Hit me up whenever."

I shower, demolish a PB&J sandwich, and crash. I'm knocked out in minutes. Soon after, a nightmare follows.

The icy rain pelts my skin with the sting of tiny glass marbles. A cold hand wraps around my own—Adam's. His eyelids are swollen.

"What's wrong?"

"I'm sorry," he croaks.

I follow his gaze...three gravestones.

My stomach clenches. Mom's, Dad's, and a new one, freshly covered with dirt. The rain blurs my vision. I drag myself closer to read the tombstone, but Adam holds me back.

"Don't," he warns me.

Terror strangles my chest and throat. "Who is it?"

He shakes his head.

I rip out of his embrace and stumble toward the grave. My steps are like cinder blocks as they sink into the wet dirt.

I wipe the rain away from the tombstone.

"In loving memory of Sidney David King."

I jerk back and blink rapidly.

No! It can't be!

A monstrous wave of despair slams into my chest. My legs buckle under its violent force. The harder I try to breathe, the more my chest caves in on itself. I try to ask Adam to call for help, but the words never reach my lips. Adam yells for help, but it's too late. The last thing I see is an angry sky before my vision darkens.

I jolt awake, wheezing and clasping my cramping stomach. I kick away the sheets, lurch over the bed, and vomit. My head throbs as I down the glass of water from the nightstand. I press on my throat to dull the sharp ache that feels like it's been raked with steel.

I check my phone for Sid's call, but he never called back. I dial him again, needing to know he's okay. Every ring escalates the queasiness in my stomach.

"Hey babe, I was just calling you."

"You're okay?" I ask.

"I'm good. What's wrong?"

"Fuck," I sigh, dropping my head into my hands. "I just… fuck…"

I swipe my eyes as the vision of his name on the tombstone flashes through my mind.

"Baby, what's wrong? Talk to me."

You were dead. My heart gave out…I took my last breath.

My entire body trembles from grief, exhaustion, and terror.

"I'm sorry," I croak. "It's nothing…"

"Was it a nightmare?"

Shame burns through me. Why the fuck can't I be normal?

"Yeah…I'm fine. Sorry. Let me hit you back." I end the call, bury my head in my hands, and scream until I'm empty.

My phone vibrates, but I ignore it.

I fold myself into a ball and lie in the quiet darkness until I drift asleep.

I'm certain my head's trying to kill me when I wake up to piss. It hurts to think. The smell of puke evokes memories of the nightmare. I drag myself to the bathroom to relieve myself. My entire body hurts. Opening the medicine cabinet, I twist off the cap of nighttime cough syrup and take a long swig. I remember the bottle of prescription sleeping pills that Adam asked me to throw away. He hated the way he felt on them. I held on to the bottle, figuring that they might help with my nightmares. I search around in my duffel until I find the bottle —eszopiclone. I swallow a few and throw the bottle in my medicine cabinet. I put the trash bin of vomit outside of my door, then crash back into bed.

Shit! Remembering how I left things with Sid, I retrieve my phone. It's almost dead. God, there are so many of his missed calls. I pen a quick text to him.

ME

Sorry for the cryptic call. Had a nightmare. I fell back asleep. Feeling like shit. I'm gonna try to sleep some more. Will hit you up when I wake up.

The phone dies as soon as I hit send, so I have no way of knowing if the message went through. Damn. I'll call him when I wake up. I throw the comforter over my head, and I'm knocked out again in no time.

I SWALLOW, BUT GRAVEL'S LODGED IN MY THROAT. I TRY REACHING for the water on my nightstand but can't move. My entire body is paralyzed. I try to rip my eyes open, but they're glued shut. There's a woman's voice, but it sounds far away. Then everything goes quiet, and I drift back to sleep.

I'm awake again...has it been hours...or days? I try to reach for the glass of water that I know is sitting on my nightstand, but I still can't move. I'm so thirsty. I try to lift my arms, but there's heavy sand where my blood used to be.

There's a woman's voice again. My eyes are cemented shut. Help me! I try to speak, but my tongue is paralyzed too. I'll never escape this.

It all fades to black again.

I gasp and jerk awake from the assault of a thousand sharp needles.

My nose burns as I huff to unplug it.

Everything burns.

"My god, that worked. He's awake! Ty, are you okay? It's me, Lily."

I groan. A sharp thumping, like someone's trying to punch their way out of my head, has me leaning forward, clasping my temples.

"L-lily?" My throat is raw. I almost don't believe what I'm seeing. If it wasn't for the scent of rose, pepper, and citrus filling the room, I wouldn't believe that Sid's mom is in my bedroom holding an ice bucket.

"Hi, dear. My Lord! What a scare you gave us. We were two minutes away from calling an ambulance. I'm on with your uncle and Sid," she says, gesturing to the phone.

"W-what are you doing here?" I pluck my shirt away from my body, and ice cubes tumble out.

"We've been trying to reach you. Sid said that you were quite distressed when you called him yesterday."

"Yesterday?"

How long have I been out?

"It's Tuesday evening."

I slept over eighteen hours?

"Yes, he's okay. I'll put you both on speaker," Lily says into the phone.

I guess my text didn't go through. Shit.

My face heats up despite being drenched in ice-cold water.

Sid and Adam speak simultaneously, and it's a jumbled mix of the same question. "Are you okay?"

"I'm fine...I'm sick and took cough syrup and sleeping pills. It knocked me..."

"That's dangerous. You shouldn't mix—Christ—how much did you take? What sleeping pills?" Sid's freaked-out voice makes me flinch.

"I don't know. The one Adam was prescribed. It's fine, I—"

"Mom, he needs to go to the hospital. We have no way of knowing if the combination is lethal."

"Ty, you were supposed to get rid of those pills. They're too strong. They made me hallucinate," Adam says.

"Mom, please." Sid's voice cracks.

"Love, hold on. I'm staring right at him. He's okay. This isn't that..."

I flash Lily a questioning stare. *What isn't this?*

"Lily, could you check his pulse?" Adam asks.

"I'm fine. I was just in pain and needed to sleep," I repeat, as Lily checks my pulse.

Why isn't anyone listening to me?

Sid's voice trembles, "Mom, listen to me, please, take him to the hospital. There's still time to intervene."

He sounds terrified. I don't get why he's freaking out. How long did it take for me to wake up?

"Please! I can't lose him."

I shrink, pulling the wet comforter up over my chest.

Lily clicks off of speakerphone. "Sidney, I can hear that you're very upset. I'm sorry you're so far away and can't be here right now. I need you to trust me. Ty's okay. I checked his pulse, and it's normal. I will hang up now so that I can pump him with water and food. If I see any sign that something's off, I will call 911 right away. I'll call you back within the hour...both of you." She lets out an exasperated breath. "I know...you trust me, right? I love Ty too. Yes, but he's not Paul, sweetheart."

I grimace. He thinks I tried to OD like Paul? I only wanted to sleep through...whatever this is. I just needed a break. I've long been able to ignore the voice telling me to end it.

Lily raises each of my eyelids like a nurse. She shakes her head. "His pupils are fine. I know you're scared, but I'm telling you he's okay. Can you do me a favor? Grab an emergency session with Adrian."

Fuck. He needs an emergency therapy session because of me? Why did I have to freak out and call him after my nightmare?

I shiver as I recall his tombstone and the drag of my last breath seeping from me.

It was so real.

Lily sighs and places the phone against her chest. "He's making arrangements to come home."

"Wait—what? No way! I'm fine."

She places the phone back against her ear. "He doesn't want you to pull out. I'll take care of him. Just take a deep breath and try to get a therapy session before your game against Australia. Okay? I'm gonna go now. I love you. Call you soon...you too, Adam. Try not to worry. Focus on your recovery. Our guy's in good hands. Call Adrian, Sidney."

My shoulders slump forward. The burden of their concern, the burden of causing concern, the weight of it is crushing.

"I'm sorr—"

"Nope. No apologies or feeling guilty. You slept like the dead, is all. I tried everything to wake you. We were all a bit shaken." She breathes a heavy sigh of relief. "You're awake now, and that's all that matters. Tell me. Where does it hurt?" She places the back of her hand against my forehead.

If only I could point to a fever. How do I explain a feeling so bleak that my entire body feels riddled with pain? I wish every-thing...everyone could just stop.

"I really just need to sleep. You didn't have to fly all of this way. I'm sorry to have burdened you."

She waves me off. "You're family, and I always take care of my family. When's the last time you had anything to eat or drink?"

"Had a sandwich when I got in."

"Okay. How about this?" She picks up the glass of water on the nightstand and hands it to me. "Drink that down. Let's get you up. I'll make you a quick bite. If you're still tired after you eat, you can go back to sleep. Deal?"

The thought of eating makes my stomach turn. I know it's generous of her to stop everything and fly out here, but I really just want to curl up in a ball and turn everything off. Maybe the quicker I shower and swallow down whatever she makes, the sooner I can be left alone.

"Sid told me where you hide the spare key...in case you're wondering how I got in."

I nod. I figured as much.

She opens the door to leave, and I'm hit with the stench of sick.

"Shoot. I'm sorry. I can get rid of that," I sluggishly move toward the wastebasket, but she beats me to it.

"I got it. Meet me in the kitchen." For a second, she sounds just as commanding as my mom, and it causes an ache in my chest.

After brushing my teeth and showering, I open the medicine cabinet and hesitate, staring at the bottle of eszopiclone. I'm too fucking exhausted to fight the looming darkness. If they understood, they wouldn't fault me. I pour a couple of pills into my hand and swallow them with water from the faucet. When I enter my bedroom, my mattress is covered in fresh bedding.

I throw on sweats and make my way to the kitchen.

"I found a can of soup in the cabinet. Not much for me to work with here. I'll run out and get groceries for us after you eat," Lily says.

I wince at the bright light, craving the darkness of my bedroom.

"Thanks." I slump down in my seat at the table. She tilts the pot of hot soup into a bowl, pops in a spoon, and slides it over to me.

"I can go grocery shopping tomorrow. I know you probably have to head back," I lie. I have no intention of going grocery shopping. If I get hungry—*unlikely*—I'll make do.

"Nonsense. I'm staying with you for the next couple of days. We'll see how it goes after. And before you protest, you should know that until I feel in my heart that you're okay, it will take nothing short of an army dragging me out of here for me to leave. So eat your soup and tell me if you have any allergies."

I have enough pills to sleep through the next week, so she can stay as long as she likes.

"No allergies." I scoop up a bite of soup and blow on it before swallowing it down. It's bland.

"Great. I'll keep it light for the next few days. If you're feeling better, I'll make the lasagna you love so much."

The thought of it makes me queasy. "Sounds good." I drop the spoon into the bowl and sip from the cup of water she placed down.

I feel the weight of her stare, so I pick up the spoon and take another bite, then another until the bowl is empty. It'll probably come back up in a few hours anyway.

"Thanks again," I say after I place the bowl in the dishwasher. "Do you need anything before I go back to sleep?"

"Nope. I put my bags in the guest room on the right. It's stocked with fresh linen and towels. I also found the laundry room and threw your sheets in the wash. I'm going to head to the supermarket, make some dinner, and then settle in. I'll be in to check on you. Don't worry. I won't wake you."

I nod. "I have an app that will deliver groceries in under two hours."

"Thanks, dear. I don't mind. I like discovering new products. Especially in a nice neighborhood like this one," she says.

"Take my car. The key is by the front door. Make yourself at home. If you need anything, let me know."

She nods.

"Oh, my wallet is also by the front door. It's low on cash, but feel free to use my card."

"That's okay. Sid opened up a bank account for me with a sinful balance. He complains that I don't use it enough. I'm gonna stock your fridge just to keep him off my back," she says, smiling.

I yawn. The pills are starting to kick in. "Was he always so generous?"

She nods. "When he was fifteen, he worked a summer job to make extra money. He was saving up for a pair of those Jordans you all love. He wanted to look hip when he went back to school. I asked him if he needed me to chip in, but he said he'd saved enough. Things were tight, but I worked extra hours to cover his new clothes and school supplies. I swear, every time I turned around, the kid outgrew his clothes. On the first day of school, he came home in a worn pair of sneakers. I asked him what had happened to the Jordans he had planned to buy, and he shrugged. After glaring at him to spit out the truth, he reluctantly admitted that Sid's best friend growing up, Paul, had his summer wages stolen by his dad. That man was the devil. He probably stole it to get high or drunk. I'll never understand how someone could be so cruel to their kid," she says, shaking her head. "Do you know Sid gave Paul all of his earnings so that he could buy new clothes? Even when we didn't have much, he generously offered what he had. He still does. No one would believe the amount he donates privately."

Now that I know him, none of this comes as a surprise. I've never met anyone who gives as freely as he does.

"I love him. I'm sorry I scared him...all of you."

She pats my arm. "He loves you too. It's a wound for him, the fear of losing loved ones. I mean, for all of us, really, but especially for him. Now that he's in love, I think it's heightened the fear. That's for him to work on healing. Don't go beating yourself up over it."

I don't think I realized how much he and I have that fear in common.

"Go on and rest. I'll call him when I get to the supermarket. I'll report in that you're fed and resting," she says.

I lean down and place a kiss on her cheek.

I take two steps toward my room when she clears her throat. "Oh, Adam's sleeping pills, dear. Where are they?"

I tense as dread creeps in. "Uh, yeah, I'll, er, grab them."

My palms are sweaty as I reach into the medicine cabinet for the pills. Sleep is the only thing that'll make the next few days bearable. I wish they understood how exhausting it is to be awake. Making a split-second decision, I pop open the bottle and pour a few pills into my pocket before twisting the cap back into place.

Lily's peering into my cabinets with a pen and paper in her hand when I return.

"Here you go."

She turns and takes the bottle.

"How are you on melatonin? I can pick you up a bottle to help you rest. It's safer than this," she says, shaking the bottle.

Melatonin no longer works for me.

"I think I have a bottle around here somewhere. Don't worry about it."

She nods. "Oh, I knitted you a sweater and socks. I'll bring them to you when I get back."

"Thank you. That's really kind."

She grins and then returns to her list.

I imagine a young Sid and Paul as I drift off to sleep. Sid's my first love, but I'm his second. I never want to lose him. I wonder if anyone heals completely after losing a loved one, especially when it's a sudden and violent death.

The next few days pass almost identically. I decided to ration the sleeping pills that I had left, reserving them for the mornings so that I could sleep through the day. The nightmares tend to stay away when I sleep in the daytime. To the outside, it looks like I'm vacantly staring at the wall, but inside, my thoughts are a haze of choppy memories, fears that my brain won't ever get back on track, and self-disgust for being so fucking broken.

It's a little after six o'clock in the evening when I hear Lily's footsteps approach my room. It's been five days since she arrived. She lets me sleep so long as I eat two meals a day. I never finish the plates, but she's satisfied I get down half.

She knocks on the door. "Time for dinner."

"Okay." I slowly drag myself to a sitting position.

She hands me a plate of baked chicken, brown rice, and sautéed spinach.

The smell of chicken makes my stomach turn. "It looks great," I say. I know Lily's cooking is amazing, and it's me that's off.

"Made with extra love." She pulls up a chair to sit with me.

This is our evening ritual. We eat dinner together in my room. She talks, and I listen.

"Adam thinks you're experiencing depression. What do you think?"

I freeze mid-chew, avoiding her gaze. I swallow the lump of food. "It'll pass."

She studies me. "You know the shitty thing about depression? When you realize you're in it, you're already waist deep."

I nod, wondering if every illness feels this sneaky.

"I don't know what you're feeling exactly, but the last few weeks put you through the wringer. What happened to Adam was scary. For him, but for you too. It's okay for you not to feel okay."

I stare at my plate. Adam lived...for now, at least. I clench the fork against my palm and remind myself that he can live a long and full life with lifestyle changes and medicine. I don't know why my brain can't accept that.

"Adam and Sid mentioned that you're reluctant to go to therapy."

I push the food around my plate. "Thinking about it."

She continues studying me but doesn't push me like Sid and Adam. "We beat France."

"Oh," I clear my throat. "On to the gold medal game."

Sid will be home in a few days, then. Tension creeps into my stomach. He's never seen me like this. I have full faith that the US will earn the gold medal. Sid will probably want to celebrate when he gets home. He deserves to be with someone who is carefree and easy. He's probably loathing coming back to me.

A few days ago, Lily mentioned that the US Men's Basketball team beat Australia and progressed to face off against France. Lily changed the subject when I asked how many points Sid scored in the match. I looked it up online and almost didn't believe the poor stats. I watched the highlights to see for myself. He missed wide-open shots that I know he can make in his sleep. He also turned the ball over a reckless amount. It's shitty knowing his concern over my health interfered with his game. I only ever want to be good for him.

He calls every day. I don't always catch it if I'm sleeping or too out of it. The calls are short because I don't have much to say. I ask him about the Olympics, but he always brings the conversation back to me. I hear the concern weighing in his voice and the careful way he speaks, like the wrong word might send me over. I hate it. I'm honestly relieved he's out of the country. I just need to disappear for a while. I don't want him or anyone to see me like this.

"Sid said he tried to reach you earlier."

I sent him to voicemail every time he called today. "I was asleep. I'll call him later."

Once I force the food down, she collects our plates and returns with a sci-fi novel. She started reading to me after dinner the day after she arrived. Her voice is comforting, though I don't have the energy to follow the story. She stretches her legs and rests her socked feet on the edge of my bed as she picks up where she left off. I catch the first few lines of the chapter before my thoughts trail off. My mind travels back to Sid. I wonder if it'll be tense or awkward between us when he returns home.

TWO DAYS LATER, I'M LYING IN BED AWAKE WHEN THE FRONT DOOR opens. I tap my phone to see the time. It's a quarter past three in the morning. Lily went to bed hours ago. I hear a chirp, indicating the security system's been disarmed.

He's home.

He wasn't due home for two more days.

A few seconds later, the bathroom door closes in the hallway. I drag my head under the covers, then scold myself for being a coward and drag myself back out. I take a deep breath. Of all the days for him to come home...today was rough. I mustered the energy to peel myself out of bed and work out. One second, I was increasing the speed on the treadmill heading into my fifth mile; the next, I was hunched in the corner, choking for air before everything went dark. I woke with a start, stretched out on the floor with Lily's concerned face hovering over me. I was so confused—I still am, honestly. I don't recall passing out. Running five miles is nothing. It doesn't make sense why it'd cause a panic attack.

For fuck's sake, I wish my body would get a grip. It's mortifying.

And now Sid's home. I had a panic attack in front of him, but this is different. I can't give him much of anything...fuck. I can't even give myself anything.

His footsteps approach the room, and I stiffen. I will myself to turn to face him, but fear that he won't like what he sees keeps my gaze peeled to the wall. His belt buckle clanks against the floor. The bed dips, and then I'm wrapped up by his arm and pulled against his chest. His grasp is strong—possessive. The gnawing feeling turning my stomach inside out eases up as his scent fills my nostrils. I choke down the unexpected swell spreading through my chest. A tender kiss is brushed against my temple. I tuck my chin, hiding my face as a quiet sob wrenches up from that raw place inside of me.

"I'm so sorry, baby...for you...for Adam. I'm sorry that you're depressed. I missed you so fucking much. I'm sorry I wasn't here," he whispers against my ear.

He was there for me in all of the ways that matter. I nestle closer to him, never remembering feeling so small in his arms. The full force of how much we've missed each other hits like thunder, rattling everything inside of me.

"Let me see you," he says hoarsely. Tender kisses land on my neck and cheek, and I relinquish the urge to hide from him. I angle my face in his direction. My fingers trail the crescent-shaped dark circles framing his watery eyes. I can tell he hasn't slept well either. Guilt scrapes my chest. I did this.

He huffs out a breath of relief. "God, I missed you so much."

The ache that's settled in my bones starts to dull. I didn't realize the magnitude of his absence until this moment.

"I love you." It comes out warbled.

"I love you too." He brushes a kiss against my lips.

I turn to face him fully and rest my face against his chest.

No more words.

We fall asleep clinging to each other.

A FEW DAYS LATER, WE'RE SPLAYED ACROSS THE COUCH IN THE living room. I just finished giving him a foot massage, and he's returning the favor as we watch the hundredth movie since he returned home. We haven't been apart for more than a few minutes. At night, I sleep against his chest. We both wake up covered in sweat, but it doesn't matter so long as we're together. The days pass easily with movies, food, sleep, and, begrudgingly, meditation. He's gotten us into a routine of meditating first thing in the morning and before we go to sleep. The last place I want to be is inside of my head, but it helps to latch on to his voice as he counts breaths, inhaling and exhaling on cue.

I was worried I'd be too mellow for his normally upbeat energy, but I've never seen him so exhausted. Going from the NBA regular season to the playoffs, then the finals to the Olympics without a substantial break is hardcore. The last few days together have been a preview of what life might be like when he moves to the Royals, and we live together. News broke that he was leaving Miami back when he was in Spain. It caused a shitstorm online. Angry Marvels fans posted pictures burning his jersey, while others posted their gratitude for his contribution to securing a championship. LA Royals fans, on the other hand, are hyped. His Royals jersey is already selling out online.

Lily flew back home this morning. Despite wanting to be left alone at first, I grew used to her company. I surprised myself by pulling her in for a tight hug in the driveway after we'd already hugged goodbye. She palmed my face and said, "If you need me, I'll come. Anytime." The ferocity of her love is humbling. I pity the idiot that'll try to hurt someone she loves.

Before she left, we ordered takeout and popped a bottle of champagne to celebrate Sid's Olympic triumph. When I skipped making a plate, Sid pulled me into his lap and fed me from his. I'm starting to come back to myself, but I still don't have much of an appetite, and I can tell it concerns him.

I haven't had the energy to work out, which has only increased my anxiety about being prepared for training camp in a few weeks. Sid keeps reminding me that my health is more important than basketball, but I can't shake the feeling that my hard work is slipping away, and I'm letting my parents down. He offered to run drills with me when I'm up for it.

I moan as he massages the arch of my foot, applying perfect pressure. A rush of desire stirs in my belly—something I haven't felt in weeks. Outside of kissing and lying wrapped around each other, Sid and I haven't had sex since he returned home. Neither of us initiated it, and I get the sense he's giving me the space to come to him when I'm ready.

My head falls back as he rubs his knuckles up the arch of my foot, and I moan.

"Yeah?" His husky voice wraps around the back of my neck like a ray of sun.

I swallow, thinking about his taste. "I miss you."

He hums. His gaze is heated and penetrating. "I'm yours."

I pull my foot back and crawl to him. He lifts as I pull down his shorts and briefs. I lick my lips when his hardened length springs free. "Need to prep?"

"Oh, it's that kinda night?" he asks, a sexy smirk on his face.

I grin. "It could be that kinda night."

"Be right back then."

My cock twitches, watching his ripped back and sculpted ass depart.

"Scoot down. I want you to be comfortable," I tell him when he returns.

"Then you won't be comfortable. How about this?" He

tosses the throw pillows on top of the area rug and grabs a throw for us to lie on top of.

Perfect. I grab the remote and turn on captions before muting the TV.

He climbs down to the floor and rests his head against a pillow. I crawl between his legs again. The soft light from the fireplace paints golden streaks across his gorgeous skin.

I straddle him, and we make out until we're both hard. Then I trail my tongue down his body. He tenses when I place a tiny lick against his head. "It's been a minute. I won't last long."

I grin. "Watch the movie...buy me time."

Trailing my tongue across the patch of his skin under his head, I moan from the delicious taste that is distinctly his. I gaze up at him, hungry for his gorgeous face filled with desire. His lips part slightly when our gazes lock. I've wanted to try this technique for a while, but I've never been patient enough. I tilt my head sideways and use my lips and tongue to stimulate the area of nerve endings between his head and shaft. I roll the skin and tissue between my lips and suckle; the tip of my tongue massages and teases, alternating pressure. His body is rigid, signaling that he's already close. He impales his bottom lip between his teeth and battles between his eyes rolling closed and watching TV. He tastes so fucking delicious—it's taking all of my strength to not suck him down my throat.

"Oh, fuccck," he groans as the first strip of cum erupts. Damn. That's a record for us. I'm torn between catching and swallowing the next strip of cum and staying where I am, licking under his head. My mouth waters just thinking about his thick cum on my tongue, and I cave.

"Goddamn," he bellows as I suck him fervently, moaning as his cum fills my throat. I don't pull off until he squirms from sensitivity.

"Fuck, you're delicious. You got fifteen minutes, then we're going again." I kiss the tip of his dick.

"Death by blowjob...a respectable way to go out," he pants, chest heaving. Then his eyes dart open. "Let me take care of you. Come...sit on my face."

"Relax, baby. This is all I want right now."

"You sure?"

I swipe my tongue across his slit, and my eyes flicker closed. "Stop trying to get in between me and him."

"Mmm." His pupils are blown as he gazes at my tongue as it swirls around his slit before I slowly pull off and turn back to the movie. He gestures to my foot to finish the massage.

"Ready?" I ask several minutes later.

He nods.

"Tell me when you're about to come."

He hums.

I place soft licks against the tip of his head, using the flat of my tongue. I close my eyes and savor the texture of his flesh.

Every one of his husky moans reverberates through me. I fight the urge to caress his shaft. He'll come sooner if I do.

He grunts. "Pop off."

I pull my head back and gaze at him as he takes a deep breath. He's so fucking sexy...especially when he's spread out like this.

"Quit looking at me like that, or this will end fast."

I grin. "Sorry." I lean forward and lick and nibble on each of his nipples. I tug his barbell between my teeth. His eyes fall closed as he bites his bottom lip.

He tells me he's ready a couple of minutes later. A few licks to his tip, and his pelvis tilts up, trying to fuck into my mouth. Ignoring him, I lick a wet trail down his shaft to his sensitive taint with firm strokes, and my mouth waters for more. I continue trailing down to his rim when a deep groan tears from him. When I rip my mouth away, it's too late. A strip of cum shoots out. I continue licking his taint while stroking his balls with my hand until he squirms away from overstimulation.

"Uh, what happened to warning me?"

"Baby, your mouth…" He shudders. "Fuck, I'm gonna come again just thinking about it." He clenches his eyes shut.

My face warms. I'm such a slut for his praise.

"Five minutes," I demand. Crawling to retrieve the glass of water from the side table.

I grin as he mutters how he'll miss my mouth in the afterlife.

I peer down at my neglected erection. I sense a mild pull to take care of it.

After ten minutes of resting against his chest and reading captions on the television, I gaze up at him. His eyes are droopy, and he's starting to fade off.

"Hey, give me ten more minutes with you, then you can sleep."

He groans but opens his legs for me.

Good man.

I suck him down until he's hard and slipping down my throat. I pause at the bottom, loving the headiness of him filling my throat, constricting air.

His hand wraps around the back of my head as I bob on him. His eyes are closed when I pull off and lick a trail down to his balls, where I use my tongue to roll one into my mouth. I hum as I suckle on it.

"Fuuuuck," he rasps, clenching the edges of the throw. When I'm done with his balls, I scoot down, slide a pillow under his hips, and wrap my arms around his thighs. His entire body trembles when I use the flat of my tongue to apply a slow lick from his taint downwards. I lick soft circles across his rim, and his thighs tremble between my arms as his low moans fill the room.

"I could eat you all night. You're amazing." I stroke my aching erection to release pressure. The scent of sandalwood emanating from him is intoxicating. I close my eyes and dive into licking and tasting him with shallow and deep strokes, alternating between licking and kissing his rim.

He babbles a mix of incoherent words and moans.

Mmm. Love those sounds.

"Uh, fuck, I need you," he pleads.

I groan. All of this edging...fuck...I'll probably explode the second I sink into him.

Pulling my tongue out of him, I crawl to the side table drawer and retrieve the edible lube.

"I need a few more minutes." I squirt some lube into my mouth and sink my tongue back into him. I get lost tongue fucking and fingering him. He's so open when I pull off.

I stroke myself with lube. "This is going to be quick."

Eyes barely open, pupils blown, I drink in his blissed-out face and body. There's nothing better than taking him apart.

I line myself up against his rim and dive inside.

"Oh, god!" I moan as he takes me easily.

As I press my forehead against his, I try not to blow.

I roll my hips slowly, eliciting a deep moan from him. Fuck me. It's the best sound.

I suck on his tongue until I need to pull back for air.

"You feel unbelievable. Damn, baby. I love you," I say, thrusting hard inside of him and biting my lip with an equal force. His body trembles when I slide against his prostate. The friction of every stroke ripples through me with a heightened intensity. I close my eyes and dive in and out of him, drowning in the sea of our pleasure. His legs are wrapped around me when I lean down to kiss him again, eating up his moans. Beads of sweat trickle down my back. Every muscle in my body thrums with life. I'm barely holding on. He bites into his spot on my neck, and I come hard with a wail, unloading inside of him. He moans into my neck as he clenches around me. For the first time in weeks, a weightless high washes over me. I pull out of him and suck him down while fingering him. He comes with a force so powerful that his torso buckles forward. It almost seems painful. I plaster myself against his chest and catch my breath as he rubs lazy circles across my back.

AFTER A LONG SILENCE, WHERE I THINK HE'S KNOCKED OUT, HE clears his throat. "Babe?"

"Yeah?"

"You scared me when you called upset, and I couldn't reach you after."

I meet his gaze.

"I know from therapy that some of that has to do with Paul, but most of it has to do with you."

I swallow roughly. "I'm fine—"

"That's just it. I don't think you are. I think you need help with the panic attacks and depression. I don't want to—" His voice breaks. "Fuck, Ty, I can't lose you."

His terrified voice sends a chill down my back.

Maybe I'm being selfish by refusing to try therapy. Maybe if I go a few times, everyone will get off my back.

"I'm sorry I scared you. I don't want you to be worried about me. I'm unsure if it's for me, but I'll try it at least. Okay?"

He nods. "I'll help you research and set up a few consultations. It'll be hard at first, but it works if you take it seriously."

I voice something that's been nagging me. "Are you sure you want to live with me when you move here? I can't promise that I'll always be me. Sometimes, I need to disappear for a while."

He resumes rubbing my back. "You don't have to worry about that. I'll love you through whatever you're battling. Always show me the real you, and I'll do the same."

"Yeah, but the real you isn't that different from what everyone sees." He shows up in interviews and games with an authenticity that draws in fans around the world. Me, on the other hand, there's a lot people don't see.

"Struggling with your mental health isn't a dirty secret. You know that, right?"

I shrug.

"Nah. Hold up. You're not disingenuous because you keep certain things private. The world doesn't get to know everything about us because our jobs involve us being thrust in front of a camera every night. That's bullshit."

"I know that, but are you sure this is what you want?"

"Yeah, I am. I love you, and I want this...badly. I want to know you're safe in our home when I'm on the road. You don't have to be alone anymore. Tommy, Kieran, and Mom are in town every few weeks, er, well, they used to be in Miami."

I hear an anxious note in his voice.

"What's the matter?"

"Would that annoy you, having my family visit every few weeks?"

"Are you serious? They're the best, and I've wanted family around forever."

I'm stoked by the thought of a house full of people and waking up beside Sid. I'll never take for granted how generous he is with his family. I used to hate that I seemed so lonely to him, but the truth is, I was lonely. Sometimes, being seen isn't the worst thing.

Now, all I need is for my mind to comply and get back on track. I'm sure things will feel normal once I get a ball in my hands again. I think about what I just agreed to. I sense he believes therapy is a magic bullet that will solve a lot of my issues. It's a lot of pressure. I wonder what it'll mean for us if I go and decide it's not for me.

Chapter Twenty
Three Months Later

"Yo, wasn't it just last season when it took three of us to guard you? ¿Qué pasó?"

Clenching my jaw, I ignore Phoenix's point guard and hit a reverse dribble, scanning the floor for an open look. Coach signals for me to take the shot. I signal for Idris to get free. Jammed up by their center, he signals for me to shoot.

Don't do it.

Seven seconds left on the shot clock.

The point guard squats low, blocking any possible drive to the rim. "Scared ain't a good look, Pretty Boy!"

"Fuck off!" I fire back.

I scan the floor again. Not only are my teammates being defended, they're all signaling for me to man up and take the fucking shot.

Damn it. I hit a crossover, step back, and fire the ball. The moment it leaves my hand, I know the shot's shit. It misses the rim, basket, and backboard entirely. Not only is it shit, it's a damn air ball.

Our eighteen-point deficit remains intact.

Our coach calls a timeout.

I hang my head as I walk back to the bench. I know what's coming. It's the third quarter, and only four of my twelve shots have landed. It's been three months since the season kicked off, and my game has been shit for most of it. A quarter of the way through the regular season, we're suffering through a soul-crushing losing streak, coming in tenth place in the Western Conference. The only thing stopping us from trading places with any of the bottom five teams is a handful of losses. We need to turn this streak around fast.

"Ty, you're out. Malik, you're up," Coach orders.

I crumple into the chair and throw my towel over my head. I stare at the floor, unwilling to meet Coach or my teammates' disappointed faces. My skin crawls with humiliation. No one knows better than me what a fucking disappointment I am. And to top it all off, I haven't a damn clue how to turn things around. When I'm not on the court, I'm training around the clock to try to make up for lost time this past summer. I'm up by five at the latest every morning to train, no matter what city I'm in. Outside of team practice, I train for a minimum of seven hours a day on my off days and four hours on game days. No other player can be putting in more work than me. Yet, I'm barely hanging on to my starter position. If I don't turn it around—forget the starter position—there's a good chance I'll be traded. I'm supposed to be the franchise's star point guard, and my shooting percentage puts me lower than the top twenty point guards in the league. I was in the top five last season as a rookie. It's humiliating as fuck.

I'm failing everyone, including my parents.

When the final buzzer rings, I beeline straight for the locker room. We got our asses handed to us with a final score of 125–92.

As I pass through the tunnel, I hear, "You suck!"

I don't bother shrugging it off.

Ain't like it's a lie.

After our post-game meeting, I'm back to work on the practice court. I bracket the ball between my palms and squeeze silently, pleading with it to work with me. Spending damn near every day of most of my teenage and adult life with a ball in my hands, I'm used to it feeling like an extension of me. My ball handling used to be my greatest strength. At times, it was effortless. I attempt plays I used to make in my sleep, and none of it lands. I don't get it.

Two hours on the practice court pass in the blink of an eye. I'm about to hit a corner three when my hands freeze mid-air.

Shit!

I promised Sid I'd make it home before he heads out for a stretch of road games. No time to shower, I run to the locker room to grab my phone and car keys. I dial him from the road to let him know I'm running late. An acidic burn courses through my sternum when I get his voicemail. GPS alerts me of a car crash up ahead, putting my ETA over an hour out.

"Fuck!" I yell, gripping the steering wheel.

I spot a "Home of the LA Royals" billboard with a blown-up picture of Sid roaring after hitting a shot. Two miles later, I pass a billboard of me mid-dribble with my new sneakers blown up in the background. It might be my last advertisement. Companies tend not to back mediocre athletes.

I pull into the driveway and jump out of the car the second it's in park.

I spot a limousine parked in front.

He's still here.

"Babe," I call out when I enter the house. As I kick off my sneakers, his phone lights up on the foyer table with notifications for my missed calls and texts from his teammate Arnaz. In addition to Sid, the Royals franchise recruited two high-scoring players to join the team: Johan Brent, center, from Atlanta, and Arnaz Cade, shooting guard, from Philadelphia. Sid and Arnaz have become a dynamic duo on the court. They read each other like they've been playing together for years. It's nuts.

I race up the steps, following music to our bedroom.

"Hey babe, sorry I—" I freeze in the doorway, my words catching in my throat.

Sid's dressed impeccably, standing in the center of our bedroom fastening cufflinks. I've seen the Tom Ford dusty pink velvet tuxedo hanging in our dressing room all week, but damn, the way he fills it in is criminal. The pink accents his gorgeous skin and penetrating eyes. He's grown out his hair. Sides tapered low, brownish-black coils piled neatly on top. Gone are the geometric shapes worn last season. A sexy beard accentuates the strong masseter muscles that define his jawline. I zero in on his defined biceps as he places his hands in his trouser pockets. Man, I've hit the jackpot. Wiping my sweaty palms against my jersey shorts, I swallow my drool. I still can't look at him without experiencing a physical reaction. I'm glad I declined to be his plus-one tonight. There's no way I could keep my hands off of him in public.

"Wow, babe. You're a smoke show."

His head darts up at the sound of my voice.

"Thanks," he says flatly. "You're still in your jersey."

"Yeah, lost track of time and didn't want to miss you...I thought we could...you know...before you left."

"Yeah, er, sorry." He stiffens. "Gotta bounce in the next ten minutes."

"That's enough time for me to blow you or—"

"No."

I grimace. "Fine." I turn to walk out. "Forget I mentioned it."

"Hey...hold up. Sorry, I just meant there's not enough time. I need to finish getting ready. Jett and Mom will be here any minute."

"Okay...it's been weeks since we've had sex, though, and I miss us...I don't know. It's like I'm being punished."

He exhales. "You're not." He unbuttons, then re-buttons his tuxedo jacket.

"Then what is it?"

"Why does it have to be anything? We've both been busy."

"Whenever I initiate, you say you're not in the mood or make up an excuse. Don't make me seem crazy." Yesterday, I woke him up in his favorite way. One minute, he's into it, opening his legs for me as he lengthened in my mouth, and then the next minute, he's tapping me to stop. A pained expression crossed his face when I pulled off of him. He climbed wordlessly out of bed and disappeared into the bathroom. When he came out, he mumbled something about hitting the gym and left.

"Are you no longer attracted to me?"

His head flinches back. "What? Where'd that come from? This has nothing to do with whether I'm attracted to you or not."

"Answer the question. Why won't you touch me? If it's not me, then what is it? Someone else?"

That earns me an icy glare. He scoffs, then brushes past me toward the door.

I dart in front of him. "What am I supposed to think?"

"Not that bullshit." He glowers. "Maybe, think about—hmph, no. I can't do this right now."

He doubles back toward the nightstand and grabs his wallet.

I tell myself to let it go, but I can't.

"Wait—what were you going to say? Maybe I should think about what?"

"Nothing, forget I said anything." He scans the room looking for something.

"That's bullshit, Sid. Be straight with me."

"Straight. Funny. That's rich coming from you."

"What the hell is that supposed to mean?"

When he pats his pants pocket, I realize he's searching for his phone.

"Your phone is downstairs on the foyer table."

"Thanks," he mumbles.

Before he steps toward the door, I dart in front of him again. "Answer me. What did you mean by that?"

He sighs, gazing past me. He shoves his hands in his pockets as if to keep from touching me or me from touching him. "You really want to do this right now?"

I nod. "Talk to me."

I try not to squirm under the severity of his gaze or silence. I'm ready to rip out of my skin when he says, "I know you've been lying to me."

"W-what?"

I try to mask the guilt on my face as all of the ways I've tried to contain my shit over the last few weeks run through my mind. I may have withheld some of what I've been going through, but it's only because I didn't want him to worry like he did in Spain. Plus, my issues are mine.

"That's your play—denial?...Cool." He tries brushing past me again.

I dart in front of him. "Wait...can we just sit and talk for a minute?"

"What's the point if you won't be straight with me?"

"I will. Just give me a chance. You're gone for a week, then I'm on the road. I don't want us to leave it like this," I plead.

He crosses his arms across his chest. "I know you've been keeping your panic attacks from me."

"H-how?" I ask, stepping back.

The lows of the last few weeks race through my mind. I thought once training camp started, things would naturally fall into place. Then camp began, and it was brutal. As expected, I was out of shape from not practicing during the offseason. No matter how much I pushed myself, my brain wouldn't jump-start. A permanent fog settled in. Then, there was the first game of the season. I attempted over two dozen shots and only a handful landed during warm up. I had never felt more resentful of my depression. Knowing I was a few minutes away from 17,000 people watching me play the worst ball of my career twisted me up. The familiar taste of bile sent me racing to the toilet, where I vomited until I wheezed. I never mentioned panicking or being sick to anyone, not even Sid.

"I know about your three a.m. practice sessions before you sneak back into bed. And don't think I bought your lie about having a stomach bug when you skipped those two games last month when I was on the road. Tell me the truth—you hit rock bottom and couldn't get out of bed." He glares at me, daring me to deny it. "The staff said you laid in the same spot in bed for four days straight and barely ate."

"Incredible." I throw up my hands. "I don't even have privacy in my own house!" Despite my indignation, the thought he's known the truth for days, if not weeks, makes my neck burn.

Stone-faced, he raises his chin. "Don't deflect. Answer me."

"Fine...yes. I crashed or was depressed or whatever. I didn't want you to worry."

"So you're lying to me now. I thought we didn't hide, no matter how ugly it gets. That's real for me. Is it not for you?"

"Yes," I mumble.

"Yes, what?" he asks, angling his head to meet my down-turned gaze.

"It's real for me. I wouldn't break that."

"Except you have."

I know. It's in my bones—guilt. It's a steel weight chained to my waist.

"I'm sorry. I didn't want to distract you. You've needed to focus on getting acclimated to the Royals. I didn't want to bog you down with my shit and—"

"I knew you would say that. That's not how we work. When you hurt, we hurt, I hurt!"

I wince. It's too much pressure. I'm constantly failing everyone. For Christ's sake, I'm just one man. Sometimes I just want to disappear. That way, I can't hurt anyone. I can just fall apart.

He scrubs his hands over his eyes. "Fuck! I feel like I'm losing you. There's this hollow look in your eyes, and I'm gutted because I've seen it before."

"This isn't that. I'm not Paul!"

"I know you're not Paul. Don't make this about him. This is about *you*. I see *you*. Your symptoms have worsened. Your nightmares have gotten worse. You're still depressed. You're checked out half the damn time unless it's about ballin'— the only thing you give a shit about. You've been keeping your panic attacks from me. You have some fucked up idea that winning a ring will bring your—"

"Stop," I hiss. "Leave them out of it."

"You need to hear—"

"Don't, Sid." I glare at him.

"They're gone, and they're not coming back. And—"

"You think I don't know they're fucking dead!" I yell, pounding my fist against my chest. "There's a chunk of me that's rotting in the ground right along with them."

"See! That!" He points at me. "That right there. It's grief, Tyler. We can get you help."

I shake my head. "I tried it your way. It wasn't for me."

He pulls on his collar. "You went to a few sessions. What the hell were you supposed to gain? Therapy can take years."

I shrug. "It fucked up my head. I've been on a losing streak ever since."

"How many times do I have to tell you that you're worth way more than ball?" His voice drops impossibly lower to a baritone rasp. Sometimes I wish he'd raise his voice instead of going low and deep. It'd be less unnerving. "You're willing to kill yourself because you believe that winning championships will bring meaning to their deaths or provide some kind of closure. It won't. Sex, money, rings—can't you see that none of it will heal the pain? You have to face your grief." He scrubs his hands over his face. "I could fuck you into the mattress until we pass out. You'd still wake up gasping for air, retching up your insides, and covered in sweat."

Oof.

I rub the acid sluicing up my chest. Now I understand. He's been rejecting my advances because he thinks it's distracting me from processing my grief. That's utter bullshit. Making love to him reaches a part of me that I can't access on my own. It's the most precious and frightening thing how much I need what we give to each other. It's always felt transcendent. It's not about getting off or escaping. It's how I feel connected to him. And some days when I'm lost, adrift, being anchored to him is the only thing that makes it all bearable. I need him to understand.

"Baby, can't you see that I might get traded if I don't turn things around? I might not even get picked up by another team. I never judge you for locking in and focusing on the game. We're supposed to support each other."

"For fuck's sake. It's always about ball with you. Why the hell are you even with me?" He shakes his head and retreats into the bedroom.

I trail behind him. "I'm with you because I love you. Ball is important, but you mean everything to me."

He stares up at the ceiling and shakes his head. "I don't doubt that you love me, Tyler." He turns to face me. "I doubt that you love yourself. Your grief is twisted so deep inside of you that it's running your life."

I went to great lengths these last few months to contain my shit and avoid the look he's giving me right now.

"Is that how you see me?" I ask, my voice splintered. He said he wanted all of me, but if I lay all my parts bare, he wouldn't be able to love something so dreadful.

The tension in his face crumbles as he moves toward me.

"Don't," I say, stepping back. I steel my voice despite the mounting fear. "What does all of this mean? I'm not sure where we stand anymore. I was honest with you when you asked for us to live together. I told you that it might be like this. I told you that I'm broken."

You said you would love me through it.

He steps back, stuffing his hands back in his pockets. "That's a cop-out, Ty. This isn't an irreversible illness. You can go back to therapy. I told you I'd love you through it. This is me loving you," he says, echoing my thoughts.

I scoff. "Pushing me away is you loving me?"

"Encouraging you to get help is loving you. I'm here. I haven't pushed you away."

"And if I don't go to therapy, what, you'll break up with me?" I swallow down the energy drink I downed in the car as it worms its way back up.

It's terrifying asking the question I fear the most.

A pained expression crosses his face. "I'm saying *I* can't keep living like this. *You* can't keep living like this. I've spent my entire life trying to heal and take care of myself. I've worked hard to live an honest life and provide for my loved ones. You know what I've been through. And every day, I watch the person I love most in the world sinking deeper and deeper into what looks like a kind of mental illness, and he refuses help," he says, lowering himself to the bench in front of our bed, cradling his head in his hands. He swipes away his tears like he's angry at himself for crying.

I step forward to reach for him but pull back, afraid I'll be rejected again. I crouch in front of him instead. I can't stand seeing him miserable. I have to fix this. I can't hurt him. We are supposed to be good for each other.

"I'm sorry. I'll do whatever you want me to. Just give me to the end of the season. I know we don't agree on why I must see this through," I beg.

After a deep breath, his shoulders slump forward. "That's too far. You need help now. Plus, how can I trust you're being honest?"

"You don't trust me anymore?"

I shrink when he doesn't answer. "So what, it'll be like this until I go back to therapy?"

"What do you mean?"

"This tension between us. You won't even touch me," I say, grimacing at how repulsed he seems by my attempts to connect lately.

He lets out an exasperated sigh. "We made love a few weeks ago."

"Since when do we go weeks without making love? Not to mention, you seemed in a rush to get it over with." My eyes drill into him, daring him to deny it.

He shrugs. "You keep asking for shit, but you give nothing in return."

"So my love and commitment to us means nothing?"

A storm of emotions crosses his face—sadness, remorse, and hurt. A glimpse of what's behind his anger.

The doorbell rings, and I flinch.

We sit unmoving, unsure of how to leave things.

Then he stands.

My pulse races when he brushes past me. We can't leave it like this. "Wait!" I reach for him.

He stiffens but pauses, waiting for me to speak.

"Please," I croak.

His head drops forward. For a second, I think he's going to keep walking—it's what I deserve—but he turns and pulls me into a hug.

"Wait, your suit. I didn't shower." I pull my tear-stained face away from his chest.

He presses me back against his body. "I don't care."

I cling to him, wishing we had more time and things could be different. I could be different.

The doorbell rings again. I pull up the front door camera mic on my phone and tell our driver Sid's on his way.

"I'll see you soon. Call me and try to take care of yourself. Please," he says.

Our teams face off when he gets back to town, and then I fly out that night for a stretch of road games. At least we'll see each other, even if it's just on the court.

I nod. "Maybe I'll remember how to ball by then."

"You've been through a lot. It'll come back," he says before tilting his face down for a kiss. It starts as a brush of our lips. When I pull back, he presses forward. A rush of heat and longing spreads through my body from the small exchange of intimacy. His tongue pushes past the seam of my lips. My soft moan elicits a deep groan from him that goes straight to my cock. Our tongues clash, lick, and glide as I clasp my hands around his neck. He pierces my bottom lip between his teeth, the pain making me rut against him. I suck his tongue into my mouth like it's his cock, swallowing every one of his moans. How he has the power to deny himself my blowjobs is a testament to his frustration with me. I groan when he pulls his lips away, but he spits into his palm. His hand dips past my waistband, and my knees almost buckle when it wraps around my erection. I moan, pressing my forehead against his chest, shuddering from each firm stroke.

"Sid," I moan, staring up into his eyes. Leaning in for another kiss, he holds my gaze with a scorching intensity that burns straight to the raw place only he reaches. This one is slow and tender. My back arches as I press closer into him. It's not close enough. If I could shed this body and meld with him,

I would. Ever since the first time our gazes locked, my soul's known its home is with him. I hate being apart so much.

"Come for me," he whispers against my lips, commanding my body in the way only he can. A shuddered breath, and my eyes clench closed. "God," I cry against his lips as the friction of his stroke ignites an inferno all over my body, and I erupt hard, grunting against his lips. Chest heaving, floating in bliss, my eyes are heavy as he takes a finger covered in my cum and sucks it into his mouth. He tilts my head back and feeds it to me before greedily drinking it in by sucking on my tongue. I massage his thick erection through his tuxedo pants. I want him so badly.

"May I?"

His gaze falls to my mouth as he bites his bottom lip. I'm certain he's going to nod, but then he grimaces. "I should go before we're late."

I nod through the familiar pang of his rejection and step out of the way so he can pass.

"Mom will want to see you," he says, walking toward the bathroom.

"Mm. I'll be right down." As I grab clean clothes, a low grunt seeps from the other side of the bathroom door. My chest deflates, and my head hangs heavy as I head to a guest bathroom. He'd rather come alone than with me.

He's climbing into the limo when I reach the front. I nod to Jett, our lead personal driver and bodyguard, as he loads Sid's bags into the trunk. Ex-military, he came highly recommended by a retired basketball legend and friend of Sid's. Despite his taciturn nature, he's super alert and perceptive. He's gotten us out of sticky situations that could have exposed our relationship numerous times. He has an uncanny ability to spot paparazzi. At seven feet, two inches with over 250 pounds of muscle and a ghastly scar starting from his right ear to his nose, jet black hair, and hawk eyes, people tend to steer clear of him.

Before Sid left Miami, he set Leslie up with a new job serving as the personal driver for another Marvels player.

"Wow, you're stunning," I greet Lily, dipping my head into the car window.

"My love! Come around and kiss me. This bustier has restricted everything short of breathing."

I jet around to the opposite side of the car, lean in, and kiss her cheek.

"Why aren't you sitting here instead of me?"

"Not up to it." I steal a glance at Sid. He's staring out of the opposite window. I wonder if he resents me for turning down his invite to be his plus one. The basketball legend who recommended Jett has a biographical documentary up for nomination. So when Sid received the offer to present the Award for the Best Documentary Feature Film, he agreed without hesitation. While we're both not ready to go public with our relationship, we attend events together from time to time. His post wishing me a happy birthday worked. The media bought our friendship. Now that we both play for teams in Los Angeles, it isn't odd when we're seen together in public.

I turn back to Lily and mumble something about Sid getting an upgrade with her as a date.

"Oh, shh! You'd kill in a strapless gown or tux."

"Pfft! I could never pull this off."

"It's Valentino and silk. 210 roses!" Her fingers graze the field of roses, trailing the length of the gown that's the same hue of pink as Sid's tux.

I nod. "You're gonna make 'em drool!"

"Let's just hope I make it down the red carpet without tripping over the train."

"Sid won't let you fall." I trace over her necklace with a blue sapphire, ruby, and emerald. "Peep the bling."

"Marvelous, isn't it? Bulgari."

"Goodness. They won't know what hit 'em. Have fun

tonight." I double-tap on the door and step back. "Hey," I say to Sid.

He meets my gaze. A strip of the setting sun casts a soft glow over his face, and a chill races up my spine as I recall a dream.

I climbed out of bed and followed the scent of pancakes and animated voices to our kitchen. I froze in the entryway as three pairs of eyes fixed on me.

"Daddy's up," Sid said at the same time two sets of tiny legs barreled over to me. I knew instantly they were our kids. Our son's resemblance to Sid was uncanny and, our daughter, with her coily puffs, resembled me. I had the dream again last night. This time, we were all in the swimming pool. Sid was strewn across a unicorn floaty, and our daughter rested against his chest. I gave my son a head start, watching him kick and flutter away from Daddy Shark. He screamed when I emerged from under the water, pretending to nibble on his ankle, making Sid and our daughter laugh.

My future belongs to Sid and our family. I need to fix us.

"Good luck presenting."

"Thanks," he replies.

"Wait," Lily says, gesturing for me to come closer.

I lean back into the window.

"Your eyes are red like Sid's. What's wrong?"

The question catches me off guard. I shake my head. "N-nothin'. I'm fine."

"Tell me the truth. What's wrong?" she repeats, gaze pinging between us.

Sid lets out a deep breath and stares back out of the window. "Let it go, Ma."

"Sidney David King, I will do no such thing."

We both remain silent.

"Someone better speak right now!" It's like whiplash the way her commanding tone reminds me of my mother.

I clear my throat, breaking the awkward silence. "It's fine,

Lily. We're working through it. Don't worry. I love you...both of you. Travel safely." I'm about to duck my head out the window and walk back to the house when she clasps my arm.

"Tell me, love. You okay?" She searches my face. "When was the last panic attack?"

I rest my palm on her hand. "I'm fine. Haven't had one in a couple days."

She studies me, reading something in my expression that relaxes her a little. "Okay," she says, releasing my arm. "Call me if it changes."

Nodding, I step back as the limo pulls away. Knowing Lily, she'll have Sid talking before they reach the end of the driveway.

I drag myself to our basketball court to get in a few more hours of practice. But when I raise the ball to release a shot, a wave of guilt and sadness hits me. I yell and catapult the ball across the gym. It's not as good as punching something, but it's close. I clench my fists as the eerie quiet of solitude washes over me. We've only lived together for a couple of months, but I miss him when we're in separate cities. His large, soulful presence radiates through the house. It's hard to think about all of the emptiness in my life before meeting him and his family.

We toured a few properties before finding this one. Sid's agent signed an NDA, so we were able to speak candidly. We fell in love with our home—a three-acre estate tucked in a gated community called Hidden Hills. The nine-bedroom, eleven-bathroom house checked a lot of our boxes. The most important requirement was that we'd find a place that needed close to zero renovation. Everything fell into place once Sid's contract with the Royals was signed. We wanted to be settled as quickly as possible.

The estate was recently re-modeled with extensive upgrades. When we entered the foyer for the first time, the natural light from the two-story wall of windows made the place incredibly warm and uplifting. The main residence is 12,000 square feet, but it flows well enough that it doesn't feel massive. The great room features an indoor-outdoor bar, an adjoining outdoor living room, and a formal dining room with a fireplace. There's a glass wine cellar, chef's kitchen, study, home theater, and entertainment lounge. The newly built gym was perfect for us. We added a few machines, an infrared sauna, a compression recovery suit, and a cryotherapy chamber. Replacing the tennis court with a basketball court was a relatively easy project. We installed hydraulic roofs, including in the two-bedroom, two-bathroom guest house to take advantage of the rain-less days in LA. A border of redwood trees offers built-in privacy. Coupled with grassy lawns, sunny hillsides, olive, citrus, and avocado trees, it's an oasis. The property came with a zero-edge saltwater pool, an eleven-person spa, and an outdoor kitchen. The spacious attached garage fits eighteen cars, which is more than enough for what we need.

After our offer was accepted, we moved in eight weeks later. We spent the first week alone christening the place. We invited Adam, Ishan, and Sid's close family members out for a housewarming, and it's felt like home ever since. Sid declined *Architectural Digest's* proposal to tour the new estate. We decided if we ever open the estate up for a tour, it would be when we're out and could show the property together.

I put on Moses Sumney's *Grae* record and read the menu pinned to the fridge left by Sharon, our personal chef and grocery shopper. Branzino, cauliflower rice, and a kale stir fry are on the schedule for tonight. Since it's just me for the next week, I skip ahead to Thursday's dinner and make a turkey burger.

As I fire up the grill, I recall the words on the tip of my tongue when Lily demanded an explanation. I almost admitted that Sid's disappointed I quit therapy. That's the crux of it, at least. I attended two sessions with a licensed psychotherapist before I quit. I chose Jaden because he checked a lot of my boxes. It's not every day you find a gay therapist who specializes in grief counseling and anxiety disorders. Our fifteen-minute phone consultation went well. Our first in-person session was even better. The minute he opened his office door and I took in his warm, earnest eyes and genuine smile, my apprehension began to melt away. He'd aged since his profile picture on his website. Salt and pepper goatee and a lanky build. He wore a cream button-down with a banded collar, dark blue jeans, and brown leather loafers. I remember staring down at my T-shirt and ripped jeans and wondering if I should've made more of an effort. I stepped into the decorated loft with exposed brick beams, a modern olive-colored couch, and a grey and white Moroccan-style rug, and my shoulders relaxed. The floor-to-ceiling windows wiped away my concern his office would be stuffy.

Jaden shared his background, including that he was called to be a therapist because of the grief he experienced when he lost his younger sister to leukemia. He asked me about my hobbies, interests, and what I enjoyed about my career. We discussed my experience growing up, attending college, and joining the league. And then it came time for me to tell him about my parents—what our relationship was like, when and how their deaths occurred. I fixated on the mountain view as I recounted my memories from that day.

"So, it was sudden and a major shock?" he asked.

I nodded. "One moment, we were laughing in our kitchen, and the next moment, they were gone. It's never made sense."

"Do you remember what you felt then?" he asked.

"When?"

"At the hospital."

I wrapped my arms around my torso. "Sick. I mean, I vomited. I cried." I shrugged, thinking the question was inane. Isn't it obvious that I'd felt fucked up?

"Any anger and guilt?"

My gaze shifted to the mounted clock above his head. "Of course I was angry. They didn't deserve to be killed. They were good people just trying to get to their kid's game. What fucking Go—"

My words died in my throat.

"What God would allow for something that horrific?" Jaden asked, finishing my thought.

I found his expression sincere and nodded.

"What held you back just now from asking your question?"

I shrug.

He set down his pen. "Tyler, what if I told you that in this space—in our work together—we need your anger? Your tears, your rage, your heartbreak—all of it. And none of it is too much. By showing up every week, we're both committing to helping you heal, which means we have to invite in everything you've had to conceal. As safely as possible, we'll need to revisit events and periods of your life locked away, consciously or subconsciously, to protect you. You faced an unthinkable loss. In a snap of a finger, you lost two of the people who loved you deeply and unconditionally. People who were in charge of raising, supporting, and keeping you safe. Two people who, by what you described, knew you best in the world. What you've experienced is one of the most difficult tragedies any of us will ever face. Your entire world was turned upside down. It's nothing short of terrifying and horrific."

My eyes burned. I bit down on the inside of my cheek and fixated on the steam billowing around his mug.

"I should be over it by now," I muttered.

"When big, terrifying, unimaginable things happen—our body, in all of its intelligence and resilience—swoops in to protect us. It takes the reins and does what's necessary to keep us safe. And for a while, we're fine. We got out of bed, right? We brushed our teeth. Maybe the next day we managed to eat a full meal. A few weeks later, we somehow manage to even enjoy the food we eat. But then, over time, things start to happen that may signal to us that we aren't okay. Nightmares, depression, chronic illness, for example. These are signs that tell us we need more support than we thought. It's important that when we're stronger and better resourced, we take back the reins by processing and coming to terms with the big, horrific thing and how it's impacted us. It's how we heal. Does that make sense?"

I shook my head.

"It doesn't?"

"No, it does. It's just they all expected me to move on. How was I—where was I supposed to go?"

"Without your parents?"

"Yeah."

"Were these friends back in school?"

"Yeah, everyone. Friends, my coach, my teachers."

"I'm sorry you didn't have the support that you needed. That must have been really rough."

A wave of fatigue settled behind my eyes as I shrugged and stared at the fog moving over the mountains.

"I should still be over it by now," I insisted.

"When a loved one dies," he explained, "it's normal to experience grief. We tend to see those painful thoughts and feelings improve over time. But for some of us, the feelings can persist and become hard to control, especially if the death of a loved one is sudden and violent or experienced in adolescence, which, in your case, it was. It becomes hard to control emotions and troubling thoughts, sleep can be impacted, and symptoms that resemble depression can occur, disrupting a person's ability to function." He explained that the symptoms I'd described point to a disorder where grief is prolonged.

"Disorder?" I winced at the world.

"It simply means something that disturbs the normal functioning of the mind and body," he replied.

I thought about how my sleep is disturbed by nightmares and the word kind of resonated.

He went on to explain that prolonged grief and depression aren't the same thing, and it can be hard to know what's wrong despite our lives being impacted. At the end of the session, he gave me a diary to monitor my grief by tracking its highs and lows every day. Specifically, I was instructed to document my experience during those moments for us to review together. I told him it might be hard to find time between traveling to different cities for road games and my practice schedule. He said it's okay if I miss a day or two, but it would suffice if I could just make a quick note on my phone. It's apparently important to create a practice of observing and reflecting on my grief.

"When people desperately try to move on, they tend to ignore their grief, but it helps with healing to pay attention to it."

I reluctantly agreed.

We went over what to expect over our next few sessions together. While it isn't required, he encouraged me to invite a loved one to a session. He said it could be helpful for a loved one to know about my experience and what's involved in treatment. They could also add their perspective on how grief has impacted me, which could be useful. I immediately thought of Sid. He'd agree to come in a heartbeat.

"Er, is everything shared by that person also protected by confidentiality?" I asked.

He nodded. "Absolutely. Why?"

I wanted to delay revealing Sid's identity, even though Sid told me he was cool with me disclosing it. His therapist knows about us.

"I mentioned I have a boyfriend…uh…since I'll most likely invite him to the session, we may need to attend virtually. We aren't out publicly."

"Oh, thanks for telling me. That's fine. It's important we

establish a consistent cadence, so I'm happy to be flexible and work with your schedule. We can do a hybrid of in-person and virtual sessions. We can also explore how being in the closet impacts you. I imagine it isn't easy."

That made me scoff. "It requires spy-level deception tactics at times. It's exhausting, but I love him, and I'd do anything to protect what we have."

That first week, I journaled every day. Just a few sentences. I noticed my grief was lowest when Sid and I made love, or he held me as we both melted into the couch after a stretch of road games. My grief was highest in the middle of the night when a nightmare jolted me awake. Sometimes, it hit when I was at home with Sid, but most of the time, it was in a hotel room while on the road. My grief was most intense during our last therapy session together. I shared this with Jaden in our second session.

"How does that make you feel?" he asked.

I shrugged. "I hate talking about how my parents died."

"It makes sense that your grief was at its highest level then, doesn't it? Part of why you feel stuck could be because it's excruciating to think about it. Remember, losing a close loved one is one of the most difficult things we'll ever encounter."

His words pressed up against a festering wound.

"Can you tell me what's coming up for you?"

Everything. I shrugged again. "I'm sick of feeling this way."

"It's really hard stuff. But, I find it hopeful that you journaled and made these observations," he said, pointing to the diary. "You came back, and that required a lot of courage. It may be during our work together, your grief feels like it's at peak levels. That's part of how healing works. To heal, we have to make space for the pain. Can you share where you are experiencing tension in your body right now?"

I released my clenched fists and pointed to my head, throat, chest, and stomach.

"Thanks for showing me. There's a technique I use to help release tension in my body. If you are open to it, I'd like to show it to you."

I nod. Anything has to feel better than this.

He walked me through a technique where I tap different acupressure points along my body, starting with the top of my head down to my chest while repeating words of affirmation. I noticed my tension reduced from a nine to a six after. He said that the longer I do it the more it will help.

"Part of our work together will involve not only revisiting the past and accepting the painful reality of their deaths but reimagining a future where you move forward without your parents in your life. A future in which you can thrive and experience contentment. We'll take it one step at a time and only do what you're comfortable with. If you say 'no' or 'stop,' we stop. If I think we're moving too quickly, I'll help slow things down to keep you safe." He asked me how that sounded, and I agreed reluctantly. The reluctance wasn't because Jaden wasn't capable of helping me. It just felt like a lot of work on top of ball. I can't be the best if I don't focus. Therapy, or healing, or whatever, felt self-indulgent.

Sensing my reluctance, he asked me about it. I told him I couldn't let anything get in the way of ball. I explained the promise I made to my parents.

He made a note in his notebook and then studied me for a few breaths before he spoke. "The goal in healing isn't to take anything away from you except for the beliefs and behaviors that no longer serve you. There's so much happening underneath the surface that we'll carefully bring into awareness to explore. Based on what you've shared with me, I know basketball is an important part of your life. It's even helped you through difficult times. We will respect and honor that. Maybe through our work together, you'll discover an alternative way to think and be in relationship with it. We're going to move slowly here. And from time to time, I'll encourage you to think about all you'll gain from this journey, however hard it may be at times."

His clear and careful way of speaking lowered my defenses. I agreed to see it through as long as my game didn't suffer. But suffer it did. The more I focused on my grief—observing it, and writing about it—the harder it became to contain its impact on me. I'd wake up depressed and out of sorts. And no matter how much Sid tried to convince me it was normal, I couldn't handle it. I found myself spacing out at practice. I saw a father and son at a game one night, and it reminded me of when Dad and I used to watch the Choppers play. I was hit with an ache so intense that I almost lost it on the court. Back in the locker room at halftime, I emailed Jaden to tell him I needed to pause. Maybe someday, years from now, I'd have the time and space to do the work, but I can't right now.

Too much is on the line.

Only now, as I look around at the empty house and think about the state of my relationship with Sid, I realize quitting therapy may have threatened more than I thought.

Chapter Twenty-One

The Royals defense is excessively aggressive tonight, and it's starting to piss us off. They've fouled us four times, and we're only in the beginning of the second quarter. Johan, center, for the Royals, committed a personal foul against Ari, our small forward, when he bruised Ari's arm while attempting a steal. Arnaz came down hard on Kaleb's shoulder when he attempted a layup. Kaleb almost lost it on him. I had to talk him down. Idris was fouled by Ussef, power forward and center for the Royals, when Ussef hand-checked him. Nicholas, point guard for the Royals, fouled Tevin by flaring his legs out and kicking him when hitting a jump shot. Their aggressive antics have put them in the lead, scoring 42–38.

The ball is in my possession with Arnaz defending me. I've missed four of my last ten shots. He usually wouldn't be able to contain me in isolation, but with how I'm struggling this season, he's glued to me. I dribble right, hit a between-the-legs crossover, and dribble with my knee forward, protecting the ball in my left hand. He squares up against me, blocking any pass opportunities. I charge forward. As he steps back, I push off of him to create space. I swiftly cross the ball and drive to the basket to complete an underhand layup. My long-range shooting is weak right now, so if I have any chance of making buckets, I'll have to shoot from mid-range or keep getting to the rim.

Sid toys with Kaleb. Bent forward dribbling slowly, he pretends he's going to charge to the rim before stepping back and hitting a ballsy long-range three-pointer. The Royals crowd gets loud for him. I roll my eyes as Arnaz chest-bumps Sid, and they exchange a special handshake that I've only seen the two of them use.

Kaleb passes the ball to me. I charge down the court as Ussef moves into position to defend me.

The crowd yells, "DEFENSE!"

Let's see if the Royals can answer the call.

I cross the ball behind my back and charge right, slipping past Ussef, only to run into Sid, who squats low, giving me enough space to read my moves but not to drive past him. I'll have to outpace him. I charge left and hit a jump fake, and as he jumps up to block the shot, I shuffle right and release a jump shot. My confidence low—I wince as soon as I release it—but it's good! I fist the air.

"Would'ya look at that? Wonder Kid's defense improves my game," I taunt.

He smirks, then races away.

On the next Royals' possession, they execute solid ball movement, passing it in succession around the perimeter. It's dizzying trying to keep track of it. One second, Sid's driving to the rim like he's going to post a layup, and then he shifts and kicks it out to Johan. Johan passes the ball to Arnaz, who wings it back to Sid. Sid spins around a defending Idris and lobs it back to Johan, who tips it in.

Idris brings the heat, firing off a three-pointer on the next possession.

The score is held at 47–42, Royals lead. For the next five possessions, both teams employ a strong defense. Their point guard is fouled by Kaleb on the next possession when completing a layup. He makes the free throw shots, increasing our deficit to 50–42.

Damn!

I charge up the court, and Johan moves in to defend me. I hit a vicious crossover dribble, and the sudden change in direction causes Johan to trip over his feet and fall backward.

That, my friends, is what you call a flawless ankle breaker!

I drive past him to post a layup—only a hand comes out of nowhere, reaching over me to smack the ball away before it hits the rim. I'd recognize that block from anywhere.

Sid, mayor of Block City.

Arnaz takes possession of the ball and wings it to Sid.

"What's wrong?" Sid asks, his lip turned slightly upward.

"Who said anything's wrong?" I reply, not taking the bait.

I attempt a steal, but he crosses the ball between his legs, moving it to his left hand out of reach.

"You're gnawing on the inside of your cheek, and your eyes are squinty, hiding the gold."

Ugh. It's unnerving how much he sees when he watches me.

"Y'all keep fouling us and see what happens," I warn him.

He smirks. "What's it to a tough man like you?"

I huff out a breath. "You've been warned."

When I'm pissed off, I play my best. It takes a lot for me to get there, but when pushed enough, I go off.

He leans in. "I thought you liked it rough."

I screw my jaw to keep from grinning as I reach in, but he backs me down and posts a floater, increasing our deficit to ten points.

With five seconds left on the shot clock, I don't even think. I launch a freak shot from way downtown. An old confidence thrums through my body as I watch it sink through the net. I'm surprised when their crowd erupts. Then again, everyone loves a freak shot. I shake my head and grin.

Things come to a head in the fourth quarter. I'm not sure what's happening with the refs, but most of the fouls that the Royals commit aren't being called. The Royals lead, but we managed to cut the deficit, bringing the score to 79–75 with under eight minutes on the game clock. I'm being double-teamed by Ussef and Johan. I execute a fast dribble combination that creates space for me to drive the ball to the rim. But once I'm mid-air, Ussef makes direct contact with my left arm. I still manage to complete the shot, but I expect a call for the foul.

"That was a foul, ref! Come on," I bark at the nearest referee, who looks apathetic.

I shake it off and get back into the game. Ari steals possession from the Royals and lobs the ball to me to post a layup. As I take flight, Arnaz jumps up and chest bumps me, knocking me out of bounds before I can finish. Ussef takes possession and books it up the court. I scoff in disbelief.

How the fuck isn't there a call on the most obvious foul in the history of the game!

"What the actual fuck! In case you forgot, it's your job to call a blocking foul," I yell at the ref.

"Back down, Washington," the ref fires back.

"What's it gonna take for you to do your damn job? Me laid out on a fucking stretcher?"

Idris pulls me out of the ref's face.

"It's fucking bullshit, man!" I yell over my shoulder.

"It is, but it's not worth getting a tech or ejected. We need you. You know how to get payback," Idris says, patting my back.

He's right. Fuck the refs, fuck the Royals. They want to fuck with me—they just cost themselves the game.

He grins. "Good of rook Ty to show up, though," he says before racing away.

Nicholas hits a three-pointer, bringing the score to 82–77, their lead. When I catch the ball on an inbound pass and hit a corner three-pointer, the refs call an offensive foul against Kaleb for pushing Johan off of him, nullifying my points. This is a joke. I laugh maniacally as adrenaline pumps through my veins. The same adrenaline I'm going to channel to annihilate these fuckers.

Sid misses the next shot.

Good, asshole!

I take possession of the ball and hit a three-point shot in the middle of the three-point line and the Royals logo.

Nothing but net!

Sid dribbles a crossover, hesitates, then hits a jump shot, bringing the score up to 84–80, still their lead. He and Arnaz smack their foreheads together again, and I gag.

As I take possession of the ball, Kaleb sets a screen, clearing my path to hit a smooth crossover, then a long three-pointer, and it's gold!

Our defense is strong on the next possession, and despite decent ball movement by the Royals, Nicholas misses a layup.

Hell yeah!

I can already taste our victory.

I dribble past half-court when I'm double-teamed by Ussef and Arnaz. I drive hard toward the left baseline, making them think I'll charge to the net, and then Johan closes in, triple-teaming me.

I smirk. *I guess I'm a problem!*

I take turns staring each of them down. They can put all five of their players on me, it doesn't fucking matter. I hit a lethal step back and release a corner three-pointer, and it's bank! And our first lead of the night. The Royals crowd gets loud.

Let's fucking go! I beat my chest, feeling fired up.

The Royals call a timeout.

As I'm headed to the bench, Johan shoulder-checks me.

E-fucking-nough! I'm tired of being pushed around.

"We got business, asshole?" I sneer in his face as I square up.

"Get your bitch ass out of here," he snarls.

I smirk. "You tight I'm wiping the floor with your team, and I just stole your crowd?"

I hit a nerve. He clenches his jaw and pushes me hard. I brace to absorb the force of the blow, but a muscular chest against my back stabilizes me.

Sid.

His arm reaches over my shoulder and grabs Johan by the jersey.

"Don't ever fucking touch him." He growls. His voice is low and terrifying.

"Dude! The fuck? It wasn't—it's not that serious," Johan stammers, confused.

I turn my back to Johan. "Ay, ay! I got this. Let him go."

Eyes molten with anger stare back at me. I silently plead with Sid by locking into his gaze and softening my expression. Refs and teammates from both sides surround us, trying to diffuse the altercation.

"You're making us look like amateurs. Knock it off," he snarls to Johan before releasing him with a sharp shove.

We separate and walk to our respective benches. I catch a few confused glances aimed in my direction.

Shit, Sid.

I could have easily handled Johan by myself. I deal with hotheads every game. I know Sid knows it, too, but he can't help his protective nature. He's intense about protecting his loved ones. And it's one thing if both teams are playing rough, but Johan made it personal. He fucked around and found out that Sid hates bullies.

"Yo, Sid just stuck up for you against his boy?" Tevin asks, bewildered. His seven-foot frame towering over me.

"It's nothing. Johan was out of pocket." I shrug off the feeling tens of thousands of eyes are on me. I don't owe anyone answers.

I listen to Coach run through plays, but I'm too amped to catch everything.

The Royals have possession of the ball when the game resumes.

Arnaz passes the ball to Sid without looking and then quickly cuts it to the basket, where Sid launches it back to him to complete a layup. They point to each other and grin.

Barf!

Kaleb passes me the ball, and I charge up the court. Arnaz and Sid move in to defend me too late. I get free and charge to the rim and dunk, bringing the score to 86–88. The crowd erupts.

Ooh, I think they like me!

Damn, it feels good to be in the lead.

Johan attempts a corner three but misses, but then Sid rebounds it and dunks.

Nicholas moves in to defend me, but Idris wedges his way between us to create a screen. I charge to the corner and hit a fadeaway jump shot.

Every time I release the ball, the arena goes wild.

They're my crowd now!

Arnaz and Tevin go head-to-head. Arnaz, in his attempt to protect the ball, loses possession and kicks it out of bounds, causing a turnover. Kaleb runs the ball upcourt but cuts it to me waiting in the wing. I kick it back to him. He immediately releases it, but Sid smacks the ball away.

Asshole.

The Royals miss their next two possessions, but I continue

my assault, hitting back-to-back three-pointers and two jump shots.

Sid's bent forward, dribbling the ball back and forth between his legs slowly, letting the shot clock wind down. Idris squats low in anticipation. With only four seconds left on the clock, Sid explodes past Idris to charge to the rim and post a floater, bringing the score to 105–92, still our lead.

Sid then moves in to defend me when I take possession. I dribble right, and he shuffles, matching my movements, squared up in front of me. I smack his hand away when he reaches in for the ball.

"Ouch!" he whines.

"Shut up!" I pull back and cross left, but still no open look. I half spin counter-clockwise, then reverse back clockwise at breakneck speed. I hold and release a jump shot over Sid's big body, and it's good!

The crowd goes bonkers.

"Wait—no secret handshake for me?" I pretend to gag, then turn and race away before he can respond.

Arnaz passes the ball to Sid, who scans the floor to see if anyone is open for a pass. Our team's defense is too strong. Sid maintains possession, using the side of his body to push forward. I charge from behind and smack the ball out of his hand to complete a breakaway dunk.

I grin as he barks, "For fuck's sake!"

Aha, fucking losers!

With under three minutes left on the clock, Coach calls a timeout to bench me for the remainder of the game. I've sealed the W for us. There's no point in keeping me in and risking an injury. As I approach the bench, I'm enveloped by my team's chest bumps, head and butt pats, and high fives. As frustrating as it's been tonight, putting up twenty-seven points in the fourth quarter and absorbing the crowd's insane energy feels fantastic. I hydrate, then crash into the chair, burying my face in my towel. I take deep breaths to release the adrenaline. I'll be too wired to sleep tonight, especially without Sid since we're heading to Charlotte right after this game.

Sid effortlessly charges through our defense to post a floater. If we were on the same team, we'd be unstoppable. I wonder if we'll get teamed up during an All-Star Game. That's assuming I'd even get selected given my shitty start to the season. Since the media still plays up our rivalry, it isn't likely we'd play on the same team. After all, it's good business for the league to give the media what it wants.

I'm on my feet when the final buzzer signals the game's end. The final score is 120–112. I place a peace sign against my heart as I take to the court to high-five my teammates. Sid, being the leader that he is, takes the lead in dapping and congratulating a few of our players. When it's my turn, he pulls me into a hug. His scent mixed with his sweat, damn. My dick perks up.

Knowing what his scent does to me, he's grinning when we pull apart.

"You were remarkable tonight. You did warn me," he says, chuckling while patting my chest.

"To be fair, the ref's refusal to call fouls didn't work too well in your favor. You put up tough shots. And that block of yours —cruel." I punch his arm.

I spot an interviewer and camera crew posted nearby waiting to interview me.

"Thanks. But *my* block?" He scoffs. "What about your stealthy steal in the 4th? Cold!"

I grin at that. It's twisted how much I love beating him on the court. "Yeah, we gave 'em a show tonight."

Our gazes lock for a beat. His eyes graze over my face, resting on my lips, and while it's no more than a second or two, I bet he's thinking what I'm thinking. I wish we could be together tonight. When we're both wired like this, we spend the night making intense love until we pass out in each other's arms. Even though things are rocky between us, I have a feeling we'd honor that ritual tonight if we could.

"Fly safely," he says before he turns and walks away. He daps Arnaz, who's waiting for him. I watch the two of them retreat until I'm approached for an on-court interview.

Chapter Twenty-Two

I throw on my headphones and hit play on Sid's post-game interview while en route to the airport. I installed privacy screens on both my and Sid's phones months ago so we could text without looking over our shoulders. He's rocking a fire truck red button-up shirt and black jeans with slate diagonal zippers down the front, some of which are unzipped, revealing his sexy skin. Damn. No one has the right to be that mouthwatering.

Fuck! I *really* need to get railed by my boyfriend.

"Sid, over here. Ned from ABC Sports," a voice off camera calls out.

Sid scans the room and nods for Ned to continue.

"There was a moment in the fourth quarter where you, Ty, and Johan looked to be exchanging words. Could you tell us what that was about?"

The unofficial rule is what happens on the court stays on the court.

Sid's face is neutral. "That was nothing. Adrenaline was pumping, and we were just blowing off steam." He scans the room for the next question.

"Sid, over here," a woman's voice calls out.

"Hey, Kim, go ahead."

"A few things seem to set Ty off tonight, such as the number of fouls committed by the Royals and not getting whistles on perceived fouls committed against him. We know that when Ty's peeved, it usually results in him playing outstanding offense. What makes it so hard to defend him when he's hot like that?"

"Well, first of all, they weren't perceived fouls or flops. We're professionals. We know the rules of the game. I don't think it was an intentional foul, but he took a lot of contact mid-air. I'm not certain what the refs were doing, but we have rules to keep everyone safe. You can understand how incredibly frustrating it is when a rule is broken, you're almost injured, and no one is held accountable." Sid's tone is neutral, but I sense frustration.

"Are you saying the refs missed a few calls?" Kim follows up.

"Yes. Look, Ty is one of the most professional and skilled players of our time. It is highly improbable, and goes against everything we've seen from him, that he would fabricate a foul and get upset for no reason. We trust the refs to do their job so we can come back night after night and compete at the highest level."

Thank you, baby. You're always the voice of reason.

Sid continues, "To answer the latter part of your question, the answer is simple—you can't defend him when he's fired up. He's too ferocious and quick. His ability to hit shots from anywhere on the court makes him formidable. We tried our best to slow him down, but even when we tried triple-teaming him, you saw tonight that it didn't work."

"Terry from *LA Times Sports*. Sid, as you prepare to host Detroit tomorrow, what adjustments will the Royals make to improve the performance that we saw tonight?"

I click out of the video to text him.

ME

> Saw your post-game interview. If I were home, I'd give you the best head of your life.

I'm surprised when my phone buzzes less than a minute later.

MY LOVE

> What I wouldn't give for your deep throat right now. You always give me the best head of my life.

My dick instantly perks up. *Fuck yeah, I'm game to sext him.* My fingers get to work firing back.

ME

> I'd lick your tip first. You know what the taste of your pre-cum does to me. Fuck. I'm rock hard just thinking about it. I'd suck you down over and over and slowly stroke you while tracing my tongue down to your balls. I'd trail my tongue back up and deep throat until you lose control and start fucking my face, then I'd enjoy gagging and swallowing your seed.

MY LOVE

> Fuuuuck. So hard right now. I love watching those pretty lips spread over my dick. I want to smear my cum all over your lips and chin and watch you slowly lick it off.

His words thrum through me like lightning. I fly to the last row of the plane.

ME

> You love it when I swallow your seed down, and I love being full of you

MY LOVE

I do. It's some primal shit how much I get off knowing my cum is inside of you. I'd suck you down slowly, bringing you close to the edge. I want you begging me to come, covered in sweat...trembling. When you can't take it anymore, I'd tie your hands to the bed and fuck you deep. I'll fill you with my loads all night. If you're good, I'll let you come when I'm done.

Thank fuck for the plane blankets.

ME

Mmm fuck, baby. It's all yours. I'm leaking just thinking about you edging and railing me. Want to know one of my fantasies?

MY LOVE

Always

I'm yours too

ME

I fantasize about your hard dick filling me for hours. You know I hate how empty I feel when you pull out. I want you to plug me with your big cock and slowly rock into me throughout the night to stay hard. After hours, when we both can't hold back anymore, I want you to wrap your hand around my neck and choke me until I almost pass out while you fuck me so rough I think about your dick every time I sit down.

I groan when I'm forced to put my phone on airplane mode as we take off.

His text comes through as soon as Wi-Fi kicks in.

MY LOVE

Fuck. I had to rub one out. Marry me. I want to be wed to your mind forever.

I grin. Despite everything we're going through, I'd say yes if he asked me for real. I know he's it for me. I don't want anyone else. My dad was right—Washington men fall hard. Sid used to playfully ask me to marry him all of the time, and I'd tell him I wanted a proper proposal with a ring and bent knee.

ME

I've been fucking myself with the big dildo, but it's nothing like you.

MY LOVE

Your hole was made for my cock

I shiver, imagining Sid's dick hammering into me. I'm so hard it hurts. I poke my head out of the aisle. Most of my teammates are asleep or have their heads buried in their phones. I reach under the blanket and tuck my dick into the waistband of my sweats. I jump up and make a beeline toward the bathroom. As soon as the door closes, I tuck the hem of my T-shirt under my chin, pull out my dick, and start stroking it. My tip glistens with pre-cum. I swipe it up with a finger and suck it into my mouth, craving Sid's taste.

ME

Fuck. I'm jerking off in the bathroom. I'm really close.

MY LOVE

Fuck, that's hot

I'm jerking off too

I picture his washboard abs contracting as he pummels me slowly, blissed-out eyes glued to his cock as it dives into me. His teeth pressed down on his bottom lip to keep from coming as he glides in and out. A string of pre-cum emerges as I stroke myself harder, imagining him choking me out while he fucks me hard, his sexy mouth kissing me and swallowing my strangled moans. I bite down hard on my lip as my orgasm tears through me, coating my chest with one long strip of cum after another.

My legs sway as I close my eyes and return to my body. Damn, I'm a mess, cum is everywhere. I wet a wad of tissues and begin to clean myself up. I'm wiping the cum off of my chin when all of a sudden, I'm thrust backward, hitting the door as a wave of turbulence rocks the plane. The pilot's voice booms through the loudspeaker, instructing everyone to buckle their seatbelt. I quickly finish cleaning up and return to my seat. I pull up my phone to respond to Sid, but the Wi-Fi is down. It doesn't return for the remainder of the flight.

I figure Sid's already asleep after I climb into my hotel bed, but I try him anyway on FaceTime.

"Hey," he says, yawning. His eyes squint from the screen's brightness.

I scan his handsome face and bare, corded shoulders and pecs. "Mmm. Damn, you look good."

He grins.

"I had to rub one out again as soon as my hotel door closed. Thank god the lights were off on the plane."

"I rubbed a few out too," he says, stretching. "Put the phone on the nightstand with the camera facing you. Let's go to bed."

I nod. I love seeing him as soon as I open my eyes.

We both make the necessary phone adjustments and then settle in. For a few moments, we just gaze at each other.

Sid breaks the silence. "I'm convinced the Creator used a miniature paintbrush and centuries of painstaking detail to create you."

"W-what?"

"How else to make sense of your beauty?"

A startled moan bubbles up. *Who says something like that in the middle of the night?*

"Good looks fade," I say, blowing him a kiss. "You'll still love me when I'm old?"

"Pfft! I can't wait until we're octogenarians. Viagra and insomnia, baby, who's gonna stop us!"

I burst out laughing.

He grins. "I bet you'd give a mean BJ when your dentures are out. I'd put fifty stacks on it."

"You're ridiculous." I shake my head, laughing. "You've apparently given this thought."

"Growing old together? Hell yeah," he says, all laughter vanishing.

I swallow down the mix of confused feelings. I can't help but think our future dangles on timing, on whether I'll get my shit together before he says enough and leaves me.

"Everything good with you and Johan?" I ask, needing to change the subject.

"Yeah. You won't have a problem with him again."

"Babe, you know I can deal with hotheads. I don't want you getting fined—"

"No one fucks with you on my watch. Ever. I don't give a flying fuck about fines."

I sigh. "I love you."

"I love you too."

"Do you want to talk about our argument the other day?" I ask.

He doesn't answer right away.

"Maybe when you're home. We should sleep."

I try to shrug off the awkward pang of vulnerability that comes with being the only one to attempt reconciliation.

I clear my throat. "Are you still able to volunteer next month for my urban garden initiative?"

"On the 18th, right?"

I nod. At the tail end of last season, I was approached by a grassroots organization dedicated to expanding urban farming in Los Angeles to make organic produce more accessible in low-income communities. I agreed to partner with the organization to host a quarterly volunteer day, recruiting both Knights and Royals volunteers to help with various projects, such as gardening or clearing out a lot that could be repurposed.

"Yeah, I'll be there. How many volunteers do you have?"

"Twenty-seven from both of our franchises, including players, coaches, and assistant coaches, as well as some peeps from Preeminent Management. Plus, about fifteen neighborhood volunteers. Surprisingly, many people are game for laying down compost, irrigation tubes, and seeds. It should be fun."

"You sure it's about the gardening and not the fact people genuinely like you and want to show support?"

I shrug. "Pretty sure it's the gardening."

He grins. "Sure."

We gaze at each other until my eyes are too heavy to keep open, and I drift to sleep feeling content to have a moment where things are a bit like before. We used to fall asleep on FaceTime whenever we traveled and our schedules allowed. I know no relationship is perfect, but what we had was pretty close. I need to fix what I broke so that we can get back there again.

Chapter Twenty-Three

"Wassup, wassup! Thanks for coming through." I dap Nicholas, the latest Royals volunteer, to arrive at my gardening event.

"Big homie! I'm down for the cause. I wish the hood that I grew up in had lots like this. It was nothing but fried chicken and car repair shops."

"Where'd you grow up?" I ask.

"Michigan. You grew up in New York, right?"

I nod. "Brooklyn, then New Jersey. I know what you mean, though. There were some spots in Brooklyn where you're lucky if you can cop anything but bags of wilted lettuce. The organization I support is nationwide. I can share my connect if you want to kick off something back home."

"Cool. I still have family there. I'll hit you up for the details." His gaze pans the lot. "Where should I jump in?"

"Any good with a shovel? We could use a few more diggers over there." I point to the plot we've allocated for citrus and avocado trees.

Sid's currently leading the digging effort. He's clad in gray joggers and a drop-arm tank. I drink in his bulging biceps as he breaks earth with a shovel, already on his third tree hole. Realizing I'm gawking, I begin to turn away, but a glimpse of Arnaz standing frozen a few feet away, staring at Sid kinda like I was just staring at him, gives me pause.

Huh.

Sid seems oblivious.

Arnaz is one of the best shooting guards in the league, and he and Sid dominate highlight reels for their team. I'd be lying if I said Arnaz isn't a good-looking dude. He's maybe three inches shorter than Sid and lean with compact muscles. His brown hair is tapered low in soft curls, with a perfect five o'clock shadow and plum-colored, bottom-heavy lips. It all comes together to make an attractive man. He's bi-racial with a white dad—a renowned, retired tight end for Pittsburgh—and a black mom.

"Yeah, I've buried a few bodies back in the day," Nicholas says, chuckling.

"Ha! Appreciate you coming, man." I pat his shoulder as he turns to pad over to Sid.

The turnout is better than I expected since most volunteers brought friends, spouses, and kids. We have nearly fifty volunteers. Thankfully, we have more than enough water and snacks for everyone. The heat is blistering today.

I fill up a wheelbarrow with compost and wheel it over to the plot we've set aside for kale, collards, and mustard greens. Kneeling, I get to work mixing the compost into the soil. Before partnering with this organization, I hadn't gardened since my parents passed away, and I've missed it. It feels like falling into a portal where it's just me and nature working with the sun and water to create new life.

"Hey, handsome! May I join you?"

I arch my head up. My gaze meets wolf-shaped eyes and a

dimpled smile. Phil, my agent, stands over me, looking like an Italian model in olive green joggers and a cream Henley. His back is to the sun, casting him with a golden halo.

I came out to him a few weeks ago. In the event I'm outed, I needed to make sure he wasn't blindsided. I also wanted his perspective on what being out would mean for my career and brand. We had a long conversation in his Beverly Hills office. He acknowledged that times have changed, and while some people may take issue, my being out in the league would most likely be supported. The NBA has made strides to be more inclusive by fining players who post homophobic content on social media, sponsoring Pride night games, and marching in Pride parades. It's a start in the right direction. He thinks it would strengthen my brand and create new opportunities, especially with more money pumped into LGBTQIA advertising. I didn't disclose my relationship with Sid, though I think it might be time. Phil shared that he was pansexual when I came out to him, and his last long-term relationship was with a man.

"Hey! Jump in as long as you don't mind the smell of manure." I extend a pair of gloves to him.

He kneels in the dirt facing me, a trench of soil between us. "Oh, manure doesn't faze me. I have an eleven-year-old dog at home who has daily accidents in the house." He smiles ruefully. "It's devastating actually how quickly she's deteriorating. She sleeps all day these days. I'm not sure how I'll cope when she pass—I'm sorry. I didn't mean to unload on you."

I put down the hand shovel and remove my gloves. "Come on." I open my arms to him, inviting him in for a hug. "I'm sorry your fur baby is sick. What's her name?" I ask, as his chin rests against my shoulder.

"Bob Dylan." He pulls back. "When I first adopted her, she'd lie on her back, offering her belly up for a rub whenever one of his records was on."

"Any favorites? Tell me it's 'Boots of Spanish Leather.'"

"That one. Though she's especially fond of 'Girl from the North...'" His voice trails off as his gaze flicks past my shoulder. "Hey, Sid."

My head whips around to find Sid's gaze leveled between us.

I know that face. "Everything okay?"

"Yeah. Got a minute?"

"Yep. Be right back," I tell Phil.

I trail Sid to the empty side of the lot.

He crosses his arms and looks out at the neighboring yard before turning to face me. "Everything good with Phil? What was that about?"

I stuff my hands in my pockets to counter the urge to reach out and touch him. "His dog is sick. He's pretty torn up about it."

"Oh. That sucks. I'm sorry." He uncrosses his arms. "Is he still calling you handsome and flirting with you?"

His uncanny ability to keep track of me while engaged in conversation never ceases to amaze me. And turn me the fuck on. He's convinced Phil's into me, but I don't see it.

"Bab-Sid," I catch myself looking around. "There is nothing there. I'm yours," I whisper.

He releases a heavy sigh. The tense lines etched between his brow softens. "I hate not being able to touch you in public."

"You want to touch me?" I whisper, inching a little closer. "Where?"

His gaze trails down my face, pausing along my lips. I slowly swipe my tongue across my bottom lip. I grin inwardly at the look of naked desire igniting his eyes.

"See something you like?"

He hums and the husky vibration drums up my spine.

"Something you want to taste?"

"Yo, Ty! Over here when you get a chance," Idris calls out.

Sid growls. "Go, troublemaker."

I wink and push out my cheek with my tongue.

He chuckles. "Subtle."

"Hey," he says as I turn to walk away. "Sorry for being a possessive asshole."

"You know I love that shit." Maybe it's twisted, but I get off on how much he wants me for himself. Plus, I miss our flirting and intimacy. I stare at my hickey-less neck every morning, and an overcast settles over my day.

"I've been meaning to ask you..." I glance around to make sure we're still out of earshot. "I'm trying to reach a new record tonight. Know anyone who can keep up with an insatiable cumdump?"

He swallows roughly, his lids dropping to sexy slits. His stare says I'm in for a marathon dick down when we get home. "Go, before you get fucked against that shed," he threatens, taking a step closer toward me.

I wink at him as I step back.

I pop into the empty shed to quickly tuck my erection under my waistband.

AFTER I HELP IDRIS PLUG AN ERRONEOUS IRRIGATION HOLE AND correct Ussef's spacing for the seeds he's planting, I head back to Phil.

"Everything okay with Sid?" he asks.

"Yep. All good. How's it going over here?"

"You tell me. How am I doing?"

I scan his work. He's almost finished mixing in the compost.

"Great. I think we can start adding the transplants now."

I have trays lined up and ready for planting.

"You want to tease the roots like so and sprinkle in a little root growth fertilizer, then place it down just like this. Fill in the sides with the compost blend we just created. Then you water. We'll top it with the cedarwood mulch over there to keep the weeds down and moisture in." I point to a wheelbarrow full of mulch.

"Easy enough. You're a good teacher," he says as he reaches for a tray and mimics what I showed him.

"Thanks. I've had practice. We had a small garden growing up."

"Do you garden at home?"

I respond quickly, remembering to change all of the "we's" to "I's".

"I started an organic fruit and vegetable garden, but I'm away so much that the gardeners maintain it most of the time."

"Maybe I can come over and see it."

My head flicks up to meet his gaze. *Fuck. Sid was right.* Maybe I could've denied his flirtatious tone, but there's no denying the way he's looking at me right now. My face grows warm.

I clear my throat. "I'm seeing someone," I blurt out.

His hands freeze in the dirt.

"Whoa, don't seem so surprised. I'm actually a catch," I joke.

"N-no, I mean, yes, of course you are! I haven't heard anything, and, well, you've been staunchly single and focused on the game. I guess I am a bit surprised." You'd be hard-pressed to miss the disappointment on his face.

"It's serious, my relationship. We've kept things private for a while now for reasons I can't disclose here," I say, lowering my voice.

Phil's eyes soften. He gets that I can't get into details about my relationship in public since I'm not out.

"Thanks for telling me. It's uh, good—I mean, I'm happy you found someone. They're very lucky."

I stare at him. In another life, I could maybe see me and him enjoying each other's company. It wouldn't be as passionate and profound as what I have with Sid. I feel safe and loved to my core with Sid. He's it for me. I just need to fix the mess that I've made by keeping things from him and not working on my shit.

"That's nice of you to say, but I'm the lucky one. What about you? Are—" I start to ask him if he's dating anyone, but my voice is overpowered by a pair of boisterous voices.

"Ty! Come over here and weigh in. Arnaz lost his damn mind," Sid says, waving me over.

"Go ahead. I can handle it from here," Phil says.

"You sure?"

He nods.

"Cool. Holla if you need me." I jump up and dust the soil off of my knees. My charcoal grey joggers and white tee are filthy. I grin at the mess. Gardening is the best.

I walk over to Sid, whose tee is now off and stuffed in the back waistband of his low-slung joggers. His massive pecs and abs glisten with sweat. He's wearing the sun hat I forced on him this morning. He looks like a porn star pretending to be a gardener. My gaze trails down his face, along his Adam's apple, his pecs and pierced nipple, over his abs and his V-shaped obliques. I have to stop myself from eyeing his crotch. I shift as my dick chubs up.

"What's up?" I ask, finally meeting his gaze.

He smirks.

I squint my eyes and turn my lip up, slightly smirking back.

Yeah, I just eye fucked the shit out of you. So what?

"Could you put this debate to bed? King D's *Pursuit of Peace* or *King of Outcasts*. Which is the better album?" Arnaz asks, voice animated.

"*King of Outcasts*, hands down. I'd even argue it's his magnum opus," I reply without hesitation.

Sid throws up his hands. "What I say! Thank you!"

Arnaz shrieks in disbelief. "Y'all smokin' rocks! 'King Blues,' 'Dead on Arrival,' 'Face Off'—"

"All solid tracks, but *King of Outcasts* is a masterpiece. I remember when I first read the lyrics for 'Top Off,' I felt chills. 'Mars,' 'Grenades,' and 'Knock-Down-Drag-Out' are all fire."

"'Mars' still slaps! It's one of the best love songs ever written," Sid jumps in.

"Isn't that your ringtone?" Arnaz asks.

"Something like that," Sid replies.

I grin. It's his ringtone for my calls.

"Oh, is the ringtone for someone special?" Arnaz teases.

I jump in, directing the conversation back to King D. "You get why the album resonates with each generation, right? He explores pain, addiction, and escapism with a radical level of vulnerability. And his commentary on the social and political structure of our society wasn't just an astute reflection of the 90s. It still holds water today, making the album timeless."

"Yo! My dude's rolling out five-dollar words like astute," Arnaz jokes.

"Told you he's got a brain on him," Sid boasts.

Sid talks about me to him?

I turn my head, pretending to look away, but my gaze flicks back to Sid, trying to read him. Despite our hot airplane sexting, he's continued to be distant. No sex. Nada. Only wintry vibes at the King & Washington residence lately.

"Bro, there's only one way to solve this debate," Arnaz says.

"Oh god!" Sid groans, throwing his head back in agony.

"Karaoke!" Arnaz exclaims. "You spit King D's bars, I'll sing the chorus."

Sid waves him off. "Nah, bruh, you've been pushing karaoke hard for months. Give it a rest. You just want to show off. We all know you have the singing voice of an angel."

"How do you know he has a good voice?" I ask.

He groans. "Whenever we're on the road, he's the first to break out in song. Unfortunately, he's the only one on our team who's spent years singing in a church choir. I want to stab my ears when he gets the other guys going."

"Worried my voice will make you melt?" Arnaz fires back.

What the actual fuck? He's flirting with him. I may have doubted his stare earlier, but now I'm pretty sure Arnaz has a crush on him.

"Not a chance. You're not my type," Sid quips.

Does he not realize Arnaz is into him?

"Hey! I could be a gorgeous actress or model," Arnaz replies.

The smile drains from Sid's face. He mentioned wanting to come out to a few close friends. I never asked him not to, but I was candid about it being risky for us. It wouldn't take much for people to know about me if they know he's bi. Or maybe I'm just being paranoid. It's clear he's become close to Arnaz, and it has to suck lying to him.

"Well, if I am no longer required here, I'll go make the rounds," I interject.

"Thanks for convincing me to listen to *King of Outcasts* on my way home, brainiac," Arnaz says.

I nod and glance at Sid. Our eyes lock briefly, and he looks sad.

I know. Even if we have reasons for not being out, hiding sucks hard.

With the help of the additional volunteers, we finish the project in under five hours. We help move all of the tools and extra supplies into the shed. Everyone poses for pictures before we head out. Sid leaves with the other Royals, but I stay behind with the grassroots organizers to shake hands with the volunteers and thank them for coming.

I find Sid showered and lounging by the pool when I get home. Frank Ocean is playing from the outdoor speakers.

"Aw, man, you changed? I wanted you to rail me in that sexy gardener porn star outfit you were wearing." I bend down to kiss him.

He kisses me back, but I sense that he's tense.

"What's wrong? Sorry if I smell like compost. I'll shower."

"You smell fine," he says, staring off toward the pool. "It's getting old lying to our friends, you know? Being around our teammates, their spouses, and kids. Having you so close and pretending we're just friends."

"I know. It felt hard for me too." I kneel next to him. "Guess what? I told Phil that I'm in a serious relationship."

I know it's not much, but it's a step.

His eyes light up. "Yeah?"

I nod. "I think you were right. He made a flirty comment, and I just blurted it out."

"Flirty, how?" He starts to sit up.

"Chill. It was something silly about wanting to come over to see my garden."

"That's fucking direct. How about I go visit him—"

"Chilllll. I told him I'm in a serious relationship and feel really lucky." I caress his neck and ears.

He captures my hand and brings it to his mouth for a kiss. "It felt good to tell him?"

"So good. I bet he could tell I'm in love, and it felt amazing to show that. I mean, I'm already out to him, so it felt easy."

He nods and leans back.

"Not to change the subject, but you and Arnaz seem like close friends?"

He seems to think about it. "I guess so. More so than the other guys. Why?"

"Is he straight?"

"I haven't heard otherwise." He squints at me. "Why?"

"I thought that maybe, uh, he might be...actually, never mind."

I decide to let it go. I don't want to be a toxic partner who's jealous of their spouse's relationship with their friends. I've grown close to Idris, Kaleb, Tevin, and Malik, and Sid's never questioned it.

"Our song. Is this a playlist?" I ask as the song changes. I recall a night earlier in our relationship when we sang the Frank Ocean lyrics to each other off-key.

He nods.

I pull my shirt and joggers off and crawl on top of him as he opens his arms and legs for me. Lying back against his chest, I settle into watching two hummingbirds flutter nearby.

"In the mood for sex?" I ask, intertwining my fingers with his.

"Maybe later. I have a headache...probably from the sun. I'm going to head in and take a nap," he says, pulling his hand away.

"Need anything?" I ask, sitting up.

"I'm good. Thanks." He offers a tight smile as he departs.

Watching him retreat, I'm not sure how much more of this distance I can take. How many more nights can I sleep next to him, our backs turned and not touching?

I think of Phil and his dying dog, and I remember Jaden once said that grief is part of being alive, and in some ways, we grieve all of the time. We turn on the news and feel grief, even if we don't know the man or child gunned down. He warned that grief shouldn't feel like all there is to life.

But what about relationships?

I grieve what Sid and I once were.

What keeps me going are memories of happier times and the too-fleeting moments of our souls grazing through an unguarded smile or touch. I'm not sure that's enough anymore.

I sense the specter of a sickness settling into the bones of our relationship.

Maybe grief shouldn't be all there is to life, but I learned early that life is littered with things that shouldn't have happened but happened anyway.

Perhaps my losing Sid is no exception.

Chapter Twenty-Four

I emerge from the locker room shower, feeling victorious after beating the Choppers. I scored twenty-three points. It's not as much as last season, but a trend in the right direction. It's our first game at home since we beat the Royals.

"What's up?" I ask the guys huddled around Tevin's phone. I towel off quickly and throw on briefs and a T-shirt.

"Yo, Sid lost it on Lucas. Check it out," Tevin says, handing me the phone.

My Sid? I steady my hands and hit play on the video.

Sid's backing down Lucas, who's defending him. Lucas is playing his usual brand of infuriating defense, pushing in hard, hands flailing in Sid's face while his mouth moves a mile a minute. I zero in on Sid—outside of a tight jaw, he seems chill. I let out a ragged breath. I need my body to chill the fuck out. My stomach flips like it's competing for an Olympic gold medal.

One second, they're ballin', and the next, they're squaring up. Lucas pushes Sid, who absorbs the force like a brick wall. More words are exchanged, and then Sid turns away. Lucas is still fired up, mouthing off, despite Sid's turned back. All of a sudden, Sid halts. His entire body goes rigid. That's not good. My breath catches in my throat as Sid balls up his fist.

Oh no.

He spins and decks Lucas hard.

Lucas's legs buckle from the force of the blow. Luckily, a teammate grabs him, breaking his fall. He looks stunned for a few seconds, but then he's right back to hurl what I imagine are curse words at Sid, who's now being held back by four teammates.

Whoa! Sid's the most controlled person that I know. What the hell did Lucas say to cause him to go off? They're both separated as the referees confer at the scorers' table. A flagrant 2 foul is called against Sid, immediately ejecting him from the game, which means he'll most likely be fined. The first time in his career. What the hell has gotten into him? Lucas is one of the most annoying players in the league, but we let his childish tactics roll off our backs.

"Crazy. That's not like him," I mumble, handing the phone back to Tevin. I throw on my clothes and race out, calling Sid as soon as my car door closes, but it rings out.

"Hi, are you okay? I saw the video. Call me."

He's up north playing the Hawks. At least he'll be home in a few hours. I put on ESPN as soon as I get home and learn that he is both fined and suspended for two games. Lucas was ejected as well but only suspended for one. Sid will forfeit his pay of roughly $600K with the two-game suspension.

My phone buzzes on the coffee table. I snatch it up, muting the TV.

"Hi, Lily."

"Hi, love. Have you heard from our guy? I tried to reach him."

"Same. Nothing yet." I sigh. "What do you think got into him?" I pace the length of the family room to try to shake the unsettled feeling in my stomach.

"I was going to ask you the same thing. Was he okay when you two last spoke?" Her voice has an innate gentleness that's instantly soothing to my nerves.

"Yeah. I mean, we've been struggling lately, but nothing to warrant this."

"I know, honey. Sid filled me in a little, and can I just say that I've been praying for you both to find a way through this together. I love you two."

"I love you too. Thank you for praying for—"

"Turn on ESPN. He's on the screen!"

I scramble for the remote and unmute the TV.

"...think your ejection was warranted?" a reporter asks Sid off-camera.

His fitted Royals cap is worn low, hooding his face. He's sitting back in the chair, one arm on the table, the other in his lap. Despite his relaxed demeanor, I notice the tension shadowing his eyes and the tightness of his jaw.

"He looks upset," Lily says.

"Yeah, he does."

Sid huffs out a breath and tucks in his legs, which are clad in black ripped jeans. "I take responsibility for my actions."

"Is it true that Lucas called you a homophobic slur?" another reporter asks.

Homophobic. The hairs on my arms stand up.

"Yes, but I'm not here to discuss that. He said something that pissed me off and, well, you know what happened from there. I've spent many years of my life vehemently protecting loved ones from bullies. His comment was ignorant, and it made me upset."

"Care to share exactly what Lucas said?" another reporter follows up.

"No. Next question," Sid replies.

The phone beeps, signaling another call. I check the screen.

"Kieran is calling. Mind if I add him to our call?"

"That's fine," Lily replies.

I accept the call. "Hey Kieran, I have Lily on the other line. Mind if I add you in?"

"Sure."

I hit the merge button.

"Okay. Is everyone on?"

"We're on. Hey, Aunty," Kieran says.

"Hey, Ty. Hey, Lily." Tommy's gruff voice emits through the speaker.

"Hi, boys," Lily responds.

"We're watching Sid's interview on ESPN."

"Us too. We didn't want you to be alone," Kieran replies, making warmth spread throughout my chest. I love this family so much.

We all go quiet, tuning into Sid's interview.

"...For the privacy of my loved ones, I won't answer that. I will say that my mother raised me to not be a bigot. In my family, we're proud of our queer family members. It takes a lot of courage to identify as gay in our society. I don't think guys realize how insidious all of the homophobic slurs are on and off the court."

"Sid, Sean from—" interrupts a reporter, but Sid raises his hand, silencing him.

"Hold on, I'm not finished. Statistically speaking, there are probably closeted players in the league because it doesn't feel like a safe place to be out."

What's he doing? He has to know the media will run with this and poke into his dating life.

"Breathe, Ty. He's not going to out himself like this," Lily says.

How'd she know I was holding my breath?

I take a deep breath.

"...should ask ourselves why that is because it's not okay. To be clear, I'm not proud of my actions tonight. I am not condoning violence as a response to bigotry. I am not a violent person, but I am human. And there's only so many times a person can face ugliness without reacting. That said, I apologize to everyone I may have disappointed through my actions tonight. It was whack. I disrupted the game and let my teammates down—" A reporter yells a question. Sid raises his hand again, commanding silence.

"We all have a choice. We can stand by and let things continue as they've been, or we can speak up. Here's my choice—I am going to work like hell to stand up against homophobia and ignorance so that the current and future generations of players can feel that it's safe to be who they are."

"Whoa. This is...powerful," I mutter, more to myself than anyone else.

"He's doing what he said he would do years ago," Kieran says.

"He is," Lily replies.

"Sid, do you identify as straight?" an interviewer asks.

All of the oxygen seeps out of the room. However brave, what Sid's doing changes everything.

"Why does that matter? I have to be gay to stand up against homophobia? Is that what you're implying? I'll take one more question."

"Sid, is there anything you want to say to the gay fans watching this interview at home who may be struggling, facing bullies or bigotry?"

He freezes for a moment, staring in the direction of the person who asked the question. He leans back in his chair and peers around the room. His pensive gaze is piercing.

I wonder what's going on in that head as I rub the goosebumps covering my arms.

He releases a long exhale and leans into the mic.

"To the people who identify as LGBTQIA around the world

—I see you. You're not alone." He pauses. Each second of silence charges the air with more electricity.

"I'm committed to doing my part to make this a more equitable place. Homophobia is vile, and it has no place in any organization or society worth its salt. I know that it can seem bleak at times, but you deserve to live authentically. You deserve to flourish. You deserve to be here."

He pauses again, and it has weight and purpose like the last one.

"This is a powerful form of resistance—living and loving proudly while shielding yourself from internalizing the ignorance out there. I know this is easier said than done. I know it isn't always safe to be who you are. I'm committing to do whatever I can to help change that, and I call upon others to do the same. You're part of a great community where there are more members and allies than you think. You're strong, brave, and resilient. Things will get better. There are many of us out here fighting to make it so. Stay safe and refuse to despair. Thank you."

The reporters erupt, yelling questions as he pushes back his chair and walks off. The screen jumps back to wide-eyed ESPN correspondents.

"I'm not crying," Kieran croaks.

"Me neither," me and Tommy say simultaneously.

"God, imagine if Paul saw a message like that from a pro football or basketball player. Who knows what kind of difference it would have made," Lily says, voice shaky.

"And not just from any player, one of the greatest players in the history of the sport. Unbelievable," Tommy adds.

"Think of all the closeted pro players too," I say.

Including myself.

God. Try as I might, I'll never fully comprehend the depths of Sid's courage. He's a natural-born leader.

"Thanks for checking on me. I'm going to try to hit him up

again," I tell everyone, the weight of the last hour bearing heavily on me.

"Okay, love, call me if you need anything," Lily replies.

"Us too," Tommy adds.

Instead of calling Sid again, I sit on the couch and think about what this will mean for us. On the one hand, I am so proud of him for speaking up tonight. I know how important this is for him. On the other hand, the next few weeks will be insane for him. No one has ever spoken out like this in the sport. Reporters will poke into his sexuality, dating history, and motives for speaking out. I want to support him, but I meant what I told him about wanting to keep my head down and focused on my game. I know there are things more important than ball, but I made a promise and need to see it through.

My phone vibrates against the table.

"Hey, Unc," I answer.

"Hey, kiddo. I just saw Sid's interview. How are you?"

I huff out a breath. "I'm proud of him, you know, but also nervous about what this will mean for us."

"Ah, well, what do you want it to mean?"

"Man, that's an enormous question." I pause and think about it. "I don't really know. I know we can't stay the way we've been. I guess I want it to be good for us overall."

"Tell me more. What does a good thing look like for you?"

I think about what I ultimately want. The answer comes easier than I imagined.

"Him happy, me happy, us moving forward. I want to be out. Get married one day. God, I've dreamed about our kids. It's crazy how real they seem. I want our friends to accept us. I want a day where we can, like, have a barbecue or something with our close friends and family. It's been lonely being in the closet. I want to keep ballin' until I'm ready to retire. I don't want to have to deal with ignorance because of who I am."

"Let's unpack that. I can tell you that being out gets easier, but I won't lie to you and say that for someone in your position, it'll be a walk in the park. Now, I was never a world-famous basketball player, but being a firefighter and Black and gay was brutal at times. I was in the closet at work for a long time before I finally came out. Fire departments are traditionally all white and hyper-masculine spaces. And there's still a lot of ignorance when it comes to people's ideas of what masculinity and manhood are and how that shows up for people who aren't straight."

I know that he's protected me a lot from knowing the full extent of the bigotry that he's faced, but I caught whiffs of it when I was growing up. He'd come by after a shift and sit with my dad. He seemed both sad and angry at times. Dad looked like he wanted to burn the world down.

"The thing is, there's no shortage of ignorant and miserable people in the world who will go out of their way to spread their misery and ignorance. You have to fortify yourself every day so that their attempted blows roll off you. Because they will try to come at you. Maybe it's a slur spewed from a coward with their window rolled down, driving by while you're on the street, or someone in the stands at a game. I remember the first time someone called me one. It was like the air was sucked out of me. Fast forward to now, those words hold way less power over me. It just tells me the person who spewed it is a miserable piece of shit, and that ain't my problem. It has absolutely nothing to do with me. At the end of the day, I get to spend my life being me, loving Ishan, and being loved in return. And I see that for you and Sid."

"How did you strengthen yourself?"

"Fortifying yourself is inner work. You need to be clear about who you are and work to love all of the aspects that make you, you. Then, no one can make you feel bad about yourself. They can try, but you'll remember who you are and that will give you power. Shame is something I had to unlearn on my journey. You also have to heal and release what isn't yours to carry. It's why I am so persistent about you taking care of your mental health."

I can't imagine what it must have been like for my uncle to come out all of those years ago. So many people have fought for the right to be who they are. Every generation that fights makes inroads for the next generation, as Sid is trying to do now.

"I know it probably doesn't amount to much, but I'm sorry for all of the hatred that you've faced, Unc. You're my hero. Real talk."

"That means the world to me."

"The league has a hyper-masculine culture too. I think if I was, like, a dentist or something, I'd have come out already. I don't know. It's like there's an unspoken code—to be a man, you have to be void of any emotions—"

"Invincible," Adam interjects.

"Yes, exactly. You can't admit that you need to be loved. You can't cry, be sad, lonely, afraid, or tender-hearted. Those are all considered weak emotions, even though I know they aren't."

Sid is the first guy I could fathom showing my whole self to. And even when I try to hide certain parts of myself, he won't let me. I've been raised by people who taught me to be true to myself. Dad was tender-hearted, affectionate with his love, and ferocious when it came to protecting his loved ones, similar to Sid. Mom was brilliant, tough as nails, and very loving. Adam is the bravest, toughest, and warmest man that I know.

"I think part of the reason that I've been struggling with coming out is that I know that our bond is special. I guess I'm afraid that if I let the ugliness of people's judgments and wrong thinking in, it'll somehow ruin it. My instinct is to keep Sid safe and protect us with everything I have."

"Well, that's just it—you fight hard to not let it in. You remember who you are. I think that's a challenge all men face. How to affirm and embrace the things that make us special even if they don't fit the notion of what it means to be a man. How to break free of the straightjacket and anemic definition of what manhood is. True freedom is being who you are and loving with joy. You gotta know, kid, that I love you as you are. You deserve to be happy. You haven't been happy in years, and it breaks my heart. You and I both know how short life is."

I rub the ache behind my sternum. Sid makes me happy... the happiest. It's just my brain mucks things up.

"You still there?" Adam asks.

"Yeah. Sorry." My voice comes out hoarse.

"If you dream about expanding your family with Sid and exchanging vows, then do it! You and Sid won't let the ugliness into your home and your hearts. You're both too protective of each other. Also, if we give ignorance and ugliness so much power over us that we are afraid to live our lives, then it has won. There will be so much love for you both. Also, you don't have to make a public statement. You can just choose not to hide and let everyone figure it out on their own. You can include a clause in your contract that when interviewed, no one is to ask about your relationship. Don't celebrities do that often to separate the personal from the professional?"

"Yeah, and I wouldn't answer anything I wasn't comfortable with. Sid wouldn't either," I reply.

"The thing is, everything we're talking about only works if you take care of your mental health first and foremost. I know you don't want to hear it, but you must go back to therapy, son."

"I know. Quitting therapy was a mistake," I admit for the first time out loud. I can't be a dad, husband, or athlete who's out in my current state. Sid wasn't wrong...things have been getting worse for me. I'm slipping deeper and deeper, and it's taking more energy than ever before to stay afloat.

"You'll resume sessions then?"

"Yeah. I can't afford not to."

"Glad to hear it."

"How's Ishan?"

"He's good. Working tonight. It's funny, you think being a firefighter your entire life will prepare you for a partner in the same line of work. I worry about him when he's on the job. I know our unit is tight, and we protect each other, but it ain't easy."

"It's frightening. I'm thankful every day that you're retired. I know that's selfish," I admit.

"I get it. I kind of wish Ishan would retire too. Then I think about all the lives we can save, and I try to pray away my fears instead of pestering him with them. Alright, let me run. I love you, kiddo. Do the inner work to get grounded and clear-hearted, then it'll become clearer what you need to do."

"Thanks. I will. I love you too."

After we hang up, my phone vibrates. I pick it up, and it's finally a text from Sid.

MY LOVE

I'm good, babe. Crazy night. OMW home now.

ME

Travel safely

I'M TOO WIRED TO SLEEP, SO I'M WIDE AWAKE WHEN SID GETS home.

"Hey," I greet him, scanning his face.

He looks exhausted.

"Hey. Didn't think you'd still be up." He leans down and brushes a kiss against my lips.

"Waited up for you. You doing okay?"

He taps my legs and I tuck them in. He stretches them across his lap and sinks into the couch, tilting his head back and closing his eyes. I frown, zeroing in on his right hand covered in gauze.

"I missed you," he murmurs after a few moments of silence.

"I missed you too...I can tell you're wiped. Let's get some sleep." I'm dying to know what happened tonight, but it can wait 'til morning.

He remains still with his eyes closed, leaving me unsure whether he heard me or not.

"He called me a fa—"

"That piece of shit." My blood boils. "What's his deal?"

He shrugs in reply. "I had enough."

"Something's wrong with that dude." I shake my head. "He's spewed crap like this before...what made you go off this time?"

His eyes rip open, and he glares at me.

I grimace. "Hold up. I didn't mean it that way." I curl in my legs as he pushes to stand. "I just meant that he's not worth getting suspended over. He does it just to get under your skin," I rush to say as he stalks away.

"Everything's always about the game with you. I'm not even surprised. I knew you—God." He turns to face me. "You know who's worse than people like Lucas? All the people who cower and turn a blind eye. The same people who look at me like I'm wild for reacting." He scrubs his hands over his face. "It's goddamn exhausting. We live in a culture of cowardice and self-numbing masquerading as maturity—"

"Hold up. I'm on your side. You have a right to be upset. I'm not denying—"

"Damn straight, I do. A homophobic fuck face insults you over and over, and everyone acts surprised when he gets his shit rocked."

I nod. "I'm not denying that or defending Lucas...Damn, can we rewind? I'm proud of you and what you said in the press conference. I should have led—"

"Whatever. I'm going to bed," he interrupts, dismissing me.

What the actual fuck?

I'm out of my seat, crossing the room before he can retreat up the stairs.

"Yo, chill. You won't even hear me out?"

"What's the point? You'll say what I already know."

I scoff. "I'm confused. Make this make sense. How is punching that asshat about me?"

He glares at me. "All day, in the back of my mind, I kept thinking about how angry you'd be at me for speaking up because it meant more attention on me. Attention that you avoid because it might impact you and your crusade to avenge your parents. And then I realized that it's always about you and what you need." He tears his arm away from my embrace and steps back. "Fuck...this relationship is me, you, and the ghost of your parents."

Oof. I stumble back, staring at him in disbelief.

If he wanted to hurt me—*bullseye.*

"I'll sleep in the guest room," I growl as I brush past him.

"Am I wrong? Were you or were you not angry?"

I freeze mid-staircase. "Actually, asshole, I must've forgotten to be angry watching your conference along with your family while we all shed tears of pride."

Remorse shadows his face.

"But since the gloves are off, I'll admit that it's one thing to push each other around to blow off steam, but trading blows isn't like us. Not to mention, the media shitstorm that—"

He throws up his arms. "Ah! There it is...*shitstorm,*" he repeats with disdain. "If I'm embroiled in one, then it impacts you. Is that it?"

I clench my fists to keep from blowing my top. "Why are you being like this? We both agreed to do whatever it takes to protect us until we're ready to come out. Why are you acting brand new?"

"I promised you I wouldn't come out until we both agreed,

but I never said anything about remaining silent in the face of homophobic dickheads. Some things are worth fighting for."

"So what's the plan, genius?" I demand, crossing my arms. "Punch every homophobe you come across? 'Cause that won't leave you broke or locked up. Why not just erect a billboard on Sunset? *Need a come-up? Call Sid King a slur and get shitrocked. Injury lawyers are on standby.* Why not just post your bank account online? Should we throw in our house? Your Lambos? What about the Astons? Wanna throw me in—"

"Enough!"

"No!" I fire back. "For fuck's sake, use your head. Speak out, but you can't afford to blow your top. Think about all that you have to lose, your teammates and—"

"It's bigger than basketball! I knew you wouldn't get it. All you—" His phone rings, interrupting whatever insult he was winding up to hurl at me. He snatches it out of his pocket.

"Yo, you copped it?" he says into the phone.

I scoff in disbelief. The gall to take a call right now.

"Yeah, I'm good. Aight. Good lookin'...I got your back too. Aight...yeah...let me hit you up tomorrow."

My jaw clenches. I'm ninety-nine percent sure I know who's on the phone.

"Arnaz?" I ask through gritted teeth as soon as he hangs up.

"Mm-hmm," he grunts, sliding his phone back into his pocket.

"Why is he calling this late?"

"I forgot my chain in the locker room, and he grabbed it for me. What's your deal?"

"Oh, I don't know. Maybe the fact that he's in love with you."

He scoffs. "That's ridiculous."

"Is it? I see the way he looks at you."

"Whatever," he brushes past me up the staircase.

"That's it? You want to skin anyone who dares to flirt with me, but when the shit's reversed, it's whatever?"

"When it's bullshit, yeah!" He throws over his shoulder as he retreats.

"Why are you getting so angry then?" I ask, trailing him.

"Because he's the only one who had my back tonight, and you're making our friendship out to be something that it's not. It's fucked up."

I freeze. "You don't think I have your back?"

I stand at the top of the landing, stunned when he doesn't answer. I try to will away the sting behind my eyes.

How the fuck did we get here? I know I messed things up, refusing to get help and lying to him, but when did all of this resentment grow inside of him?

He's the only one who had my back tonight.

I wipe my eyes quickly.

It's the shittiest thing he's ever said to me. It's simply not true. I can disagree with some of his actions and still stand by his side. Why the fuck are we together if he doesn't know that? A fresh wave of anger hits. I need to be far away from him right now. Trembling, I beeline to our dressing room, slam the door, and start jamming clothes into a duffle.

He's the only one who had my back tonight.

I wipe my eyes on the sleeve of my T-shirt.

Why's he with me then?

I rip my jeans off of a hanger when his chest presses against my back, and his hands cover my own. "You're not leaving like this. You're upset. I'll sleep in a guest room."

Pulling away from him, I clasp onto the duffel. "No!" I reply, wiping my face quickly. "I'm leaving. We both need space."

He lets out an exasperated breath. "I'm tired of space."

I shrug. "Fine. I need space then."

"Wait, slow down," he says as I move to fill another duffel. "Don't leave. This is our home. I'm sorry for being a dick. Let's just sleep and try again in the morning," he pleads against my ear. The rawness in his voice threatens to thaw my icy resolve.

He notices my grip on the duffle softens and continues pleading with me. "It's just a fight. Stay with me, baby." My traitorous body lights up from the feathery brush of his lips against my ear. I find myself tilting back slightly against the press of his chest. He brushes a kiss against my neck. I hear my whispered moan when his hand reaches under my shirt and rests on my abdomen. "We're both wound up." His fingers trail down, slipping past my waistband. I moan when he takes hold of me. I hold back from grinding into his fist. "It's been too long. It's my fau—"

I jolt when his ringtone blares through the room. He snatches it out of his pocket. "Kieran's notoriously bad timing," he groans as he tosses it on the bench across the room.

He's the only one who had my back tonight.

The words balloon inside of my head. I rip myself out of his embrace. I clench my jaw at the thought that Arnaz could make him happier.

"I need to go." I zip up the duffles and move toward the door.

He darts in front of me, blocking my exit.

"Move, Sidney," I grit out.

"I'll never forgive myself if you leave here angry and something happens. Let's just talk."

I shake my head, trying to dislodge the vision of him with Arnaz.

"Move!" I bark. "It's been weeks of you rejecting all of my advances, and what, now you want to fuck me?" I stick out my chest, swollen with rage.

"No, that's not what—"

"I'm not a sex doll for you to fuck when you want. You're lucky I'm loyal, but don't push me," I snarl. "Just because you're the only man I've been with doesn't mean I can't have another big cock inside of me whenever the fuck I want. Finding someone who enjoys being deep-throated until they pass out can't be hard. In fact, maybe I should call—"

"Enough!" he bellows, eyes narrowed and dark like coal. "Keep goin' and see how it works out for the fuckers you name. Go on. Put shit in my head that I can't get out. Try me."

I swallow my words.

"You degrade what we have. It was never about sex with us."

I wince at his voice's serrated edge.

"Goddamn!" He walks across the room and stares up at the ceiling, shaking his head. "So that's it. One rough patch, and you're out?"

"I can't. It's not just one. It's like we're growing apart. Look at us. We've been off for a minute. I know I messed up, but you're hot and cold. There's all of this distance...I feel abandoned and—"

"How?" He whips around to face me. "I've given everything to you. My heart"—he bellows—"my dedication"—he pounds on his chest—"my soul. Everything!" He swipes away tears before they have the chance to fall. "How have I abandoned you, Tyler?"

His voice bounces off of the walls, causing me to flinch. This is the first time he's ever raised his voice.

"You keep rejecting all of my attempts to connect. You know what our intimacy means to me. It hurts and—"

"I'm not allowed to be hurt by your decision to not get help?" he asks. "You told me that sometimes you think about ending it."

My eyes widen. "W-when did I say that?"

He scoffs. "You don't even remember. You think I abandoned you because we stopped having sex? How am I supposed to stay hard when I'm so fucking scared I'm gonna lose you?"

"When did I say it?" I ask again.

"After your panic attack the night after our first week of games."

I'm frozen in place as I recall a hazy memory from that week. I'm so stupid. I can't believe I let that slip out.

I flinch when the doorbell rings.

"This fucking day!" he thunders, storming out of the room.

I resist the urge to slide down to the floor and rest my head between my legs. Instead, I grab the bags, phone charger, and kicks. As I approach the bottom floor, I hear Jett's, our security guard's, voice.

"...to interrupt. I heard yelling and wanted to check that you're both good."

His concerned gaze pings between us as I reach the bottom of the landing.

"Thanks. We're good," Sid says, quickly wiping his eyes.

Jett scans the room and he nods.

"Oh, sir, I was going to hit the wine shop on my way home. What's the name of the wine you gifted me last year?"

This is a coded question that Jett taught us in the event there's ever a home invasion, and we need to signal for help.

"Sancerre," Sid confirms, which is code for we're okay.

"Yes, that's the one," he replies before he glances between us and then leaves.

I gaze at Sid's back and will myself to brush past him. Every step feels impossible. Hand on the doorknob, I pause. "I'll be in Topanga."

I can't turn around to face him. If I do, I'll never make it past the threshold.

"Don't leave, Ty." His voice is hauntingly sad.

I didn't think leaving would hurt this much, but I need space to fix this.

He's right. I need to start ridding us of my ghosts.

Chapter Twenty-Five

It's been three weeks since the night of our fight. I tossed and turned for nights after, replaying everything we said to each other. What messed me up the most was Sid's assumption that I would be angry at him for speaking out. Well, that and his claim that Arnaz is the only one who has his back. It's clear I haven't done the best job of showing him how important he is to me. I regret threatening to step out. It was stupid, and even more, it was an empty threat. I miss him and our home, but being back in my house in Topanga feels right for now. I need space to think so that I can fix this. One thing I realized pretty quickly after I left is that I can't fix everything alone. I need help. So, I returned to therapy with Jaden for two sessions a week. In some sessions, we focus on my separation from Sid. Others focus on my grief. When I revealed to Jaden that Sid was my partner, I was relieved that he didn't make a big deal out of it.

Sid's comments at the press conference are all anyone talks about in the league. Most of the public celebrated his speaking out. There was a backlash from online personalities and ignorant fans who claimed he was trying to corrupt the league by advocating for gay players. Sid's sexuality has also been questioned on a few gossip sites, piquing my anxiety. Within the league, the response has been mixed. While a good number of players vocalized their support for his efforts, Sid was approached sporadically by players who told him to his face that they don't think gay people belong in the league. Of course, the players wouldn't ever admit to being homophobic in public. Sid fired back that he didn't think homophobic fucks belonged in the league either, so it's a good thing players aren't in charge of draft selections. This was reported to me by Lily, who calls every day to check in. Without being asked, she updates me on how he's doing, and I'm pretty sure she shares updates with him about me. I'll never admit it, but I look forward to her calls every night. After convincing her that I wasn't spiraling into depression, she admitted that Sid's been in rough shape since our fight. He regrets things that he said and worries that he lost me. I hate to think of him hurting. It's all made me double down on my work with Jaden.

I overheard some teammates discussing Sid's comments in the locker room. Vlad, a recent transfer from Milwaukee, wondered about Sid's motives and if he was just pretending to be an ally for publicity. He also didn't get why gay people needed to come out.

I unclenched my jaw to respond, but Kaleb beat me to it.

"Yo, you can't be serious with that question. Has anyone ever assumed that you're gay when they met you for the first time?"

Vlad shook his head. "So what?"

"Alright then. People assume you're straight. You never have to clarify. That's a privilege you have if you're a straight dude. Gay people don't have that. They constantly have to clarify when people, like, misidentify them. That's part of what coming out is. People will assume you have a wife when maybe you have a husband. Coming out shouldn't be a big deal, but mofos are still homophobic."

His response stunned me. Later that night, when I thought about the entire exchange, it hit me that I've never heard homophobic banter from him.

"Fine, but I don't need to know if someone likes it up the ass," Vlad replied.

"Bro, what the fuck? That's homophobic."

Vlad scoffed. "How?"

Oh, I don't know, fuck face, maybe because you're reducing an emotional, erotic, and romantic identity to a singular sexual act?

"How?" Kaleb squints at Vlad. "Because it's bullshit. That's like me saying I don't want to know if you're straight because it means you eat pussy. Also, not every gay person fucks with anal, and stop fronting like straight people don't do that shit too."

Yes, Kaleb!

I pulled my jaw off of the floor to jump into the conversation. "Also, Sid's not doing this for attention. That's got to be one of the dumbest fucking things I've ever heard. I know that this matters to him. Next, you're going to say that you don't want a gay teammate checking you out in a locker room. It's certifiably ignorant to think that just 'cause someone's gay, it means that they want you just because you're a man. Human attraction is complex."

"Exactly," Kaleb says, patting my shoulder. Then he smiled at me in a way that left me wondering if he knew about me or me and Sid. How could he, though?

"So, in summary, no saying homophobic shit on our team. Work on being a better ally," Idris piped up in his veteran no-bullshit voice.

"Listen, love is love and all of that, but in my religion, being gay is a sin," Ronen, our center, who is more of a benchwarmer, piped in.

"Ro, no one asked you to change your religion. But at the same time, don't ask me to change my beliefs. I don't believe that being gay is a sin. Therefore, we have to respect that we have different beliefs. For the record, you're a professional athlete. Not saying offensive shit is expected of all of us," Idris fired back.

"Word!" Tevin added.

"Like my mama used to say, if you don't have anything nice to say, then shut the fuck up. I'm paraphrasing, obviously. She'd threaten to wash my mouth with soap if she heard me swearing," Malik chimed in, grinning.

I took one thing away from that conversation. If I ever decided to come out, I'd start with Kaleb, Idris, Tev, and Malik.

During my first post-game press conference after Sid spoke out, a reporter asked me what I thought of his remarks. I wasn't surprised by the question, but it was loaded. If I declared my support for him, I risked the media looking at our friendship in a different light. Even when we were out together at events, we always maintained distance. Still, all it takes is one heated glance between us captured on video for there to be speculation. No matter how careful we've been, in the back of my mind, there's always the fear that we weren't as careful as we thought. But if I didn't declare my support for him and speak from the heart, then I wouldn't have been able to live with myself. He's standing up for what's right, and so many of us will benefit from it.

I lifted my chin and leaned into the mic. "I'm deeply moved by Sid's bravery and support his efforts. I've witnessed the ignorance that he mentioned, and it's messed up. I stand with the LGBTQIA community. Fighting for progress and equality is important to me. It's up to every generation to fight for progress, so we're handing the next generation a world better than we had. Sid's been doing that for years. I got his back and will do my part."

As for the man himself, he's demonstrated nerves of steel. He's used the momentum to announce partnerships with non-profits focused on LGBTQIA suicide prevention. His first post-game conference after his suspension had over a million views in a couple of hours. As soon as my hotel door closed, I pulled up the clip. My heart ached to see him for the first time since our fight. He looked strong and serious—more serious than I've seen him up there. When asked his thoughts regarding the online backlash at his comments, he responded:

"Honestly, I couldn't care less about the opinion of homophobes. I've heard it all my entire life. Bigots call gay people crazy, sinful, blah blah, which creates a stigma. I don't believe any of that. It's garbage. Gay people are people like everyone else. I'm not interested in taking on the mental and emotional labor of trying to change people's beliefs. My time and energy are better used advocating within the league for protections that will help foster a safe space for all players. I understand that some people will have a problem with that. That's honestly their problem. Burn my jerseys, and post your hateful comments online. I will still be here tomorrow, fighting to make this world more equitable. And when my career is over, I'll still be fighting bigotry."

"Actually, your jerseys are sold out in most places and are being resold for 5x the retail price online. Why do you think that is?" the reporter replied.

Sid nodded. "Well, there are good people in the world who believe what I believe. They also want people who identify as LGBTQIA to be able to live their full and authentic lives. They've seen the rates of suicide, depression, and violence the community faces. Maybe they're part of the community or know someone who is. The hate is loud online and can distort reality, but the world isn't what we see on social media. There are communities in the real world with people who share my values and beliefs. We're out there. I recently posted online resources for people looking to engage and find support."

"Sid, over here, Ren from *Sports Daily*. Do you think the league has done enough to make it safe for LGBTQIA players? Do you think homophobic bullying is endemic in the league?"

"I think the league is trying to increase its efforts, but there's always room for improvement, not just in basketball but all sports. There should be a baseline of decorum that's enforced. As a professional player in any sport, if you make offensive comments—whether it be racist, sexist, or homophobic—you should be suspended and fined. And if you're a repeat offender, you should face tougher penalties. People should be able to show up and do their jobs without encountering slurs of any kind. Some of us are parents and relatives of people who identify as LGBTQIA. Some of our fans are part of the community, and we wouldn't have a league without fans. At the end of the day, people will be people, so we look to the league to enforce a healthy culture."

Since Sid's initial comments, the league made a public statement that they are committed to ensuring everyone feels safe. The players union reached out to Sid to understand his ideas for improvement and devise a list of recommendations to present to the NBA Board of Governors, the management body overseeing the league's operations. The union will also run a survey to collect feedback from other players since there's strength in numbers. I told our team's GM that I was happy to meet with the union to lend my support. I also tapped my teammates.

Then, a reporter asked him, "Much has been written about your rivalry and friendship with Ty Washington. Ratings skyrocket whenever your teams face off. You received support across the league, but what did it mean for you to receive his support in particular?"

Sid's face remained neutral when he replied, "I'm honored

by his words and support. He's a consummate professional. He may be ferocious on the court, but off, he's one of the kindest and most honest guys you'd ever meet. I consider myself lucky to know him and call him a friend."

My shoulders slumped. His words are nice, tidy even, but his tone couldn't have been flatter. I spent way too many hours that night overthinking his response. I mean, I know the score with us, and maybe he was trying to protect me by putting up a canned response. But a part of me wished he gave something— anything—to give me a sense of where we stand.

Chapter Twenty-Six

Today's session with Jaden left me wrung out. I'm at home spread out across the couch like fresh roadkill. My stomach is stuffed to the hilt after crushing a Big Mek burger and strawberry milkshake. Jaden said I should reward myself for all of the hard work. Something about balancing painful emotions with more uplifting ones helps with processing grief. I was instructed to choose a reward I wouldn't usually allow myself. I immediately thought of the burger Tev had told me about and placed an order for delivery as soon as I got home. It was hands down the best burger I've ever had. Nothing's better than Adam's cooking, but the burger definitely makes the top five.

We spent most of today's therapy session revisiting the events leading up to my parent's deaths. Jaden explained that revisiting helps me process their deaths emotionally so that I can feel connected with them more healthily. It's also supposed to help dull the intense feelings that come up. As I retold the story in painstaking detail, Jaden stopped me periodically to assess the intensity of emotions I felt on a scale of one to ten, with ten being the most intense or painful. The first time we did the exercise, it was tens all of the way. I rewarded myself after that session by skipping my usual late-night practice and watching an action movie.

Today, the intensity level dropped to an eight and a half, which is progress, I guess. Jaden kept reminding me that facing painful experiences gives us a chance to process them. When I asked him what that meant, he said that in my case, it gives me the opportunity to face and accept what happened, however unwanted, so that I can find a way to live with it.

Sometimes, it's too much to wrap my head around, but I refuse to quit. I need to do this for myself. I need to do this if I have any chance of a future with Sid. Some days, I leave the weight of my sessions with Jaden to give myself a break and be able to focus on practice and on the court. It's the only way I can keep going back week after week.

I pause the movie that I'm watching when my phone vibrates. Flipping it over, I see it's Kaleb calling, and I send it to voicemail. Then it vibrates again. This time, it's Idris calling. That's odd. We text more than we talk on the phone. I let it go to voicemail. A minute later, I get a text from Tevin with a link. My pulse immediately kicks up. This can't be good.

I click on the link, and an article pops up.

"To Be a Gay Player in the NBA" by Arnaz Cade.

Oh shit!

I jolt upright and expand the page to read the full article.

"Over the last few weeks, there's been a lot of talk about what it's like to be a gay basketball player in the NBA. Specifically, whether or not it's safe to be out in the league. There are some people even questioning whether gay people belong in the league at all. As if being gay in any way correlates with a person's ability to play basketball. Ability is really the only thing that should matter. Do you have the talent, discipline, and hunger to compete at a high level? Can you learn from your failures and use them to strengthen your game? Can you put aside your ego and show up for your team night after night,

season after season? Can you show respect to your teammates, coaches, and fans, even the ones with different beliefs and backgrounds?

As I reflect on my journey as a basketball player, I'm proud of my career so far. I've played 571 games, and I've tallied 13,892 career points. I've torn my ACL, sprained my ankle twice, and healed from several contusions and a shoulder injury. I've put everything into my career while hiding an important part of my identity.

I'm a basketball player, and I'm gay.

Unless closeted, you can't possibly understand the toll it takes to deny who you are because it isn't safe to be out. I've suffered from chronic depression and suicidal ideation since I was a teenager. I've always known that I was gay, but I learned quickly that if I wanted to pursue my dream of playing basketball, I'd have to hide that part of myself until I'm close to retiring from the league.

Sid King is right.

If you're a player in the league, you hear homophobic stuff often, and it has to stop. It's not okay. It's unwelcome behavior that leads to mental distress and humiliation, which no one should have to endure, especially in a professional environment.

Today, I pledge my support in helping to make the league a safer place for all people, especially for my LGBTQIA family.

Sid, thank you for your bravery in standing up for those of us who are too terrified to stand up for ourselves. By fighting to create a safe space using your voice and platform, you inspired me to speak my truth. It means a lot knowing that I'll still have you as a friend after this is published. Thank you for your allyship and advocacy.

To those of my teammates who I've witnessed stand by Sid over the last few weeks, thank you! Your support has inadvertently helped me with my decision to come out.

I made the personal decision to come out based on my needs. I've seen the media question people's sexuality over the last few weeks. I urge them to STOP! Sexual identity is private. People are not required to come out. It is a complex personal decision that comes down to a myriad of factors, including self-identity, sense of safety, and personal needs.

Respect that.

Lastly, I have never been more committed to playing basketball and supporting my teammates. I hope to continue playing basketball for many years.

Go Royals!"

WOW. I RE-READ THE ESSAY AGAIN, STUNNED.

Arnaz is gay.

Arnaz is gay, and he just came out.

And Sid's actions directly inspired him.

Whoa.

My thumb hovers over Sid's number in my phone. I'm dying to know what he thinks. Wait—what if he knew all this time? Did he lie to me when I asked him if Arnaz was straight? Does he really not know that Arnaz has a thing for him?

My phone vibrates again. This time, it's Malik calling. I toss the phone across the table and bury my head in my hands. Fuck, I'm exhausted. I turn off the lights and head to the shower. I stand under the hot water for a few minutes, lost in thought. Arnaz coming out feels enormous, but a part of me wishes it didn't. I wish I lived during a time when it wasn't such a big deal. After crawling into bed, I pull up Arnaz's essay and re-read it. The essay has over 5,000 comments. I take a deep breath and read through the top-liked ones. Most are positive, congratulating Arnaz on living his truth. Some are from religious folks saying that they will pray for his soul to be saved. There are blatantly hateful ones that make my stomach turn. I click out of the essay and see the missed calls from earlier. I hit Kaleb back. He picks up on the third ring.

"Yo!"

"Wassup," I reply.

"Yo, you saw Arnaz's post?"

"Yup, wow, eh?" I huff out a breath.

"Right? Wowzers! I'm happy for him."

I hear a kid crying in the background.

"Your house always sounds like a playground."

"Yeah, it's a f-u-c-k-i-n-g zoo." He sighs. "Why do you think I'm the first to turn in when we're on the road? Peace!"

I chuckle. "Still spelling out swear words when the kids are around?"

"Yeah, I'm too cheap to put money in a swear jar."

"I'm not sure that's how that works. Hey, I've been meaning to ask you. You meant all that stuff you said to Vlad the other day, you know, as an ally?"

"Yep, every bit of it. Why? Someone giving you shit?" he asks, sounding like he's ready to go to war for me.

"No." I chuckle nervously. "Why would someone give me shit?"

Fuck! He does know! How?

"No reason...Uh, why'd you ask?"

"I was just curious."

His wife yells for him to bring something called a "boppy."

"Let me let you go. Sounds like you're needed."

"Yeah, I get two minutes of peace every hour in this house. Listen, I'm here if you ever need to talk about...whatever."

"Same, bro. I appreciate you."

My mind's a cesspool of thoughts—Arnaz's coming out, the ugly comments people posted under his article, whether Sid knew about Arnaz, if Arnaz coming out will change Sid's feelings for him, if Sid's in love with Arnaz, and the high probability that Kaleb knows I'm gay.

There's one question that I can get an answer to now. I unlock my phone.

ME

Did you know?

I swallow roughly when bubbles appear under my message less than a minute later.

MY LOVE

He never told me. I wouldn't lie to you.

My head falls back to the pillow, and I blow out a breath of relief.

I want to call and ask him how he's doing and tell him about my sessions with Jaden, but something holds me back. I need a few more sessions to prove to myself that I'm committed to seeing this through. Though it's been nine days since my last nightmare—a new record—last night, I woke up in the middle of the night feeling raw. All the sadness I ignored in the day weighed heavily on me. I miss him terribly.

Chapter Twenty-Seven

Arnaz's name is everywhere over the next few days. He's received enormous support from celebrities, teammates, and even politicians. Most of my teammates posted messages of support online, myself included. It's clear from Sid's and his teammates' comments online and postgame interviews that the Royals feel protective of him and have his back. The league has been doing a great job of immediately ejecting bigots out of games for shouting slurs when the Royals are on the road.

My phone rings.

"Hey," I answer, bending down to lace up my kicks.

"Yo, you ready?" Kaleb asks.

I asked him to grab an early dinner, knowing how precious his kid-free evenings are locked in his hotel room. My mind was already made up, but after talking through it with Jaden, I felt surer than ever that I wanted to come out to him tonight.

"Yeah. Actually, can I swing by your room real quick? There's something I need to tell you, and I'd rather do it privately."

"407. See you in a bit," he says, then hangs up.

I grab my wallet, key card, and jacket. I'm hungry, but I know the rumbling in my stomach is more from nerves.

I stare at myself in the mirror.

You got this. Kaleb is safe, and he likely already knows.

I take the stairs the two flights down, not wanting to run into any of my other teammates. When I reach his door, I knock twice, and the door flings open.

"Yo!" Kaleb nods at me. "Come in."

"Thanks. Dude, your room is bigger than mine," I complain, staring around at the king-size bed, couch, desk, armchair, and ottoman.

"Yeah? Good to know the player that scores the most points doesn't get the best digs," he says, chuckling.

"They have to keep me humble somehow."

I cross my fingers to stop myself from jinxing things. My basketball skills are slowly coming back.

"Look, I'll make this quick." I perch against his desk. "What I'm about to say needs to stay between us. Can you do that?"

"Of course man."

Just rip the bandaid off!

I rub my sweaty palms against my thighs. "I'm gay."

His eyes go wide. "Um...oh...wow."

I jump to my feet. "Fuck. I knew you knew already. How?"

If I hadn't spent two seasons with him, I might have bought the somewhat believable acting.

He grins. "Don't be mad. It's just you never seem interested in the endless pussy conversations in the locker room or on the road. You show up with hickeys but refuse to tell us anything about it. You seem really uncomfortable whenever we prod. You turned down every lap dance on your birthday. You actually seemed kinda turned off by the idea. I wasn't sure, but I had a feeling. Idris and Tevin kind of guessed too. But we'd never ever say anything. We got your back."

"I need to sit down." I fall into his desk chair. "Y'all know?" I ask in disbelief.

"Kind of...maybe Malik too, but that's all. I swear. I've been trying to find a way to tell you for a while that I'm safe, you know, if you needed someone to talk to, but I also wanted to respect your privacy. It's the same for the other guys. Sid kind of kicked the door open, and it finally gave me a chance to speak up in the locker room."

I feel like such an idiot wasting so much energy to hide when they knew all along.

I clear my throat. "So, you're really cool with me being gay?"

"Fuck yeah! I hate homophobes. My favorite cousin is bi, and my nephew is gay. The little dude was bullied last year in school. My sister, bro-in-law, and I went up there, met with the parents, and dealt with it. It changed him, though. He's in therapy now, but I wish there was more I could do."

"Man, I'm sorry. That's rough."

"Yeah, but it makes what Sid and Arnaz are doing that much more important. My nephew loves basketball, and seeing out players will make a difference. It's only a matter of time. That generation ain't fucking around."

I grin. "Word."

"Tev, Idris, and Malik are cool too. If you ever want to come out, we got your back. Real talk."

"Dude." I shake my head. "I need a drink...or ten."

"How about a hug? Bring it in." He opens his arms.

I shake my head as I climb to my feet.

When we separate, he asks, "Are you gonna tell me about your secret boyfriend?"

I laugh and pat him on the shoulder. "I think that might be enough secrets for one day, but soon, I promise."

"I'm a patient friend. Ready to roll?"

"Yup," I reply, shaking my head again.

I PICK UP MY PHONE TO TEXT SID ABOUT COMING OUT TO KALEB, but then I freeze, remembering our separation. The lightness that I felt just a moment ago turns to lead. I scroll through social media instead and freeze when I see Arnaz and Sid's names trending.

"You look like my kid when we force him to eat anything other than pizza and mac 'n cheese," Kaleb says, returning from the bathroom.

"Sid and Arnaz made this year's Time 100 list of the Most Influential People in the World!"

"Get the hell outta here. That's boss," Kaleb says, reaching for the dinner rolls.

"Yeah...it's incredible." I pull up the article.

Time 100 selectees are recognized for changing the world. It's a wild list of people of all backgrounds—dictators, athletes, activists, you name it. I wonder who they bumped to add Arnaz, considering he just came out. There's a commemorative gala being held in June in Manhattan. Will Sid make a speech? Who will be his plus one? I'm crushed he didn't tell me. I know we're separated, but this is huge.

I WAKE UP AT TWO O'CLOCK IN THE MORNING TO PISS AND FIND thirty minutes later that I can't go back to sleep.

I check my phone for messages and zilch. I missed Lily's call when I was out with Kaleb, and it was too late to call her back once I got in. I responded to the group thread with Kieran and Tommy. They text every day, sometimes asking how I'm doing, other times sending funny memes. It's their way of being there for me.

Scrolling through social media, I see the Royals trending and click on one of the reels that Nicholas posted of himself, twerking to Kelis' "Milkshake." I chuckle at his really animated twerk. He swings the camera around, and it looks like they're at a gay bar with buff dancers. I spot Sid and Arnaz and pause the video. Sid's arm is slung around Arnaz's neck as they laugh at Nicholas. My stomach turns even though it looks innocent. It's just—they look really good together. Johan and Ussef jump in, attempting their own twerk. Ussef squats down low while humping the air, tongue sticking out, causing Sid and Arnaz to buckle over with laughter, then the feed dies. I scan the comments—most are playful, while others are offensive. I freeze when I see a comment shipping Sid and Arnaz. The comment has 752 likes and a few replies about how they look hot together.

Ugh.

This shit is not helping my insecurity. Throwing my phone across the bed, I yell into the pillow.

I'm stuck wide awake for the rest of the morning.

I don't play well against the Marvels later that day. My teammates chalk it up to road fatigue, but I know the truth— my head's just not in it. 1,552 is the number that keeps circling my thoughts. That's the latest number of likes for the comment shipping Sid and Arnaz. 1,552 people think that my boyfriend, the man I want to marry, looks hot with another person. I know I'm supposed to ignore comments, but my brain is stuck on it. It's wormed its way into my head, bloating my insecurities.

So what if they look hot together? Sid and I are in love, and we look pretty fucking hot too. Someone even called them a power couple for making the Times 100 list.

"Dude, are you listening?" Kaleb asks.

"My bad. What?"

"Are you going to Ussef's party on Saturday night? Our team was invited. It's at his crib in Beverly Hills."

"Uh, yeah. Idris invited me. You?" I tell myself that I'll go to drink and live a little, blah blah, but Sid will most likely be there, seeing as Ussef is his teammate, and I can't resist the chance to see him, even from a distance.

"Yep, I think most of the team's down. Dude's parties are lit. This one is supposed to be a swanky suit and tie affair."

I nod. "Heard something like that. I'll hit you up when I get there."

I need to get my head straight. Seeing Sid and Arnaz's names everywhere has me trippin'. Not to mention, their magic on the court together keeps improving. For the first time, I can't bring myself to watch highlights of Sid's games. I tried a few nights ago, but the seamless way they read each other on the court fueled my insecurity. I hate feeling this way.

Chapter Twenty-Eight

It's Saturday night, and I'm home getting dressed for Ussef's party. I stare at the new, tailored Gucci suit hanging from my closet.

"Here's to hoping you lift me out of my funk, homie."

Buttoning up the white band-collar shirt, I clasp on my favorite Dior, gold, oval, cufflinks that I stole from Sid. Then, I slide on the slim-cut, forest green wool and cashmere blend trousers and matching blazer, buckling up a cognac-colored, leather belt that matches my Prada leather Chester boots. I reach for an oatmeal-colored beanie, then decide against it. I mean, I did get a fresh cut earlier. I slide a gold bracelet on one hand and a gold band on the opposite ring finger.

I admire myself in the mirror.

Not bad.

The party's already lit by the time I arrive. I run into Kaleb and Idris less than twenty feet from the door.

"You look like a fucking model. Is that alpaca?" Kaleb teases, extending a dap.

I grin. "Is that velvet? I peep the whole sleazy-chic vibe you got going." He looks like a boss in a black turtleneck, an indigo-blue velvet blazer, and black trousers.

"Well, we can't all be pretty, but I try," he says with a lazy grin.

"What's good." I dap Idris and scan his slim-fit, ash grey suit with a mock-neck, white tee underneath. "You clean, bro."

"Thanks. Props to my stylist. I have no style."

"We know," Kaleb and I say simultaneously, causing us to crack up.

"Knights fam, thanks for coming through."

Our heads whip around to face Ussef.

"Look at the birthday boy's drip," I say, scanning the navy blue trouser shorts with the seams exposed around the knee and a matching cape.

A cape.

He's shirtless, flaunting his tats, which run from his neck to his toes, and his navel and nipple piercings.

He smirks. "Drip for miles, bredrin. You know how I do."

Word. His style is the most avant-garde of everyone in the league, right up there with Sid.

"Happy Birthday," Kaleb says.

"Thank you, thank you!" His full lips spread into a hazy smile, crinkling his glassy eyes.

He offers his blunt to us.

"Nah, I'm good." Weed bugs me out.

Idris takes two pulls, then passes it back. "Good lookin'."

"Let's head upstairs. The lounge area is chill," Ussef says, leading the way through the crowd.

We stop to dap people along the way, and by the time Kaleb and I reach the second floor, we lose Ussef and Idris to side conversations.

I turn to Kaleb. "I'll be right back."

I scan the rooms, looking for Sid, but come up empty.

I try to keep my energy up despite the disappointment creeping in.

"You good?" Kaleb asks.

"Yeah, I'm straight. Was looking for someone," I say, rubbing my neck.

"Come on. Let's head up."

I trail him to the third-floor lounge, where my mouth goes dry as I spot a group of Royals and their wives.

He's here. I can sense him.

I dap a few players as I push through the crowd. My skin prickles when I hear it—his voice. I follow the sound, reversing direction and dodging a server balancing a tray of drinks.

I freeze in my steps when I spot him sitting on a couch, immersed in conversation. I take in his slim-cut, garnet checkered suit and a cream dress shirt with a wingtip collar, topped off with a crisp pocket square. Sitting to his right, Arnaz is in a three-piece, navy-blue suit, accented by a pink rose lapel and a blue and white polka dot pocket square. The fucker cleans up nicely.

I recognize Johan's wife, Lainee, to his left.

Kaleb starts a conversation nearby with a woman who looks vaguely familiar—maybe an agent. I zone them out and glue my attention to Sid. He angles his head toward Arnaz, giving his full attention. One of Sid's gifts is his ability to be fully present. He makes you feel like you're the center of the world, and it's one of the things I love about him, but right now, I hate it. Arnaz leans closer to help Lainee catch what he's saying. When Sid turns away, Arnaz stretches his arm across the brim of the couch and turns into him slightly.

Back up, fuck face.

A few seconds later, I grin when Sid shuffles to give Arnaz space.

Good job, baby.

My breath dies in my chest when Sid laughs at Lainee's joke, and his entire face transforms. I never understood the laws of gravity until I experienced Sid's laughter. Its cavernous rumble knocked me into a new orbit, where I'd gladly circle eternity, bathing in its sound and gazing into his sun-glinted eyes.

Arnaz's lips part slightly as his eyes trace over Sid's face with meticulous detail.

And now I'm watching another man uncover the mystery of gravity.

I clench and then unclench my fists.

He wants him, that's undeniable. But I haven't seen anything that tells me that Sid wants him back.

Fuck. The thought alone makes me want to hurl a building at Arnaz.

Lainee excuses herself, leaving them alone. Sid reaches inside his blazer and pulls out his phone, but Arnaz nudges his shoulder and says something to him before he can unlock it.

So desperate for his attention.

I know it's ridiculous, but I'm annoyed that Sid hasn't looked up once. Is it out there to wish he'd felt my presence by now? He probably heard my team was invited, but I doubt he'd expect me to show up.

As if I've willed him telepathically, he scans the room, glancing toward the door.

Look to the left.

His gaze pans to the right of the room, then back to the door. He absentmindedly nods at something Arnaz says while searching. He stares at the door and stares and stares, his eyes dimming with each passing second.

Over here.

Finally, his gaze swoops to the left.

*Yes...come on...almost...almost...*Our gazes meet, and a jolt of heat rushes through my body. For a split second, I worry he isn't happy to see me, but recognition hits, and his face breaks into a smile so brilliant that I can't help but mirror it. He's out of his chair a second later. My pulse takes off as his gaze trails down my body.

Down, boy, I tell my dick.

"You're here," he says, enveloping me in a hug. "I hoped you'd come."

God. That voice.

I hold on longer than I should, but he isn't letting go either.

When we pull away, he stares into my eyes, searching. A pained expression darkens his face. "Fuck, I've missed you."

There's so much I want to say to him.

I've missed you too.

I'm ready to come home.

I'm sorry I hurt you.

I'm sorry it took me so long to get help.

I was wrong for thinking I didn't need help.

I miss my best friend.

I've had tough days.

Healing sucks sometimes.

I met our kids.

They visit me sometimes when I sleep.

I've spent hours wondering what it means.

I think it's a sign.

I need to make peace with the past.

Our future is our family.

I miss your laughter.

I love you.

I've never loved you more.

I want to body-slam Arnaz for falling for you.

It's easy to fall for you.

Do you still want me?

"Hey, are you stealing my arm candy?" Kaleb jokes as he slings his arm around my neck. "We know you like 'em pretty, but this one is taken for the night."

I flash Kaleb a tight smile.

The worst timing in history.

Sid raises his hands, eyes locked on mine. "I heard he was taken."

His eyes drop to my dimples when my lips part in a tiny grin.

"How's the party?" I ask, changing the subject before we give ourselves away.

"Pretty chill up here. I haven't made rounds," he says.

He moves to my side so the three of us face the room.

Kaleb angles his head forward toward Sid. "Good game against the Choppers. You and Arnaz put on a show. Wasn't it something like seventy-four points between the two of you?"

"Thanks, man. Yeah, seventy-six. Their defense was off, more so than usual. It felt like an exhibition game."

I keep track of Sid's stats, but I still can't bring myself to watch his highlights—too much of "The Sid and Arnaz Show."

Speak of the devil...

"What's good?" Arnaz daps Kaleb. When he extends his hand to me, I expel a slow cough into my hand and shoot him a tight nod instead. Petty, I know, but it's the only thing keeping me in pocket right now.

"We were just talking about the buckets you two put up against New York," Kaleb says.

"Ay! That was hella fun. I can't take credit. If you ever play with this guy"—he nods to Sid—"you can't help but get after it."

Oh, fuck off with your thirsty compliments.

"It has nothing to do with me. I've played with a lot of guys who don't put up your numbers. That's all you," Sid replies matter-of-factly.

"Yeah, okay. I'm not number three in the league averaging thirty points per game," Arnaz fires back.

"31.4," I grit out.

"What?" Arnaz asks.

"He's averaged 31.4 points per game, not 30."

"My bad," he says, bunching his brows.

The urge to deck him has never been more attractive. I'd revel in watching him hit the floor. I'd stick out my face, encouraging him to get up and swing back just so I can drop his ass again.

"Did Sid tell y'all that ESPN is doing a segment on us for the—" Arnaz continues.

Us. Ugh.

"I need a drink," I interrupt, walking off.

I order a double neat of mezcal. When my drink arrives, I bring the glass to my lips and an involuntary shudder courses through me as I breathe in Sid's scent.

"Are you okay?" He asks, leaning against the bar and facing the room.

I clench the glass. "He's the only one that had your back?"

He seems confused, and then his eyes widen. "I didn't mean it that night. I'm sorry."

My gaze pings Arnaz approaching us, and I grunt. The fucker can't stay away.

"Got to find Idris." I down my glass and stalk away.

I reach the staircase and hear, "Get the hell out of here!"

Jeff Banks. I'd know that voice from anywhere.

He pulls me into a bear hug. Jeff's still one of my favorite people from college to face off against.

"I didn't know your team was in town."

He shakes his head. "Just me. I'm on *Late Night with Tina* this week."

"My manager keeps trying to get me to go on there."

"I can talk to my agent if you need a connection," he offers.

"Nah." I wave it off. "They want me on the show, but I turned it down. It's not my thing."

He grins. "Same ol' Ty. Hates the limelight. On your monk shit. I haven't seen you at any of these parties ever."

I shrug. "You know me. Married to the game. I'm getting too old for this—"

"Yeah, whatever! You look barely a day older than you did in college...same serious eyes, just more muscle. You're a vampire or some shit."

I grin. "How's June and your boy?"

"Beautiful. He's already trying to dribble. I'm heading out soon to catch a plane back. What about you?"

I can't find the energy to lie. I can say I'm seeing someone without divulging details. "Yeah, actually. I'm—"

"Pardon me."

Sid. His palm grazes my lower back as he slides past us with Arnaz.

"My bad," I reply, stepping to the side.

"Those two are fucking, right? You can't take a shit without seeing their faces," Jeff says once they're out of earshot.

My jaw ticks. "Those two? Nah. I know they're just friends."

"If you say so."

He's suddenly the most annoying person in the world after Arnaz.

"Got to piss. Have a safe flight back." I brush past him down the stairs.

I'm fuming by the time I reach home. It was a mistake showing up to the party. What was I thinking? If I can't get the images of them plastered every fucking where online out of my head, how'd I think it would go seeing them in person?

Sid's demisexual when it comes to men, and it's clear he's formed a close connection with Arnaz. That doesn't mean much, except they have an intimacy that extends to their game. And I know for sure Arnaz wants him.

Or has he had him already? I push the thought away despite knowing how easy it is to cheat. Dudes throw entire NDA parties to fuck around. It'd be so easy for shit to go down with Sid and Arnaz on the road after a win, drunk, and headed back to the hotel.

I ball my fists. I'm so tired of these thoughts racking my brain.

After I down a glass of water, I head to the patio. I stare at the sky, desperate for a reprieve from the gnawing images circling my head. Pulling out my phone, I delete all my social apps and power it down. I take a deep breath and stare out at the dark trees and mountains. I didn't think I'd be back here tonight. I thought...I shake my head. It doesn't matter what I thought.

I start to undress as I head to the bathroom to brush the taste of alcohol out of my mouth. My hand trembles as I pick up my toothbrush.

I really need to punch something.

Or fuck someone.

Like an optimistic idiot, I prepped tonight on the chance Sid and I would reunite.

I hang my head as I climb into the shower. After I scrub myself, I lean against the wall and let the hot water unknot my muscles. I recall the press of Sid's body against mine when he hugged me. God, he felt good in my arms. My fingers trail down and wrap around my dick.

His scent and the intense way he stared into my eyes...

I pump myself faster, and my head falls back. Fuck. I can already tell my hand's not going to be enough tonight. I need to sink into—

"Ty!"

I jump, startled by Sid's voice, as the bathroom door rips open. "What the fuck? You just bounced? No bye? Then you ignore my calls?"

I start to respond, but my brain wipes out when his gaze trails down to my erection, and despite his glare, he does a shit job masking his desire.

Neither one of us moves. I can sense he's battling with himself, but there's no denying he wants me. And, fuck, if my erection is anything to go by, I want him badly too. But I can't touch him—not until I get answers.

I release my dick and brush past him. "I'm surprised you noticed." I snatch up a towel and stalk away.

"What's that supposed to mean?" he asks, trailing me into the bedroom.

I towel down and then reach into the drawer for briefs. I yank them on and stare up at the ceiling. "Are you fucking Arnaz?" I ask, turning to face him.

He grimaces. "The fuck? No! Never. How could you ask me that? I've never been unfaithful."

"Are you falling in love with him?" I cross my arms, bracing for the answer.

"No! I'm in love with you. Seriously, where is this coming from?"

How doesn't he know what everyone is saying?

"I saw how close you two are tonight, and I know what an emotional bond with a man can mean for you. I hear what people say about you two."

"Whoa, whoa, what did you see tonight? What have you heard? I'm not fucking him. He's just a friend. I'm not allowed to have friends now?"

"C'mon, Sid. He's in love with you. You're telling me that you can't see it?"

"I'm telling you that I haven't seen it. He's never tried

anything with me. But even if he did, I'd tell him I don't feel the same. What's the big deal?"

I throw up my hands. It's like we live on two different planets. "You're everywhere together! I can't look at a screen without seeing you together or comments with people linking you. It's a nightmare."

"The stuff online is bullshit. The media's trying to twist my speaking out and Arnaz coming out to get clicks. I've spent the last few weeks miserable because you left, and what, this whole time, you thought I was fucking him?"

My voice chokes as doubts plague my thoughts. In my core, I don't believe they've fucked, or he's cheated—I'm not sure it would even be considered cheating since we were separated. But, fuck, it would eviscerate me. Just the thought...

"What are you doing?" I ask as he starts to remove his blazer. Ignoring me, he rips it off and hurls it on the armchair. Then he begins undoing the buttons on his shirt while staring at me with an intensity that tunes every cell in my body into him. I throw him a questioning look.

"What are you..." My brain times out as he unbuckles his pants and drops them, along with his briefs.

Fuck.

My pulse takes off as he reaches into the drawer and pulls out the lube, slicks his cock down, then stalks over to me.

My spine tingles as I take him in.

Damn, I've missed his beautiful cock.

I grimace as I imagine Arnaz down on his knees, wrapping his lips around it.

"We need to tal—"

"Shut up. Come here." His mouth slams against mine—our tongues crash with a ferocious hunger, wiping out my thoughts. Our moans are rolling thunder, echoing back and forth, crackling the air with heat.

"Sid!" I gasp as his lubed finger penetrates me.

"I've missed you moaning my name." He brushes a kiss against my lips as he curls in another finger and fucks me. My head falls to his shoulder as I savor the burn of the stretch. My knees tremble as I dig my fingers into his waist to keep them from buckling.

"Get in bed," he orders.

My mind spins from déjà vu as I crawl into bed, remembering our first time together.

"Fuck," I groan when he pulls my dick between my legs and sucks it.

"Gonna come," I warn him.

"No," he snaps, racking my body with shivers.

I clasp the comforter and try to hold on, but fuck, I was on the edge in the shower.

My forehead digs into the pillow as his tongue fucks my hole. He slides in a finger and then another as I push back, fucking myself on him.

He yanks me back against his chest and growls in my ear. "I thought I told you—this dick is yours and yours only." He wraps his hand around my cock and strokes it. "You forgot?"

I whimper and shake my head.

"Liar." He clasps the back of my neck and shoves me toward the pillow. "I'll fucking remind you."

Fuck, fuck, fuck.

All of the blood in my body rushes to my dick as he thrusts inside and pounds me. My ears blare with grunts, the slap of flesh, and the scrape of the bed hitting the wall.

"Sid," I rasp.

"Hmm?" He leans forward, squeezes my throat, and fucks me senseless. The pressure in my head builds and builds until the room starts to spin. I arch my back, gasping for air, and fist the sheets as I teeter on the edge of a mind-bending orgasm.

He drags off my throat and pulls out of me.

"Please," I whimper from the sudden loss. I push my ass back, scrabbling for his dick to fuck myself on.

"No," he barks, smacking my hand away, then he spreads my cheeks and spits in my hole. I plead for more as his tongue laps at it. He ignores me, squeezing my ass as his tongue dives in. My body throbs as he tugs on my balls—the sensation so intense that dots of white blur my vision. He sinks his cock back inside of me, wrapping his fist around my dick so that I am fucking his hand on every thrust.

I turn my head to look at him, and our gazes lock.

"Fuck. Don't look at me," he grunts as his thrusts turn uneven.

He leans forward and clasps my lower lip between his teeth. The sharp pain flushes my body with a warm, tingling sensation. He kisses my bruised lip and whispers into my ear, "Whose dick is this?"

"Fuck, Sid!" My eyes roll closed as I whimper against his lips. He pushes me flat on my stomach and grinds into me, his chest pinning my back down. My eyes burn with tears as the friction from my dick dragging across the sheets has me tremoring on the brink.

"Shh," he says, into my ear, as he intertwines my fingers with his and rolls his hips, fucking me impossibly deep. "Tell me, baby, whose dick is this?"

"Ungh—fuck," I rasp, voice barely audible.

"Look at me. I've missed those gorgeous eyes."

My eyes inch open.

"Listen to me carefully. I'm only in love with you," he grits out, slowing his thrust to a glide, stroking my prostate, and flooding my body with pleasure. "You're mine. I'm yours. This is mine," he says, reaching underneath to rest his palm over my heart.

"Sid—" The pain of the last few months rises to the surface, and I bury my face into the pillow.

"No hiding," he whispers, pushing the pillow away and kissing my lips.

"God," I sob as he snaps his hips and bottoms out inside of me.

"Say I'll be your husband and a father to our kids."

A hoarse moan sputters up from the ache in my chest. He speaks my dreams so fluently.

I resist the urge to bury my face again as my eyes flood with tears. There is no hiding from him. Our love is a cipher. It cracks me open and lays bare the immensity of my heart.

"Tell me," he repeats, his voice coated with a tenderness that strums an ache in my core.

"Mine," I choke out.

"Only yours. I won't let anything break us."

My lungs expand at his words. For weeks, I've breathed like I feared I'd run out of air. "I can't lose you."

"You won't lose me." He drags us up so that I'm in his lap and spreads his thighs. My head falls back against his chest as he sucks on my neck, and I grind on his dick. He kisses the spot, then clasps my hips and raises me up and down on his dick at a controlled pace. I'm fucking delirious as I take over, fucking myself on him with a punishing force while jerking myself off. I cry out as the most intense orgasm of my life hurdles to the surface.

"Whoa, fuck, wait," he rushes out as he lifts me up and pulls out.

"Fuck's sake," I wail, turning my head to glare at him.

"Mmm. So sexy when you're angry." He brushes a kiss against my lips, drilling into me with beautiful, watery eyes. "But I need more time with my hole."

I lean forward and spread my legs.

He groans as he massages my rim with the head of his cock. I hold my breath, waiting for his penetration, but it never comes.

"Please," I beg.

"Need a second," he grunts, squeezing the base of his cock.

I suck my middle and index finger into my mouth, back and forth slowly. Dripping wet, I reach behind and sink them into my hole. I huff a dissatisfied groan because it's not enough. Not even close.

He growls, smacks my hand away, then thrusts hard inside of me. Pulling out, leaving just the tip in, he slams back inside.

"Yes," I hiss as I grip the sheets.

My whimper turns into a moan when he leans forward and whispers, "It's been too long. I'm thinking I should fuck my hole all night and let you come in the morning." The room blurs as his words send fire through my body.

I have to come.

His fucking scent.

I need to come.

My stomach contracts, my balls draw up, and I cry out as a rush of blood floods my dick.

"No," he growls, smacking my ass hard and pulling out.

I groan, feral with need, and whip around and shove him to his back.

"What are you—fuuck." He gasps as I wrap my mouth around his cock.

My eyes roll closed as I lap up his pre-cum, and a tingling sensation shoots up the back of my head.

Husky moans sputter out of him, the vibration so hot that I have to press the base of my dick to stop myself from coming. I reach for the lube and squeeze some on my cock and his hole, and finger him open. I'm on the edge as I line my cock up and dive inside.

"Fuck, Ty," he groans.

I roll my hips slowly, savoring the tight velvet grip on my cock. *He feels like heaven.* I stare down at his gorgeous face and bite my lip hard to keep from blowing. I'm tracking every shift of his face when he winces.

"Hurts?"

"No. Feels good. Fuck. You're just really deep."

I grin. "I miss you coming on my dick." I lift his legs to fuck him deeper and reach down and stroke his dick. His soulful eyes disappear behind his lids as his abs contract, curving his pecs. I swipe up a pool of pre-cum glistening on his tip and suck it into my mouth. I gaze over his sexy V down to where my dick disappears inside of him.

"Damn," I rasp. I stroke his dick harder as my balls draw up. On my next thrust, he clenches hard around my dick, and I fucking lose it. A thunderous orgasm has me folding him in half and hammering his tight fucking hole. I ignore his grunts filling my ears and his cum painting my chest, and I fuck him mercilessly. He's clenching my sensitive dick so hard that my vision wipes out when I crash on top of him and burrow my face into his neck.

I shudder when he spreads my legs and slips his dick inside of me, plugging my hole. I melt against him, unable to tell our racing hearts apart, and for the first time in weeks, an inner peace settles inside me.

I'm starting to doze off when Sid breaks the silence. "Baby?"

"Hmm?"

"I'm sorry I was hot and cold before we separated. I wanted to help you, but nothing I did helped. I didn't mean the comment I made the night of my fight. I know you have my back."

"It messed me up," I admit. "I couldn't get it out of my head."

"I'm sorry," he says, raising my chin to meet his gaze.

"I'm sorry, too, for threatening to step out. There's no one else I want."

He arches down and kisses my forehead.

"I need to feel you, Sid. I need our connection. I'm fucked when I can't feel it."

"I know. I need it too. These weeks apart..." He shakes his head. "Never again."

"I've hated it too."

"This is crazy. I've never loved like this."

"Never?"

He shakes his head. "Being separated was rough."

I lean up and kiss him, and he matches my tenderness. I hate to think of him hurting. After I pull away, he says, "I'm a jackass for not seeing how the attention on me and Arnaz impacts you. I assumed that you knew it was all garbage. With everything that's happened, he and I kind of leaned on each other—just as friends—to cope with the homophobic back-lash. It was never ever anything other than platonic for me. I'm clear about that."

"Baby, I can trust that it's platonic for you, but I don't think it is for him. Even at the gardening event, I caught him staring at you intensely when you weren't looking. I saw it again tonight when you were both on the couch. Trust me, I know how it looks to desire you."

"He never said or tried anything. I swear. What do I do about it? I can't avoid him. We're on the same team, and with everything going on, how can I cut him off? He's been a good friend."

"I'm not asking you to cut him off. The obvious next step is for you to tell him about us. He thinks you're single, which is unfair to him. He could be misreading your kindness as something more."

"Of course. I hate hiding us."

"I know you do. I do too." I rest my head under his chin. "There's so much I want to tell you, but how's it been since your press conference? Lily filled me in some."

He reaches for my hand and kisses my palm.

"A mixed bag. The stuff that bothered me more than the idiots online were the dudes in the league who said ignorant shit that proved my point."

"I heard about some of that. What did you do?"

"Like, how'd I cope?"

I nod.

"Besides telling them to eat shit and die?" He grins. "I don't know. It helped that everyone on our team had my back, even Coach and management."

"I'm glad you had that. I hated not being with you. I wanted to call you just to talk."

"Me too. If it weren't for my mom's updates, there's no way I could've stayed away. Is it true about therapy?"

I nod. "I went back the week of our fight. Some of the sessions leave me wrecked,"—I huff out a breath—"but I'm not quitting this time."

"Yeah? I regret pushing you."

"Nah, don't. I'm grateful for you and Adam. I needed to do this for me, but also for us and my family."

"We all love you."

I grin. "I haven't had the nightmare in a while, and I came out to Kaleb. He knew already somehow and said Malik, Tev, and Idris knew too. Something about the hickeys and how I seem private and go blank whenever they talk about sex." I guess I could have done a better job of faking it.

"Whoa." His eyes widen. "What was that like?"

My stomach growls. "Tell you over cereal?"

"I'm glad we're both home for the next few days," he says, shuffling to stand.

I peer up at his muscular frame and beautiful face, and a wave of gratitude washes over me.

We have another chance.

Tonight was a turning point for us for the better.

I clasp his extended hand and pull myself up.

We climb back into bed with our bowls of cereal and stay up talking for hours.

Chapter Twenty-Nine

I wake up a man on a mission. It's been a week since Sid and I reconciled. I hit up the group text with Kaleb, Malik, Tevin, and Idris last night, asking if they could swing by my old place for beers and a quick catch-up. Tevin and Idris immediately texted back that they were in. I grab my phone and see that Kaleb and Malik are in too. I'm glad that they're all in. It makes what I am about to do easier.

I smile, taking in Sid's equally sexy and adorable sleeping face. How the man can ooze sexiness, possess intelligence, courage, and wisdom beyond his years, and be so damn adorable is a mystery. Gently climbing out of bed, I tiptoe to the bathroom to get ready. I moved back into our house the day after we reconciled. I noticed our bedroom looked barely slept in but didn't think anything of it. Then I passed one of our guest rooms and noticed the bed unmade. I asked Sid if we had a guest, and he sheepishly admitted to being unable to sleep in our bed without me. I dragged him to our bed and made love to him all over again.

Dressed and ready to dip, I'm retrieving my phone from the

nightstand when Sid stirs and reaches for me in his sleep. His eyes shoot open when he pats the bed and doesn't feel me.

"Hey." I climb in next to him. "I was gonna sneak out to meet up with the guys to tell them about us. I wanted you to sleep in."

His head drops to the pillow, and he scrubs his hands over his face. "Wow. It's really happening."

"Yep." I snuggle my nose in the crook of his neck to inhale his scent, and he wraps me up in his arms.

"Cool if I meet up with Arnaz to tell him about us?"

I nod, recalling what we discussed.

The night that we reunited, we decided that we were ready to come out to the people we trusted. With all the momentum building from Sid's and Arnaz's efforts to bring about changes in the league, it feels like the right time for us. Of course, it takes one slip-up for it to get out to the public, but it's a risk we're ready to take. As long as our close friends and family support us, that's all that matters. I told Sid about my conversation with Adam the night of our fight. How he said that we're so protective of each other that we'll fight to keep the ignorance and hate out. Sid replied, "Damn straight!"

"Seriously? I want to respect your feelings about Arnaz and the media garbage."

"He should know about us. Obviously, I don't like that he has a thing for you, but from what you've told me, he's been a good friend and teammate. I already deleted my social media apps to give myself a break from seeing pictures and comments coupling you. I'll get over whatever irritation I feel toward him. If I'm keeping it real, our issues were never about him."

"No, they weren't. Still, you have a right to be annoyed. Putting myself in your shoes—it would be a lot for me if every time I jumped online, I saw idiots linking you to another team-mate. You know how I get."

I snort. Sid would try to tear the internet down if the shoe was on the other foot.

He grins. "Shut up. I was never like this before you."

I roll my eyes. "Uh-huh."

"It's true."

"It's unnecessary. You're it for me. Where am I going?"

He smirks. "Stop acting like you don't like it."

I grin. No point fronting.

"Back to Arnaz. There's no need to tiptoe around me with him. I trust that you know how to be careful with him. He has feelings for you, and he's going through a lot."

"For sure. I won't ghost or anything. Should I mention that you're uncomfortable with some of the media attention we're getting?"

"That makes it about me, though. Are you not uncomfortable with it?"

He shrugs. "It seems ridiculous to me, honestly. Because I am vocal about fighting homophobia and he is an out basketball player, we have to be together? Why? All straight people aren't attracted to each other."

"Yeah, but it's not just that. You're friends, and as annoying as it is to admit, you're magic together on the court. He looks at you like you're a championship ring. There have been affairs based on far less."

He sighs. "I think it's ridiculous, but I understand what you're saying about optics. I'll just mention that I don't want you to be hurt by all of the misguided media attention our friendship is getting. Cool?"

"I think so. I feel crazy because a week ago, I wanted to hurl a building at him, but today, I'm asking you to be gentle when you tell him." I slap my forehead.

"Oh babe"—he snickers—"I hate to be the one to tell you, but you've been off your rocker."

I burst out laughing. "Shut up."

He grins. "When are you back? I want to order takeout, close the shades, and watch movies all day." He grins. "I wouldn't be mad if there were a few blow jobs sprinkled in."

I quirk an eyebrow at him. "Just a few? What do you think is the world record for time spent giving a blowjob? Bet we can beat it."

"So competitive," he says, trailing his thumb across my lips.

"Or we can lazily 69 while watching movies?"

"Worthy endeavors if there ever were." He massages his erection tenting his briefs and stares at me with hooded eyes and a criminally sexy as-sin smirk.

"Nope."

"What?"

"Uh-huh. Like I don't know that face." I grab the lube from the nightstand and toss it to him. "Use your hand."

"Okay," he says, pulling out his morning wood and stroking it slowly.

Fucking hell.

I screw my eyes closed.

I have to go. Even if I wanted to...traffic is horrific at this time, and I can't leave the guys hanging on my doorstep.

But fuck me, I open my eyes and take in his glistening head, and the next thing I know, I'm kneeling over, licking his tip. I hum a spine-tingling moan when his pre-cum hits my tongue.

"Damn...love your mouth," he sputters, putting gentle pressure on the back of my neck. I press his hand down, encouraging him not to hold back. Something in me goes wild when he claims my mouth and starts thrusting his hips. I gag, relishing the tears pricking the back of my eyes.

When my mouth reaches his base, I hold my breath, pull up, gasp, and then swallow him back down.

I'm so hard I start stroking myself, but he slaps my hand.

"That's mine." His commanding voice goes straight to my balls.

I bob on his cock, pulling off to spit on it and suck it back down. I rub his dick across my lips, a fiend for his scent. I slowly lick under his shaft until I reach his balls. I massage his taint with forward strokes. My tongue trails back up to his head until I'm deep-throating him again.

His sleepy eyes are glued to my lips as his smoky voice utters filthy words and delicious moans. The slurping, gurgling sound, the heady scent of his morning wood, the way his head hits my uvula as it slides down my throat...

His head falls back, and when he raises it again, his pupils are blown.

So. Fucking. Hot.

Too fucking hot.

Oh, fuck!

I pull off him and bite my fist as my balls draw up, and a toe-curling orgasm hits. My head falls back as I moan and coat my jeans and shirt with cum.

"So sexy how much you love it," he says, swiping my cum into his mouth while stroking himself with his left hand.

Damn. I rest my forehead on his thigh. I wipe my cum dripped hand on the sheets. I've lost count of how many times I've orgasmed from giving him head.

"Need a head doc. Love it too much," I pant.

He laughs. "That's the double entendre of the year."

It takes my post-orgasmic brain a second for the joke to land, and then I lose it. We're buckled over laughing when he randomly snorts, and the look of bewilderment that crosses his face has us cracking up so hard tears stream down my face, and Sid has to press down on his stomach to stop cramping.

He wipes his eyes. "It's perfect how much you love it. Never change."

"I don't know," I splutter. "Think I might need an impartial opinion."

Never one to leave a job undone, I suck him back down.

Less than a minute later, he tenses up and puts pressure on my neck. I massage his balls in tandem, causing him to fuck my mouth. Spitting on my finger, I massage his rim.

"Fuck, Ty," he sputters and damn near levitates off the bed as he unloads in my mouth. I continue to bob, suck, and swallow him until he's wrung out.

I wipe my mouth, then punch his arm.

"Ow," he whines, though he's too dopey to have felt it.

"I'm late now because of you." I look down at my cum-covered outfit. "And I have to change and clean up all over again. You know better than to show me your erection when I have to be somewhere." I scowl as I climb out of bed and waddle to the bathroom with my soaked briefs and jeans.

"Can't pretend that I'm sorry when you just sucked my dick like you're possessed by the god of fellatio, then swallowed my cum like it's ambrosia."

I shake my head and burst out laughing. "I don't even have time for breakfast now."

He scoffs. "I just fed you protein, zinc, B-12, and vitamin C. Breakfast fit for champions."

"Of course you looked up the vitamins in semen, you health nut." I strip out of my clothes. "Is it crazy that I'm already counting the minutes until we watch movies and 69?"

"Let's go crazy together, baby, because so am I."

"Are you sore from last night?" he asks.

"Yeah. You?"

"A little, yeah."

"You don't have time to take an Epsom bath with me?"

I throw him a wet washcloth to clean himself up. "No, babe. I really have to go."

"At least pop in a CBD suppository before you go."

As I reach for one, his phone rings.

"Hey, Ma!"

I quickly clean up, change, and then jog over to kiss him goodbye.

"Ma, one sec," he says.

"What time do you think you'll be back?"

"Six, the latest."

"Cool. I'll aim for the same. Love you. Come back home to me," he orders.

"Aye, aye, captain." I salute him. "You drive safely too. Love you."

"I love you, Lily," I call out as I leave the room.

"You heard him?" Sid asks into the phone.

"She loves you too," he calls out as I jog down the steps.

I slide into our Rosso Corsa hybrid LaFerrari Aperta. We rarely take it out for a spin since only two hundred were manufactured globally, but I'm amped today. I quickly order a couple of pizzas and beers to be delivered to the Topanga house before I pull out.

"You're the baddest of 'em all," I say to the car as my hand wraps around the sleek leather steering wheel. The car is super responsive to every micro-shift of the wheel. It's like no other car in our garage.

Luckily, I'm the first person to arrive when I pull up to the house. The pizza and beer arrive shortly after. I open the windows and stream music through my speakers. Filling an ice bucket with ice and beer, I set out plates and napkins, then check that the bathroom is stocked with soap and toilet paper.

Tevin arrives first, followed by Idris, and then Malik. Kaleb arrives last. He hugs me tightly and thanks me for getting him out of the "shit fest" at home. When I asked him what that meant, he murmured something about his kid having the shits.

We're sitting around the patio table when I pipe up. "Thanks for coming. I know it was short notice. I, 'er, want to share something important with you."

I have their undivided attention.

"Spit it out. I have only a few minutes of freedom left," Kaleb says.

I nod. "Okay. 'Er, well, you know that I consider you all my boys. Y'all had my back all season, even when my game was trash. There's something I haven't told you that—"

"We know you're gay," Malik blurts out.

Tevin smacks the back of his head. "Dude, you have to let him come out. We talked about this."

"Ow!" Malik says, rubbing his head. "I felt bad for the guy. The four of us know already."

Tevin glowers at him.

"It's true. We didn't know how to tell you," Idris says matter-of-factly.

"Yeah, Kaleb told me that you all suspected as much. Are you all cool with it, for real?"

They respond at the same time, and it's a mix of, "Of course," "Hell yeah," "No doubt," and "Duh, dummy."

"Cool, because I've been dating someone pretty seriously since last season."

"The hickeys gave that away. Ready to tell us who the lucky guy is?" Kaleb asks.

"Is it your agent Patrick?" Malik asks.

I frown. "Phil? No. Why?"

Tev's forehead crinkles. "The dude's hella thirsty whenever you're around. Either he likes you, or you're his favorite client."

How am I the last to know these things? Sid is right. I have no radar for flirts.

I huff out a breath. "Nah. Not him."

I rub my sweaty neck as I take in the four pairs of eager eyes.

Here goes nothing.

"It's, uh, well, you know him, actually." I wince, bracing for their reaction. "It's...um..." I clear my throat. "It's Sid."

I've never seen four jaws drop at once—until today.

"Sid who?" Kaleb asks.

"Sidney King," I reply.

Idris cackles. "Shut the fuck up." He turns to the guys. "He's fucking with us." They haven't pulled up their jaws yet, so they don't respond. He turns back to me. "You're fucking with us, right?"

"Does that explain why that Ferrari is in your driveway?" Tevin asks.

I cross and then uncross my arms. "Yes. We own a house together too. I haven't lived here in a while. We just keep it for appearances."

"No way. We're being recorded. Where are the cameras?" Malik asks, looking around.

I decide to fast-forward things, unlock my phone, and pull up a picture of Sid and me kissing. I figured it might come to this. I show them the picture, and then another one, and their eyes go wide as reality sets in.

"Sid is gay? What about the women he's dated?" Idris asks.

"I'm gay. He's bi and demi. Have you seen him date anyone publicly recently?"

They seem to think it over.

"Exactly," I say.

"He's the one that's given you all the hickeys?" Kaleb asks.

I nod. "We've been official since All-Star Weekend last season. I'm sorry for keeping it from you. I was terrified that it would hurt us, my career, and our team."

The room falls silent, tightening the knots in my stomach. I'm glad I haven't eaten yet. Well, except for Sid's breakfast of champions.

Kaleb speaks first. "You deserve to be happy. It's just— damn you and Sid King." He shakes his head. "I need a sec to wrap my head around it. It doesn't change anything, though. We got your back." He looks around at the guys. "Right?"

They respond at the same time, and it's again a mix of, "Hell yeah," "No doubt," and "Duh, dummy."

My shoulders drop as I exhale a rush of air.

Malik scrubs his hand over his face. "Dude—I mean, I get it. I'd go gay to be with Sid. I didn't even know I had a shot. Damn!"

Tevin smacks his head again. "Not the time, bro!"

"I'm just saying, he's undeniably hot. You don't have to be gay to know that's a sexy muthafucka. Plus, he's like a gazillionaire," Malik says, shaking his head.

Kaleb and I burst out laughing.

"We're planning to come out soon. It's only a matter of time before it gets out."

Malik nods.

"It won't come from us. Thanks for trusting us with this," Kaleb says, standing and patting my shoulder.

"Yeah, it took mad heart for you to tell us," Idris says. "Anyone gives you shit, holla at me."

"Me too," says Tevin.

"Since last season?" Kaleb asks, shaking his head.

"How'd y'all keep it under wraps that long?" Tevin adds.

"Ain't easy. We're both focused on ball. Plus, you know how crazy our schedules are. Only our close family members know...Yeah, but it kind of came to a head recently. Had to take some space to figure things out. We want to get married and have kids. We can't do that in the closet. I had to work on myself and shit."

"You shouldn't even have to be in the closet. That's whack, man," Idris says.

"Y'all go hella hard competing whenever our teams face off. How the hell does that work?" Kaleb asks.

I shrug. "We like competing and want to be the best. We don't really talk about our face-offs at home. I love demolishing him on the court," I admit, grinning.

"Kinky," Idris says, making us all laugh. "Real talk. I've never seen you show the Marvels or Royals any mercy." He shakes his head. "Wild!"

"Never. I'd never do anything to hurt our team. I fought too hard to get here, and I don't only ball for me. My parents sacrificed a fuck ton for me to be here. I can't fuck it up."

"We know, man," Kaleb says, meeting my gaze.

Hearing him say it is a relief. I think I've proven my dedication and loyalty to our team. I'd be crushed if they doubted it.

"We don't get initiation rings or cloaks for joining the inner sanctum?" Malik jokes.

I point to the pizza and beer. "What do you think that's for?"

Idris laughs. "Cheap bastard."

"Marriage and kids. Youngin', have I taught you nothin'? Did you not hear that I escaped a shit fest? You can't marry your first boyfriend," Kaleb says.

"Uh, you can when it's Sidney Fucking King," Malik says. "If he won't, I will."

I laugh as Tevin raises his hand to smack him again, and then quits mid-air, shaking his head.

"Going forward, y'all are welcome to stop by and hang with us anytime. Just hit me up."

"Maybe watch your man around this one," Tevin says, nodding to Malik. "While we're sharing shit, confessing, and whatnot, I kinda have something I need to get off of my chest."

I nod. "The floor is yours."

"I've been dealing with anxiety and depression for years. I've kept it on the low, but hearing Arnaz talk about depression and suicide made me wonder how many more of us struggle. You know?" he says, scratching his arm.

Idris, Kaleb, and Malik nod, but they're speechless.

"Thanks for sharing that with us. I suffer from depression too. Ever since my parents...It gets really bad sometimes. Sid and Adam encouraged me to try therapy. It helps," I say.

Tevin meets my gaze. "Word? I didn't know. I see a therapist too. I'm on Lexapro."

"My mom suffers from clinical depression. She has for as long as I can remember," Malik says.

"Yeah? What was that like growing up?" I ask.

"Rough," he says, shifting in his chair. "She withdrew a lot... always exhausted...sad. She was diagnosed with clinical depression after I joined the league, but it was there all of my life."

I shake my head. "I can't imagine what that was like. It must have been really difficult."

"Thanks, man. Yeah, to this day, we don't really talk about it. She's a closed book."

"My parents are closed books too. It's something about that generation. They've learned to suffer in silence," Kaleb says.

"Real talk," Idris chimes in.

"I know we don't always know how to talk to each other about this stuff. It's taken me years to finally go to therapy. I'm here, though, if you ever need to get shit off your chest," I offer.

"Me too," Kaleb says.

"Me too. What's therapy like?" Idris asks.

I look to Tevin to answer, but he nods for me to respond.

"Well, I guess it's different for everyone. I'm relatively new at it. Despite my best intentions, it can be painful to face hard truths and shit. It feels alright, though, in the end. For what it's worth, the way therapy is depicted on TV is trash. Y'know the cold therapist who just nods at whatever the person is saying for an hour? That's garbage."

"Word? Glad you said that. It looks hella whack on TV," Idris replies.

"You don't have to be depressed to seek therapy. We all have shit to work through. Know what I mean? It doesn't hurt to have a confidential and qualified ear. It's like a slow-release vitamin. Over time, you realize it's working because that thing that used to fuck you up doesn't anymore. And when new things fuck you up, there's someone to help you avoid falling off the deep end. It won't solve all your problems, but it helps," Tevin adds.

"That's real," I say, reaching for a slice of pizza now that my stomach is finally chill. My phone vibrates. I take a quick bite before digging it out of my pocket.

MY LOVE

You good?

ME

Yep. Pretty sure Malik has a thing for you. Your side?

MY LOVE

He has good taste. Just left Arnaz's. You were right. I'll fill you in when you get home.

ME

Can't wait. Should be done here soon.
Love you.

MY LOVE

Love you too

The guys and I talk for another hour before we all head out. I'm grinning from cheek to cheek when I pull out of the driveway to make my way home. Coming out to them went way better than I imagined.

Chapter Thirty
Months Later

How is it that we run out of ice or beer every time we host? I squeeze into one of the last remaining parking spots and climb out of the car. I've been gone less than thirty minutes, yet the cars in our garage have doubled from when I left.

"Need a hand?"

Arnaz.

"Hey." I turn to face him. "Yeah, thanks."

He rolls up his car window and climbs out. He takes a second to pat down his white tee and salmon-colored swim trunks. Besides on the court, I haven't come face to face with him since Ussef's birthday party. Sid's had his teammates over a few times, but it's always when I'm on the road. When Sid came out to him about us, he said Arnaz's disappointment was palpable. He felt foolish for not seeing Arnaz's crush before. They've been good, though, overall. Both their friendship and dynamic style of playing are still strong.

"Ice. Can never have enough, right?" Arnaz says, pulling me into a dap.

"Seriously. Sick Bugatti. Divo?"

"Yep. Thanks, man. You're welcome to take it for a spin. Sid mentioned that he's eyeing the Centodieci. It's supposed to go from a full stop to sixty in under two and a half seconds."

"Yeah. 1,600 horsepower and only ten made. Hard for him to resist." I continue stacking the ice. "How are you?"

"Alright. Ready to chow down on your uncle's famous cooking. Sid wouldn't shut up about it all week."

"It really is that good."

"Elite season, bro. You're about to clinch the top point guard spot. What was it, like sixty points against Denver last week?"

I grin and hand him a bag of ice. "Thanks, man! Y'all up there too."

The Royals are in first place. We climbed our way to the third spot in the Western Conference. Everyone on our roster is locked in night after night. And it shows in the way we made a comeback this season. I've never wanted it more. I had to go deep to redefine what ball means to me. Jaden helped me realize that I get to choose how I honor my parents. Processing my grief and climbing out of the darkness is the greatest honor I could bestow upon them. I remembered something my mom used to say. She said that whenever you're sinking in life's muck, you reach out for help and keep going. I was too young to understand it then, but I do now.

One day, I stepped on the court and felt like the kid at my first game again, staring at the sea of fans, buzzing with awe. I love this game. I have the opportunity to leave an indelible mark in the history of one of the greatest sports in the world. I plan to see how far I can take it.

"Hey," Arnaz says, shifting his feet, "my bad if I in any way made things uncomfortable for you both. I saw the posts."

He catches me off guard, and I freeze for a few seconds. It's big of him to step up to clear the air.

"Thanks." I rub my neck. "It was frustrating, but I know it wasn't on you or him. We're good."

I hand him another bag of ice.

"You two are lucky to have each other. It's not easy finding someone to trust."

I pause and look him square in the eyes. "He's everything to me—my best friend and my family. There's nothing I wouldn't do to protect him and what we have."

He nods. "I got that loud and clear from him too. He's obsessed with you," he says, smiling, though there's something else there in the shadows. Sadness.

"Is that so?" I continue stacking the ice. "From what I've heard, you're getting hit up by mad dudes. Some closeted, some out." I recall what Sid told me about Arnaz's status as one of the most sought-after bachelors.

He grins. "Wellll, I never said I had a hard time getting laid. Just haven't found the real thing."

"Fucking stud." I playfully punch his arm.

Once we divide up the ice, we make our way to the backyard.

"Hey, when I came out to my boys, it opened up the gates for us to get stuff off our chest. It got me thinking about maybe starting a meetup for players. Real chill, just beers and an open floor to talk. Any interest?"

"Sounds dope. Since I published my article, a couple guys reached out to share their struggles. I'll spread the invite if that's cool."

"Definitely. The more the merrier."

The barbecue is in full swing once we get inside. Bob Marley is booming from the speakers. Adam's manning the grill and smoker. Ishan is shirtless in the pool, lying back in a rainbow-colored chaise float, talking to Tommy, who is treading water beside Phil. Kaleb's three kids, his wife, and Nicholas's girlfriend are chilling in the shallow end. Sid, who looks edible, clad in only trunks with cobalt blue and tangerine freeform shapes, is at the center of a conversation with Malik, Tevin,

Idris, and Kaleb. Ussef and Nicholas, whom Sid also came out to, are throwing a frisbee back and forth.

I lead Arnaz to an ice barrel cooler where we offload the ice.

"Thanks, man. Help yourself to a drink. I'll go see if the food is ready."

The caterers dropped off trays of rice and peas—both a regular and gluten-free version—and vegan baked macaroni and cheese, baby kale and endive salad, baked salmon, and vegan sliders earlier today. Sid and I made sure to cover everyone's dietary restrictions.

Kieran and Lily are putting the finishing touches on the picnic table. A natural, woven runner sits under cream pillar candles and bouquets of fresh cream flowers with green stems. The gold and cream place settings round out the celebratory theme. I pat my pants pocket to confirm the ring is still there. Adam, Ishan, and Sid's family know about my plan to propose to Sid today. Kieran and Lily volunteered to take care of the decorations. They knocked it out of the park. Everything looks perfect!

"Hey, Unc. Need a hand?"

"Hey, kiddo! I'm just about done here. Can you take those three trays to the serving table? Finishing up the dogs now. Five more minutes."

"Cool." I peel back a tray's lid to get a whiff of the jerk chicken. Another tray has BBQ chicken and a third has burgers.

"Dayum! Smells insane!" I can't resist peeling off a piece of the juicy and perfectly grilled meat and popping it in my mouth.

"It's the smoker! Man, I have to cop one of these. Sid did his research."

"He researched and compared a dozen options, spent hours watching reviews. You know how he goes in."

I make a mental note to gift order the smoker to him and Ishan.

"Hey, everyone, all the food will be ready in five minutes. Now's a good time to wash your hands, start making yourself a plate, and grab a seat at the table. Grab the chicken while it's hot if you know what's good," I announce.

"Thanks, babe!" Sid calls back.

After moving the trays to the server table, I take my advice and run inside to the restroom. Staring at myself in the mirror, I wash my hands and take a deep breath. I dry my hands and pull a piece of paper from my pocket even though I know what's written on it by heart, having written and recited it a gazillion times over the last month. It's too long, I think, starting to freak out.

There's a knock on the door. I quickly stuff the paper back in my pocket.

"It's me, honey," Kieran says.

I rub my sweaty palms on my shirt and turn the lock.

He slides inside. "You ready?" He tiptoes to embrace my shoulders.

"No, yes, ugh no," I stammer.

"Y'all are already married in my cousin's eyes. This is just a formality."

"I know, but, like, what if he prefers a private proposal?"

He tilts his head to the side. "Sid? Private? Not a chance. This is perfect."

"I know, I know, but what if he hates the ring?"

I reach into my pocket and pull out the most stunning 24-carat emerald-cut eternity ring I've ever seen. Norah, my jeweler, really outdid herself. It was a challenging ring to make. The difficulty came down to trying to match emerald-cut diamonds for eternity bands. Specifically, aligning the carat weight, clarity, and color. Given the layout, she looked at close to eighty diamonds to find the seventeen that would fit Sid's ring size. The project took weeks. I've never spent so much on a piece of jewelry. Good thing I only plan to get married one time.

"It's magnificent, Ty! You know he'll love it. Your descendants 400 years from now will love it."

I grin at that.

"Now, take a deep breath."

I close my eyes and inhale for five seconds, hold for seven, then release for nine.

"Good. Now erect your spine, shoulders back, head high," he says.

Spine straightened, shoulders down, and chin up.

"Hey," he says.

I nod.

"You're about to get engaged!"

I grin and pluck him up into a bear hug. "I love you, man!" I kiss his cheek.

"Why am I always surrounded by giants who lift me like a doll?"

"It's 'cause you're so lovable. We can't resist your hugs," I reply as I put him down.

I pocket the ring, take another deep breath, and signal Kieran to lead the way.

He pats my chest. "I love you too. Now, go get 'em."

EVERYONE IS ALREADY SEATED AT THE TABLE WHEN WE EMERGE from inside.

Sid's left the head of the table open for me and is seated to the right of me. Lily is seated at the head on the other end.

As I approach the table, Sid stands. We agreed to say a few words before the feast.

I thumb the ring in my pocket. *This is it.*

I wrap my arm around his waist as he slings his arm over my shoulders.

Our simple embrace garners everyone's attention.

"Ty and I want to thank you all for joining us today. It's been a hell of a year, as y'all know from the headlines. It's also been a tremendous year of growth for our relationship."

You can say that again.

On top of our individual sessions, we started seeing Leah, a couple's therapist, for extra support. Her fiery, no-nonsense, homophobes-can-fuck-off attitude is helping us prepare for coming out publicly.

"We're thankful to have your support, trust, and friendship. Cheers to all of you!" Sid says, raising his glass.

A cacophony of cheers, applause, and Kaleb's "woot" fills the air.

"Before I turn it over to Ty, I just want to say a few words," he continues, glancing at me before turning back to the group.

"The first time I saw Ty, I was at home packing for a game. The TV was on in the background. His team was playing against Pittsburgh, I think. I happened to look at the screen just as he tore through their defense to post a lethal leftie underhand layup. His finesse was staggering to watch. When the camera zoomed in on his face, I didn't see the gloating or smugness I'd expected. Instead, I saw a fire in his eyes. Well, fire and a heart-wrenching amount of sadness. To say that I was captivated is an understatement. Every cell in my body lit up watching him. He was familiar, but I knew for sure that we'd never met. I later spent countless hours searching the internet to find as much information as possible about him."

"You never told me this," I whisper.

"I know," he says, brushing my lips with a kiss.

"I decided to fly in to see him play during my next free afternoon. I hid by a side entrance to avoid being seen by fans and the press. After helping to clutch the W, he was hoisted in the air. That's when our eyes locked. Do you remember?"

I nod. "My college game. There wasn't anyone in the crowd for me that day, but you were there."

He smiles. "Time stood still when we looked at each other. It was chilling." He turns back to our guests. "When I boarded my plane, I couldn't shake the feeling that he was someone important. Then a few months later, I received a call that ESPN wanted us to do a one-on-one interview to commemorate his breaking my record, and I remember thinking, of all the people to break it—of course it had to be him. I wasn't even salty about it."

Sid shoves me playfully when I mouth, *Yes, he was*, causing laughter around the table. I'm joking, of course. If he was salty, he never showed it.

"Then it was time for the interview. For a reason I didn't understand then, I was nervous on my way into the ESPN office. But the minute I approached him, it was like finding a long-lost best friend. We sat down together in front of a room full of people, not to mention a camera pointed at us, and we had one of the best conversations of my life. Again, it felt like that day in the gym—no one else in the world existed but us."

He turns away from our guests and stares into my eyes. "Here's the thing—I started falling for you the first time I saw you, and I've been utterly in love with you ever since. Even though that day on TV was the first time my eyes laid upon you, my soul recognized you. Its grace and wisdom led me straight to you."

I turn away from our guests to bury my face in his chest as my vision turns blurry. He kisses the top of my head and whispers, "No hiding, remember."

I freeze when he pulls away from me and reaches into the pocket of his swim trunks.

Oh my god!

My legs tremble as he kneels and presents a magnificent platinum ring with a brilliant oval diamond.

A wave of murmurs and gasps vibrates around the table.

"Tyler, I want to spend the rest of my life with you." He clears the emotion out of his throat. "You, whose beautiful soul is cast from love. I will strive every day to ensure that our family knows true joy, protection, and peace. Ours is an everlasting love forged through life's fires. Whatever storms may come to pass, we'll bear them together and come out stronger. Our family will find refuge in our union. Because of you, I know that love is the greatest of mysteries, and true humility is accepting its breathtaking and unfailing path. I am already yours, but would you do me the honor of marrying me?"

I cover my mouth with my hand. The world reduces to a blur as all of the love in my heart for him pours out of me.

No, no, no.

I should be the one down on a knee asking for his hand. It's him who would do me the honor of being his husband. His unfaltering love has held me together on days when I could barely muster the strength to get out of bed or feed myself. He's loved me despite my fears and insecurities. He's given me more joyful memories than I have any right to in a lifetime.

The light in his eyes dims. *What's wrong?*

Our guests are suddenly so quiet that I'm about to look up to see if they're still there when Sid asks, "No?" while blinking rapidly.

Oh, Christ! Did I say "no" out loud?

My hand drops from my mouth and reaches into my pocket for the ring.

"No, because it's I who would be honored if you'd marry me."

I hold up the ring and take a knee.

A loud wave of murmurs and gasps echoes around the table.

"Oh, thank God," Sid mutters as his shoulders fall forward.

"Sidney David King, I know in my bones that—"

"Yes!" he exclaims.

"Yes?"

"Yes, of course, I'll marry you!"

"Duh," Kieran yells, and we burst out laughing as Sid hobbles the short distance and pulls me in for a kiss.

Our friends and family erupt with cheers, laughter, and applause.

Our kiss is wet and messy. "I love you so much," I say, our foreheads touching. I wipe his tear-stained face.

"I love you more," he says, wiping mine. He even wipes my snot like it's not super gross.

I take his hand and slide the ring onto his finger. The sparkle from the diamonds against his gorgeous skin makes my heart ache.

His eyes go wide as he takes it in.

"You like it?"

"Like? It's stunning. Like nothing I've seen before. I love it."

He laughs when I look over at Kieran and wink.

"Give me your hand," he says.

He slides the mesmerizing engagement ring onto my finger.

"Sid, it's gorgeous...too gorgeous." I make him laugh when I exaggerate the weight of it and pretend to need my other hand to hold it up.

"I thought of you the second I saw it," he says.

I shake my head. I'd kill to see myself the way he sees me.

He kisses my hand, then turns to our guests and exclaims, "We're engaged!"

There's an explosion of shouts of congratulations. We're enveloped in hugs as soon as we're on our feet.

When I reach Kieran, I catch him full-blown crying and blowing his nose.

With a side-eye, I ask, "You knew he was planning to propose?"

"I plead the fifth," he says, beaming through sniffles. "Tommy has it all on camera. Just for you two to show your kids one day. It was beautiful," he says, patting my chest.

I pull him into a hug. "You and Tommy are amazing."

"Let me see your ring. I helped him pick it out. Guess how many carats?"

I stare at it. "Twenty? It's unbelievable."

"Thirty-one!"

"Holy fuck! Wait, when did he pick it out?"

"When you were separated."

My jaw drops.

Jaden and I've been working on building my self-compassion, and while I've made some progress, I still cringe when I think about my refusal to get help. Even though it led me back to therapy, it's still rough to think about the weeks that we were separated.

I clear my throat. "K, why would he get me a ring when we were on the rocks?"

Kieran waves it off. "It was always you for him."

I wipe my eyes as I try to wrap my head around that.

"Both of your rings will become priceless heirlooms. Sid said he only plans to get married once."

I grin. "That's funny. I told Norah the same thing." I brace his shoulder. "What would we do without you and Tommy?"

He stares off, and it's like he and Tommy have a private line into each other. As soon as Kieran looks at him, Tommy meets his gaze and smiles.

Kieran turns back to me, a soft blush dusting his face. "We have your wedding to plan."

"Can't we just do a small ceremony on V or here?"

"Ooh, an intimate yacht wedding." He thinks it over. "The idea has potential. Or we can rent a private island. Or a chateau." By the sound of his faraway voice, I'm sure Party Planner Kieran has taken over, and I've lost him. Sid and I will have to recruit Lily and her frugal nature to temper Kieran's imagination, which rivals Walt Disney's.

"I'm happy you'll be my cousin," I tell him.

"Pfft. You've been my cousin. Even if the world turned upside down and you two broke up, you were ours since the first Christmas Sid brought you home."

And there I go, choking up again. "Means a lot."

"Kiddo!"

I turn and fall into Adam and Ishan's embrace.

"Congratulations!" they bid together.

"Thank you. I can't wait for your big day!"

Adam proposed to Ishan a few months ago, and their big day is less than six months away.

"We went for a fitting with the tailor you recommended, and the funniest thing happened," Adam says.

"Oh yeah, what's that?"

"He refused our money. Said he received a sizable advance payment."

I stick my hands in my pockets. "Strange."

"The same thing happened with the venue we selected. Oh, and then last week, a wedding planner called. Said she was hired to make our wedding dreams come true. She asked for our availability to stop by and make—what was it—a mood pad or something?"

"A wedding mood board," Ishan confirms.

I stare at my feet. "Geez. That's insane."

"Uh-huh, you wouldn't know anything about this, would you?"

"Of course not! How's the heart?" I ask.

"My heart's fine. You know that, seeing as you were on speakerphone during my last check-up. So, back to the string of peculiar events. You really don't know anything about the tailor, the venue, and the wedding planner?"

I shake my head. "Scout's honor."

"You were never a scout," Adam retorts.

"Hmph. True. Of course if my parent, who is also my favorite uncle and only living relative, gets married to his dreamboat boyfriend"—I wink at Ishan—"I would listen when he tells me that he's using his retirement savings to pay for the wedding. Especially—"

"Hey, wait one second—" Adam starts.

"Especially, when he refuses to use the savings account I set up for him, or let me buy him a bigger house."

Adam sighs.

"Look at that—I think I finally met someone more stubborn than you," Ishan says, grinning.

"Ha!" Adam exclaims. "When it comes to this kid's stubbornness, we're all outclassed." He steps forward and places a kiss on my forehead. "Thank you. No more, kid. Okay?" He rubs the back of my neck. "Parents shouldn't take from their kids. Rose and Morris would agree."

"Yes, you've made that clear. And I've made it clear that you aren't taking if I'm giving to you of my own free will."

"Semantics." He waves it off. "No more."

I nod. "Welllll, there's just one more—don't be mad—we might have bought you both a new truck as a wedding gift. Ishan's is on its last leg, and you need to get to your appointments when—"

"Kid!"

I wince. "Okay. Okay, I'll stop. But, like, if a travel planner calls to book your Safari honeymoon, maybe don't hang up."

Ishan laughs as Adam throws his hands up in disbelief.

"Pardon my interruption. Just want to wish Ty here congratulations!" Phil says, extending a handshake.

I clasp his hand.

"Start thinking about the wedding of your dreams. Toni's mood boarding sessions are known to be epic," I say to Adam and Ishan.

"Thanks! I appreciate you being here today," I say, turning to Phil and releasing his hand.

"I appreciate the invite. You and Sid make a very handsome couple."

I find Sid in the crowd. He's showing his ring to Kaleb's wife and Nicholas.

"Thanks. Will you hang around? I want to hear about Bob Dylan."

Phil grins. "Ol' girl's still kicking. I'll be here. I'm famished," he says, patting his stomach. "And I have a few more science questions for your brainiac friend, Tommy."

"Amazing! He finally has someone else to geek out with."

"Go," he says, "make your rounds. We'll catch up later."

I clasp his shoulder and then make my way over to Lily.

"Oh, congratulations, my love!" she says.

"Thank you!" I bend down to kiss her cheek. "Did you know he was proposing too?"

She doesn't answer, but her smile tells me she did.

"I know I never met them, but every loving parent wants their kids to be happy and loved, to have someone to go through life with. I think your parents would be so happy for you today. Adam has told me beautiful stories about how close the three of you were. I hope you know by now that I will continue loving you like an overbearing mama, and there's not much you can do to stop me. I love you very much, dear."

She opens her arms for a hug.

"I love you too," I reply as we separate. "Thank you for loving me."

She clasps my cheek. "We were meant to be in each other's lives. I just know it."

I nod. I feel it too.

I've thought a lot about my parents this week. They'd have loved Sid. My dad would have cried more happy tears than me. By Monday, Mom would have gone into serious wedding planning mode with lists and spreadsheets. She would have worked hard to make our day special.

"Where's Malcolm?" I ask, looking around for Lily's boyfriend. She surprised us when she announced that she had invited her new "guy friend" to dinner last month. Sid interrogated the man all night, but he withstood the heat and ended up sealing Sid's approval.

"Just sent him out to get more beer. We're running low."

I nod. "Thanks! I think we stashed a case or two in the house. I'll grab them."

After I throw the beers on the ice, I make my way over to the guys.

"Bruh! Congrats! Sick double engagement," Idris says.

"Let's see da drip!" Malik says.

I show them the ring.

"It's beautiful, man! Looks expensive as fuck. Don't let my wife see it." Kaleb sighs. "She'll want to renew our vows just to get an upgrade."

"Too late. I just saw her eyeing Sid's," I warn him.

Idris pats Kaleb's back. "Sorry, bro. You're fucked."

Tevin slings his arm around my neck. "'Ours is an everlasting love forged through life's fires.' That was fucking beautiful man. I'm cold-blooded, but that made me tear up."

Cold-blooded, right. Dude's one of the warmest guys I know. I pat his chest. "Thanks, big bro."

"Which one of us is your best man?" Kaleb asks.

I take a page from Kieran's book. "I plead the fifth."

I love these guys, but it will be Adam for me and Kieran for Sid.

"Any chance Sid has a very similar, if not identical, brother hidden somewhere?" Malik asks.

Tevin scoffs. "Dude! Are you even bi?"

Malik scoffs back. "Like you wouldn't go bi for Sid!"

We burst out laughing.

"Nah, sorry. He's an only child," I reply.

"You have a beautiful family," Kaleb observes.

I follow his gaze to Tommy laughing with Kieran, Ishan sitting on Adam's lap, feeding him a bite from his plate, and Sid and Lily embracing each other as they return to the table.

I beam with pride. "Yeah, I do."

"Hey," Sid announces. "Our engagement interrupted our feast. How about we all return to our seats and eat Adam's delicious food?"

Kieran passes around glasses of champagne as we settle back into our seats.

I can't resist bending down and kissing Sid's gorgeous lips, which are parted in the most radiant smile. As I take my seat next to him, he immediately reaches for my hand. I trace his ringed finger with my thumb and grin hard.

Brittany Howard's voice croons through the speakers.

Arnaz leans over to fist-bump Adam. "Best frickin' jerk I've ever tasted," he says.

"You should open a spot in New York," Idris agrees, licking his fingers.

Adam laughs. "Thank you! You all should visit the east coast and check out the amazing Caribbean restaurants."

"Okay! Just give me a bite," Camilia, Nicholas's girlfriend, says as she reaches for his chicken.

He moves his plate out of reach. "Not a fat chance. You made me promise to get you over the line."

"Nicholas Steel, give me a bite right now or no s-e-x for a month," she declares, spelling out the word because Kaleb's kids are at the table.

"You told me that if I caved, I wouldn't get s-e-x for a month. I can't win."

"Someone want to fill the rest of us in?" Idris asks, wide-eyed.

"Cam is doing one of those vegan thirty-day challenges, and she's five days away from completing it," Nicholas says.

"Whatever! Twenty-five days is sufficient. Thigh, now!" She demands.

Nicholas looks to us for help. Sid swipes his hand across his neck and mouths, *Don't do it.* At the same time, Kaleb says, "Give the lady what she wants."

"Screw this," Nicholas says, and we burst out laughing when he attempts to shove an entire breast and thigh in his mouth.

I retrieve the tray of jerk chicken from the serving table and walk it over to Cam. "Nick can't be punished if I cave. Here you go, milady."

She plucks up a breast and rips off a huge bite. Her eyes roll closed as she moans. "Praise be to you!" She points the half-bitten breast to Adam before ripping off another bite.

Even Kaleb's kids are cracking up.

"I'll just leave the tray here," I say.

I pat Nicholas on the back as he pulls the chicken out of his mouth.

While Cam mutters about marrying meat, Nicholas grabs my elbow and mouths, *I owe you.*

I wave it off. No sex for a month is cold. I've been there.

"I still get credit for vegan 30, don't I?" she asks Nicholas.

He throws his arm around her shoulder and kisses the side of her head. "Sure, honey. Twenty-five is the new thirty."

After we feast, Malcolm, Arnaz, Adam, and Lily break off to start a game of spades. My money is on Lily and Malcolm. Tommy, Kieran, Phil, and Ishan laze in the pool.

"How about a pickup game? Four on four. You, Tev, Kaleb, Nicholas against me, Ty, Ussef, Malik," Idris challenges Sid.

"Best of 20," Sid replies, grabbing his T-shirt from a chair.

"Come on, Cam. How about we take the kiddies to the pool and sip margaritas?" Gaby, Kaleb's wife, says as she shuffles the kids toward the pool area.

"You're not gonna watch?" Kaleb calls out.

"Love you, sweetheart, but I need a margarita," she says, blowing him a kiss as she retreats.

"Savage," Kaleb says, shaking his head and making us all laugh.

Sid and I hand our rings to Kieran before we make our way to the court. We all stretch quickly to warm up.

Sid's team wins the coin toss, so they have first possession.

Tevin passes the ball to Nicholas, who lobs it to Sid. He runs it in to attempt a layup, only I smack the ball away before it hits the rim.

"I'm the new mayor of Block City," I boast.

Sid laughs. "You're not even going to ease up on me on the day I proposed to you?"

I stick my tongue out at him. "Never."

He flashes me a mischievous grin, leans in, and says, "I got something for that tongue."

And damn if my dick doesn't perk up.

"Hey, you two! No foreplay on the court," Idris says, grinning at us.

Sid moves in to defend me, but Idris creates a screen. I get the ball to Malik, who hits a corner three-pointer.

On the next possession, Sid passes the ball to Kaleb, who lobs it back to Sid, who then passes it to Tevin, who posts a layup.

"Good ball movement," Sid calls out.

"Remember, they're Royals!" I tease as I take possession of the ball.

I pass the ball to Idris, then create a successful screen against Tevin, who is guarding him. I spin and drive to the basket as Idris lobs me the ball mid-air to complete a layup.

Pick and Roll, an oldie but goodie.

"That's 5–2," I call out.

"You mean 5–5," Sid says, raising the ball and hitting a long three-pointer that's all cash.

Damn. For a second, I forgot Sid's game is equal parts talent and big-dick energy.

We go toe to toe until we're tied at game point. If we make a three-pointer, we win. Sid's team only needs two points to win. Unfortunately for us, Sid's team has possession. Kaleb passes the ball to Sid, whom I move in to defend.

Sid leans forward, dribbling the ball between his feet. "Think you can hold me?"

"Think you can get in my head, dickhead?"

"Such a filthy mouth." He raises his hand to cross the ball between his legs, except I intercept and smack it away.

We both dive for it. I pin him down and crawl up his back to take possession. I immediately wing it to Ussef, who posts a layup, moving us one point away from a win.

"You move like a turtle," I taunt as he tries to buck me off him.

I signal Idris and Malik to double-team Sid, but he's too quick. As soon as he takes possession, he cuts through them with a spin, crossover, dribble combo, then leaps into the air and slams the ball down with a one-handed dunk, winning the game.

He roars as Nicholas chest bumps him, and Kaleb smacks his butt.

"Fu-uck!" I groan, palming my temple.

Kaleb laughs. "You, like, really, really hate when your fiancé beats you."

Something in my chest leaps at the word fiancé, and I break out in a wide grin.

"Congrats or whatever," I grumble to the winners.

Sid chuckles. "So salty." He pulls my back against his chest and then kisses my sweaty neck.

I angle my head up to give him a congratulatory kiss.

We wrap our arms around each other as we walk back to the pool area with the gang.

A couple hours later, everyone clears out, leaving only family, all of whom are spending the weekend with us.

Sid and I spent the last two hours making individual rounds with our guests. He and Kaleb faced off in a water balloon fight, and Sid teamed up with Kaleb's middle child, Benji, against Kaleb and his eldest son, Theo. Sid protected Benji from a barrage of balloon fire, then picked him up and used their combined arm strength to launch a counterattack. Benji's sweet giggles mixed with Sid's boisterous and animated voice made my heart ache. I look forward to the day we're parents.

"Master Blaster" by Stevie Wonder comes on. Lily loves this song.

"May I have this dance?" I ask her, extending a hand.

"You sure you can keep up?" she teases, taking my hand and following me to our makeshift dance floor.

She sways her hips while clapping her hands together above her head. I match her pace, swaying side to side with a two-step.

Kieran joins us, spinning and throwing his hands in the air. Unlike me, he was born to dance.

Sid turns the music up and cheers us on, standing to the side while downing a glass of water. Ishan joins in, taking Kieran's hand and spinning him around. Tommy, Malcolm, and Adam watch fondly from where they're seated at the spades table. As expected, Lily and Malcolm won every round.

Ed Sheeran's "Thinking Out Loud" comes on next.

Malcolm approaches Lily for a dance.

Sid's chest hits my back.

I turn and wrap my arms around his neck. He holds my

waist as we sway. I tilt my chin up for what becomes a spine-tingling kiss.

"Wow," I whisper when we come up for air. The string lights and candles from the picnic tables cast a golden glow over his face.

"Wow yourself," he says, smiling.

"Today was perfect. I think it was the happiest day of my life."

His breath hitches. "I only want happy days for you."

He brushes another kiss against my lips. "It was the happiest day of my life too." He grins. "Right up there with the first time we made love."

"All-Star Weekend?"

"Yeah, I was already done for by then. That night was perfect."

"First time I ever cried during sex."

He nods. "You asked me what I was doing to you?"

"And you said I could ask you the same thing." *We were both done for back then.* "I can't believe you never told me about seeing me on TV for the first time."

"I didn't intentionally conceal it. It just never came up," he says.

"God, I love you. The odds of you getting a lot of sleep tonight are slim."

"Let the record reflect that I'm not the one who almost dozed off with my dick in their mouth during our last movie and 69 night," he whispers against my ear.

I burst out laughing. "It was a long day, and we both came already in the sauna."

But now that he's brought it up...

"Mmm. I want you. Let's clean up quickly?"

He grins.

We roll the large garbage bins over to the tables to start the clean-up process.

The eight of us are done cleaning in no time.

We say goodnight to everyone and jet upstairs.

"Top or bottom?" I ask. "Or switch?"

"Top. You?"

I nod. "Perfect."

"You're not too full?"

"Nah. I purposely left space for this."

The corners of his lips hitch up. "Start in the shower?"

I answer by stripping down.

The hot water washes over us, steaming up the bathroom. He immediately gets to work licking and sucking my neck. His erection rubs against my rim as I pump body wash into my hands and reach behind me to gently stroke him with it.

He moans against my ear, sending a shiver down my spine. Grabbing body wash, he rubs circles over my chest and under my arms. He eventually makes it to my erection. We both reach the edge, stroking each other.

"Don't want to come yet," I pant.

He grunts but releases me.

We laugh as we get tangled trying to kiss and fondle each other while drying off. His teeth latch onto my neck as I lead us to the bedroom. Without warning, he lifts and hurls me on the bed, and fuck if his strength doesn't make me leak more.

He pumps lube into his hand as his hungry gaze feasts on my body.

"We've never fucked as fiancés," I whisper.

"I've never fucked you."

"Fine. We've never made love as fiancés."

"Mmm." He takes hold of my shaft.

My eyes roll closed as I melt against his touch.

His warm tongue licks back and forth across my rim.

His fingers stroke me in long pumps.

"Need you," I plead.

He works his fingers inside of me while continuing to rim me.

"So good, fuck." I push down on his fingers and tongue.

"Damn, you taste delicious," he groans, sticking his tongue in deeper.

He finger fucks me, adding a third curved finger.

I moan and push down, trying to fuck his hand.

With a grunt, he stands up, stroking himself.

I swallow, staring at his erection. "Come here."

He crawls up the side of my body.

Swiping up his slit with my tongue, I suck him down.

I moan when he reaches down and penetrates me with his fingers.

I put my finger into my mouth parallel to the angle of his sliding cock and suck it to get it wet. While I'm bobbing on his cock, I reach my finger around and massage his rim.

"Mmm. I won't last if you penetrate me," he warns.

I slide off his dick. "You will. Your cumdump needs you tonight."

He groans as I lap up the bead of pre-cum glistening on his slit. I insert my finger inside of him at the same time and wrap my lips around his length and suck him back down.

"Shit. Aghh," he cries out, his fingering becoming jerky inside of me.

I add a second finger as he fucks my mouth harder and loses control.

I love him like this.

I sputter and gag around his cock as we finger fuck each other.

"I'm really close," he grunts.

I bob on his dick, then pop off, leaving a wet trail down my chin. He grabs the back of my neck and tongue fucks my mouth. I swallow his dark moans as I continue finger fucking his hole.

Removing my fingers, I flip to my hands and knees.

"Hard," I tell him over my shoulder.

"Fuck...so sexy," he grunts, stroking himself as he relishes the view.

He grabs the lube and stuffs a fingerful inside of me.

I moan, knowing what's coming—he adds extra lube when he's planning a punishing fuck.

He lines his head up and rubs it back and forth over my rim.

My dick is throbbing, and I'm trembling with need.

When he finally enters me, we both groan.

He holds for a few seconds and pulls out halfway before slamming back in.

"Oh fuck," I cry.

He clasps the front of my neck, partially restricting oxygen as he fucks me so hard that the bed slides across the floor.

"Stroke," he grunts. His way of telling me that he's close.

My body is under siege by the thrum of ecstasy coursing back and forth from my head to my toes. I can't bring myself to move or speak.

"Baby," he whispers into my ear as he slows down and deep strokes me. "Stroke your sexy dick for me." He sucks my ear lobe.

He changes angles, and my eyes roll to the back of my head.

Realizing he's fucking my brains out so I'm incapable of heeding his command, he reaches around and wraps his hand around my shaft. He rails me so hard my eyes sting with tears.

"Shh," he whispers, turning my face and licking inside of my mouth. He pulls back and bites his lower lip. "Fuck. I love how well you take it."

"Sid," I yell when he slides out and then slams back in so deep that a blinding orgasm expels me from my body.

Sucking on my neck, he stills and, with a chest-ripping grunt, releases inside of me. Tiny quakes and shivers tingle my muscles with each of his shallow thrusts and panted breaths. I float forward as he collapses on top of me.

His heart races against my back.

His cock is still inside of me as he rolls us to our sides so that we're spooning. I whimper when he slips out of me as I doze off.

I wake with a hoarse cry sometime in the night when Sid enters me again.

"Baby," I moan, delirious from sleep and his fullness.

"I got you," he whispers, nestling me closer to his body. He fucks me tenderly. "I can't wait to marry you."

His words, husky voice, the thrum of his heartbeat against mine...

I turn my face to kiss his lips.

My eyes roll closed as he deepens his stroke.

"Yours," I murmur.

"Soon your husband," he whispers.

My eyes fill with tears sprung from that tender place that only we reach.

"Your soulmate," I gasp when he lifts my thigh and thrusts deeper.

"Yes, and you're mine."

"I love you so much."

Wiping my tears, he continues to make love to me.

"I love you more." Thick emotion coats the coal timbre of his voice.

"I'm going to come inside of you again," he whispers into my ear.

I hum with pleasure.

He starts stroking my cock. "Can I stay inside of you?"

I shiver and rut against him.

"Tell me," he says, driving in deeper.

"Baby," I gasp, moaning into the pillow.

"Tell me what you want."

He shifts to peg my prostate on every thrust, and I fall apart, babbling curses and pleas.

I whine when he suddenly pulls out of me. My head spins, and I glare at him.

"Don't look at me like that. It only turns me on more." He squeezes his base before thrusting back inside of me. "I wish I could stay inside of you all night."

I clench around his cock, eager to keep him in me.

He pants. "Fuuuck. I feel how much you want it."

With slow, deep, and powerful thrusts, he makes love to me. A prickling sensation builds as I suck on his tongue. I fist the sheets and moan into his mouth when he starts stroking my tight balls.

I cry out as I come and come and come.

He grunts. "Ungh—oh fuck."

I rut against him so that I'm completely impaled. Aftershocks of my orgasm vibrate through me as he fills me for the second time tonight. I continue clenching around his length, milking him of every drop.

"Stay," I whisper, telling him what I need. I love hearing his panted breaths against my ear. I love his intoxicating scent. I never want him to pull out.

Turning my face, he gives me the most tender kiss of my life, wipes my tears, and nestles me closer. "Always," he whispers into my ear as he rocks into me softly, spreading zings of pleasure down my spine. He pulls the blanket over us and cradles me in his arms.

I melt against his chest as I stare at our intertwined, ringed fingers.

Always. Another answer to an unspoken prayer.

If anyone showed me this moment six years ago when my world fell apart, I would've recoiled from the cruelty of witnessing a happiness that I could never possess. Not in my wildest beliefs could I have imagined this.

Then again—beliefs are fickle things.

The truth is, I can't control the day or when my loved ones fall ill or depart this life. I can't predict when grief's bitter hand will shatter my world again. I don't know when my final breath will expel from my lungs. There's one thing I am certain of—I love deeply.

At times, it's felt like a curse and the root of my pain. Yet, it's the one thing that's been unfailing through everything. Although I haven't always felt worthy, I've mustered the courage to accept love in return. I *believe* in Sid and our love and will spend the rest of my days appreciating the time that we have.

The same goes for our family.

There are some beliefs that turn to dust under a new sun and some that fall away with life's seasons. There are some that break your heart or lead you down a woeful path of destruction.

Yet, there's one more powerful than them all—love.

When it comes to love, it's a sure shot for me.

TURN THE PAGE FOR A SNEAK PEEK AT ARNAZ AND SALEM'S DUAL-POV love story, *Scoring the Player*. It's only fitting that brave Arnaz gets his happily ever after. If you're craving more of Sid and Ty, you're in luck! The lovebirds will make a few appearances.

Sidney David King,

I ~~feel~~ know in my bones that you and I have been friends for a very long time. How long? Well, it's said the soul is eternal, so if I had to approximate, my intuition tells me to start there. This is not hyperbole. Like Neptune's moons, I believe we've been locked in a celestial dance for countless lifetimes. I was once a man too broken to possess strong beliefs. Confusion and grief have sullied my thoughts for such an absurd portion of my life. Depression convinced me that everything, even existence, was meaningless. Then you entered my life, and with you came your profound care, kindness, and reverence. Not only did you enter my life, which was a dream in and of itself, but you offered your entire world to me. When I tried to hide the wounded parts of myself, you insisted on seeing them. When I mustered the courage to let you in all of the way, by some kind of supernal wonder, what you saw, you loved. The transcendent force of your love helped me heal and find joy again. You taught me that even a broken heart can give and receive love. You taught me that love is souls sailing Home together. You taught me that love is the most powerful of beliefs.

Sid, I love you so deeply that they'd only need to study my body to prove love is real. A single mention of you and my brain resembles a galaxy, lit up like a hundred billion stars covering the infinite sky. I want to love and watch over you for the rest of your days and thereafter. I'm where you rest your worries and innermost thoughts for safekeeping. We're soulmates, you and I, and yet, it would be the greatest honor of my life to be your husband.

So what do you say, will you marry me?

Scoring the Player

Salem

It's the second quarter when Coach puts me into the game. The crowd makes noise to commemorate my return. After five months of healing a stress fracture in my left foot, I'm ready to make the comeback of a lifetime. I've played for two other teams in my pro career, but ain't no crowd like the Brooklyn Lions. A lot has changed this season. For one, we have rookies who are pulling their weight. Then there's the bench that's proven to be deep enough to keep us in the running for playoffs when, like me, our star point guard and center succumbed to respective shin and shoulder injuries. Then, finally, my favorite change this season—the league has an openly gay player! And I've had a thing for that player for as long as I can remember. Anyone in the league coming out as gay is exciting, but Arnaz Cade coming out...it's the greatest discovery since electricity, or Einstein discovering that light is the fastest thing in the universe. Some might argue that my comparing Einstein's Theory of Relativity to learning my crush is gay is absurd. However, to me, the discovery is just as astonishing. I think my dude Einstein would feel me. He explained relativity as an hour talking to a pretty woman feeling shorter than a minute of having one's hand on a hot stove.

Unfortunately, Arnaz's rumored to be dating his teammate on the Los Angeles Royals, Sid King, but until it's been confirmed, I'm not giving up hope. Considering that we play for teams on opposite sides of the country, I have to be creative when I make my move. Someone who has the balls to be the first openly gay player in the league deserves a bold play.

Jason, power forward for Minnesota, makes a fast break down the lane.

Cute!

Before he can complete the dunk, I'm charging through the air. My shoulders eclipse the back of his head as I reach up to smack the ball away.

Not in my house!

Jason clasps his head and complains to the refs that I fouled him.

"Nah, bruh! That block was immaculate," I fire back.

I charge up the court and catch a pass from our center.

I evade Minnesota's defense and attempt a fadeaway jump shot. It bounces off the rim, but Cillian, our shooting guard, rebounds and floats it in.

Damn, it feels good to be back!

Cillian kisses the horseshoe tat on the back of his hand, then winks at me. That's my homie. When everything went down with Arnaz and Sid, our team, like I imagine every team in the NBA, discussed it in the locker room. I hated the offensive jokes being made. I was tired of that shit. A new dawn had arrived. I could join Sid and Arnaz or stay quiet and let things remain the same. I remembered something my dad said about when one person chooses to evolve, however painfully, they inadvertently influence the people in their radius. I made a choice.

I stood up and faced my teammates.

"Yo! Chill. Some of y'all are talking recklessly. Watch that igno-rant shit around me. I think it takes balls to do what Arnaz and Sid are doing...And for the record, I'm gay! Not that it's any of y'all business."

Everyone went silent as expected. I stared into their faces, silently asking, "We got a problem?"

Cillian spoke up first, "My brother, Liam, is gay. He's the best."

All eyes turned to him. He stood up, reached inside his cubby, and pulled out his deodorant. He swiped some on and faced me like we were in the middle of a conversation.

"Uh—yeah? Is this the, uh, brother that you introduced me to when we played Toronto last season?" I asked.

"Yeah, that's right, you met him. I forgot about that. His husband, Eli, couldn't make that game. Remember the picture of the Frenchie I showed you? That's their dog."

"The grey one?"

"Yeah, Loki. I love that dog, but he's a terror unless you give him treats. He has a weak stomach, so they buy him these crazy expen-sive small-batch treats with probiotics and a crap ton of healthy stuff. He goes wild for 'em. He begs by standing on his hind legs and spinning in circles. It's the only trick he knows."

I grinned. "Sounds like a character."

"Hey, if you're seeing anyone, you should bring them by for the next game night. Laila and I would love to meet them."

"I'm single, but thanks, man."

He nodded. "You ever need a wingman, I got you! I'm not saying I take all the credit, but Liam has me to thank for Eli. I'm the greatest wingman."

Over a dozen pairs of eyes ping-ponged between us. Cillian had to have felt it too, but he didn't seem to give a shit. It was so Cillian to have my back without saying he had my back. I shouldn't have doubted that he'd be someone I could trust to come out to.

Ezekiel, one of the guys taking jabs at Arnaz and Sid, hung back after most of the guys had cleared out.

"What's up?" I turned to face him.

"Hey man, my bad with the jokes. If I knew you were, you know, I wouldn't have said anything."

"Gay. The word is gay. Your dick won't fall off if you say it. Whether you knew I was gay or not isn't the point. That shit's vile, man. It's hate speech. You never know who is or isn't gay around you. Every time you say shit like that, you're spreading hate and potentially hurting other people."

He rubbed his neck and winced.

"Anything else?"

He shook his head. "Just my bad."

"You know, it's interesting how you insult in public but apologize in private. Next time, man up in front of everyone or save it."

I slung my bag over my shoulder and brushed past him.

I know so many dudes like him—constantly shitting on other people to assert their manhood. They're so committed to proving and performing their masculinity that they can't see how it's reduced their humanity. And if that's not fucked enough, they go and try to impose that crap on other people. To hell with that. I've spent too many years of my life feeling insecure about my manhood because of it. I have no interest in belittling and dominating other people to prove that I am strong, and I sure as hell won't be subjected to it from other people.

The opposing team's point guard gets jammed up by our small forward. He passes the ball to Dominic, their center, who runs three feet to lay it in. Dominic never sees me coming when I charge in from the wing, reach in, and block the shot. He attempts to retrieve it but ends up sprawled on his ass.

I gesture to the crowd that they aren't loud enough. They heed the call and scream their lungs out. I stumble back, pretending to be blasted off of my feet.

After the next three possessions, I force a turnover when their shooting guard squares up for a three-pointer. I run up behind him and smack the ball out of his hand before it's released.

Gimme that!

Our point guard, Onyx, takes possession and hits a three-pointer.

I end up playing a little over eighteen minutes before Coach benches me. She never keeps us in long during our first game back from an injury.

I'm tapped to join the post-game interview after I shower. Changing into matching pale blue corduroy pants and a long-sleeve, button-down shirt, I leave the top three buttons undone, partially revealing my chest tatts.

"Salem, over here. Tom from CBS Sports."

I nod.

"Firstly, welcome back. It's official, Salem the Silencer has returned!"

The room erupts into laughter, myself included. My defensive style has a way of silencing the opposing team's crowd, hence the nickname.

"You've been called the soul of the team, one of the toughest defenders the franchise has ever seen, and you can hold your own offensively. After five long months, how did it feel to be back on the court?"

"Thanks, Tom. It's been tough, but so many people behind the scenes helped me rehabilitate. I'm grateful to each of them. It felt amazing to be on the floor with my teammates again. It's good to be back."

"Salem, Erica from ESPN, you tallied five blocks, six points, a steal, two rebounds, and three assists to help the Lions clinch a W, 117–102. What do you think was the secret sauce behind today's win?"

"We got great stops and played to each of our strengths. Cillian made a huge splash in the fourth quarter, banking seventeen points, twelve assists, and four blocks. He's amazing.

Ezekiel guarded the rim ferociously. Zyair was one assist away from a triple-double with eleven points, ten rebounds, and nine assists. I mean, I could go down the line. I'm proud of the guys."

"Salem, Sloan from NBA TV, you're coming back from an injury to play in a league with an openly gay basketball player. What do you think about Arnaz Cade's and Sidney King's actions to promote inclusivity in the league for gay players?"

I grin and take a beat to formulate my response.

I think it's the best thing to happen to the league. Imagine if we could enjoy all of the perks of our straight teammates who often have their spouses and kids in the stands. Imagine if we could be out and not have that be the focus of our story as professional players.

Then there's Arnaz and his kaleidoscope eyes that resemble light grazing ocean waves, coloring blues a bewitching green. Handsomeness wrapped in a toffee complexion, plum lips, and a perfect five o'clock shadow with a kind smile. You take my seasoned interest in him and the fact that he's gay, and, well, damn, I have a lot of feelings about that.

"Sloan, I'm proud of the work that they're doing, and I stand in solidarity. It shouldn't matter if a player is gay or straight, but for some reason, it does, and that's a problem. I have no tolerance for homophobic speech or behavior."

As the words leave my mouth, it hits me—a way to get Arnaz's attention!

Nah, it's too out there.

But, I mean, wasn't bold always the plan?

I rub my neck.

This could go one of two ways. One's great and gives me a shot with the literal man of my dreams, the other...eek. Everyone will know I took a shot. It'd be mortifying. I once read about a government black site somewhere in the Arctic Ocean. Maybe I can hole up there for a decade until...okay, I sound scared again.

Is the AC broken? I swipe the beads of sweat lacing my hairline.

Yeah, okay, I'm definitely scared.

Is it my scared or rational voice?

Does it matter?

It's Arnaz.

Arnaz!

Okay, okay...

Argh...here it goes...

I clear my throat, ignore the tap dancing in my chest, and lean into the mic. "But on a more personal note, I'd like to know if Arnaz is single 'cause I'd really like the opportunity to shoot my shot."

I flash Sloan a sweet smile.

Like a blown fuse, the buzz in the room wipes out as my admission registers on the faces of the reporters. Then a backup generator kicks in, as a burst of frenetic energy careens reporters out of their seats, competing to ask the next question.

"I'll take two more questions!" I yell above the excitement.

"How about you?" I point to a guy with the *Brooklyn Daily News*.

"Thanks, Salem. Are you coming out as gay right now?" He shouts his question to be heard over the fray.

I plaster on my best shocked face. "I have to be gay to like him? Shoot!" I frown. "Nobody told me I had to be gay to like a guy."

Sloane's jaw drops.

"Can I just be gay for Arnaz?" I ask, looking into the camera.

I let the question sit unanswered. The energy in the room teeters close to combustion from the suspense. It's like I'm doing the equivalent of screaming "Fire!" in a crowded theater.

I stop fucking around and temper the tension.

"Yes, I'm gay. I have been since day one, and I've had it bad for Arnaz for a while now. Y'all got any advice for me?"

Kevin's eyes widen in shock.

Okay, to be fair. I didn't know I would be coming out

publicly today, but the way I see it, when it comes to your dream guy, you gotta put up or shut up.

"You could ask him out on a date!"

I follow the voice to its owner. "I could, Ciara, but I don't really know what he likes."

"How do we know you're being serious?" someone yells out.

"Y'all don't believe me?"

Another hush falls over the room.

"Y'all journalists always need receipts."

I shake my head and fish out my phone from my pocket. I dial my dad on speakerphone. His call goes to his generic voicemail. I hang up before his number is read out loud. I try my mom next, and she picks up on the second ring.

"Hi dear, is everything okay?"

"Hey Mom, I'm good. Listen, I have you on speaker—"

I signal for them to quiet down as laughter spreads throughout the room.

"That's good, baby. Your dad is driving me nuts. He's been in the kitchen for hours. He's on his third attempt at the double lemon cardamom cake you selected for this month's challenge."

I place the phone against my chest and whisper, "I can prove it—gimme one sec."

"Ma, I'm in a press conference. I'll call you later about that. Can you confirm for my friends here the name of the guy I've been crushing on hard since my second year in the league?"

"Arnaz, of course, darling. You've been smitten since the first time you played against him. For what it's worth, I don't think he's with the Wonder Kid. If I were you, I'd go after him."

The room erupts into more laughter.

"I'm trying, Mom." I smile into the phone.

"Listen, please call your dad back right—wait, here he is."

"Wait, Mom, I really have to g—"

"Hey, son!" My dad's sonorous voice emits from my speakerphone. "You picked a hell of a recipe this month. I don't know where I'm going wrong, but it tastes awful."

"Wait, Dad, I have to call—"

"It'll only take a minute. I added the lemon curd to two-thirds of the buttercream, then I—"

"Dad, I'll call you ba—wait, did you say two-thirds? Isn't it one-third of the buttercream to two to three tablespoons of lemon curd, and then you use the remaining two-thirds to mix in the cardamom extract?"

"That can't be right. Wait a minute. Let me put on my glasses."

I shake my head at the amused reporters as Dad mutters instructions.

"Holy cow! You are right. I don't know how I made such a mess of it. Thanks. Oh, and I agree with your mother. You're a handsome young man, and life is short. Stop pussyfooting around and go after Arnaz. I ain't raise no punk."

I burst out laughing, joining the reporters.

"Thanks, Dad! Call you later."

"You're a baker?" Ciara asks once I hang up.

"Amateur. My parents stayed with me after my surgery to help with things, and we binged *The Great Bake Off*. As you all now know, my dad and I started our own monthly challenge."

"Bake something for Arnaz!"

My head tips to the side as I toss the idea around. "Huh." I think of the countless recipes that I've bookmarked on my laptop at home. It'll give me the chance to flex my skills and make my interest in him clear. I'd have to figure out logistics since I live on the other side of the country, but I could use my parents, who live in Los Angeles. I could fly in during an off day —it'd be tight, but it's possible. Pretty quickly, the idea blooms into a thrilling plan of action.

"That's actually brilliant, Ciara."

I need more information, though. Best to go to the source. I peer into the camera.

"Hey, Arnaz, wassup? I have two questions for you—are you single, and what's your favorite dessert?" I ask in my smoothest voice.

And with that, I jump up.

"Thanks, y'all. This was fun. Until next time."

I turn my head to Ciara. "I owe you one."

She mouths, *Good luck.*

I ignore pleas to answer one more question as I head toward the door.

Cillian is leaning against the entrance wall, smiling. "Aight, lover boy. I peep you. Just one minor question, how the actual fuck am I supposed to follow that? They're going bananas. You gave 'em shock, howling laughter, and romance in under five minutes, not to mention a surprise cameo by your parents."

I chuckle as he stares at me in disbelief.

"My bad. I owe you one. You think I got a shot, though?"

"I mean, that was crazy romantic. I'd say so. Sid might kill you if they're dating, but I'm rootin' for you, bro."

"You're a real one."

"And you do owe me. I want your millionaire's shortbread with extra ganache."

I pat his chest. "Say less. I got you, bro."

"Salem the Silencer, my ass," he grumbles as he heads toward the microphone. Somehow, the reporters are louder than before.

I grin as I watch him settle in to take the first question from Kevin. Knowing him, he's about to feast on their hunger for a soundbite.

"Cillian, what's your reaction to learning Salem is gay?"

"Pfft, old news." He dismisses the question with a wave, tilting back in his chair.

I burst out laughing.

"Oh, my bad, did you all only just find out?" he asks, wide-eyed. "Awkward," he whispers, staring at the table. "I wouldn't take it personally. I knew because we're, like, besties, but not many people know." He seems to consider that. "Well, technically, his coach knows, his family and friends, our entire team, my girlfriend, our cat Edgar..."

He offers a wry smile, meeting the gaze of the reporters.

"But, hey, none of it means anything. Surely, it was important for him to tell all of you. Because, of course, you would respect his right to privacy and not insist on asking every person on his team and across the league for their opinion on his sexuality. I'm sure you only asked me as a one-off because you know he's my brother from another mother. Given he's one of the greatest defenders in the league, and we're all here to discuss basketball, whaddya say we focus on that?"

It took less than two minutes for the challenger, Jo "Bull" Murphy, to knock out heavyweight Sal Corsetti. Cillian may have him beat tonight. It's like a giant ice bucket's been released over the room, dousing the collective fever. Silence permeates as the reporters exchange slightly dazed and embarrassed looks.

Cillian finds my beaming face and winks.

Extra ganache, caramel, and buttery shortbread, I decide as I head to the locker room.

Operation Bake a Cake That'll Win the Guy of My Dreams begins now.

Acknowledgments

Writing *Loving the Legend* was a profoundly healing, humbling, and enriching experience. I tossed the story around in my head for countless months, and over time, the characters became so alive that I had to pen them—if only to free up mental space. Themes around grief, mental health, and sexual awakening are some of the few explored in the book that are deeply personal. Like Ty's mom's utopia, writing this story warmed my bones whenever I needed refuge from life.

Writing a story is only part of the publishing journey. Another part is finding the courage to ask for help. I'm immensely grateful to all of the people who helped me publish this book.

First and foremost, to my partner and best friend, thank you for your steadfast support and enthusiasm. When I shared my idea to write a sports romance, your face lit up, and you said, "You'd write an amazing story! I can't wait to read it." Then you read the manuscript, laughed and cried, and in doing so, it instantly transformed from a personal project to something that could maybe live out on its own in the world. We've been on this journey together for ten years, and I'm still in awe of your kindness. One day, I'll discover words extraordinary enough to tell our story. What an epic tale it'll make!

To my editor and social media manager, JoAnna Bachar, my goodness! How could one person be so gifted, brilliant, and generous? You are a true powerhouse! Thank you for the tremendous effort spent ideating and executing all things book publishing. I came to you for help with book promotion, in which you excel, and discovered a gifted and passionate editor with top-notch instincts. I plan to continue partnering and learning from you for many years. I'm sorry in advance for the blaring squeals and ginormous hug if we ever meet in person. I promise I won't try to hug your brilliant brain!

To my beta readers, Bekka, your insightful feedback notably impacted the manuscript. Thank you! Alyssa, waking up to your manuscript comments became the highlight of my morning. I know your official title is PA to the PA, but you are invited to alpha/beta read my manuscripts anytime. Please and thank you!

To Michelle Hazen, I learned a great deal from your developmental edits and critique letter. Your feedback helped guide the revisions. Thank you! I am grateful to you and Katie Golding for coming up with the first two book titles in the series, *Loving the Legend* and *Scoring the Player*.

To author Marina Vivancos, from the minute I discovered your books, I knew two things: one, you're a marvelously gifted author, and two, you were someone I was meant to know. When I sent you that first email, I had no clue that it would be the beginning of a friendship. Thank you for sharing your publishing wisdom and encouragement.

Author Abigail Hunter, thank you so much for sharing your sage publishing wisdom! I appreciate your generosity.

To all of the authors who allowed Jo and me to pop into your readers' groups to promote *Loving the Legend*, thank you! As a huge fan of many of you, I am humbled by your kindness.

To my ARC/Hype Team, thank you for sharing your excitement and helping to promote the book! I saw every repost and comment.

And thank you, dear reader, for reading the book. I hope you enjoyed it.

About the Author

When not immersed in the pages of a book, Kit Grey yearns to be, except when crafting love stories. Then, there is no other place she would rather be.

Indulge in the seductive world of her plot-heavy romance novels, where intricate characters interlace with emotional depths, weaving passionate love stories that leave an indelible mark.

Stay connected and be the first to know about Kit's latest releases and exclusive content by subscribing to her newsletter on her website at www.KitGrey.com. Engage further with Kit on Instagram and Facebook, and discover more about the alluring world behind her stories.

amazon.com/stores/author/B0CRF7Z9MF/about

instagram.com/authorkitgrey

facebook.com/authorkitgrey

Playlist

Visit @AuthorKitGrey on Instagram for the full playlist.

"Mount Everest"—Labrinth

"Is This Love"—Bob Marley & The Wailers

"What Are You Doing on New Year's Eve?"—Ella Fitzgerald

"Intimidated"—KAYTRANADA featuring H.E.R.

"DO 4 LOVE"—Snoh Aalegra

"PILLOWTALK"—Zayn

"Chocolate Hills"—Khruangbin featuring Leon Bridges

"Bluebird"—Alexis Ffrench

"Count Me Out"—Kendrick Lamar

"The Feels"—Labrinth

"River"—Sault

"The Rapture Pt.III"—&ME, Black Coffee, Keinemusik

"Cut Me"—Moses Sumney

"Atmosphere"—James Blake

"Godspeed"—Frank Ocean

"Love Like That"—Snoh Aalegra

"Stay High"—Brittany Howard ft. Childish Gambino

"Thinking Out Loud"—Ed Sheeran

"Nervous"—John Legend

"You Save Me" Alicia Keys featuring Snoh Aalegra